A Hero for
Miss Hatherleigh

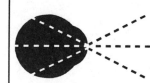

REGENCY BRIDES:
DAUGHTERS OF AYNSLEY

A HERO FOR
MISS HATHERLEIGH

CAROLYN MILLER

THORNDIKE PRESS
A part of Gale, a Cengage Company

GALE
A Cengage Company

Farmington Hills, Mich • San Francisco • New York • Waterville, Maine
Meriden, Conn • Mason, Ohio • Chicago

LIBRARY OF CONGRESS CIP DATA ON FILE.
CATALOGUING IN PUBLICATION FOR THIS BOOK
IS AVAILABLE FROM THE LIBRARY OF CONGRESS

ISBN-13: 978-1-4328-6902-1 (hardcover alk. paper)

Published in 2019 by arrangement with Kregel Publications, a division of Kregel, Inc.

Printed in the United States of America
1 2 3 4 5 6 7 23 22 21 20 19

For my sons, Jackson & Tim

Gifted by God with intelligence,
creativity, and scientific curiosity.
I love you!

CHAPTER ONE

London
November 1818

Surely a prospective husband must elicit greater feeling than the comfort experienced when wearing one's favorite slippers? Caroline Hatherleigh adjusted her skirts as the Berkeley Square door knocker tapped three times, and then glanced at the gentleman beside her. With his high shirt points and carefully sculpted sandy hair, the Honorable Edward Amherst looked the very picture of respectability. But then he should, being the second son of the Earl of Rovingham, and destined to enjoy the same social standing of which she also partook.

Really, she thought, eyeing him, if Ned wasn't a second son, and someone she considered as a brother, he would almost do as a husband. He was so generally well-disposed to be pleased, and inclined to obey her smallest summon, as his accompanying her on this afternoon's outing demonstrated. In fact, if it wasn't for a faint suspicion that a certain other young lady might never forgive her, she would almost dare to lift a finger and see if the approval she always met in his eyes could warm to something sweeter.

Before she could pursue these thoughts further, the door opened and a servant enquired of them. All thought of matrimony was abandoned as she announced herself and her companion. "I am sure Lady Carmichael will see me, seeing as we are old school chums and all."

"If you'd be good enough to wait here." The elderly retainer gestured to a small room, filled with art sure to please the recent bride — Serena had always been inclined to artistic endeavor, while Caroline had always possessed more appreciation for artwork than skill.

She smiled as memories of their former art master grew large. Mr. Goode had proved to be quite a good teacher, as his help in developing her sketching ability from mediocre to passable had shown. Of course, his efforts in other affairs had shown him to be anything but good. His later attentions to Serena had led to a scandal of no small size earlier this year when he'd been seen dragging her away at the Summer Exhibition, or so Lord Burford Snowstrem had said, a man whose proclivity for gossip even eclipsed Caroline's own. But such a situation had somehow resulted in Serena securing the attention of Lord Henry Carmichael, the very-soon future Earl of Bevington, or so society whispered, due to his father's poor health. Perhaps a bit of scandal did not hurt a young lady's prospects to the degree that Mother believed after all.

"What are you smiling about?" Ned whispered. "I always mistrust that look."

"Something which says far more about your sad, suspicious nature than it does about me," Caroline countered, her lips tilting higher. "I am simply glad to finally be able to visit my friend after her recent, most advantageous marriage."

"Won't she think it strange that I accompany you, rather than your mother or sister?"

"Perhaps. But Serena is too well bred to ever exhibit curiosity about such things. Besides, Mother made it clear that I was to fulfill my obligations and pay a visit today." Though she probably did not expect Caroline to be so fortunate as to encounter Ned on her way to Berkeley Square and demand he serve as her escort, rather than Mary,

Caroline's maid. Not that it mattered. Mother thought of him as a son.

She shrugged, aiming for nonchalance. "Mother is too busy seeing to Cecilia these days, preparing her for next year's come out."

Tension knotted her chest. Would her younger sister be more successful in her first season than Caroline had been in hers? Mother had not been cross. Not exactly. But she had made no secret of her desire to see her eldest daughter secure a husband as soon as possible. How to explain to Mother that no young man had ever elicited more than a general warmth in the vicinity of her heart? Not that she expected to marry for love — such feelings were common, and far beneath the daughters of Aynsley, so Mama always said. But if one were to marry, Caroline would much rather feel there to be a degree of mutual respect and esteem for herself as a person, rather than mere respect and esteem for her dowry.

"Forgive me, Caro, but your frown suggests I might be considered an intrusion."

She tossed her chestnut curls impatiently. "They will not think that, seeing as you are with me."

He chuckled. "Always so self-assured, aren't you?"

"Of course. Why ever would I not be?"

Ned shook his head, his smile stretching, but she knew he meant no harm. For she only spoke the truth. As Lord Aynsley's daughter, her position in life had been assured since birth. She would marry well — how could she not when she was guaranteed a dowry of fifty thousand pounds? — and she would live in a large estate not too far from her parents, and she would fulfill the role her parents had been training her for since she was a small girl: the doyenne of her community, wife to a peer, and one-day mother to his children. Such was the role mapped out for her. She smiled, not without complacency.

"Caroline!"

She glanced up at the door, quickly pushing to her feet. "Serena." She held out her hands. "I knew you would not wish to deny me. How are you?"

As she spoke she quickly scanned her former school friend. A tinge of dissatisfaction stole through her. If Caroline was to be completely honest, it would appear that Serena did not look absolutely delighted to see her, indeed seemed to almost hold a vague look of impatience in her expression. Her chest knotted. Surely Serena had not misunderstood their last encounter at Somerset House six months ago?

"I am well," said Serena. "What are you doing in London?"

"Oh, we're here preparing for Cecilia's come out." Noticing her friend's glance at Mr. Amherst, she performed the introductions. "I don't believe you have met before."

"No." There was no look of speculation in Serena's eyes, nothing to indicate any degree of interest in the young man at all. But Caroline supposed that was nothing much to wonder at, seeing as Serena had always been more interested in her art than anything — or anyone — else.

After a polite exchange of shared reminiscences, Caroline finally managed to convince Serena as to the benefits of a longer visit, and they were invited into a blue drawing room. There she was surprised to encounter, not Lord Carmichael as she had hoped — for it would be quite something if she could boast to Mama and Cecilia that she had spoken with the dashing young lord whom Serena had secured — but a young lady she had never met before, a very pale blonde whose features seemed strained, and whose comical expression of surprise suggested that she had been waiting for someone else.

"Forgive me for intruding," Serena said.

"A former school friend of mine has called, and I thought I might introduce you. Caroline, this is Mrs. Julia Hale. Julia, this is Lord Aynsley's daughter, Miss Caroline Hatherleigh."

Mrs. Hale? Now why did that name ring a faint bell? Schooling her expression to hide her curiosity, she dipped a small curtsy. "Pleased to meet you."

She glanced at Ned as Serena continued the introductions, disconcerted by the look of keen interest in his eyes. He had certainly never gazed at Caroline like that.

"How do you do?" he offered with a bow.

Caroline glanced at Julia before returning her attention to Serena. "You must forgive me, but when I learned you were in town I could not pass up the opportunity to see you again. It has been so many months since Miss Haverstock's, and I cannot but wish we had stayed in closer contact this past year." She chattered about some *on-dit* of town, before saying, "Oh, it is good to see you again, Serena."

It did not take long before her friend's initial frost thawed, and they were engaged in swapping recollections of shared confidences from their times at Haverstock's, and other occasions when Serena had visited Aynsley Manor.

13

She eyed her friend, trying to peer beneath the inscrutable mask that led to an expression so like her name, but Serena remained calm, indeed seemed to own a new, somewhat disconcerting sense of peace. Unlike the other young lady, whom Ned had taken to most unexpectedly. Had he not heard her introduced as a married woman?

As if sensing her displeasure, he caught her eye and gave a tiny nod before returning his attention to the young lady and offering a small bow. "Caroline, I believe it is time for us to depart. Thank you, Lady Carmichael, for the chance to meet you, and your lovely friend."

Serena inclined her head in a gesture befitting a countess, and murmured something of her pleasure at the unexpected visit, but made no mention of hopes for a return call.

Hmm. Caroline lifted her chin. Well, if Serena chose the likes of the nondescript Hale woman — where *had* she heard that name before? — then so be it. Serena should know not to expect an invitation to Aynsley again.

"And after all we did for her," she muttered, as they descended the steps to the waiting carriage.

"I beg your pardon, my dear?"

She shook her head, waiting until they

were inside the carriage and the servants could not hear. "I am simply surprised, that is all. After all, we condescended to invite her to Aynsley not a few times, and did so, despite her father proving himself to be a most debased man, gambling his family into decrepitude. And this is the thanks we are to receive!"

"From my conversation with her rather lovely friend, I gather it was not meant to be a slight but rather an expectation that family would soon arrive."

"Oh. Well, that is different then." Somewhat appeased, she smoothed her skirt then peered at him. "You certainly seemed to enjoy your time."

"Mrs. Hale is a very lovely young lady."

"A very lovely young lady who is *married*."

"Yes, well, that is a tad unfortunate."

She blinked. This was a side to her neighbor that she had not seen before. "Surely you would not wish to pursue a married woman?"

"No." He sighed. "I confess, though, that spending time with a pretty creature like that would be more amusing than . . ." His brow creased.

"Than what?"

"Oh, you know, than trying to fend off the young ladies so often casting lures my way."

"It must be *so* trying."

"Well, you would know. I have seen more than a few young gentlemen interested in you for your fortune."

Offense heated her chest. "And my good name and connections," she reminded him sharply.

"And that, too, of course," he soothed. "That goes without saying."

But when she had returned to her family's town house in Hanover Square, his words continued to steal through her earlier complacency. Was it true that the gentlemen she preferred to mildly flirt with were more enamored of her fortune than her face? Granted, she was not as fair as either Serena or Mrs. Hale, but she had received many a pretty compliment on her fine looks. No, she thought, looking at herself in the looking glass. She might not be *quite* so fair, but she was certainly not a hag. Besides, why should any of that matter? She was destined to marry someone who held the same values, who cared about family connections as much as the amount she might bring to the marriage. Such an alliance would bring assurance, would bring satisfaction, would bring contentment, just as it had for her parents. She peered more closely at her reflection, noting the shiny red beginnings of a spot next to her nose, and frowned.

So why did something deep inside whisper for something more?

Sidmouth, Devon

If he could but reach that one rock more . . .

Wind whistled, whipping his collar, the spraying sea salt dampening his hair. Erasmus Gideon Kirby Carstairs felt his grip on the rocks slip. His fingers tightened. Breath hastened. Legs dangled. His pulse scampered like the furious pounding of waves far below. Skin scraped against stone, yet he would not fall, could not fall, not when duty, not when love, demanded he live.

He gritted his teeth, hugging the layers of shale and rock as misty rain grew more insistent, driving into his skin, drenching his clothes, the drops stinging like pellets from a shotgun. How could he have known the weather would turn so quickly? How could he have known the tide would surge so fast that escape was only possible through a cliffside ascent?

Muttering a prayer for strength, he hauled himself — inch by blessed inch — to the clifftop and pushed over the edge and onto the slippery grass. He heaved a deep breath. Dragged the sack and satchel from his shoulders. Waited as his frantic pulse slowed.

When his breathing steadied, he rolled to his back, staring up at the dripping sky. That had been close. Perhaps he should have heeded Emma's warning, for today's expedition had come perilously close to being his last. But how was he to know the cliff would start to crumble so dramatically?

His lips twisted. Well, he should have known, should have listened to Belcher's warnings that the cliffs surrounding Sidmouth were none too safe this time of year. Gideon had thought Belcher had referred to something more clandestine than a mere search for fossils; this stretch of coastline held a number of interesting crags and coves less scrupulous men might like to use. Regardless — he glanced at the sack lying limply on the sodden grass — he should have paid attention to those locals who had looked at him askance as they answered his questions about Sidmouth's surrounds.

Pushing to his feet, stumbling upright, he gazed down at the treacherous froth of white below. Guilt soared within. Was his quest so very necessary? What if the unthinkable had happened, leaving Emma all alone? How would she cope? What would become of her?

"God, protect her," he muttered into

the wind.

Was it so very reckless to have left all they knew for his search of the as-yet unknown? He suspected their brother believed so, but he'd prayed and felt reassurance that hiding in plain sight could still work. And surely this yearning inside was not completely self-centered, was about more than wanting to derive personal attention and acclaim?

"God," he addressed the heavens, "You know I do this to understand You more."

He felt assurance wash within, and released a breath, but soon sensed the familiar discouragement lap his soul. Perhaps God wanted Gideon to know He could not be brought down to the level of a man, that His ways would forever remain incomprehensible to those formed from the earth's dust. Was that why Gideon remained findless still?

The rain eased, the fog shifting to permit study of the shoreline, the white cliffs of Beer Head shining in the distance. Intense examination of William Smith's map *A Delineation of the Strata of England and Wales* had convinced him this section of coastline could hold the same mysteries as those farther east. The geology was not so very different, after all. Indeed, William Buckland's recently published table of strata suggested these cliffs held similarities with certain sections of the Continent, sections which the French naturalist Georges Cuvier believed held species entirely lost to the modern world.

So why had his expeditions proved fruitless? Yes, he had found the odd specimen here or there, but nothing yet wondrous. Logic suggested that this stretch of coast would hold treasure similar to that found in Lyme Regis just seven years ago. His heart burned. If only he could be the one to unearth it.

After wiping the worst of the mud from his hands and sleeves and straightening his apparel, he collected his belongings and turned toward home, following the grassed path that led from the cliff edge to the tamer village surrounds. He knew his appearance might come as something of a surprise.

He strode up the last of the rough-hewn steps to the cottage atop the hill. A smile quickened to his lips at the sight of the well-wrapped young woman sitting in a chair in the garden of their new abode.

She looked up. "Gideon!" The lines of suffering marring her face smoothed as her eyes lit. "You finished far sooner than I expected."

"And far sooner than I had anticipated."

Or wanted. He hid the disappointment with a grin. "But such things permitted my seeing you the sooner."

"You are sweet."

"Although I must confess I did not expect to find you sitting out of doors."

"I have been here but a minute," she assured him. "I simply needed some fresh air."

Gideon glanced at the middle-aged woman standing behind Emma. She gave an almost imperceptible nod. His heart eased, and he nodded dismissal.

"So, what exciting discoveries did you make today?"

He sighed, sinking into the chair beside her. "Nothing too dramatic, I'm afraid. A few fish bones, I believe, but nothing to warrant the term *exciting.*"

"New discoveries still await you." She patted his hand.

He smiled at her. "And this is why I love you. You are always so quick to see the positive, eager to encourage. You are a true blessing."

"Now you are being silly. How can I not be enthused when we are so fortunate as to enjoy such a situation?" Emma motioned toward the sea, now tinted with silver, reflecting the leaden clouds above.

"Still, you should not be outside —"

"Oh, pooh!" she said, waving off his concern with a surprising energy. "I had no desire to remain indoors, despite what Mrs. Ballard might say."

"She's only looking out for you."

"I know, but I am stronger than I appear."

"It is just that I am worried about you."

"I know. But really, you know you should not." Her smile grew a little crooked. "Do you not remember what Father used to say? Are we not supposed to present our worries to the Lord?"

"I try."

"I know you do," she said, green eyes gleaming. "And I also know you are very trying."

A chuckle pushed past the tension, his heart gladdened by her return to the air of mischief he remembered from long ago. "But that will not stop me from doing all I can to preserve your health for as long as possible."

A trace of pensiveness crossed her features. "Just escaping to come here has done that." Her gaze grazed his upper cheek, marred by the raised, red scar inflicted two weeks ago.

He shook his head at her, willing her to banish the guilt he knew hovered on her tongue.

"Every day I have to pinch myself that this is real. Oh, Gideon, you cannot know how glad I am that you brought me here."

"I have some idea," he said, forcing up his lips, even as a strain of sadness stole within. He would do all in his power to ensure Emma's days were filled with as much brightness as possible. For a world without her in it —

"Please don't," she murmured, as if sensing his spiraling thoughts.

"I cannot help it," he muttered. "I wish there were more I could do, more that the doctors could do."

"Which is a form of worry, is it not?" Her hand squeezed gently, too gently. "Believe me, I know of your concern. And I am simply thankful that you cared enough to bring me here, and we can spend more time together."

His throat tightened, and he shook his head, willing the emotion away, willing the tease and banter to return. "You are good to say so, especially when I leave you for hours on end every day just to explore cliffs and coves."

"I am so very understanding, aren't I?" She sighed. "I suspect that if I did not allow such things, then you would pace the house like that caged lion we saw years ago at the

Royal Menagerie, and I would be forced to suffer the pain of listening to you espouse for the hundredth time the importance of scientific discovery, all the while pretending interest in something I dare not admit bores me silly."

A chuckle pushed past his earlier melancholy. "Yes, I've seen exactly how bored you are, asking me question after question. You, my dear, might profess to all the world to be a pious young lady, but I know just what a liar and a schemer you can be."

"Me? Scheme?"

"You. Scheme. No, don't go widening your eyes at me like I might not actually know you. I know you wrote letters to potential benefactors and sought funding for an expedition to France. I can never forgive you, you know."

"Never?" A smile tilted her lips.

"Never!"

She laughed. "Yes, well, I have seen just how much you have hated being here, being beholden to me."

He drew closer and gave her an affectionate hug, kissing her brow. How good it was to see the return of her spirits.

"Oh! Before I forget: a letter arrived for you."

"Do you know from whom it is?"

"Well, seeing it was addressed to E. Carstairs, I might have just happened to examine the return direction, especially as it had a seal and all."

Interest flickered. "A seal, you say?"

"A seal, I say." She nodded solemnly. "And naturally, I could not let such a piece of correspondence pass into your hands without first assuring myself it did not belong in my hands —"

"Naturally."

"— so I felt myself obliged to open it, whence I discovered it most properly did belong in your hands, so here it is."

He received the letter stretched towards him and flicked it open, scanning through the closely written pages. "It is from Lord Kenmore."

"Yes." Something about the way she said that made him look at her closely, but her dark green eyes only stared back benignly. "Well? What does he say?"

He should have known, despite her teasing words, she would adhere to the code of honor they both had clung to since they were small. He quickly scanned the contents, releasing a low whistle. "Well."

"Well what?" She eyed him avidly.

"It appears our Irish friend wants to visit in the spring."

"Really?"

He narrowed his eyes at her, but her gaze remained composed. "This is not more of your doing, is it?"

"Why, Gideon. How can you ask such a thing? Surely you cannot think me so underhanded as to invite your closest friend to a short stay on the beautiful Devon coast?"

"I don't know what could have given me such an idea."

"And surely you cannot think I have lost all propriety as to write to an unmarried man?"

"You are certainly not the poor innocent you like people to think."

"Again, you make me sound like I'm a schemer, when I am anything but. Now don't look at me like that! If you must know, I *might* have mentioned the potential for an invitation in my letter to Lady Cardross, and if she happened to mention it to her brother, well, I cannot be held responsible for that. Nor for any inclination of his to want to see you. Nor for the fact Aidan might find your work here of great interest."

"Aidan, is it?"

"That *is* his name. Really, I do think you are most unkind to your poor Emma."

"Poor Emma indeed," he said, flicking the

26

letter back and forth.

"Well, if you don't like the idea, then write and tell him no. It makes no difference to me."

"Does it not?"

A trace of color filled her cheeks. "It does not, and casting aspersions to the contrary does you no favors."

"Well then, there is only one thing for it." Gideon held out his hand and helped her to her feet. "We best return inside before those clouds resume delivering the rain they appear to promise, so I can write my reply."

Her hand grasped his forearm a little tighter. "And that reply would be?"

"That I prefer he arrive at his earliest convenience."

The hand clutching his arm relaxed. "Truly?"

"Truly," he said, escorting her inside just as spits of rain recommenced.

For why shouldn't he want his fellow scientist and closest friend to assist him as they sought to unravel one of the greatest mysteries in the natural world?

CHAPTER TWO

Aynsley, Somerset
December 1818

The snap and hiss of the fireplace drew Caroline's attention, tugging a smile to her lips as she slowly stroked the sleeping pug on her lap. Mittens uttered a low snore. Really, there was nothing better than being warm and comfortable at home, and now, with the bluster and flurry of London behind them, they could look forward to a lovely Christmastime before the true social season began again next year.

She leaned back against the sofa, the slouched posture something she would never let her mother see, on account that she might rail at Caroline like she always did at poor Verity, who did not seem to care a whit for social niceties. Why, just yesterday her youngest sister had returned from school without a word of hello for her family or their guests, insisting on greeting her

28

horse instead! Her smile flickered. Mama had been so cross, but Verity *did* need to learn to control some of her madcap impulses. How ever would she get a husband otherwise?

The door opened, and Caroline straightened as her mother sailed into the room, Cecilia following like a little stray pup.

"Ah, here you are. Well, my dear, it appears dear Lady Heathcote is about to be our guest. I spied the carriage coming up the drive."

Caroline nodded. "I'm sure she will have the latest news."

"Yes. It is good, is it not, to have a neighbor we can rely upon to share what is truly important in life?"

"Truly important" was a euphemism for society gossip, or so Verity would say. But if one was truly to care for others, as Reverend Poole preached, then surely it was important to know all one could about one's neighbors. And if one truly cared, then one was obliged to share. It was, indeed, only the right thing to do. Caroline exchanged a speaking glance with her sister and smoothed down her skirts.

Minutes later Lady Heathcote was escorted in, and the two matrons exchanged greetings and said all that was proper.

Caroline enquired after Lady Heathcote's children, Stephen and Sylvia, and learned that they were in good health. Stephen was her age, and quite good company, even if inclined at times to a certain childishness which led him to provoke those younger than himself to absurd and silly pranks. Why, once he convinced Verity to ride her horse up Aynsley's back staircase! Mama had been furious, not believing Verity's protestations about her innocence as to the origins of the idea. Granted, Caroline had not believed it either, until Stephen imbibed a little too much at a ball soon after and admitted it was his idea and dare. Of course, by then it was far too late to cause further ructions, so she had let it pass and not said anything to Mama. Otherwise her mother would be sure not to permit such a gentleman into her house, and Stephen *could* be very amusing . . .

"Well, it is good to have you all back," Lady Heathcote said eventually. "The neighborhood felt desolate without you."

"I'm sure," Mama said complacently.

"I don't suppose you've had a chance to hear the latest news?"

"That is what we count on you for, dear Lady Heathcote."

"Well, I know this might come as a surprise, because I understand he was in London with you not a few weeks ago, but it concerns our dear friend and neighbor Mr. Amherst."

"Really?" Mama's eyes widened with interest.

"Indeed it does. I understood from your letters, Lady Aynsley, that he was *quite* the favorite with some of the young ladies in town."

This last was said with a tilted head and such a fixed smile at Caroline that she was forced to acknowledge the truth with a nod, even as unease pulled within.

"Yes, yes, but what has happened?" Mama asked.

"Apparently" — Lady Heathcote paused as if awaiting the moment of greatest dramatic impact — "he was shot!"

Breath sucked inwards. What?

"No!"

Caroline glanced at Cecilia, who had suddenly paled.

"Yes, I'm afraid so, Miss Cecilia. It is in this morning's newspapers. And as he's a man whom we all know and care for *so* deeply, I knew I had to come immediately, knowing that we are so fortunate as to receive our papers a fraction earlier than you do here. Stephen spotted the item but

31

an hour ago."

Caroline couldn't help but wonder about his feelings on the matter. It was well known in local circles that there had never been any great love lost between Stephen and the man he seemed to regard as something of a rival. She shook her head at her cynicism and returned her attention to her sister, who still had not quite managed to cover her shock.

"Apparently," Lady Heathcote continued, "he might die!"

Cecy gasped.

Oh no! How very dreadful! A frisson of fear rippled over her. "I'm sure he cannot be that bad," Caroline said, as much to re-assure herself as Cecilia.

"Well, I don't know if you can be so sure, my dear," Lady Heathcote said. "It appears a bad case of it. The magistrate is after the villain."

"This is terrible. Simply terrible!" Mama said.

"I know," Lady Heathcote affirmed, but no sign of horror lingered in her eyes. Rather, she had adopted an almost preda-tory aspect, like one of those vicious crows that tormented the Aynsley estate dogs, one of whom had even gone so far as to peck out the eye of poor Bunty.

She blinked. Truly, she must be growing as fanciful as Cecy to think such things.

But Lady Heathcote did seem a trifle too glad to have a meaty item of news to dissect, leaning back in her chair, her eyes and teeth glinting. "One can only hope and pray that he will live."

Caroline glanced at Cecy, whose face had taken on a whitish hue, and shot her a frown. One did not create a scene, especially not in front of Lady Heathcote, who needed no enticement to speculate further.

"Yes, we should pray for him," Mama said agreeably. Caroline knew she said it only because it was the proper thing to say. Her parents held no stock in prayer, and had always disdained those who went about advertising their personal beliefs. Imagine, telling the world you found comfort in an invisible being! Such things were the crutch of the poor and weak, of no use to those of sound and strong mind.

"It appears that the young man had been escorting a certain Mrs. Hale around Hyde Park. Mrs. Hale! Who is this person? And here I was thinking he had something of a *tendre* for you, my dear."

This was said with a sidelong look at Caroline that forced her to fight a blush as she said stiffly, "I'm sure there is an innocent explanation."

"Oh, I'm sure there is, too," Lady Heathcote agreed quickly, yet her voice held a note of doubt. "It, well, it makes a person wonder, that is all."

"I met Mrs. Hale in London," Caroline continued. "She seemed all that was virtuous."

"Well, she cannot be *that* virtuous if she's permitting a gentleman other than her husband to escort her. Never would I have imagined Amherst doing such a thing, carrying on in this jingle-brained way. But there have been rather wild whispers of other activities he's been involved with, too. Something about a bet that sent a poor man to his grave? I don't know the specifics, so dare not speculate, but really, can you imagine? And he, an earl's son! Poor Lady Rovingham."

"Hmm." Mama looked at Caroline with slightly narrowed eyes. "I would never have countenanced such a thing, either. His behavior is quite beyond the pale."

"Indeed it is."

Caroline met her mother's scrutiny with a look she hoped did not give away her misgivings. Mama would not be best pleased to learn Mr. Amherst had escorted Caroline — at her request.

Cecy stood, somewhat unsteadily. "Please, Mother, may I be excused? I have something of a headache."

"Of course." Mother waved a hand. "This news is shocking, and I would not have you perturbed, my dear."

Judging from the anguished look on Cecilia's face, she was certainly a great deal past perturbed. Caroline would have to check on her sister after their guest took her leave.

"Poor thing. I'm afraid the past few weeks in London have been something of a trial," Mama said, with another wave of her hand. "Cecilia is a good girl but not used to crowds."

"Of course," Lady Heathcote murmured. "She has always been a trifle shy."

"We enjoyed ourselves in London, did we not, Caroline?" Mama continued, as if unwilling for Lady Heathcote to cast aspersions on any of her daughters. "*You* have never had any compunctions about meeting new people, have you, my dear?"

"No, Mother," she said, relaxing once again as she saw the approbation in Mama's eyes. "I quite enjoy it." Really, Caroline thought, she and Verity were as different from Cecy in this regard as Caroline and Cecy's chestnut curls differed from Verity's straight black locks. Such confidence had always made Caroline think she would make a perfect hostess one day, just like Mama. Now to find a gentleman who might see and appreciate these excellent qualities.

As Mother and Lady Heathcote continued, Caroline returned to her usual daydream about her perfect suitor. He would be rich, handsome if at all possible, someone who enjoyed the finer things in life just as she did, someone who would wish her to live in comfort all her days. And if they could share a degree of mutual affection, then so much the better. Finding such a man would not prove too difficult, would it? After all, her first season had been simply a practice run, to get used to society's ways. Next season she would begin her hunt for the perfect husband in earnest. Hunt! She smothered a smile. How ridiculous to think *she* would be the one to do the hunting —

Mama's mention of her name broke into her musings. ". . . a lovely time this past season, did you not, my dear? Attending the drawing rooms, and meeting the royal dukes and princesses."

"I enjoyed myself very much," Caroline said with a polite smile, as if they had not had this discussion many times before.

"I'm sure you did," Lady Heathcote said, a faint trace of exasperation in her eyes.

Ah. Best to change the topic. Mother did not seem to notice that her stories were not always fresh enough to guarantee continued interest. "I do hope Mr. Amherst gets better."

"Oh yes. Well, I'm sure you do, seeing as you are such good friends and all. And of course, we all wish that young man a speedy recovery."

Mother cleared her throat. "Such talk seems a little gruesome. I'm sure I would much rather talk about pleasant things, like dear Cecilia's plans for her presentation." Mama determinedly returned to her previous topic. "I wonder if they'll even hold it next year. It's been rather inconstant these past years, what with Queen Charlotte's sickness, and then the deaths of the poor Princess and the Queen."

"A sad time for them all," Caroline murmured. One could only wonder whether the King might soon succumb as well.

"I do hope they will still hold the Drawing Rooms next year," Mother said. "I know Sylvia still has a few years until she is presented, but I would not like Cecilia's come out put off for any great period of time."

"Yes, that would be most unfortunate," Lady Heathcote said in a flat tone. She rose abruptly. "You must excuse me. I'm sure you are as busy as we in this Advent season. I just wanted to come and wish you the joy of the season."

Caroline stared at her. By telling them this awful news about Mr. Amherst?

"And we hope you will have a pleasant time also," Mother said. "Thank you for coming."

"A pleasure." With a nod, Lady Heathcote gathered her skirts and exited.

"Well!" Mama said, sinking back into her chair. "That was most unexpected. Poor Mr. Amherst. I should probably write to Lady Rovingham and send our condolences."

"Ned is not dead, Mama," she said, stifling a trickle of fear.

"But he might very well soon be. And then what will happen?" She sighed. "This is a terrible business. He has always been rather too fond of the company of you girls. And I cannot help but regret that we allowed him so much latitude in his interactions with you. I would hate to think you might be ostracized by society, and no man willing to make you an offer."

Caroline's chest grew tight as her earlier pretty daydreams shattered to the floor. "We did not know what would happen, Mama."

"What if people were to learn he had escorted you alone?"

Mama knew?

"Oh, don't look at me like a simpleton. I know you visited Serena with him."

"I am sorry, Mama."

Her mother waved an impatient hand. "Never mind that. We must make it very clear that he means nothing to this family. People might start speculating about you the way they speculate about poor Amherst."

Caroline schooled her countenance to hide her rising panic. Did Mother truly fear for Caroline's reputation?

"I cannot like it," she continued. "I see now that we have erred, and it will not do for your matrimonial prospects to be adversely affected because of this. I think it best if you were removed from his vicinity, so that no one can make assumptions. Perhaps we should see if your grandmother is amenable to having you stay."

"Grandmama?"

"Yes. I don't mind admitting to you, my dear, that I did not particularly care for the way Lady Heathcote studied you. Nor, for that matter, how she eyed your sister. Really, I would have expected Cecelia to have more self-possession than what she displayed!

Aynsley ladies do not embarrass themselves, or others, and they stay away from any whiff of scandal. At least I can trust you, Caroline, to always behave in a manner worthy of the Aynsley name."

The sop to her pride was no doubt intended to mollify Caroline's objections to the scheme to banish her. "Mother, truly I have no wish to leave. Perhaps Cecy would —"

Mama sighed. "It is apparent your sister needs more instruction in matters of propriety, and would benefit from a mother's careful guidance, something that would perhaps be achieved more easily without her sisters in attendance. With Verity returning to school in the new year, if your father can persuade his mother that you would benefit from a stay by the seaside —"

"But it's winter!"

"That is neither here nor there. Yes." Mama nodded resolutely. "Once Christmas has passed, I'm sure you will find a visit to Saltings to be of great benefit."

Protest erupted in her chest. Why was she being banished when she had done nothing wrong? "Forgive me, Mother, but I do not think this fair, and I cannot agree with you."

"But you would agree it best to avoid further speculation about your supposed attachment with such a man, would you not?"

"There has never been any attachment," she insisted.

"Exactly. Which is why we must do all in our power to ensure no gentleman is put off by thinking that there is." She rose. "I will speak to your father at once."

Mother swept from the room, leaving Caroline in a welter of confusion, rejection, and with a decided feeling that she most certainly did *not* wish to go to Saltings. South Devon in winter? She shuddered.

This Christmas held a number of firsts for Gideon. The first spent in Devon. The first — his heart wrenched — without their parents. Yet the first, in what felt like a long time, that held a measure of hope. He glanced at Emma as she dutifully paid attention to the minister in the pulpit, then turned his head to do likewise. These past weeks of attending services had led him to believe Reverend Holmes's sonorous tones demanded attention, if not respect. Not that Gideon had anything against the man — his father was a minister before circumstances changed, and Gideon generally held men of the cloth in high regard — but this reverend seemed a little too certain of himself, as if his version of the world must be the only correct one, and anyone who did not agree was a sinner of the greatest magnitude.

Gideon had come across this attitude before, with people whose learning only seemed to increase their loathing of anyone who dared see the world in a different way. He couldn't help but think such attitudes a little pharisaical and narrow-minded. Yet his own understanding of the Bible had been challenged of late, forcing him to delve deeper into the meaning and context as he struggled to balance his faith with his science. And he knew that reasoning and logic weren't everyone's forte.

"Let us pray."

Gideon started guiltily, and bowed his head in acquiescence, listening as the reverend beseeched and implored and advised God. Amusement tugged at his lips, and he filtered out the reverend's prayer and lifted his own pleas to heaven.

Heavenly Father, thank You for all Your good blessings, for our new home, for Emma's health. Keep her safe, and help us to serve You, and use us for Your kingdom.

"Amen."

He echoed a second later, earning a glance from Emma. He patted her knee, then assisted her to rise for the closing hymn.

Within minutes they were outside, waiting for an older lady to finally finish speaking to the minister, an older lady who clearly thought herself more important than the rest of the congregation, seeing as she didn't seem to mind leaving everyone else to shiver in the queue behind.

He swallowed a complaint, glancing at Emma again. Cold weather was never helpful for her condition, and being left to stand here like this . . .

"Hurry up, dearie," a voice lilted behind them, a voice inflected with the rolling *r* this part of Devon was renowned for.

Gideon drew Emma closer, patting her arm gently. "I'm sure it won't be long now."

"Don't count on it," came the disgruntled woman's voice again, forcing Gideon to peer over his shoulder. "Her highness thinks it 'er duty to let the minister know what he can improve upon for next time."

"Her highness?" Emma said, eyes widening.

"Well, more of a duchess or a countess, really. The Dowager she be known by 'round these parts at any rate. Thinks she can dictate the sermons simply because she pays the minister's wages."

"Fancy that."

Emma pinched his arm, whispering,

"There's no need to talk so."

"Talk like what? Can I help it if we both know a certain someone who behaved in much the same way?"

"Father was not the only man in the family whose methods could be thought a trifle high-handed at times."

"You wound me."

She smiled, and the line finally released to begin moving again, the duchess or countess or whatever she was moving in a stately fashion to a waiting carriage.

"Well, and here we are. Hello, again." The minister clasped Gideon's hand briefly, but his gaze had — as usual — slid straight to Emma. It was not surprising, Gideon supposed. While not generally considered a beauty, she possessed a great sweetness that made ordinary men act in ways that could lead to discomfiture and no small degree of awkwardness.

And worse.

Gideon put his arm possessively around Emma. "Thank you, Reverend Holmes. We shall see you in services next week. Good day."

"Ah, yes, of course. Thank you. And to you, of course."

Gideon herded Emma away to where other congregants chatted, by the great yew that centered the churchyard. Beyond, he could see a row of horse-led vehicles lining the field on the other side of the gravestones. "I'll be back after I've checked on Nancy."

"No need to worry. I shall be perfectly content here."

After removing Nancy's blanket and readying the gig, he returned to find Emma talking — or rather listening — to their somewhat critical fellow congregant. Emma drew him to her side. "Gideon, I'd like you to meet Mrs. Baker. Mrs. Baker, this is my —" He eyed her sternly. "Mr. Kirby," she finished with a blush.

"Ah," the woman said, eyeing him curiously. "I been seeing you these past weeks. Messing about near the cliffs."

He inclined his head. "I am interested in the petrifications."

"Is that it? I wondered. Well, you just be careful. There be rockfalls and such to beware of, as well as certain other things." She gave him a significant look, then with a "Mrs. Belcher!" waddled off to talk to someone else.

"What other things?" Emma asked.

He led her past the low stone wall of the churchyard to where Nancy waited patiently, breath huffing white in the frosty air as she tossed her mane. "I do believe that was a veiled reference to the free traders."

Her eyes widened so the green became pronounced. "Smugglers?"

"I don't believe that's a term these people particularly appreciate. But" — he handed her into the gig — "it can hardly be wondered over, given the nature of these coves."

"I suppose not," she said, glancing back at the congregants still milling about. "Do you think some of the people here are involved?"

"Undoubtedly."

She chuckled. "So, you think the Belcher, and the Baker —"

"And the candlestick maker are involved? Yes, yes I do." He gently snapped the reins. "I have, in fact, heard stories where even the church minister allowed the church premises to be used for the storage of French brandy and the like in the cellars."

"Surely you jest!"

He smiled, but shook his head. "I'm afraid not. Some people prefer to skirt the law than pay taxes, and when one thinks of the ridiculous sums being demanded for all manner of things" — he gestured to the windows of a large stone house they passed — "then it cannot be a surprise that some people would object."

"I suppose not. Although I can't quite see Reverend Holmes being party to such a scheme."

"Perhaps not." Although Gideon could see him being coerced into turning a blind eye. Money had a way of doing such things.

She exhaled and huddled into her warm coat as he encouraged Nancy to a trot. Really, the sooner Emma could be inside the better. At least the weather was milder than what they had grown up with.

"We shall just have to be very careful."

"Well, *you* will," she countered. "It is not as though I will have much opportunity for encounters with smugglers."

"I should hope not." He slid her a look then guided Nancy through the white-washed stones marking their drive. "But I still think it important to continue the fiction we agreed upon."

She eyed him, biting her lip. "But what about when Lord Kenmore comes?"

"He knows the truth, so of course we shall have to reconsider things then."

"But won't it make things awkward?"

Her eyes held a somewhat pleading quality, causing his own to narrow slightly. Was it possible Emma held something of a *tendre* for his Irish friend? He shook his head. No, such a thing was impossible, could never work. Why, he might as well set his sights on the likes of the imperious duchess from the services.

His grin grew wry. Not that either of them could do such a thing, not while they maintained this illusion of marriage.

CHAPTER THREE

January

"I just think it important that you be careful, Cecy," Caroline said, smoothing down her pelisse. "You should not let a gentleman be too confident in your affection, else he will become complacent, and not treat you in the way you deserve."

Cecilia eyed her with a mutinous look but said nothing. Really, Caroline thought, the chit almost deserved to know about Ned Amherst's decided non-interest. Especially after all her carrying on during Lady Heathcote's visit; why she had acted as if she thought herself in some way bound to the young man — a young man who very likely never gave her a moment's thought!

Such behavior was certainly not worthy of an Aynsley, Mama had later said. Young ladies did not give in to the baser emotions — and especially did not exhibit those emotions to young men who cared little for them. Not that she would say such a thing to her sister. Well, she might to Verity — very likely she *would* say something like that to Verity, but not to Cecilia. Cecy, the shy, sweet, sensitive sister.

Cecy averted her gaze, her tightly compressed lips suggesting she was withholding further comment and had no wish to engage with her older sister. And on the very day said sister was leaving. Irritation at Cecy's determined silence finally made her say, "I'm sorry, Cecy, but Ned is simply not interested in you."

As her sister's mouth fell open, her eyes filling, then spilling with tears, Caroline felt a moment of remorse. Apparently she *was* that kind of person, after all. But wasn't it better to live in reality than daydream about impossibilities?

"I am sorry if what I say sounds harsh."

"You don't sound very sorry," her sister said, wiping at her damp cheeks.

"Cecy, I *am* sorry. I simply care about you too much to let you indulge in foolish fantasies. Ned Amherst is not the man we thought him, and I simply cannot advise you to seek him out."

"But he is our friend, and he is injured — he could have died!"

"And his actions have brought great

embarrassment to his family and, need I say, by association, to ours. As it is, Mama is none too pleased Lady Heathcote's gossip means I am being forced away" — a pang struck; Mama didn't *really* want Caroline to leave, did she? — "so I do not think it wise to compound her displeasure and distress by speaking about the man who is responsible for our parting."

Cecilia shot a glance at the mantelpiece clock, as if anxious for Caroline's departure.

Regret filled her chest, leading Caroline to force her lips up and adopt a conciliatory tone. "I have no wish to part with discord between us. I only wish for your happiness."

"I know," her sister muttered.

Caroline enfolded her in a hug. "Then let us say farewell. Know I shall be thinking of you."

"And I you."

But what precisely her sister would be thinking, Caroline did not care to contemplate.

A knock came at the door, revealing a footman. "Miss Hatherleigh, your mother wishes you to know the carriage is ready."

Caroline nodded and then turned to her sister with a smile. "I shall see you in a few weeks."

"Wonderful," Cecilia replied, without a

whit of enthusiasm.

Caroline shot her a narrow look then shrugged, sweeping from the room to bid her parents farewell. Verity, unsurprisingly, was nowhere to be seen.

"We hope you have a pleasant journey."

"Thank you, Mama, I'm sure I will."

"Mary and John Coachman know what to do."

Mary, Caroline's maid, and Aynsley's long-serving coachman — though Caroline was fairly sure his name was Timothy, not John — would provide sufficient chaperonage for the two-day journey.

Her mother clasped her in a light hug before quickly straightening, as if the display of emotion had occurred in a moment of weakness. "We shall see you in the spring."

Caroline had to fight the flicker of resentment elicited by her mother's words. She knew why she had to leave — any further association with Ned would be detrimental to her reputation — but it still seemed somewhat drastic and a mite unfair to be sent away. Still, she thought, lifting her chin, smile plastered on, she would simply view this as a brief aberration to her plans and regard this as an adventure. She scooped Mittens from a footman's waiting arms and nodded.

"Goodbye."

She was handed into the carriage, and after settling herself, she glanced back at the Palladian mansion that was Aynsley. Its long, imposing frontage — over four hundred feet she'd heard her father boast — glowed golden in the wintry sunshine, the façade speaking to the legacy of the family who had lived here for countless generations. She would return in just over seven weeks, and life would resume as before, and the season — her season to find a husband — would begin. Who knew? She might even have gained some tips from Grandmama on how to get the right man to propose when she finally met him.

The carriage turned out of the drive heading south. She smiled at Mary and squared her shoulders. Let the adventure begin.

Lyme Regis, Dorset
The cliffs towered over the surrounding landscape, menacing, yet promising so much. Above, the sky spat water droplets, remnants of last night's storm that made this morning's mission all the more urgent. He had to access the beach before the tide turned, and before the other fossil hunters arrived and scavenged the best finds.

Lyme Regis hugged the coast, protected

from the southwesterly winds by the lee of the hill. It was a fascinating locale, where the wealthy came to breathe salt air and the poor tried their best to sell their exotic natural finds. The driver muttered to the horses as the hired cart creaked steadily down the long hill, the steepness of which had necessitated leaving his gig at the top. Ahead, he could see the Cobb, the harbor protected by the curving seawall extending into the English Channel, against which waves pounded endlessly. He drew in a salt-tinged breath, eyeing the dramatic scenery. Anticipation thrummed within his veins. Perhaps today would be the day of dramatic discovery.

Gideon glanced to his left, where the cemetery full of tilted mossy headstones clung precariously to the crumbling Church Cliffs. Beyond, perched the ominous craggy face of Black Ven, a place, so the locals had said, where bad things happened, where a misstep might plunge a man hundreds of yards to his death on the rocks below. But a place where one of the most remarkable relics from the ancient past had been unearthed after years of being locked in layers of shale and sand.

With such finds to be discovered, it was little wonder desperation led a man to do dangerous things. His lips twisted. He knew that only too well. On his previous visit, an encounter with a local had led to discussions of some of the more notorious characters who had visited in recent times. The old timer had nodded, then said in his thick Dorset burr, "Aye, it be said that they know this stretch so well that even when running ashore on blind nights they can tell the location from a handful of pebbles."

Gideon couldn't help but wonder at the truth of this. But years of geological study had revealed the variations of so many types of stones and mineral matter that he should not be so surprised. After all, the locals had long sought to gain from the interest their curios evoked. One such collector, a Captain Cury, was known as a confounded rogue, following others as they searched the beach for curiosities, then riding out to the Exeter–London turnpike to meet unsuspecting travelers with samples of "his" finds. His audacity and determined efforts to sell his inferior wares before visitors arrived in town — and had opportunity to see the markedly superior shells and strange stones of less brazen collectors — had made him most unpopular amongst fossilists and the good people of Lyme. He'd heard stories of another man, a Mr. Cruikshanks, who used to traverse the shoreline hunting for curios with a long pole that resembled a garden hoe. Such men, like so many of the other poor, depended on the sale of what the locals called "verteberries" in order to supplement their meager incomes, to keep themselves a few shillings beyond being forced to receive poor relief from the parish.

He felt a moment's pang. This was why he never felt completely comfortable in searching the cliff shores at Lyme, knowing so many were dependent on selling the curios simply in order to have enough money to buy food or fuel to survive the chilly, damp Dorset winters. Gideon at least had a modest income, and would never have to go hungry, no matter how desperate matters reached. He would always be able to provide for Emma.

But still, the thirst for discovery — the thirst for understanding God's world — spurred him on. Consumed his dreams. Energized his resources, like nothing else, save the rescue —

"Here we be, sir."

Gideon nodded, instructed the driver to return in three hours, and forced his thoughts to his present surroundings with their remnants of long ago. After retrieving his equipment, he moved towards the shore and descended to the sand-strewn rocks. Here he began a slow sweep of the beach, carefully examining the stones and debris that had been pried loose from the cliff by last night's winds and rains.

By the time the sun reached its zenith, his arms had grown heavy. Despite the storm's promise, this morning's venture felt like something of a failure, the best he'd managed to find was a few mollusk fragments of such poor quality he'd left them on the beach for some other soul to find and sell, rather than take them and deprive someone of the opportunity to possibly make some coin.

He trudged back to the cart, directing it back to the township, back to where the mouth of the River Lym fed into the sea. A bridge of cottages spanned the river mouth, and it was to one of these he directed the driver. The modest cottage had a table outside, upon which rested numbers of shells and stones, which went by the names of "John Dory's bones" or "ladie fingers." To the untrained eye, they simply looked pretty, but Gideon knew they contained the remains of ancient specimens.

Had any new discoveries been made? He nodded to the woman at the door, put his question to her, received a negative reply.

His heart eased a fraction, then, recognizing his selfishness, he prayed to overcome his envy. He shouldn't compare his efforts with others, but sometimes it was hard to remember God's plans were good for him also. He sighed, looked up. A large and very beautiful ammonite, a "corremonius" in the local dialect, gleamed from the window, its elegant whorls like the spirals of a coiled serpent. No wonder locals called it a snake stone, had even believed it to hold magical power as a talisman against serpents, as well as a cure for blindness, impotence, and barrenness.

A long, pointed belemnite drew attention. Was it any surprise such oddly shaped stones were once said to be thunderbolts used by God, and were known colloquially as "Devil fingers," or — by the more pious — "St. Peter's fingers"? Ancient tradition held that powdered belemnites could cure the infections afflicting horses' eyes, could even aid the scourge of intestinal worms. Fossils had always elicited a mix of superstition and science, a place where facts sometimes did battle with his faith. But truly, how could he not concur with those who believed that fossils were God's inner ornament for the earth, much like God used flowers to adorn the earth's exterior? Fossils were simply the remains of those creatures swept away in the Great Flood described in the book of Genesis, when "the fountains of the great deep" were broken up. The existence of such ancient relics certainly did not take God by surprise.

"Interested in such things, are ye?"

Gideon glanced at the older gentleman who'd sidled near and murmured affirmation.

The older man smiled a greasy smile and whispered, "They sell much too 'igh, 'ere. I knows where ye can get things for the merest trifle."

"Do you?" Gideon said politely.

"If ye would be so good as to follow me, I'll show ye —"

"Thank you, sir, but," I really would prefer not to have my head split open as you lead me to a den of thieves, "I'm afraid I have an appointment at the Bridge Inn." Well, his stomach did, anyway, he thought, glancing at his pocket-watch. "And look at that, right now, as it so happens."

"Is that so?" came the flat response.

"Good day to you," Gideon said, before turning and walking away at a smart clip. A smile flickered across his face. Really, it would be almost disappointing if he was not accosted by one so-called collector or another. This stretch of coast was lined with thieves and those who would be if the opportunity presented itself. But the poverty of so many was not reason enough to let them gull him so easily.

He reached the Bridge Inn and made his way to the taproom. The room was abuzz with conversation; every so often he heard mention of rocks or excavation or fossils. Something within eased. These were people whose language he spoke, among whom he could both understand and be understood.

He took his nuncheon and coffee to a large table that accommodated far more than the solitary gentleman seated at the end. "Excuse me, sir. Would you mind if I joined you? It appears the other tables are full."

"Be my guest," the bespectacled man said, his attention returning to his plate of ham and cheese.

"It's rather busy at the moment," Gideon offered, testing to see if the younger man would respond to friendly overtures.

"Amateurs hunting for fossils," the man said with a sniff, before shoving in a fork of cheddar.

Gideon's smile twisted. Would he be classified as such by this supercilious gentleman?

"Forgive me," he said. "My name is Gideon Kirby." Well, it would be so here, and likely remain so, unless he was fortunate enough to discover the fossil that would demand wider attention from those interested in matters of undergroundology.

He held out a hand which was finally taken and briefly shaken with a muttered, "Peter Wilmont."

"Do you hunt for such things also?"

Wilmont dipped his head. The art of conversation did not appear to be this young man's forte.

"Have you seen the creature called the *ichthyosaurus*?" Gideon tried again. Not that he was desperate for conversation, but in his hunt for fossils, it could be helpful to know what stretches of beach had already been searched by those who knew what to look for, as this young man clearly seemed to think he did.

Wilmont picked up his tankard, took a long swallow, and placed it back down on the table. "I've seen the *ichthyosaurus* many times," the young man affirmed, first adjusting his eyeglasses and then removing them to polish the lenses. "Truly, it was one of the most wondrous things I have ever seen. Over seventeen feet, with that great skull with hundreds of teeth. One can only imagine what it must have been like to have first come across such a thing."

"Indeed."

On his previous visit to Lyme, Gideon had been fortunate enough to meet the remarkable young lady who, together with her brother, Joseph, had found the creature — and several other interesting fossils since. Mary Anning's family might be poor, but they had a rich collection of fossils, and so he had made a point of visiting the young lady whose self-taught understanding of fossils would put to shame an Oxford-educated man three times her age. Truly, she was one of the most remarkable people he had ever had the good fortune to meet.

She had been polite, but not particularly enthused, and he had soon gathered that she was more concerned about the next great find than she was in answering many of his questions. No wonder. Not if it was true that the price she had been paid for the *ichthyosaurus* had been a fraction of the amount paid when the buyer resold it to Mr. Bullock, that famous London collector with his Museum of Natural Curiosities at 22 Piccadilly.

"I gather you have seen it also."

"Yes."

"I have heard whispers that William Bullock plans to sell it to the British Museum. Now that is a far more appropriate place for such a fine specimen to reside, where it can be studied at length by those who are truly interested in understanding these matters, rather than gaped at by the illiterate masses."

Gideon swirled the dregs of his coffee. "Do you truly consider that those less fortunate in their attainment of education would not understand such things? Miss Anning herself is widely regarded as having knowledge far superior to anything most men may ascribe to. And this despite her frank acknowledgment that she received virtually no schooling."

"Yes, well," the younger man blustered. "That is different."

"She certainly has a thirst for knowledge that must rival my own. And yours, too, I imagine."

Wilmont made a noise somewhat non-committal.

"All people deserve a chance to get to know something more about this marvelous world we live in, and if that be in a museum for the masses then surely that is good. I believe it would be a sorry thing if all those considered illiterate were not encouraged to marvel at God's wondrous creation."

"Now you begin to sound like my cousin. He's always going on about this amazing world we live in and how we should honor its Creator. I have no patience for such things."

"You do not believe finding fossils adds to our understanding of creation?"

"I consider myself a man of science, and do not care to consider that which can neither be observed nor measured through scientific ways and means."

Gideon swallowed a smile. The young man's fervor for scientific discovery put him in mind of his own somewhat naïve approach when his interest had first been piqued. A rare family trip to the seaside had seen the collection of shells, one of which held a particularly unusual and intricate structure, something he later learned was not a shell but the remains of an ammonite, thought by some scandalous men of science to predate Adam and Eve. Father had been horrified, decrying that interest in such matters was scarcely befitting the son of a minister, and hinting darkly that he might withdraw his support for Gideon's studies of natural sciences and insist he be sent instead to study theology at Cambridge. It was only his siblings' support that had swayed Father; chiefly James, to whom Gideon still counted himself firmly indebted.

"Your cousin sounds an intelligent man," Gideon said.

"Well, I cannot complain, I suppose. He has funded me quite generously these past years, and I have been able to find some interesting ammonites to add to my collection."

As he talked about his time in Europe, and his opportunities to examine recent specimens, and even hear the great Cuvier lecture in Paris, Gideon fought pangs of envy. While he was thankful for the potential of funding from a rich patron, such patronage would also bring obligation, with the expectation that any finds would be presented to him. Gideon was scarcely in the position of being able to fund a personal collection as this young man apparently was.

"And who is your cousin?"

"Lord Winthrop."

He sat back as Wilmont continued sharing, oblivious to the clashing emotions his words had provoked within Gideon's chest. To learn the floppy haired young scientist was also the cousin of one of England's wealthiest men, Lord Jonathan Winthrop, was one thing. Word of Lord Winthrop's philanthropy had reached even Gideon's ears, and the connections one might make through such an impressive man could be most beneficial. But then he discovered the young man was also in proud possession of a considerable estate in Wiltshire known as Avebury, albeit with no intention to return there soon. "For this fuels my passion as nothing else has."

Gideon nodded and soon made his excuses, seeking out the great stone seawall alongside the Cobb as envy continued prickling within. He walked the long stretch of breakwater, thinking, praying, as waves crashed beneath him and droplets sprayed across his face. How nice it would be to be financed and carefree, to know that one day an extensive estate awaited him, that he wasn't burdened with the constant fear of discovery. That he would be free to follow his passions, to follow his heart.

His fingers clenched. Unlike some.

CHAPTER FOUR

Saltings, Devon

"Grandmama. How lovely to see you." Caroline tried to inject warmth into her voice, but really, given her grandmother's decided look of annoyance upon Caroline's arrival, she could understand why Mama had chosen not to accompany her to Devon.

Her grandmother received the peck Caroline bestowed on her cheek, her familiar scent of lavender lifting from the cool, papery skin.

"Caroline." Her name was said in the same tone someone might state the month, with nothing in voice or face to suggest her grandmother took any pleasure in Caroline's arrival. "You remember Miss McNell, don't you?" She waved an indifferent hand at the gray-haired lady seated in the other chair, her arms filled with a white-furred cat.

"I do," Caroline said, nodding to the

former school friend of her grandmother's, whose straitened circumstances had led her to the unenviable position of acting as Grandmama's companion.

"It's a pleasure to see you again, Miss Hatherleigh."

"Hello, pussy," Caroline said, putting out a hand to pat the animal, which promptly hissed at her, causing her to stumble back. Miss McNell murmured in a tone that mixed apology and pride, "I'm afraid Jezebel doesn't often take to new people."

"I hope she will not mind Mittens."

Miss McNell stared at her, her pince-nez teetering dangerously. "Mittens?"

"My pug. I left her with the butler in the hall —"

"You brought an *animal* with you?" Grandmama looked horrified.

"She is just a small pug, and so lazy she hardly ever barks —"

"Nobody said anything about you bringing a *dog* to Saltings. We have enough silly creatures here as it is," her grandmother said, with a look at Miss McNell and her cat that made Caroline wonder precisely to which silly creature she referred.

"Oh, but Grandmama, she truly is a sweet little thing —"

"I cannot think that Jezebel will like other

company," Miss McNell said worriedly. "She has such *particular* tastes —"

"Enough chitchat," said Grandmama, with a decided nod that put an end to that matter. "Remind me, Caroline, how long are we to have the pleasure of your company?"

"Until March, Grandmama."

"I see."

Judging from her grandmother's tone and look of disappointment, Caroline could see, too. If only Mother had not banished her . . .

Ah well, she thought, hitching up her smile. She'd always known Grandmama preferred that scamp Verity to herself, so she shouldn't be surprised, or feel this strange slight strain of hurt. Perhaps Grandmama might thaw after some conversation.

"It is rather cold out."

"Snow usually indicates such a thing," her grandmother said with a sniff.

"Of course." Caroline held onto politeness with an effort as she searched for something else to say. "That is a pretty view."

"You've seen it before."

"Well, yes . . ."

"Hmph." Grandmama eyed her narrowly. "Really, if that's the best conversation you can offer then one must question how you spent your time at that expensive school. Such a sad result for all the fees your father paid."

Caroline forced her smile not to waver, willed her expression to appear pleasant. How had she forgotten her grandmother's propensity for acerbity?

"A season down, and no offers?" Her grandmother shook her head. "Perhaps if your conversation rose above the commonplace you might have been able to acquire a husband by now."

Heat ballooned within. But didn't such unconventional behavior mark a lady as somewhat desperate? Surely gentlemen would prefer a wife who was guaranteed not to invite speculation. And as her mother always said: Aynsley ladies do not embarrass themselves — or others. Her lips pulled tighter.

Grandmama sighed. "Well, I suppose if you are to stay then you had best be taken to the Rose room. Dawkins."

A silver-haired butler appeared, his demeanor everything proper. "Yes, m'lady?"

"Please ensure my granddaughter is made comfortable. And see to" — her gaze flicked to Caroline's maid — "see that this, er, person, is directed to appropriate lodgings also."

"At once, m'lady."

He glanced at Caroline, gesturing to the wide stairs beyond the drawing room doors. She curtsied to her grandmother then followed as Dawkins led the way to a bedchamber on the first floor. A footman opened the door.

"I trust you will be comfortable here, miss."

"Thank you." She nodded dismissal — it was not as though she'd never stayed here before, after all — and moved to the large windows overlooking the gardens and dark sea beyond.

Bleak. Everything dulled and dispirited. Even the gardens seemed to have given up, smothered as they were by a thin layer of snow.

Her face drooped. What would she do here for the next seven weeks, ensconced in a house with a grandmother who seemed to neither like nor want her here?

Her shoulders sagged, and she shivered.

The first days passed with a modicum of civility, Grandmama tossing Caroline the odd remark like a butcher might toss a scrap to a stray dog. Caroline couldn't help feel somewhat like that stray dog, wondering why she had been virtually banished for something not of her own doing, forced to suffer the consequences of another's crime. Not that Ned had committed a crime as such, more a breach of propriety, which was well and truly enough to be counted criminal by society's gossips.

Caroline peeked up from her stitching to where her grandmother unfurled a garden catalog that had arrived in today's mail. She bit back a smile. What had her world come to, when the highlight of the week was the arrival of mail? But at least she had received some correspondence, letters from home having arrived from Mama and Cecilia. Mother's letter had been short and perfunctory; Cecy's at least contained some news of local matters, chief of which was that Mr. Amherst was on the mend.

Really, Mama would have been far greater served by sending Cecy to Saltings than Caroline. Indeed, Cecy's interest in the young man appeared not to have abated, despite the knowledge he had escorted a married woman around London, amid other unsavory rumors. Really, Caroline thought crossly, how much self-respect did Cecilia lack to want a man like that to notice her? She would be far better off someplace else where she could meet new people. Or at least have the potential to meet new people.

Caroline hadn't met anyone new yet. Grandmama seemed disinclined to socialize, her chief point of contact with others appearing to be attendance at services in Sidmouth on Sundays, the rest of her time spent ensconced in Saltings' spacious rooms. Caroline's days so far had been spent writing letters, perusing the shelves of the rather magnificent library, and stitching in front of the fire. Matters had reached such a desperate level of boredom she almost desired to attend the small gray-stoned church on the morrow, which said much, seeing as she had long ago adopted her parents' disinclination for obligatory services. She usually much preferred to spend her Sundays in bed, drinking hot chocolate and reading novels. But too many days doing exactly that had led to this feeling of mind-numbing boredom. Surely anything — even discussing a sermon! — had to be better than this. She glanced over to where her grandmother sat perusing the gardening catalog. They might even be able to have some conversation that way.

Next day
Well, perhaps thinking the minister's sermon might contain something worth discussing

later had been a trifle optimistic. Caroline clenched her jaw in an effort not to yawn, swallowing the heated bubble of air even as her eyelids closed in another heavy blink. The minister's voice droned on and on, forcing her to concentrate all the harder. Not on the sermon subject matter — which apparently revolved around someone called Jerubbaal or Jerubabbel, or was it Jerrububble; regardless, someone long dead she had absolutely no interest in. Rather, she concentrated on maintaining her posture of polite and appropriate interest: head up, eyes forward, unwavering expression, as if she truly paid attention and was not thinking how much more boring this had proved than matters of past days. Really, much more of this dissertation on the evils of sin might be enough to send her to an early grave! She tugged at the sleeve of her blue pelisse, chewing the inside of her bottom lip as another yawn threatened escape. Could the service be any duller?

At least she had the benefit of looking at new sights. The church was pretty — even Grandmama admitted as much on the drive over — with its arches and stone carved pulpit. And the congregation, whose reverent pre-service buzz had been chastened to holy awe at her grandmother's procession up the aisle, might deliver someone whom the dowager viscountess might deign to approve as a potential conversationalist. One could only hope so.

The minister's mutterings rambled to a close, the last hymn endured, and they were released to follow the minister down the aisle, Caroline conscious once more of the keen interest in the expressions of those facing her. As she drew up her chin and followed her grandmother, a slight cough drew her attention to the right. A young woman — no, a young lady — dressed in a faded pink color that did nothing for her complexion, glanced up with a murmur of startled apology. Behind her stood a young man, his plain features marred by a vivid red scar, whose height and slight air of possessiveness led her to wonder if he were the young lady's husband. His look of sardonic amusement as he gazed evenly back at her brought a fluttery sensation to her midsection, sent heat to her cheeks along with the strangest feeling of breathlessness, and returned her gaze back to the door.

Goodness gracious. What had just occurred?

Gideon exhaled past the heat rushing through his chest, forcing his gaze not to follow the figure in blue. *Lord, forgive me.* He wasn't supposed to be thinking about the attractiveness of a young lady in church; he should be thinking about the sermon, or at least about God. But right now, it felt like his brain had blurred to ignorance about everything save how her curls held ruddy highlights, and the startling depths of blue in her gaze, and the feeling hat as soon as she'd looked at him he'd felt a kind of knowing deep within, something that seemed to say "here she is" and "she is yours."

Which was ridiculous. Utterly ridiculous! Anyone with half a brain could see she occupied a social rung higher than he could admit to. Anyone could see she possessed at least a measure of the haughtiness her elderly companion embodied. He'd been trying, in his pathetic way, to assume his own mask of supercilious amusement when those eyes had pierced his armor, sending his pretensions to the dust. Still, he couldn't help but feel like a connection deep and marvelous had suddenly wrenched into awareness, something he'd be forever helpless to ignore. *Lord, help me.*

The sound of a cleared throat drew a different type of awareness, awareness that those behind him were waiting for his removal from the pew, and that Emma awaited him in the aisle.

"What is it?" she whispered. "You look as though you've seen a specimen to rival one of Miss Anning's finds."

He gave his sister a mock frown. "Better?"

"I'm not sure." She clasped his arm. "You look a little peculiar."

"Why thank you." Was *she* out there? Who was she? What was her connection to the imperious older lady? How could he possibly gain an introduction?

As if in answer to his unvoiced prayers, his ears sharpened to the conversations around him.

". . . believe she's the granddaughter . . ."

". . . visiting from near Bridgewater way . . ."

". . . a Miss Hatherleigh of Aynsley, I believe . . ."

Aynsley? His heart stuttered. Was she related to the viscount of the same name?

By now they had reached where the minister waited to shake their hands, was murmuring something to Gideon that only required a noncommittal response. It was like his brain couldn't think, like every fiber of his being was straining for him to turn and search for —

"Mr. Kirby?"

He forced his brain to focus, his senses to narrow down to the man standing before him, a look of puzzlement wrinkling his brow. "Thank you for the encouragement this morning," he finally managed. "I appreciate the reminder to fix our eyes on and trust in our Lord, no matter the circumstances."

"Oh! Well, I, er, I am glad."

This was said with such an air of surprise Gideon could not help but wonder whether the good reverend had even had such a thing in mind. But it would never do to speculate on another person's beliefs; was always best to give the benefit of the doubt.

The reverend's attention was claimed by the next group of congregants, freeing them to the snowy churchyard. Noticing Emma's shivers, he muttered about collecting the horse, releasing her to the conversation of the apothecary's wife, which freed him to suck in a deep lungful of air and release it in a cloudy breath.

Dear God. What had happened in there? He could not afford to indulge in fantasies of such a nature. It would be best to forget, to ignore these strange and urgent feelings pulsing through his body. Would be best to turn his attention to thinking on the sermon, his studies, to anything really, anything other than those mesmerizing blue eyes that had slain him with one glance.

"Dear God, help me," he muttered, lifting the reins over Nancy's nose, tugging them into place then climbing into the gig. "I cannot afford distractions. I don't want distractions. I need You to help me think about Emma, what is best for her, what is best for us."

He turned the gig around, lifting a hand to claim Emma's attention. She smiled, nodded to those she stood with, and made her slow progression to the waiting carriage.

Gideon helped her up, grasping her hand tightly, as if he could infuse strength. Guilt panged. What was he doing allowing another to steal his focus from Emma, from a good woman who needed him? He was little better than a scoundrel.

"Well! That was a more interesting service than I anticipated," Emma said, sinking back against the cushioned seat. "Lady Aynsley's granddaughter is visiting for a time, or so Mrs. Goodacre says."

"Oh." He was aiming for noncommittal, but from the look Emma was giving him, Gideon didn't think he'd succeeded.

"Yes, oh," she said with what looked like a smirk. "Don't pretend I didn't see you noticing her. She *is* quite attractive."

"I prefer redheads," he said, glancing at her copper tresses with a smile.

"Well, that only proves your capacity for mendaciousness. We both know such a statement to be false," she said, amusement lurking in her eyes.

"I hope you are not referring to a certain unwise incident that may have been committed by my younger self."

"There was no 'may' about it. But a man of science endeavoring to serenade a university dean's daughter is something that should never have been attempted."

"I know," he said humbly.

"How I wish I could have seen it," she said with a wistful air, tugging up the blanket.

"How I wish dear James had never mentioned it."

"Well, an elder brother is forever destined to mock his siblings."

"It is in his blood."

"Yes." The look of humor in her face faded, as if she were reminded of the more lethal mélange her blood held.

He snapped the reins, encouraging Nancy to a faster trot. "You were speaking with the apothecary?"

"Mr. Goodacre said he has some new medicine that may help."

Wasn't that what apothecaries were paid to do? "I suppose it cannot hurt to try."

"No."

The least harm he could offer Emma the better. Which reminded him —

"Oh, there she is. Look."

As if unable to disobey her command, he found himself looking through a glass window into the plush carriage passing by, straight into the widened blue eyes he wanted to forget. Breath constricted, and he had to drag his gaze away, to refocus on the deeply rutted road ahead. He exhaled heavily.

Beside him, he heard a soft chuckle. "I thought so."

"You thought what?"

"I thought I recognized that look."

"What look?" he snapped.

The chuckle rounded into laughter. "*That* look. The one with red cheeks and fixed aversion that only cries embarrassment."

"I'm not embarrassed."

"Of course you aren't."

Really, sisters could be most provoking.

"Why would you be? Just because you saw a pretty young lady, and she noticed you, and I noticed you both noticing each other — why would you be embarrassed?"

"Emma," he said, in what he liked to think

was his warning voice.

"Gideon," she said, mischief dancing in her eyes.

"You are truly the most obnoxious, irritating —"

"Irritatingly wonderful sister in the whole wide world. I know," she said complacently, before adding, "it is probably best not to encourage your hopes, anyway, judging from the look of her grandmother. She looks like she'd as soon as have you cast into the sea as speak to you."

He guided Nancy through the gates, but not before casting a quick look at the gray sea skirting the village. The dowager viscountess possessed a degree of authoritativeness that made such an action not unlikely. Well, perhaps a little less likely in this day and age. But were this a different century, she seemed the sort not unwilling to cry "off with their heads." Or at least see him pinioned in the stocks.

"I think you would do better, sister dear, to think on the sermon we just heard, and refrain from idle speculation."

"But refraining from idle speculation is so boring, Gideon." She sighed. "You always prefer the logical and measurable. You know such things can make you very dull."

But such things also kept one from making a fool of oneself. After his one sad flight into romantical fancy eight years ago, he had no desire to embarrass himself again. Not even for a rather striking young lady with blue eyes. "Are you finished yet?"

"No."

He pulled the reins, drawing Nancy to a gentle stop, waiting for Emma to finally finish what she wished to say. Better here than inside, where one of the servants would hear.

"You know you will need to marry one day."

"I can't. I won't. I would never leave you —"

"You can, and I truly hope you will. It grieves me to know I am the reason you have not yet found happiness."

"But —"

"Please, Gideon." She leaned her head on his shoulder. "I know what you will say, and I know you've heard me say this many times before, but you cannot know how much I wish you could find a lovely young lady who would make you happy. Such a thing would make *me* happy."

His throat clamped. But while they remained incognito, and her illness remained so unresolved, so prone to episodes of tremors and nausea and weakness, so ferociously uncertain, she remained his responsibility. Would forever be his responsibility. "I love you, Emma."

"Then if you love me, please do something that will make you happy."

"But I am." He gestured to the back of the house where he'd established his study. "You know how much I love my research here."

"I also know that you want more."

He swallowed. How could his baby sister have discerned so much about things he barely recognized himself?

"Please, Gideon. Please don't dismiss all possible young ladies from your future, just from some misguided sense of honor."

"It's hardly misguided," he muttered.

"I know," she said, patting his arm. "But I feel you should know that I would quite like to have someone I could consider a sister. It's been a challenge, let me tell you, putting up with two brothers all my life."

"Probably not nearly as challenging as James and I have found putting up with such a termagant of a sister."

"I am a termagant, aren't I?" Her eyes gleamed, her mouth tilted in a grin.

"The biggest termagant I know."

"Only because you do not yet know Miss Hatherleigh's grandmother. I have the feeling you might find her more formidable than even me."

"Impossible."

She laughed, and he helped her down and into the house, before leading Nancy to the stables behind, his thoughts tracking back to the young lady he'd tried to avoid thinking upon. He shook his head. A young lady like that, consider him? Those rocks he liked to study might as well live in his head.

CHAPTER FIVE

Caroline stroked the tan coat of Mittens, whom she had successfully persuaded her grandmother to keep, provided Grandmama never had to see or hear the pug. At least she had one friend here, she thought, rubbing her cheek against the top of the pug's head. And at least Mittens seemed to know her place, scarcely stirring from her basket near the fire, which was unsurprising, given the weather they had endured of late.

She took in the view from her bedchamber window, the long stretch of gardens leading to the cliffs, beyond which the sea glinted, an alluring gemstone, sometimes blue, sometimes silver, always changing. Sunday's rain had persisted for days, culminating in last night's wild storm, a storm of such ferocity that she had wondered whether the wind might succeed in tearing off the shutters. Today had calmed somewhat, and the moody weather called to her, the gray skies beckoning her to escape the confines of Grandmama's house. For once she could understand Verity's constant desire for escape, to be loosed from the noose of unspoken expectations. Her lips twisted. Perhaps one day she might even understand this youngest sister of hers.

Her thoughts shifted to her other sibling, and a sigh escaped. Poor Cecy. She did not seem to be dealing with the disappointment of Mr. Amherst very well, as Mama's latest epistle appeared to attest. Perhaps Caroline should suggest Cecy come visit her at Saltings. Then at least she might experience new things that would distract her from constant disappointment.

Though heaven knew this was perhaps not the best place to think about something other than intriguing young gentlemen. Another sigh released, and she shook her head as she placed the now-sleeping pug back in her basket. Why must she think on him still? He was obviously unsuitable, somewhat genteel if not precisely a gentleman. How could he be a gentleman with that scar on his cheek? Truly, he seemed somehow disreputable, almost like a pirate.

She smiled at herself. Yes, definitely a pirate, for one could see he did not care particularly for appearances, as the careless arrangement of his neckcloth attested. Neither did he seem to care for social etiquette, as his too-bold expression had declared; no gentleman she knew would have ever looked at her with such impudence. Yet he obviously cared for the young lady by his side, and she for him. They must be married, or betrothed, at least. A pang struck. What must it be like to be safeguarded in such a way, to have a young man not merely respect her but willing to protect her, perhaps even desire her?

A peculiar fluttery sensation crossed her chest. She put hands to her hot cheeks, annoyance growing within at the strange twisted thoughts. This was foolishness. She would marry a perfectly respectable young gentleman, not for love but for financial benefit and political alliance. She had always known that. Anything different was . . . was being very silly indeed! Was making her almost as silly as Cecy!

She drew in a breath. Glanced at the beckoning skies. Yes, a walk in cool winds might blow some sense into this very foolish brain!

A short time later, pelisse buttoned up, shawl and bonnet tied on firmly, sketchbook and pencils in hand, she made her way down the stairs and found her grandmother in the drawing room, exchanging quiet conversation with Miss McNell.

"Ah, Caroline. Are you planning on going out?"

"I would like to see the rose gardens, Grandmama. They appear most lovely from my window. I thought I might see if I can find something worth sketching."

"Well, it's good to see you have some sense. They've nothing on them at this time of year of course, but come summer they are most spectacular. I have been wondering about the wisdom of trying a new variety. I'm persuaded that the Scotch variety might cope with the sea air a little better . . ."

Eventually her dissertation on the benefits of one rose variety over another wound to a halt, allowing Caroline to murmur an excuse and make her escape. She moved along the terrace and down the steps to the garden, as she had said she would. The rosebushes did look sad, little more than gnarled sticks stiffly shaking in the breeze, but well she remembered previous summer visits when her grandmother's pride had not been misplaced, and the roses had bloomed in all their heady-scented glory.

She hurried past them, down to where the paved path led to a small fenced vantage point. Here she could hear the crash of waves, could peer down to where the thin stretch of pebbles and sand hugged the cliffs. These cliffs were not white as those she had seen farther east; rather they were more a reddish color. Which seemed strange, now she thought about it. Which thought itself seemed even stranger, that she would even *think* to think about such things as the colors of cliffs. She shook her head. Clearly time at her grandmother's was affecting her ability to reason as she ought.

The call of birds snagged her attention, and she watched their weaving through the wind that threatened to pry loose her bonnet. She closed her eyes, savoring the scrape of coolness on her skin, the scent of salt and earth, the delicate tickle of curls wisping across her cheeks. Something tugged within, to know more of this raw world in which she now stood, to be unfettered like the birds, not bound to societal expectation and obligation and propriety.

To just be.

Restlessness pulled again. She could recognize the feeling now for what it was; she held no peace, no contentment. The quiet doings of the past ten days had only induced boredom — and she did not want to be bored all her days. Her eyes snapped open. Is that what marriage to a perfectly respectable young gentleman would result in? Something where she was forever made to feel shielded, insulated, more a spectator to life than a true participant — is that what following society's rules achieved?

That tug in her heart wrenched once again.

Was life truly dictated by one's social position, or could one live beyond what was expected, beyond the confines of the known? How did people even do that? She occasionally heard stories of eccentrics, people who turned their back on what was expected and lived their lives to please themselves, following their passions and dreams regardless of the consequences. Such people as their distant cousin, the scandalous Lady Hester Stanhope, born to a life of privilege, yet casting it off to explore the ancient ruins of the Holy Land, or so Mama had once mentioned in dismissive tones. But regardless of improper behavior, Caroline could not help but secretly admire the courage such decisions demanded; what passions must consume their lives. She rather thought she lacked either courage or passion to stray too far from the life mapped out for her, but if she did, what would her life look like? Would such a thing lead to happiness greater than this boredom?

She exhaled, the sound swallowed in the cool breeze. Such thoughts felt nearly treasonous with their potential ramifications. She was not that sort of girl; that manner of thinking was Verity's domain, not hers. These thoughts were best smothered, best placed back inside the foolish box from whence they'd come, and never allowed air again.

Caroline glanced at the sketchbook she still held. The view here was certainly inspiring, but she wanted something different, something more, something that made her less a spectator and more involved as a participant in the scene. She peered down at the beach below. Perhaps something there might be suitable —

"Excuse me, miss."

Caroline turned, unsurprised to see her maid, presumably sent by her grandmother to ensure her safety. A huff of exasperation escaped. Surely Grandmama did not expect any harm to come across Caroline's path on her very own grounds?

"Yes, Mary?"

"Lady Aynsley sent me with this" — she held out an umbrella — "in case it rains."

Caroline glanced at the sky. It did indeed

still hold an ominous tinge of gray. "Thank you."

Mary remained, hovering, as if uncertain whether she would be dismissed or needed.

Caroline swallowed another sigh. "I believe I shall take a walk of a more substantial nature."

"I beg your pardon, miss?"

"I wish to go down there," Caroline said, pointing to the beach below. "Do you think this gate leads to the shore?"

"I'm sure I would not know, miss."

"Well, in that case, there's only one way to find out." And with a tilt of her chin, Caroline moved to the gate and the grassed path beyond.

"Miss? Are you sure?"

Caroline ignored her, taking not-quite-ladylike steps, as if the lengthened stride might help her escape her grandmother's notice more quickly. Why she felt this sudden urge to escape the bounds of propriety that only seconds ago she'd felt she must succumb to she knew not, save that if she didn't, she might well always feel a sense of regret.

The gate opened with a slight squeak, a sound almost lost in the call of seabirds, and the roar and hiss of the waves. She followed the path along the cliff top to where it twisted in descent, then gingerly trod down the worn earth-hewn steps, strands of seagrass scraping her skirts.

"Be careful, miss!"

"Of course I'll be careful." Really, what did people take her for? She had never presented as a fainting miss, had she?

"I'm sorry, miss, but I don't think your grandmother would like to know you were traipsing about around here."

Caroline turned to eye her maid. "Then it's best she doesn't know, isn't it?"

Mary flushed. "Y-yes, miss."

A few steps more and they had reached a small sandy track that led to the beach. A strange sense of anticipation thrummed through her veins.

She stumbled onto the beach, her slippers sinking in the damp sand, sliding on the pebbles. Really, this was most ridiculous, a sentiment echoed in her maid's mutterings behind her.

"Please remember I did not invite you to accompany me," Caroline said.

The maid flushed, and lowered her eyes.

Caroline pressed her lips together. Perhaps she could be just a little too sharp with her words at times, but — she tossed her head — one simply did not apologize to maids.

She scanned the beach. Red-gold cliffs

bounded yellow sand, and round gray rocks of varying sizes littered the shore, like a giant's abandoned marbles. Shaking her head at her foolishness, she warily stepped closer to where the waves lapped the shore, their hush and sucking almost mesmerizing, the sigh of the sea holding the slightest strain of sadness. Yet somehow the sight and sound were soothing, easing the restlessness within. Caroline closed her eyes. She could understand now why people enjoyed living by the sea.

"Miss?"

Mary's voice held a note of worry. She must present an odd picture standing here, the water lapping nearly at her feet. She opened her eyes, and, aiming for a conciliatory tone, said, "This is quite lovely, is it not?"

"If you say so, miss."

A tiny shell caught her attention and she bent to pick it up, examining it carefully in her gloved hand.

"This is certainly a pretty piece. Look at the color, how it glows." She held it out for her maid's inspection.

Mary sniffed. "Why, yes, if you like that sort of thing."

Conscious of a sense of disappointment, Caroline glanced away. When had her maid become more proper than she? When had she started caring what her maid thought? Oh, why had she dared scorn propriety and venture down here?

She stilled, breath suspended, as a figure emerged from behind a rock, drawing her attention. The man seemed to be searching for something, if his stooped posture and careful examination of the ground was anything to go by. What could he be searching for?

As if he'd sensed her thoughts he paused his activity and glanced up. From this distance, she could not precisely determine his features, but with his dark hair and breadth of shoulders he looked similar to that young man she had been thinking on earlier. A thrill of expectancy rippled through her. Who *was* he? And why did he have this effect on her?

She knew only one thing: this young man, whoever he may be, seemed to know something about escaping life's restrictions, and such knowledge held a tantalizing promise indeed.

Gideon glanced up from the specimen and almost dropped it. Her! He took a step forward, then paused, noting the terrier-like aspect of the maid-type creature beside her, eyeing him with a look that could only be described as suspicious. The young lady she guarded, however, seemed to be holding something more akin to interest in her expression, interest that fueled hope she might be amenable to his approach. Of course, it was scarcely the done thing to speak to a young lady without prior introduction, but he sensed he needed to speak with her now, before the winds of chance separated them again, perhaps forever.

This knowledge hounded his steps as he made his way to the pair, standing at the water's edge.

"Good morning," he called.

"Good morning," the young lady said, as the maid beside her hissed, "Miss!"

"Forgive me for approaching you, but I cannot help but wonder at the sight of a young lady roaming these sands as I do. It is not at all usual."

A smile flitted across her face as she replied, "I am quite aware it is not the usual thing. But today the sea seems to hold a mournful quality that I simply had to come see."

Did it? She did not strike him as the fanciful sort. But he was a fool to hope she had ventured down here simply because she had spotted him, and was as curious as he to learn about a mysterious stranger.

He smiled at himself, and gestured to the shoreline. "It is certainly an interesting place to be, especially after the storm last night. Who knows what sort of treasures the sea and cliffs might give up?"

She held out a small pink shell. "I found this just now."

"Ah, a cephalopod. It is a very pretty specimen."

"I thought it very pretty." She retracted her hand. "But Mary here doesn't agree."

He glanced at the maid who looked resolutely elsewhere. "Not everyone is enamored of such treasures."

"No." Her head tilted, and he was given opportunity to study her features, a porcelain skin that obviously was not used to the out of doors, seeing as it even now was reddening against the icy wind. Blue eyes of a milder hue than the sea behind her. Strands of rich ruddy-brown hair curling in wisps across her forehead, tugged by the wind.

Her gaze met his, and he was again conscious of that delicious thrill he'd felt last Sunday. Why her gaze should affect him he dared not think upon.

"And may one enquire as to whether you are collecting sea specimens also?" she asked, to her maid's horrified squawk of "Miss!"

She lifted her eyes to the heavens.

"I could only oblige you with an answer if you would allow me to make myself known to you. My name is Gideon Kirby."

She curtsied and smiled prettily. "Miss Hatherleigh."

He grinned. He didn't need her introduction; her name had been burned into his brain last Sunday. "I'm very pleased to make your acquaintance."

The maid cleared her throat, forcing him to glance at her. She scowled.

He returned his gaze to Miss Hatherleigh. "In answer to your question, yes. I am searching for some of nature's treasures."

"Nature's treasures?"

"Fossil specimens." He smiled. "Like that of your pretty shell."

She glanced at her shell doubtfully. "This is a fossil?"

"Yes. We believe a tiny creature would have lived within it, once upon a time."

As her maid uttered a sound of disgust, the young lady looked at him, brows raised. "We?"

"My fellow scientists and I." Was it vainglorious to say such? But he *was* a scientist, even if his father had mocked his pretensions. "Never tell me that you are interested in such things?"

"I never will."

He chuckled. "I wonder if I would be right in assuming yourself a visitor to these parts."

"That is correct."

"And may I be so bold as to enquire from whence you came?"

"Hasn't stopped you so far," muttered the maid.

"Mary, how about you go stand over there?" Miss Hatherleigh said, pointing to where a series of steps were carved into the hillside, and then waiting for the maid to obey before returning her attention to him. "Forgive her. I do believe my maid thinks herself part watchdog. Now, you were saying?"

"I simply wished to know if you are a visitor to these parts as I am." Well, that wasn't all he wished to know, but he couldn't afford to ask anything but the most innocuous questions.

"You are a visitor, too?"

"My family originates from the Midlands."

She nodded. "I have heard my father speak of visiting near Leeds, though I have never been."

Her father, the viscount, who must be well-to-do if he could travel and his daughter was afforded a personal maid and such fine clothes. Not a peer forced to nip-farthing measures. His chest tightened.

"And you are from . . . ?"

She shrugged, and looked suddenly coy. "A little place in the west of Somersetshire."

He nodded. Was that a little place called Aynsley? He dared not reveal his interest and enquire too closely.

"And may I ask what brings you to this part of the country?"

"I am staying here with my grandmother," she said. "And if I returned the question?"

"I would say I am staying here with my family also." What half remained of it, anyway. A twist of sorrow curled within.

"You would say? Is that not true?"

He bit back a grin and inclined his head. "As sharp-witted as she is beautiful."

She gasped.

His cheeks heated. Had he truly just said those words aloud? "Forgive me, I did not mean —"

"No, of course not."

"I . . . I would never normally . . ."

"I quite understand."

"I appear to have had all reason knocked from my brain, and as a result I am struggling to make sense, and I . . . I am sorry."

"Don't be." She suddenly smiled. "It is

simply the nicest thing anyone has ever said to me."

His heartbeat scampered as her eyes lent assurance to her lips. Warmth flooded through his chest.

They exchanged a few more trivialities, during which he learned that she was finding her time in Devon not especially exciting, that in fact she seemed a trifle lonely, which determined him to introduce her to Emma as soon as possible. But as grave a breach of etiquette as it was for him to speak to her, it would be even more so if he were to invite her to his accommodation. But perhaps . . .

"Would it be terribly forward of me to express a wish that we will meet again soon?"

She shook her head, her blue eyes dancing. "I don't believe so, although" — she leaned forward and said in a hushed tone — "I believe Mary might think so."

"Well then, it's probably best I don't speak with her if she feels that way."

She gave a tinkly laugh, a response that gladdened his heart, but which at the same time seemed to induce her maid to shout a warning that they best get back.

Miss Hatherleigh sighed. "I suppose I should return." She held out a hand.

"Thank you for being so bold as to speak with me."

He carefully grasped her gloved hand, wishing for the boldness he'd seen Kenmore use on more than one occasion in lifting a young lady's hand to his lips. He settled for a murmured, "My pleasure."

"I am so glad, and somewhat relieved, as it quite removed the need for me to come speak with you."

Now it was his turn to laugh, something which seemed to make her look at him with wondering eyes. He grinned again, and determined to persuade Emma to the benefits of paying a social call as soon as possible.

He waited, watching as Miss Hatherleigh turned and walked away, exchanged a few words with her maid — who cast him an acidic look — before peeking over her shoulder one last time and smiling. He lifted a hand in farewell.

Gideon exhaled. Who would have thought today's expedition would result in the discovery of a young lady with whom he seemed to share such a disconcerting bond? He was supposed to be looking for fossils, not finding that he shared a sense of humor with a most unconventional miss. What would Emma say? What would Lady Aynsley? A sinking sensation filled his chest. He could just imagine her expression of distaste, what she would feel it necessary to say to him, just as she felt it necessary to speak to the church minister about the content of the sermons. His lips twisted. He could just imagine what choice words she would have to say if he dared lift his sights to her granddaughter, dared assume such pretensions as the man he currently presented to the world.

There was no point in further speculation; it was obvious Miss Hatherleigh was possessed of a tidy fortune, and any guardian would sneer at his pretensions just as the uppity maid had. Who was he trying to fool? Hadn't history taught a man of humble birth not to aim for the stars?

And he returned to his examination of the cliff's geological layers and forced himself to concentrate, albeit with an oh-so-foolishly distracted heart.

Chapter Six

The next day was brighter, the sky making a welcome return to patches of pale blue, as if yesterday's winds had blown away the gray smudge she had come to associate with this part of Devon. If only it could now blow away the misgivings that smudged her soul.

She had been foolish. Irresponsible. Mary had been right to admonish her, both yesterday, and now with her rigid silence of affront. Who was she to act in such a manner, almost like one of those poor misguided damsels she had seen in London last summer, damping down their muslins to draw attention to themselves, before acting all coquettish and coy in their assumption of surprise at male attention? She now saw her moment of impetuosity to be exactly that: she had known herself to desire his notice, and had succumbed to her baser self and allowed herself a free and easy manner she knew to be wrong, and definitely *not* what

Mama would approve. So far she had managed to keep Grandmama in ignorance, but with Mary's thinly concealed threats she knew she could not count on her maid's silence.

No. She would have to remember her rank, that she was a daughter of Aynsley. She raised her chin. Mama's lessons had not been for naught.

"Caroline, here you are."

Caroline turned away from the drawing room's bay window to greet her grandmother with a smile. "Here I am."

"Hmm." Grandmama's brow lowered. "I wondered if today we might make a short visit to Lady Dalrymple. She is a friend of mine, and I think it would do us all some good to get out of doors now the weather had improved. Miss McNell can come, too."

"That would be very nice."

"Well, I don't know if very nice is how I would describe a visit to Lady Dalrymple, but it is sure to prove enlightening. That lady knows nearly all that is worth knowing in local affairs."

Caroline's heart quickened. Perhaps this friend of Grandmama's might know something about the young gentleman on the beach. Although — No, she spoke to herself sternly. That was foolishness. He was married, and would be as nothing to her. "And when would you like to go?"

"At once if you please."

Within the hour, Caroline was in a many-gabled stone house, sipping tea as she listened to the flow of conversation about her. For the most part, her role seemed to be that of spectator, merely observing polite niceties or offering the odd comment when addressed by one of the older ladies. Her ears quickened when she heard mention made of a Mr. Kirby.

"I understand he is of a scientific persuasion, that he is often seen examining our shorelines in hopes of the next big find. I believe his inclinations run akin to that strange Mary Anning person of whom we hear such stories."

"So peculiar," Grandmama said, with a visible shudder.

"Miss Hatherleigh." Lady Dalrymple turned to her. "I'm not sure if you have heard the stories about Miss Anning. I understand she is something of an amateur fossil collector, someone the residents from Lyme are always boasting about. Apparently she found the bones of a sea dragon."

"A sea dragon?" Caroline asked, swallowing the temptation to laugh. Perhaps she wasn't the only one who indulged in strange fancies.

"Something of that sort. No, don't look at me like that, my dear. One cannot argue with facts. Apparently the bones may be seen in some London museum. And here is another piece of local lore: the girl, Miss Anning, is revered by the villagers as something of a miracle. Seems she was struck by lightning whilst just a babe in arms. Three women with her were killed, but she was spared." She nodded. "Quite miraculous."

"Indeed," Caroline said, wide-eyed. Were miracles not merely the stuff of biblical legend after all?

"Yes. She is most peculiar. As seems to be this Kirby fellow."

"Such an odd person," murmured Miss McNell. "And very unattractive."

"Yes, well, I cannot think that *certain* members of our community would be particularly thrilled to know he is interested in combing the beaches so carefully. Indeed, I believe there were some who suspicioned him to be an exciseman!"

"And we all know such a man would never be warmly received in these parts," Grandmama said with a sly chuckle.

"Indeed not," agreed Lady Dalrymple. "Just why a man from out of town would choose to settle in our part of the world is a strange thing. Perhaps it has something to do with his wife, poor thing. She holds such an air of fragility she must be here for the sea air — although it is an odd time of year to visit, to be sure. No one ever seems to see her, apart from at services, and even there they never stay long enough to learn anything."

Caroline swallowed a smile. Was it any wonder they did not linger to satisfy local curiosity?

"I'm sure there must be something wrong with her. The only person she ever spends any time talking to is the apothecary and his wife, but trying to find out information from him is like asking a clam to talk. One learns simply nothing at all."

Feeling like poor Mrs. Kirby's health had been talked over long enough, Caroline cleared her throat. "Would you know where they are from?"

Her grandmother looked at her rather hard but said nothing, as Lady Dalrymple said she did not know, before asking, "Why do you wish to know?"

"I just wondered," Caroline said airily. "I happened to notice him last Sunday, and thought he possessed rather an interesting face."

"Yes, that big scar on his cheek gives him such a fearsome aspect —" Miss McNell began.

"That may be the case, Caroline dear," her grandmother interrupted, "but it is most unlikely that they be of *our* class, and therefore they are not people we should waste any energy in speculating about."

"Of course not, Grandmama," she said in as meek a manner as she could, stifling another smile at the absurd request from someone who had made her own interest in the young man and his wife very plain indeed.

But the conversation merely reignited the interest from before. Even if Mr. Kirby was not of their class — and hadn't his forward behavior in talking to her without previous introduction proved that? — he was still the most interesting person she had met since her arrival nearly two weeks ago.

Hopes of putting her interest to one side was further challenged on the return journey, when they neared the churchyard and met an approaching gig containing two persons.

Mr. Kirby touched his hat, Grandmama inclined her head regally, and Caroline fought the blush heating her cheeks. Why his merest attention should draw such a reaction from her she knew not; it was only to be hoped that neither Grandmama nor his wife noticed at all.

His wife.

Caroline peeked up from under her lids as the gig passed, stealing another look at the young lady seated beside him. She would never be classed by the *ton* as pretty — red hair was so unfashionable, after all — but her features were even, and her countenance, though pale, possessed a gracious calm. Her heart writhed. Regardless of her appearance, it didn't change the fact that the young lady was still his wife, and as such, Caroline needed to force her thoughts away from him, from them. She withdrew her gaze and looked determinedly at the crescent-shaped bay stretching away to the side.

"You seem very interested in that young couple, my dear."

"I am not used to seeing many scientists, I'm afraid," Caroline hedged.

"Why you would be interested in this one I do not know."

She could not answer.

But still, that absurd something deep inside tugged at her to get to know him. Despite her conscience. Despite all the obstacles. Despite all her misgivings. She sensed that somehow, this man held the keys to her future.

Gideon hurried up the stone steps gracing the garden's outermost corners. He had been away too long, the plans he had mentioned to Emma this morning having unexpectedly altered after a most unnerving encounter on the shore near the village of Beer. He hadn't expected to see Peter Wilmont venture quite so far in this direction, and the sight had filled him with dread-laden anxiety. It was foolishness, he knew, but Gideon felt he'd laid claim to the surrounds of Sidmouth, and that Wilmont was an interloper, trespassing on his territory. He'd had to fight feelings of possessiveness, fight his insecurity, as he mustered up an expression he hoped conveyed pleasantness, and not what he truly felt.

To his credit, Wilmont had been amicable, although surprised to learn Gideon had based himself in Sidmouth and not where so many of the other fossil hunters were in Lyme. They had even exchanged a few observations about the stratifications along this section of cliffs, before Wilmont had ended their discussion rather abruptly, with the words, "I've wasted enough time as it is. Good day to you."

The disconcerting feeling that farewell had left him with — was Gideon truly wasting his time hunting in this region as opposed to farther east? — had only been compounded by his noticing a group of men huddled around the base of the cliffs. He had tried to look uninterested, but he was sure they would have noticed his foraging along the shore, even as he tried to avoid eye contact with fellows he suspicioned were not strictly on the up-and-up. Were they members of the local free-trading community? The somewhat hastily obscured marks of what must surely be a dragged rowboat suggested so, as did the way they paused what they were doing and sent flinty-eyed glares in his direction until he passed. But as he had no great interest in their doings, and did not halt to speak with them, he hoped they knew him not to be a spy for the excisemen who sometimes visited these parts.

Still, the encounter had left him uneasy. He'd felt himself being watched as he bent to examine the rocks and scattered stones, and he struggled to focus on the task at hand.

The grayness of the skies and chill wind that scarcely let up made it near impossible to know how much time had elapsed, which made him doubly anxious now. Emma had been alone all day, no doubt wondering where he was, seeing as he'd been unable to send word of his changed plans, let alone inform her of any delay.

His heart quickened, much like it had the previous day when he'd once more seen the lovely Miss Hatherleigh, but instead of being tinged with something joyous, he felt something more like apprehension riding his steps. Was it truly best for Emma's health that he had brought her here? While cold, Devon did not hold the same vicious bite as Leeds tended to, and her winter cough did seem marginally better than what he recalled last year. And — he reminded himself — the most important thing was that Emma was safe. He would do all within his power to ensure she remained safe for as long as possible.

He pulled himself up and hurried along the cockleshell-lined path. From here he could see the cottage, could hear the sound of — laughter? Feminine *and* masculine laughter?

His steps slowed, paused. Who could be here? He had wondered sometimes if she might ever laugh again. Surely she would never laugh like that with her husband?

Gideon picked up his pace, pushed open

the front door, moved to the sitting room, and flung open the door. The scene greeting him drew a relief-tinged bubble of laughter from his throat. "You!"

"Why certainly it is I, though why my dearest friend should think it necessary to greet me in such an uncouth manner I will never know."

The Right Honorable The Viscount Kenmore pushed from the sofa to his feet and held out his hand. "It is good to see you, Gideon."

He drew close and hugged him. "Not nearly as good as it is to see you, Aidan."

"Well, that is to be expected," the Irish peer's son said humbly.

Gideon chuckled, smiling at Emma whose face had taken on a glow. She had always enjoyed Aidan's company. "What brings you here so soon?"

"Why your note, of course. You may be surprised to learn that even such a superior being as myself lacks supernatural intelligence, and cannot pluck from the air the name of a village where you *might* be. I have tried; it is impossible."

Gideon gestured to where the cut glass decanter stood poised, ready to give their infrequent visitors refreshment. "Would you care — ?"

"None for me, I'm afraid. Your good sister here has already ordered tea."

A certain sense of gratitude stole through him, which no doubt aligned with Emma's relief, signaled by her relaxed shoulders. No wonder. Since witnessing the extremely unfortunate consequences of Pratt's ruinous propensity for drink, Gideon had refused to taste another drop, unwilling to ever give his sister cause for alarm. He smiled. Between his beliefs and such actions, he was almost finding himself worthy of the Quaker-like name his father had given him.

Gideon settled into a chair. "As I recall, your note said something about spring."

"Yes, and I do hope you don't mind my arriving a little earlier. I'm afraid family matters necessitated my removal from Ireland at this time." A shadow crossed his face.

"Your father?" Gideon asked gently.

A dip of Aidan's chin. "He is not fully recovered as yet."

"Oh, I am sorry to hear that," Emma said, sympathy tweaking her lips. "He must find this illness a great burden."

"Sweet, compassionate Emma. I knew you would understand. Yes, he has carried this illness for some time now. But I am pleased to report the doctors believe he is on the mend, which was enough for me to be released to London. He wanted me to attend to some estate business on his behalf." His grave expression lightened. "One of the joys of being the son of Lord Kilgarvan."

Gideon smiled. "You are *so* heavily burdened, my friend."

"Well, I'll admit I do not have it quite so hard as some, but I do appreciate your kind consideration."

"It is ever yours."

Aidan's eyes glinted. "Such a good friend. I don't know what I have done to deserve you."

"I rather thought it was the other way around," Gideon murmured *sotto voce* to the Irishman's soft chuckle.

"We will pray for Lord Kilgarvan's health, that God will show His grace at this time," said Emma.

"Thank you, Miss Emma." Aidan gave her a considered look. "*Is* it Miss Emma? Forgive me, but I am struggling to remember how I should address you."

Emma glanced at Gideon, her own expression twisting. "I confess I hardly know myself. Sometimes it is very hard to remember just what role I am to play. All I know is that I am exceedingly grateful to not be anywhere near Leeds anymore." She rose, forcing both men to their feet. "Forgive me, I must see what has happened to our tea."

She left the room, and Aidan sent Gideon a questioning look. "I'm sorry, I did not know —"

Gideon shook his head, saying in an undervoice, "Pratt was a brutal beast. He made her life a misery. When she finally told me of the threats he made when he was in his alts, I could not bear to leave her a second longer. By God's grace I found her in the nick of time, and we stole away here."

"And that?" Aidan gestured to the scar adorning Gideon's left cheek.

He described how it came to be, then went on to explain about the use of his name, a disclosure that had his friend's face lighten momentarily from the darkness his mien had assumed.

"Then I shall be a simple mister, too."

"I am not quite sure what the locals think. Some may think she is my wife, but it does not matter as long as she is safe and he cannot hurt her."

Aidan's face had darkened once more. "He beat her?"

"The bruises have cleared now, and the local apothecary has been excellent in his ministrations to assist her recovery." *Thank*

God. And thank God his sister held no other awful legacy of that beast. If she'd been with child he feared such news might further injure his sister's delicate state of mind, and lead his friend into hotheaded actions to match the color of his hair.

Even now the Irishman was muttering quietly. "How anyone can think of harming such a gentle creature as your sister I do not know. The man must be a fiend!"

Gideon nodded.

"How such a union could ever have been countenanced — Forgive me. I have spoken out of turn. It is not my place to cast aspersions."

"My father was under an illusion in thinking Pratt as honorable a man as his father. I hate to think how blinded we were."

The other man's face closed. Gideon's friend had once expressed a preference for Emma's company, a preference scorned by Gideon's father and elder brother because they had no wish to see Emma forced to move to the west coast of Ireland, so far from the proper medical care afforded by proximity to London. Too soon was Emma introduced to Lord Pratt and persuaded to put aside any thought of another. Too soon had the good and dutiful daughter exchanged her vows and moved to Keighley, before they could learn the truth about her husband — and Aidan could learn his sweetheart had married another.

"Time heals, so the poets say," Gideon offered gently.

"Perhaps. But they never say how much time, do they?" Aidan offered a queer twisted smile, before shaking his auburn head. "Anyway, it is good to see her safe, and looking well. And you, too."

"And how long might we have the pleasure of your company?"

"A week or two? I shall need to return to London at some point, then I must return to Father. The estate is not flourishing as it ought, what with Father's poor health and our attentions being taken up with that."

"That is understandable."

Emma reentered the room, closely followed by Mrs. Ballard carrying the tea tray. Emma's eyes looked suspiciously red, her smile tremulous. "I am sorry it has taken so long."

"No apologies necessary," Aidan said, his expression lightening, gentling, as it did whenever he gazed upon Emma. "I understand it would take quite some time to sail to China, pluck the tea leaves, prepare them as one ought, then return to England. Your absence was far more expedient."

The slight look of strain around her eyes eased as she chuckled, then murmured something about his nonsense. And Gideon felt hope softly stir. Perhaps his friend's visit might provide a mite of ease to his heart also.

CHAPTER SEVEN

The next time at services Caroline did her best to recall why she attended, to fix her thoughts on the service, and not on the gentleman seated two rows behind her on the left. The fascinating gentleman, the gentleman with the scarred face, the gentleman who was dressed somewhat carelessly again, but in clothes of a superior quality, that showed his trim figure and broad shoulders to advantage. She would not think on him. She should *not* think on him. For did he not belong to another?

But those good intentions had been knocked almost asunder by the intriguing sight of another gentleman beside him, a handsome young man with hair a reddish hue, and an expression that gave rise to thoughts he could prove mischievous. She'd quickly averted her eyes, but the wondering remained, all through the catechism, and the sermon on Levitical tithes, and the prayers, and the closing hymn. Earlier she had resolved to not look or speak with him at all, but such intentions were impossible to fulfill after they had shaken the cleric's hand and she was waiting while Grandmama talked with Lady Dalrymple. She couldn't help notice the two men smiling as the young lady shook hands with the minister.

Something that felt a little like envy streaked through her chest. Why did that young lady have so many young men look at her like that while Caroline had none? She fought the desire to fluff out her hair and smooth the Pomona green velvet of her pelisse. Surely it did not matter what these people thought. Only, she was, perhaps, a *little* lonesome . . .

". . . looks rather too fond of himself," Grandmama said, jerking Caroline's attention to their conversation again. "And do you know that young gentleman's name?"

An expression of distaste crossed Lady Dalrymple's face. "A Mr. Kenmore. Irish, I'm afraid."

"Oh dear."

"But I think . . ." Lady Dalrymple's brow knit. "I'm nearly sure I once read in *Debrett's* of a Kenmore being related to an earl, so I suppose that makes up for it."

Grandmama sniffed. "It might go some way, I'll allow, but if an Irish earl, it scarcely signifies."

"Well, such things cannot be helped. But we may find he has some notion of drawing attention to himself, so if I were you, I'd be keeping an eye on that granddaughter of yours."

"I do not think Caroline would countenance such a connection, even if the man were an earl himself. She knows what is expected of her."

"I thought as much," said Lady Dalrymple, as if she hadn't just suggested the opposite. "One can always tell a brought-up gel, and one could scarcely envisage you with a family member who did not know her rightful place in this world."

"Thank you," said Grandmama, a look not wholly pleasant in her eyes, not dissimilar to that worn by her crony a minute earlier. Was it possible Grandmama could see through the other lady's pride and sad pretensions and realize them for the empty things they were?

Caroline blinked and turned away, and in that instant became aware that the young lady who had elicited feelings of envy just moments before had drawn close.

Their eyes met, the other lady smiled, and

Caroline found herself responding in kind.

"Excuse me. I know we have not yet been introduced, but I could not help but notice you before."

Caroline's brows rose.

"Nothing to alarm, I assure you. I merely wanted to know where you obtained such a pretty pelisse."

"Oh!" Caroline felt herself thawing. "This old thing? I'm afraid it is last season's, but I love the color so much that I could not bear to let it go."

"I see."

Remorse struck Caroline in the echo of her prideful words. Judging from the other lady's somewhat shabby pelisse, a new wardrobe was scarcely within her means. How could she make amends? She put out her hand and smiled. "I am Miss Caroline Hatherleigh."

"Emma," she said before adding, with no small degree of hesitation, "Emma Kirby."

Caroline's heart sank as she noted the confirmation of Mrs. Kirby's marital status. Well, she smiled, drawing up her chin, that was not supposed to concern her anyway. She also noted that Mrs. Kirby's grasp was featherlight, as if she had no bones. Was she ill? She peered more closely at the pale face, but the delicate features held nothing that indicated illness; instead, her eyes shone with a kind of luminous contentment. That feeling of envy again prodded deep within.

"I am pleased to make your acquaintance," Caroline said. Something about the dark green eyes gazing so directly into hers suggested this young redhead was as free from pretension as her husband. What was it about this couple that drew her so?

"From the first time I saw you, I felt like we were destined to be friends, and not just because we seem to be the only two young ladies in this parish. My brother says —"

"Caroline, come here."

"Excuse me." Caroline turned obediently to her grandmother, who was glancing at Emma askance.

"We have been invited to Lady Dalrymple's manor for tea. Hurry up now, we cannot keep her waiting."

"Goodbye, Mrs. Kirby," Caroline said, dropping a slight curtsy, which met a deeper one from the other young lady.

"Oh!" She blushed. "But I'm not —"

"Caroline! At once if you please!"

"Forgive me, I must go." She hurried after her grandmother, still refusing to look at the two gentlemen who had moved either side of Emma.

Although, as Caroline joined the older

ladies, she couldn't help wondering what Emma's husband might say, and why she once again felt the disquieting sense of being a mere spectator in life.

"Now who is that lovely lass?"

"That is Miss Caroline Hatherleigh," Gideon was glad to hear Emma say. He was still processing how much a smile could transform a lady's face.

"Hatherleigh, Hatherleigh." Aidan's brow creased. "Why does that name ring a bell?"

"That is something only you can answer, my friend," Gideon said, in an attempt at joviality.

"Well, she's got a fair sense of style about her, though the lady she be with has a look on her that'd turn a funeral down a country lane," his friend continued, as the object of his attention ascended the sour-faced woman's carriage, her gaze fixedly averted.

Gideon's heart panged. Why would she refuse to look at him when she had been so bold as to speak with him before? Something didn't make sense. Had she somehow learned of his family's sad situation? Was she now disinclined to associate with them?

"She appears a wee bit toplofty," Aidan said, speaking Gideon's very thoughts aloud. "I don't know if I would care to get to know her."

"She seems quite nice," Emma said stoutly. "Although I do think she might have been a little confused."

"What do you mean?" Gideon asked.

"I believe she thinks I . . . that is, we . . . are married."

Perhaps that was why she refused to look at him. The tension lining his heart eased, a smile hovering about his lips at his foolishness, until the reality of their situation caused him to sober once again. "You know it is not such a bad thing if we are thought to be married."

"I know. It is for my protection."

"Exactly. We do not want that man to learn where you might be."

"No."

"Hmm." Aidan glanced between them. "I know you think this a grand plan, but I cannot help wonder about its wisdom."

"Yes?"

"Tell me, what should happen when you meet a young lass you would wish to make your bride?"

Gideon's throat tightened. He swallowed. "I can assure you I have no thoughts of matrimony when things remain uncertain with Emma."

"Really? Because from the way you've

pretended to not notice Miss Hatherleigh, and the way she seemed determined to not look at you, one has to ask the question just why there is so much averted interest."

He felt his cheeks grow hot at the smirk on his friend's face. "I can assure you, there is nothing to be gained from pointless speculation."

"Really, Gideon?" Emma said, worry pleating her brow. "Because if there is any interest, I would not have you deny your happiness at my expense."

"And I cannot be happy unless I know you are safe, so we are at an impasse, are we not?"

She shook her head sadly at him. "I wish you could trust God with this."

"I am, which is why we have removed you here."

"Is that trust? Or is that simply hiding?"

"Would it have been trusting God to leave you in such a circumstance?"

She bit her lip.

"Please, do not ask me to consider another when your safety will forever be paramount to me."

"Forever?" Aidan said, one brow hooked.

God help him. However long it proved necessary.

CHAPTER EIGHT

Caroline glanced along the bookshelves, the dust of which suggested it was not often frequented. While Wallis's Marine Library couldn't quite compare to the circulating libraries of Bath or London, she had been pleasantly surprised to learn such a small village boasted its existence. Clearly the books were stocked by someone whose taste ran very different to her own, but she was nevertheless thankful that the library provided further opportunity to be out and about, and not stuck at Saltings with thoughts she was ashamed to own. Grandmama's companion, Miss McNell, was at the haberdashery securing some ribbons to trim a bonnet. Caroline had declined the excursion. She had no interest in ribbons, not when all her thoughts were caught up in wondering about Emma Kirby.

They had encountered one another a couple of times in the past week. Once, when Caroline had been sketching near the harbor; another time when she had come across Emma leaving the apothecary. On both occasions they had done little more than exchange nods and the briefest of greetings. Such encounters had only served to increase her curiosity about this woman who had been so quick to offer friendship.

Could she feel lonely like Caroline did? Would she one day have opportunity to rectify this? How did one keep a friend, anyway? Friendship seemed a delicate balance of openness about oneself whilst showing interest in others. Had propriety made her too aloof? Perhaps sharing her true feelings might help people see past the polite façade to know her for herself. She winced as memories of past friendships fueled by self-interest crept into mind. Is that where she had failed with Serena? Surely proper behavior did not eschew interest in others, no matter how humble their position in life may be. Perhaps this quest for friendship would be better served if she asked other people about themselves, rather than sought opportunity to display her thoughts about everything.

But could she ask such a thing of Emma? This past week, Caroline could not help but ponder the nature of Emma's illness. She still owned that paleness, that air of fragility, yet she possessed a peace that made Caroline wonder about it all.

"Hello, Miss Hatherleigh," came a female voice.

Caroline glanced up from the table of seaside-themed knickknacks. "Mrs. Kirby!"

The other lady blushed. "Please, may we talk?" At Caroline's nod, she gestured to a room beyond them, one used for reading, currently devoid of anyone save themselves. "You must forgive me," Emma said in a lowered voice. "I find I am quite puzzled as to what to do."

Caroline waited, sure she would hear an explanation soon.

After much biting of her bottom lip, Emma continued. "I am sure I can trust you, can I not?"

"Of course."

"You . . . you have not been near Leeds, have you?"

"Never."

A look of relief crossed the other woman's face. "Then I *shall* tell you, no matter what Gideon says. I cannot stand for such a lie to stand between us, not when I have hopes that you will be my friend."

Interest mounted within but she forced herself to say politely, "Only tell me what you are sure you will not regret, Mrs. Kirby."

"Such solicitude has quite decided me. You see" — she leaned close — "I am not Mrs. Kirby."

Caroline blinked. "Forgive me." How scandalous! "Then what is . . . ?"

"Gideon is my brother."

"Oh!" Something tight within her chest released. "I didn't realize. I thought you were married."

"I'm afraid it is a little complicated." The pale cheeks tinted rose. "You see, I *am* married, but my husband is, well, he is a terrible man, and he hurts me, so I have escaped here with my brother."

"Oh my!"

"Yes. It is a little awkward to feel I am deceiving people by not using my proper name, but I cannot risk people finding out the truth. It could be scandalous for Gideon's career, and would be so awkward to explain. And I simply cannot risk my husband learning the truth and finding me."

"You poor thing."

Emma gave a small smile. "I am not so very poor. I might not have very much compared to some people, but I know my brother loves me, and that makes up for more than most things."

"That is a wonderful attitude to have."

"Isn't it?" came the surprising response, along with another of those disconcerting smiles. "Forgive me, I'm sure you are not quite used to my sense of humor yet."

"Your brother seems to share it also."

"You have spoken with him?" The green eyes sparked with interest. "I did not know."

"I . . . I met him on the beach last week."

"Well, he certainly was closed-lipped about that." Her red head tilted. "I wonder why."

"I'm sure I cannot say," Caroline said, stifling the sudden surge of eagerness that demanded to know such things also.

"Well, I am glad you have managed to speak with him."

"Yes?"

"It will make things far easier when I invite you to visit tomorrow. I hope you like tea."

"Indeed, I do." Caroline clasped her hands together. "Well, for my part, I fear it only fair to warn you."

"Warn me?"

"That I have every intention of accepting."

"Well, that *is* good then," Emma said with a chuckle.

And, heart thrumming in anticipation, Caroline's smile became the most genuine it had ever been.

"You did what?" Gideon asked, eyeing his sister across the table.

"I invited her for tea."

"But why?"

"Because as kind as Mrs. Ballard is, I would like some female companionship that does not consist of a servant."

"Were you planning for me to be here?"

"No, not at all. Except it would seem strange if you were not, especially as you have met before, and you would not want to give the impression you did not like her, would you?"

Gideon looked at his sister very hard, working to ignore the twinkle in her eye, and the laughter he could hear being not very successfully choked back by Aidan. "I do not know why you feel it necessary to interfere."

"It is not interference, is it, to extend Christian charity? There she was at the lending library, looking quite as lonely as I felt, and, well, it would have been cruel to have left her there without an invitation."

"But you know nothing about her."

"Well, that is about to be remedied," his sister said, eyes wide. "You would like that, would you not, Gideon?"

He was forced to bite back his answer as his friend gave a disconcerting chuckle then said, "I remembered last night where I knew the name. Hatherleigh is the family name for Lord Aynsley, a viscount from some place north of here." Aidan eyed Gideon with an upraised brow. "Apparently, the daughters — he has three — are worth fifty thousand each. With such sums of money he must be very well-breeched indeed."

Gideon's heart sank. And would doubtless be thrilled to know that a man of very tame fortune wished for his daughter's affection. He willed his countenance to assume indifference, prayed for his heart to do the same. Really, he should not entertain such desires, not until he knew they shared faith as surely as a sense of humor.

"I do not care if she is related to the Prince of Wales," Emma said. "I am glad she is coming, and I hope the two of you will help me entertain her as our guest."

"You do know that I have plans tomorrow?"

"In the morning, which should leave you plenty of time to get that organized and be ready for tea at four."

"I, for one, would be more than willing to sacrifice my afternoon in order to meet the viscount's daughter."

Gideon stared at Aidan hard. Did he have an interest there? Surely not.

"Why the frown, my friend? Surely you don't suspect me of harboring intentions?"

He forced his lips up. No, he suspected his friend of having an interest in a very different direction. Poor chap. He turned back to Emma. "You really are quite the manager, are you not?"

"Why thank you." And her smile elicited his reluctant grin.

The next afternoon saw the arrival of Miss Hatherleigh in style, arriving as she did in the town coach Gideon suspected belonged to her grandmother. Of late, it was not too often that he had seen a crested coach, and even rarer when he had been the recipient of such a visit.

Miss Hatherleigh was today dressed in deep blue, a shade that complemented her eyes, brought out the honey-red tones in her hair, and made her skin appear to glow.

Emma gave the introductions, and Miss Hatherleigh gave her greetings, her gaze lifting to meet his in another moment that caused his skin to tingle. He could not help but admire her, to find her all that was appealing, and in the conversation he struggled to find much to say beyond the commonplace. Eventually he found himself on surer ground when she asked Aidan questions about how he spent his time.

"I will admit to a secret, Miss Hatherleigh," Aidan said, to her widened eyes. "This may come as a surprise, but I have spent quite some time in Ireland."

"Have you indeed?" she said, a dimple moving in and out as if she tried to suppress a smile.

"Aye," he confirmed. "Such tends to be the lot of one born there. But I was blessed with the good fortune of making the acquaintance of Car—" He coughed. "Excuse me. Of making the acquaintance of Kirby here at university." He clapped Gideon on the shoulder. "This grand man, this wise, courageous, clever man. Even if at times Kirby tends to have a wee dash of recklessness."

Miss Hatherleigh's blue eyes turned to Gideon, brows aloft.

"I am at times a little reckless," he admitted, thinking of some of his actions up north, "but I would not say it is irredeemable."

She nodded, her polite smile seeming a trifle uncertain.

"Gideon believes that most things can be redeemed," explained Emma. "But then that is what happens when one comes from good parsonage stock."

"Your father was a church minister?"

Was that surprise in her voice? Disappointment? "He was."

"Was?"

How could he explain the complicated path that saw his father move from humble parson to a social rung they'd never dreamed of? What could he say that was truthful? Truth was a dangerous commodity when one wished to hide.

"Our parents died last year," Emma said.

"I'm so terribly sorry." And her softened countenance and voice showed that she was. "That must have been a dreadful time for you all."

"It was."

And it had been. Despite his at-times complicated relationship with his father — one fractured by disapproval concerning his choice of friends and studies and their arguments over Emma's marriage — the loss of his parents' anchoring presence had nearly overwhelmed him, until his sister's problems gave renewed focus.

For a moment, it seemed as if the conversation had reached a stubborn standstill. Even Aidan — never one without a word to say — seemed at a loss.

Miss Hatherleigh glanced around the room, then straightened and faced Gideon. "I wonder, would you mind telling me more about your scientific pursuits?"

"Gladly." His heart lit with gratitude as her words dragged him from the pain caused by the past. He began to speak on geology and recent scientific discoveries that suggested it would only be a matter of time before a complete fossil skeleton was uncovered.

"You should see his drawings," Emma said. "It is remarkable how well he manages to capture the likeness."

If his sister's praise and the look of pride in her eyes weren't enough, then the soft glow of entreaty in the blue orbs of Miss Hatherleigh was quite enough for him to acquiesce and fetch his sketchbook. He drew closer, pointing out various elements of the fossil skeletons from sites he had visited in Seamouth and Lyme Regis. Miss Hatherleigh asked such intelligent questions that it was some time before he noticed that Emma and Aidan had withdrawn to another part of the room and were conducting their own whispered conversation. He glanced up, met Emma's smile and Aidan's roguish grin, and suddenly realized their intention. But what was the good of fostering a relationship that could never afford to live?

He drew back, closing the pages of the sketchbook with a snap. "I trust you now understand what it is an undergroundologist does, Miss Hatherleigh." His tone — harder than he had intended — seemed to make her withdraw, her face adopt a stiff politeness, an expression he'd seen his own mother wear when faced with those who had sneered at the reverend's new title. He winced internally.

"Thank you, yes." He hadn't mistaken it. Her cool tone, her mien, conveyed a measure of disappointment. "I" — she glanced at the others, who watched them both with expressions of keen interest — "I feel I should best take my leave."

"Oh, no, Miss Hatherleigh. It is much too soon," complained Emma. "We have barely had time to talk."

"My grandmother would be concerned if I return much later than what I previously said."

"Very well then. You may be excused this time. But you must promise to return. Perhaps next time Gideon can show you some of the places where the fossils have been found."

"Emma," he said warningly.

"Thank you, Emma, but I would not have

Mr. Kirby do anything he does not wish," Miss Hatherleigh said without looking at him.

"I believe Mr. Kirby's feelings would be far from not wishing to do such a thing," Aidan offered with a sly grin.

Gideon glared at him, sparking a muffled giggle from Emma who drew closer to Miss Hatherleigh. "Please ignore my brother. At times he forgets how to be gracious."

Miss Hatherleigh looked at him uncertainly, sparking a new streak of guilt. "It is not that I have no wish to take you to see such things," he managed. "Just that it might be deemed somewhat untoward for me to accompany a young lady without appropriate escort."

"Is our escort not enough?" said Aidan, the spark of mischief in his eye becoming more pronounced. "I would have thought your sister and I respectable enough company."

"But your thoughts pale in comparison to what Lady Aynsley might think, and I would not wish to cause Miss Hatherleigh concern."

"You are all consideration," she said softly, before rising to her feet and holding out her hand to Emma. "Forgive me, but I really must depart. I trust you will be well."

The piercing look accompanying this comment was enough to make him wonder at what else Emma had told her, but now wasn't the time to speculate, not when Miss Hatherleigh was offering him a slight curtsy. "Thank you for taking the time to show me your illustrations. This afternoon has proved most informative."

"I . . . am glad you enjoyed yourself," he murmured. But judging from the aloof look she offered him, he wondered if enjoyment was overstating things.

"Goodbye, Mr. Kenmore," she said. "It was a pleasure to meet you."

"And you, Miss Hatherleigh."

She nodded, gave Emma a small smile, then within the minute had left.

Leaving him ruing his response, ruing his friend's and sister's interference.

"I am sorry she did not wish to stay." Emma's brow lowered. "I wish you might not have appeared quite so cool towards her."

"And I wish you did not feel it necessary to manipulate me into something I have no wish for."

"No wish?" Emma cried. "How can you say such things?"

"Easily," he said, ignoring the jab of conscience.

"Too high in the instep for you, is she?" Aidan asked.

Gideon shot him a glare before refocusing on his sister. "I repeat: I do not have any interest in someone like her." He couldn't afford to. Literally.

Behind him, a squeak denoted the door's opening. He spun around to see Miss Hatherleigh's pink face, her gaze firmly averted once more.

"Forgive my intrusion, but I came to retrieve my gloves. The front door was open . . ."

"Oh, please do not concern yourself with that," Emma said, handing the gloves to Miss Hatherleigh before casting Gideon a swift angry glance, "or with whatever you might have heard my foolish brother say."

But it was no use. She had gone. And with her any hope of explanation.

CHAPTER NINE

She should never have gone. What kind of fool was she to think he might have held her in some esteem? She had thought when he had been explaining about his studies and his time visiting various geological sites that he enjoyed talking with her; had indeed been so foolish as to think he'd watched her while she examined his sketches, had thought she'd felt the weight of his gaze on her skin.

But she was wrong. Had he not said he held no interest in her? She could not have misheard that; it had been very plain what Emma and Mr. Kenmore were doing, leaving her and Mr. Kirby together for such a long time. But they had been proved wrong, too.

Her lips pressed together as the carriage rattled towards Saltings. To know herself so humbled was a new, disconcerting experience. Was she the sort of young lady no man would ever be interested in? Ned Amherst had mentioned the young gentlemen interested in Caroline for her fortune, but none of them had ever demonstrated interest in her for herself. What's more, none of them had piqued her interest the way Mr. Kirby did, but neither had he shown himself interested in her, save for a friendliness she suspected was a family trait.

Tightness filled her chest. What was wrong with her? Was she so unlikeable? Was she not attractive enough? She held no pretensions to great beauty, but had received too many compliments not to consider herself somewhat attractive. Or was that flattery merely as practiced as one's ballroom dance steps could be?

Her eyes filled with tears. She angrily blinked them away. By the time the carriage drew into the drive, she had approximated an expression more suitable for the daughter of an Aynsley.

"Ah, here she is," Miss McNell said as Caroline entered the drawing room, the woman's welcoming demeanor contrasting to the hissed greeting of her cat.

"How was your visit?" Grandmama said, in a tone not devoid of interest.

Caroline lifted a shoulder. "It was well enough, but I do not think I shall go again."

She ignored the twist of pain at the thought.

"No? Why is that?"

"I think her rather insipid." Her heart protested her lie. "And Mr. Kirby rather contrary."

Her grandmother's brows rose. "Hmm."

Somehow her grandmother's indifference drew her pique, drew her anger, making her want to say something that demanded attention. "You know they are not married, don't you?"

Miss McNell gasped.

"Really?" Grandmama finally did look interested, as her companion fanned herself and murmured something about the depravity of sin.

Remorse struck at her careless words. How could she let such a stain dishonor two people she had hoped to one day call her friends? Worse, what if the brute discovered Emma's whereabouts because of Caroline's loose-lipped pique? "I . . . I mean to say that they are brother and sister," she said, studying Miss McNell in a way she hoped would curb that lady's wide-eyed speculation. "They have done nothing wrong."

Her grandmother made a high-pitched sound in her throat, her mien shifting back to indifference. "Well, it's probably best you do not associate with those kinds of people anymore. They seem most untrustworthy."

Caroline managed what she hoped was a pleasant expression, her smile sliding away as she trudged upstairs to her bedchamber and removed her bonnet.

Mittens barked a hello and Caroline scooped her up and held her close. She closed her eyes as the gentle thump of a canine heartbeat reverberated against her chest. At least someone here liked her, she thought, swallowing the lump within her throat, though that one be but a pug.

Mary came in all aflutter, but Caroline sent her away sharply. She had no desire to listen to her maid's remonstrations. Was she really so unlikeable? She knew herself to be rather inclined to gossip, and to backbiting, as evidenced just moments earlier — she winced — but did such things make one a bad person? Didn't everyone enjoy indulging in a spot of gossip every now and then? Surely it never hurt too much.

Guilt gnawed at how she had partly exposed Emma's secret, but really, who was Grandmama going to tell? And it wasn't as though Emma had revealed her husband's last name, so surely she would be kept safe.

No. She stared at her reflection in the looking glass. She was going to have to find another way, another friend with whom to spend her time.

Two days later she came back from a walk to see a gig drawn up at the *porte cochère*. Misgiving slid through her. She was no judge of horseflesh, not like Verity anyway, but unless she was mistaken, that horse belonged to Mr. Kirby.

Her suspicions were proved correct when she entered the house to hear voices coming from the drawing room: her grandmother's voice, and the unmistakable low tones of Mr. Kirby. After a moment's hesitation, she stripped off her gloves and bonnet and handed them to the footman, braced within, and entered the open door.

"Good afternoon." She glanced at her grandmother, Miss McNell, and the three guests, offering them a cool nod and her best masked smile. For a few moments she was able to engage in polite nothings, until Mr. Kenmore engaged her grandmother in conversation, leaving Caroline to face Miss Kirby and her brother.

Emma cleared her throat. "Miss Hatherleigh, I hope you do not think it presumptuous, but we simply could not let another day pass without hoping to explain ourselves regarding that last unfortunate encounter."

"Explain yourselves? Forgive me, but I do not take your meaning."

Mr. Kirby remained standing, hands behind his back, his expression grave. "I am very sorry, Miss Hatherleigh, if my words sounded unmannerly on Tuesday. I am sorry if you were upset."

"Upset? I don't know what you mean." The imp of perversity propelled her on. "It's of no interest to me, Mr. Kirby, what kind of person takes your fancy, I assure you."

He flushed satisfactorily, and she turned her artificial smile to his sister. "I hope you will forgive me, but I have just come in from a walk and find myself in sore need of a rest. It was nice of you to call. Goodbye."

She snuck a peek at her grandmother's face and quickly turned from her outraged expression, exiting the room with her head up, her poise steady. Until she reached her room.

Her shoulders slumped. Dear God, what had she done? She had been immeasurably rude, clutching desperately to pride like a torn garment to hide her vulnerability. She knew her actions had displeased Grand-mama, for as often as she might declare the Aynsleys were of noble heritage, she was just as adamant that the honor due to such a proud lineage as theirs only existed as a result of the respect they showed their fellow man. And Caroline had shown neither honor nor respect. Especially to those she had once so foolishly hoped might be her friends.

Her heart hollowed, and a lump wedged in her throat. She was such a bad person. But sometimes it felt rather too hard to be nice, to pretend hurts didn't sting. She would be better off returning to Aynsley at once.

A squeaked floorboard announced a visitor, and Caroline sat up on the bed and hurriedly brushed her wet eyes.

"Young lady, I have never been more ashamed in my life."

Her chin tilted. "Grandmama, I am sorry to disappoint you, but you did not hear what he said the other day."

"I do not care what he said! You, a daughter of Aynsley, have no right to behave in such a manner. Those people might be below us — although the Irish one might be your social equal, I'm not sure, as I found it hard enough to listen to him let alone understand much of what was said — but regardless, that gives you *no* excuse to speak in such a way."

Caroline's gaze faltered before her grandmother's hard one. "I know. I am sorry. I should return to Aynsley —"

"You are going nowhere until you apologize to them."

"They are still here?"

"I have instructed Dawkins to show them the gardens. We shall perhaps posit your earlier removal as a chance to change your attire rather than as the snub it appeared to be."

Guilt panged again, and she nodded.

Grandmama exited, and the door closed gently, with the restraint befitting an Aynsley.

Caroline quickly exchanged her walking dress for something a little nicer, and made her way downstairs to find the others at the end of the garden, in the place overlooking the beach where she had spied Mr. Kirby last week. Trepidation filled her. How would they respond?

She swallowed. "Hello again."

Three figures started, then turned, their movements so identical it raised a small smile.

"Miss Hatherleigh." Miss Kirby smiled warmly. "Thank you for condescending to see us."

Caroline's cheeks heated. "I am sorry about . . ." She waved a helpless hand.

Mr. Kirby bowed. "I fear my ungracious

words have hurt you more than you allowed before. Please forgive me."

He was apologizing to her? She shook her head. "You must forgive me, Mr. Kirby. My ungraciousness just now was entirely my own doing, and something for which I must apologize."

He offered her a look halfway between wry and understanding. The hard knot in her chest eased a fraction.

"Well! I'm glad to see this little misapprehension has been cleared up," Mr. Kenmore said.

Caroline glanced at Miss Kirby, whose nod suggested it had indeed been resolved.

"I wonder if perhaps I might be so bold as to propose a little excursion," the Irishman continued.

What? "I am sorry, but I do not see . . ."

Her words faltered as he held up a hand. "I must beg for your patience, Miss Hatherleigh, and ask that you hear my reasoning. Truly, I feel the only way Gideon here can make it up to you is if you agree to a tour of some of the local sites where his precious fossils may be found."

"Oh, but —"

"Are you perhaps not so keen on such things? I can understand that the discovery of tiny creatures from long ago might not suit everyone's tastes, so perhaps another venture could be arranged. I know! I have heard mention of a set of caves nearby, where once there was a hidden chapel."

"A hidden chapel?" Caroline repeated blankly.

"I have heard of it also," Emma said. "Mrs. Baker was telling me of some of the local sites, although she said such a place was simply used now as a quarry, and held nothing of interest save some bats."

Caroline shuddered.

"Bats," Mr. Kenmore echoed. "Well, I don't mind admitting that I am quite partial to the little creatures. They always seem to be misunderstood, something I find myself rather prone to also."

Mr. Kirby made a noise that sounded like a snort of disbelief. "Your trials are heavy, my friend."

"I'm so glad you understand," Mr. Kenmore continued. "It has been a sore trial to me these past years thinking that perhaps you did not."

"Aidan," Emma voiced in soft reproach.

"Forgive me, my dear," he said, sending her a warm smile. Just how well did they know each other? "Well" — his attention returned to Caroline — "I believe I am heartily in need of visiting such sites myself, and I have high hopes that Emma here may be persuaded to accompany us."

"But if you have been warned not to go . . ." Caroline said doubtfully.

"Was it a warning, my dear?" Mr. Kenmore turned to Emma.

"I . . . I could not be sure."

"If so, I wonder why such a warning might have been given." His upraised brows at Mr. Kirby were met with a firm shake of the head. "Ah well. Perhaps an excursion to another interesting locale might be in order. I've heard talk about the ruins of a Roman fort?"

"It is near the western end of the village," Mr. Kirby confirmed.

"Excellent! Now, if only Emma might be persuaded to attend with you, we can make arrangements for a grand adventure." He shot Emma a glance which was met with her soft rebuff. Disappointment crossed his features, and was quickly smoothed away into the geniality Caroline had by now assumed was his usual mien. "No? Well, I am sure we can find someone else to say yes and thus offer their chaperonage. Do you think your grandmother might be so inclined?" He raised his eyebrows at Caroline.

"I'm afraid not." Why the idea!

"Her companion?"

"No."

"Your maid?"

"Somehow I do not think caves or ruins in line with Mary's interests."

"Ah, but we never know what can interest us unless we search to see. Why, you may find yourself developing an intense enthusiasm for a time long past. Such a thing can be most liberating indeed."

"I'm sure it can," she offered. But for all his friend's enthusiasm, Mr. Kirby still had not offered to sponsor any such excursion, and she could not — would not — be presumptuous with him. She had no intention of being misled by foolish emotions again.

"Miss Hatherleigh," Emma said, her brow knit, "I would be most happy to accompany you on a journey to the fortifications, if that would make you feel better, but I must admit to a certain degree of fear in entering confined spaces, should there be anything of that nature."

"Dearest Emma," Mr. Kenmore said with a smile. "You are truly the most excellent of women."

Emma blushed, averting her gaze.

"Oh, but . . ." Caroline faltered.

Mr. Kirby's head inclined. "Please, Miss Hatherleigh. We would truly appreciate your company on such a venture."

Her smile of politeness froze. *We* would? Did that imply he had no pleasure in her company himself, save for what she could offer his sister?

"And if another expedition could be arranged, I would enjoy the opportunity to show you where certain fossil specimens have been found so far."

Oh! She relaxed as the warmth in his gaze sent heat through her chest. Perhaps if he could be gracious so should she. "I will speak with my grandmother." She offered a small smile. "She seems to think it quite marvelous that the local free traders have not taken issue with your searching near their caverns."

He exchanged a look with Mr. Kenmore over Emma's head that made her think perhaps issue had been taken, but he had no wish to alarm his sister.

"Really?" Emma said, looking between them. "Is smuggling a problem here?"

"I do not believe the smuggling is the scourge we are sometimes led to believe," Mr. Kirby said.

"I personally do not think it a scourge," murmured Mr. Kenmore.

"How can you say such a thing?" Emma said, eyes widened.

"Quite easily, if I believe the government demands brutal taxes. I mean, really, do you believe exorbitant taxes on liquor justifiable? No, the free traders have my sympathies, as all good Irishmen would agree." He gave a decided nod.

"But surely you cannot approve their means?" Caroline ventured. "I have heard some are cutthroats, and deal with those who oppose them most ruthlessly."

"Please do not misunderstand me, for of course I do not support their methods of intimidation. It is simply that I can understand why they feel they must resort to illegal means." He smiled. "But I'm sure our excursion need not involve the lairs of smugglers. What say you, Gideon?"

"I thought you were only here for a short time," said Mr. Kirby.

Mr. Kenmore shrugged carelessly. "I find I am able to extend my stay, provided my hosts are amenable." He glanced at Emma with such candor in his eyes that she blushed.

"I . . . have no objection," she finally managed.

"I am glad," he said in a low tone, that seemed meant for just the two of them.

Caroline watched Mr. Kirby curiously. How would he feel about this very obvious demonstration of partiality, especially when his sister was still married? How could such a thing ever work? She had heard that divorce was incredibly difficult and expensive to obtain; so how could this attraction blooming between them ever end happily?

Mr. Kirby met her gaze, and in his gray eyes she found a wealth of emotion: understanding, frustration, despair.

Sympathy tugged within, and she offered a small smile which elicited a similar response from him. Conscious of a growing awareness, she glanced away, to where a small boat listed in the dark sea. "Do you think that might be a smuggler's vessel?"

Three sets of eyes swiveled to look. "I cannot see smugglers being fool enough to risk being spotted in the daylight," Mr. Kenmore scoffed.

Mr. Kirby glanced at her, warm humor hovering around his mouth. "I do not think you need to concern yourself with free traders, Miss Hatherleigh, not if you would be so good as to accompany us on a visit to one of the local fossil sites." He grinned. "I promise to protect you should any smugglers make an appearance."

"And do you always keep your word?"

"Yes."

His look grew serious, intentional, his eyes

warm as he said in a lower voice, "Please Miss Hatherleigh, I would be honored if you deigned to accompany us on an excursion this week to see the Roman fortifications. Please say you will come."

Her heart fluttered, for in his look she could read intention far beyond mere introduction to fossils. Had he indeed lied about his interest in her? The fluttering became more agitated, her nerves pulling across her midsection. For despite the interest she recognized in his eyes, she knew that, just as with Emma and Mr. Kenmore, this attraction had no hope of succeeding, not with the very likes of Grandmama and her parents sure to lend opposition.

But something within her begged to see how far this attraction could go, to dare to participate in life beyond the role of observer that society dictated.

Conscious he awaited her answer, she dared. "Yes."

Gideon glanced at his companions as they clambered through the fortifications of the Roman Age. Whilst he knew his time would be much better put to use examining cliffs, he understood today's outing was necessary for a number of reasons.

Emma needed opportunity to enjoy some

fresh air, and time to further connect with her new friend. Aidan, like Gideon, was also reveling on this unseasonably mild day in the chance to be out of doors, as they explored the ruins from long ago. And, Gideon thought, watching the two young ladies chatter, he didn't mind the opportunity himself to observe Miss Hatherleigh in such relaxed surroundings, albeit under the eye of the maid that Lady Aynsley had insisted attend her.

Miss Caroline Hatherleigh remained a mystery. Her manner vacillated from careful propriety to something more relaxed and charming, as evidenced earlier with her exclamation of startlement when they had visited the harbor to collect supplies, and a boatload of mackerel had been dispersed at the dock. The shiny fish, their colors gleaming in rainbow hues, proved a most rustic and charming picture, something Miss Hatherleigh herself had noted, exclaiming with an expression of delight. Yet contrast this to the stiff manner in which she at other times held herself and it was enough to make him wonder. Was her agreement to accompany them borne from the wish to escape her own boredom, or did she, like him, long for something more?

Regardless of her motivation, he could not

complain about her company; she was as good for Emma's spirits as she was for his own eyes, eliciting quite a few chuckles from Emma as they ate their picnic lunch on a cloth spread on the grass. The donkey that had brought their cold provisions was tethered nearby, his occasional *hee-haw* drawing smiles. The view over the ocean agreed with the travel guide to Sidmouth that Emma had borrowed from the library, a view that "defied the most sumptuous edifice created by the hand of art." He drew in a deep breath and released it slowly.

"Miss Hatherleigh is proving a charming companion," Aidan said quietly. "I am glad for your sake that she chose to acquiesce to our expedition today."

"For *my* sake?" Gideon asked.

"Aye," Aidan said. "You cannot know how concerned I have been about you, my friend. And now for such a personable young lass to have piqued your interest . . ."

Gideon's eyes narrowed.

Aidan chuckled. "Don't look at me with such daggers. I am pleased for all our sakes. You may even find she is amenable to other excursions. It is good for your sweet sister to have something to distract her these days."

"Something other than a certain Irishman

you mean?"

"No, I do not mean that at all. I would quite happily distract Emma for the rest of my days if I could, but I suspect the Church might frown on such a thing."

"Not to mention James."

"I try to make it my policy never to think on him, I'm afraid."

A moment, weighty with the past, stretched between them.

"Tell me, dear Gideon, what do you plan to do about Pratt? Forgive me, but I cannot think it best for your sister's health if she is dragged from pillar to post as you try to elude notice. And while I do heartily applaud the inclusion of such ladies as Miss Hatherleigh to the Carstairs circle, the more who know Emma the more likely it is that someone will say something that will let her secret out. And I do not like the feeling of the unknown hovering, vulture-like, waiting to pounce."

"Very descriptive," Gideon said, in an attempt at lightness. But when Aidan said nothing more, obviously waiting for Gideon to continue, he was forced to finally admit the truth that kept him awake at night. "I do not know what I would do if he was to suddenly appear. I live, half in dread, half in desperate prayer, wracking my brain for what to do should that happen. I long to know she will be safe."

"You had put it about that you were overseas. Could you not take Emma and escape to someplace far away? While your disguised names might be some protection, I cannot think it will prove quite enough to hide your true identities forever."

"I could not alter things overly —" he began.

"No, I know why you chose it so, but I do think it best to consider what your strategy should be if Pratt arrives in town."

For the next few minutes they talked quietly, discussing stratagem, making plans, discarding them, before Aidan finally sighed. "I do not envy you, my friend. But I trust you know you can always find refuge at Kilgarvan if you require. Or even if you don't," he added, that sparkle of mischief back in his eye.

"I thank you most sincerely," Gideon replied, heart touched. "But I would not wish to further jeopardize her health by taking her so far from the specialists in London. It is a comfort to know we can be there within the day, if necessary."

"I understand," Aidan said. "It is as I expected."

"Gideon!" Emma called. "Would you

164

come and look at this? I believe it to be most interesting."

"Of course," he said, getting up, and moving quickly to the ladies. He smiled at Miss Hatherleigh, then turned to his sister. "For someone who purports to be bored by matters of science it is surprising just how often you draw my attention to these specimens."

"I am a most dutiful sister," she said in a tone of innocence, but with a sly look at her companion that gave lie to her words.

"Now, what is it you wanted me to see?"

"This." Emma produced a small shell and dropped it in his hand. "Caroline was very keen to hear from the resident expert about such things."

"Oh! I — that is, no, I —"

He smiled inwardly at Miss Hatherleigh's rosy confusion, smoothing his expression to approximate something appropriately scientific. "Look, Miss Hatherleigh," he said, drawing closer. "See the pale pink ridges here? They tell something of the age."

She shifted closer, so he could smell her sweet scent, like the lily of the valley flowers he remembered hidden in the woodlands of home. "And how old would you say this shell might be?"

"It is difficult to say. Perhaps hundreds of years."

She touched the shell gingerly as it lay in the palm of his hand. "It is very lovely."

The whorl of her ear, the scent of her hair, the very softness of the appearance of her skin wafted tendrils of desire within. He tried to speak. Was forced to clear his throat. "It is."

She glanced up at him, her gaze capturing his in the way it had several times before, but this time they were so much closer. So close that he couldn't help but notice the violet lines that circled her iris, a color so intriguing he felt he could easily gaze deeply into her eyes for days; a closeness that lent itself to an intimacy he only wanted to prolong.

She blinked, the moment dissolved, and he cleared his throat again. "I believe this type of shell was recently inhabited by a tiny crab."

"And where is he now?"

"He has probably grown too big for such a small house, and has moved to somewhere bigger."

"Is that a common practice?" Her look grew wistful. "You might think me foolish, but it seems a shame that a pretty place be abandoned in the hope of something bigger. Surely that which is bigger is not necessarily better."

Her words caused him to pause. Was she simply talking about the crab shell, or was it indicative of something deeper? Was he a fool to wonder if she might be happy with a humbler life than that to which she was obviously accustomed?

"May I ask why you believe this, Miss Hatherleigh?"

"Oh." She gave a small shrug. "I appreciate the warmth to be found in smaller dwellings."

She spoke as if used to a palatial style residence, which renewed his swirling doubts. But he remembered the surprising change in circumstance which had led his family from a parsonage to something far more grand, and how much closer his family had been before the weight of titled obligation. "I agree."

"I suspect one is forced to interact with others in a more personal way than when one is surrounded by so many rooms, and can find escape or distraction more easily."

"Ah, but such close interactions might be driven by necessity, not necessarily by choice. I cannot think the poor prefer to live in a single-roomed house."

"I suppose it's not the size of the house itself, but rather the quality of the interactions I admire, such as is demonstrated between you and Emma. I would like to have such a thing," she added in a softer voice, almost as an afterthought.

"This may come as something of a surprise, Miss Hatherleigh, but I do not always find myself in agreement with my sister. We disagree, but I have always hoped to follow the maxim given us in the book of Romans: 'If it be possible, as much as lieth in you, live peaceably with all men.' I do not always manage it," he admitted, "but I try."

"The book of Romans?" she inquired.

"In the Bible?" he prompted hopefully.

"Ah, yes."

But her look suggested she was not much acquainted with that particular book. "It is found in the New Testament. Paul's letter to the church at Rome."

Her brow puckered for a long moment, then she sighed. "Well, regardless of your reasoning, I find myself challenged to reconsider my interactions with my own sisters, and see the times when I have fallen short."

"I am sure we all have times when our dealings with others have not been as they ought." His last encounter with Pratt leapt to mind. Perhaps he had been a *trifle* heavy-handed . . .

"Indeed."

Another moment, soft with accord, stirred between them.

Then her smile flashed. "I must say it is somewhat refreshing to talk to a gentleman who does not hide behind false civilities, someone who would say, 'Oh, I'm sure you mistake the matter, Miss Hatherleigh; you would never exchange a cross word with another person in your entire life.' "

"You mean you have?" he said, opening his eyes wide.

She laughed, a rich, sweet sound that reminded him of warmed honey. "Yes. And I might be so bold as to say I rather think *you* have exchanged hard words on occasion also, if that look of yours but a moment earlier was to be believed."

He inclined his head. "I am but a sinner, and will confess to behavior that has not always made me proud."

"But pride is a sin, is it not?" she asked, innocently.

A chuckle escaped, and he shook his head. "You make me forget myself, Miss Hatherleigh." He offered his arm. "Now, where is that sister and foppish friend of mine?"

CHAPTER TEN

The conversation lingered in Caroline's memory, pursuing her into sleep, the conviction that she had not treated others as she ought almost like a tangible thing, chasing her into spending the following day writing kind letters to Serena and to her own sisters.

To Serena she offered apology for her self-interest over the years, and her hopes to rekindle a warmer friendship.

To Cecilia, she expressed regret at the hurtful words she had communicated on the day of her departure; Cecy's letters had possessed a polite stiffness, as if all trace of warmth had gone from their relationship. And while she could not regret Cecy knowing the truth about Ned Amherst's lack of interest, she realized now that her communication of that fact had more to do with her own pride than with a desire for Cecy's well-being.

Her letter to Verity was more of a challenge — how could she extend an olive branch to someone who was so dissimilar in every single way? But perhaps, she reflected, perhaps she and Verity were not so very different after all; they both cared for others, even if their demonstration of such care varied widely. And Caroline could now finally glimpse a little of what Verity seemed to long for in seeking to rebel against societal rules, wanting to be free. For herself, Caroline was not yet sure if she possessed enough courage to follow her passion — whatever said passion may be — but regardless, she now knew that not all people might be content to settle for the grooves established by society. To Verity she finally managed to write something of her regret at her treatment over the years, that she had not proved to be the supportive sister she could have been.

The writing of such letters would doubtless be frowned upon by Mama, who always thought apology a sign of weakness, but Caroline felt so much better, more at peace, more at charity with the world, like invisible cords within her heart had been untied. Perhaps there was more to be said for aspiring to live at peace with others, as the Kirby siblings believed.

Perhaps there might even be something to

seeing what other words of wisdom might be found in the Good Book they liked to read.

That night following dinner, she decided to see if she could find the passage Mr. Kirby had quoted. Grandmama had gone to the Assembly Rooms, but Caroline had pleaded a headache — not wanting to admit that the only people she wished to speak with were unlikely to be there. Neither the Kirbys nor Mr. Kenmore gave the impression of being terribly wealthy, nor that attending society events would be their preferred way to spend time. So instead of trying to maintain the polite fiction of caring about insipid conversations, she was snuggled in the four-poster bed, carefully turning the pages of the rather large and heavy family Bible she had liberated from the library.

Really, it felt strange to be even holding a Bible, let alone reading it. Surely only church ministers did such things? But something about the Kirbys' sincere belief had compelled her to see if this book contained truth like they thought — though heaven knew what her parents would think if they saw her now. No doubt they would say something about the foolishness of believing old myths and trusting in an invisible being.

She located the book of Romans that Mr. Kirby had quoted and began to skim the words, looking for the part about living peaceably with all. A section in the third chapter gave her pause. Really? God thought they were all sinners? Well, she certainly wasn't; it wasn't as if Caroline had ever murdered someone! The old indignation rose before memories of her words yesterday gave renewed pause. Hadn't she herself admitted to being less than perfect? And hadn't she acknowledged the times she had fallen far short of what she had known was right? And this with people she was related to, that were her friends, that she was *supposed* to love. If she had failed to love them appropriately, how much less righteous were her actions towards those she did not know so well?

She bit her lip, and read on.

In the sixth chapter she found another verse that seemed to parallel the previous one. Her heart sank at the first words: *the wages of sin is death.* How true that could be; even if it did not mean physical death, sin still had a way of poisoning one's heart, of deadening one's soul, of making someone uncaring and unkind. She could see in her own life how pride had stolen her compassion. Even if God wasn't truly real, this verse still held some truth.

But — she felt her frown lift — if the second part of the verse was true, the part about the gift of God being eternal life through Jesus Christ, then how wonderful was such a gift! That is, *if* Jesus Christ had really lived. Although, now she thought on it, if Jesus hadn't really lived, then it seemed strange that so many people believed He had, especially those interested in history and science, like the Kirbys and Mr. Kenmore. Was her parents' opposition to faith due more to tradition or unwillingness to examine their own lives than based on what the results of real study had given?

She read on. The next chapter talked about the law, about commandments, things that seemed somewhat confronting and challenging to understand. But one part did make sense, that concerning the good left undone, and the evil — well, the sin, at least — she should not do that she had done. How often had she tried to *not* say something hurtful only to speak unkindly mere moments later? But it was at the end of the chapter she found words that really struck her soul. "O wretched man that I am! who shall deliver me from the body of this death?

I thank God through Jesus Christ our Lord."

The way, the means, to salvation lay in this person Jesus Christ. The way to freedom from the law of sin and death, the way to freedom from her pathetic attempts at righteousness that always fell short. Such freedom was found in Jesus Christ.

"Jesus Christ." The words spoken aloud sounded almost blasphemous, but also seemed to hold a curious strength. Had He truly come to save a person from the guilt and shame of sin? Could He truly help her? Was He even really real?

"Please help me understand."

To whom she spoke, she could barely admit, the words rippling forth from her soul, chased as they were by doubts. If this was real, then this was wonderful; if not, then she'd be a fool. But she'd be a fool in excellent company. And somehow, she had recognized elements of truth in what she'd read . . .

She waited, listening, anticipation thumping in her heart. Would she hear some sort of reply? Or was expecting such things evidence that she had plunged to the depths of madness?

Outside, the wind held an eerie moan. Inside . . .

Silence.

Then there came a patter of feet before the door opened and Mary peered in. "Excuse me, miss, did you call for me?"

"No, thank you, Mary," Caroline said.

"Oh. I thought I heard voices."

Caroline swallowed a smile, then gave strict instructions not to return — yes, Caroline was quite capable of tending the fire and putting herself to bed — and sent her maid away.

Conscious of a curious sense of disappointment — had she really expected an invisible being to speak to her? — she began to read the rest of the book, and found the section Mr. Kirby had quoted. "If it be possible, as much as lieth in you, live peaceably with all men."

She closed the Bible's hard covers gently, mind spinning over the implications of this, and the other verses she had read tonight, the doubts of the past battling with the promise found in a book much older. Was God real? Was Jesus Christ His Son? If true, what would this mean for her life, for her family, for her future? Or was this all an elaborate deception?

Caroline shook her head. No, she had tasted something real within these pages, something that made her want to change.

Regardless of anything greater, one thing was certain.

"If it be possible, as much as it depends on me, I will live peaceably with others."

She shifted and blew out the candle.

The day for their next excursion proved fine, allowing for time to appreciate the contrast of colors between cliff, sky, and sea. As the others engaged in conversation, Gideon focused on the cliffs, the storehouses of history that he longed to know. The deep-ribbed red cliffs around Sidmouth showed the wear of centuries, erosion eating away at the rocks, revealing tiny skeletons and fossils from eons ago. When he had first shown an interest in studying natural science and geology, years before on a family holiday to the south of England, his father had been shocked and not a little dismayed, decrying the pursuit of understanding an ancient past as something that was ungodly. "Why would you wish to dig up that which can never be again? Surely such a desire to learn how the world was made is in essence trying to become like God, and as such, is blasphemous."

"Father, my study has nothing to do with blasphemy, and everything to do with honoring our Creator."

A twinge of guilt had crossed his heart. Perhaps Gideon's own interest stemmed from honoring God, but he knew there were others who sought an explanation for the world's formation that denied God's sovereign power; indeed, there were some who denied the existence of God altogether. For these fellow scientists, he could only pray that the endless quest they had for answers might one day result in finding the greatest answer of all, the Answer who gave hope and purpose to life, rather than reducing all existence to mere happenchance.

Father had eventually come around, persuaded that Gideon wanted nothing more than to learn about the magnificent ancient creatures referred to in the Bible as leviathan or the behemoths of ancient days. Were such things somehow related to the *ichthyosaurus* skeleton discovered in Lyme Regis? How he wished he might discover something for himself.

"Darling brother, at the risk of sounding like a bore, may I enquire if we have much farther to travel?"

"Not much farther, I promise you."

He smiled at his companions. Emma — God bless her — had agreed to accompany them despite not feeling well, which had permitted Miss Hatherleigh to attend also.

His pulse scampered. To have Miss Hatherleigh here seemed barely believable. As much as he wanted her to visit, he would never have imagined her grandmother would grant permission for two outings within the week. But when Emma had posed the question, Lady Aynsley had assented, which meant Miss Hatherleigh was here, and he would have further opportunity to get to know her, while taking great delight in displaying the layers of time as revealed in the rocks.

The path turned then lowered alongside the beach and he soon drew Nancy to a halt. Aidan helped the ladies descend while Gideon secured the horse then retrieved his materials, which allowed a moment to surreptitiously observe his special guest.

Miss Hatherleigh wore a yellow gown that perfectly highlighted the gold in her russet curls. Her bonnet and gloves detailed her father's wealth and her own exquisite personal style; she looked as neat as if she might be attending a London soiree rather than a trek through sand and dirt to inspect rocks. He smiled. For whatever reason she came, he was grateful.

"Are we ready?" he asked as they approached the stone-specked shoreline.

"Are you sure it will be safe?" Emma said,

with a worried glance at her friend.

"We shall be quite safe," he assured them both. He'd checked the tide; it was going out.

"And I shall be here to protect you," Aidan said, with another of those disconcerting looks at Emma that reminded Gideon of his urgent need to talk to his friend. But any time he ventured down that path Aidan diverted him with discussion of recent fossil finds, and Gideon, to his shame, had too easily allowed himself to be distracted.

To draw Emma's attention, he pointed out the little pools between larger rocks, bending to show the elegant corallines.

"What is that?" Miss Hatherleigh said, pointing to an example of an *anemone,* the curious animal flower of fungus consistency but with a Medusa-like head of small snakes.

He explained, and she sounded interested, so he went on to explain about other of the brightly colored creatures that could be found in this locale.

"They seem a form of natural treasure," she said.

"Indeed they are." Much like the treasure hidden in the cliffs.

"Speaking of treasure, are you sure we

shall not meet any smugglers?"

He grinned, offering Miss Hatherleigh his arm as they reached a section of slippery sea-washed stones. "Ah, now that I cannot guarantee."

"I do think that would make for quite a story."

"I'm sure it would, but perhaps I will show you the merits of this story . . ." He gestured to the rock wall which they now faced, a wall whose different layers of colors told the story of millennia.

Unsure just how much Miss Hatherleigh knew, he gave an abbreviated version of scientific discovery, sharing how just like excavations had led to discoveries of Roman forts and houses, history of a natural order had been preserved in the rocks until discovery in more recent decades.

"So, it is not blasphemous to discover what has been, as the land is simply a record, enabling us to learn about the past."

He saw that she had no reaction to his talk about blasphemy, which boded well. Perhaps she was more enlightened than his father with his strict puritanical beliefs. Or perhaps it stemmed from a lack of interest in God generally. He shook away the disquieting thought.

"See this here?" He pointed to a small

shell-encrusted ridge. "This is often where we can find ancient shells that are actually types of ammonites."

There were murmurs from the ladies that suggested interest, even though he knew Emma had seen similar specimens before. Aidan, he knew, had often seen such specimens; had in fact accompanied Gideon on some of his fossil-finding expeditions.

"And how long ago do you think such things might have lived?" enquired Miss Hatherleigh.

"There are different accounts as to how old they might be," he said carefully. "Some believe the world to be seven thousand years old, others believe it to be much older."

"Why would people think the earth to be seven thousand years old?"

"Because of certain ways of reading and interpreting the Bible."

"I see." Her head tilted. "Do you mean to suggest that the Bible is to be taken as a literal account?"

Here was the crux of the matter. If as a scientist he wanted to progress in his field then perhaps adhering to literal accounts was injurious to being treated seriously. Indeed, there were several professors at university who had scorned any attempt to reconcile biblical accounts of the formation of the world with scientific views, had indeed treated such beliefs as quaint and misguided. For his own part, Gideon could not reconcile how people who purported themselves as being open to discovery and reason seemed so closed to viewpoints not their own, and indeed went to extremes to make alternative viewpoints appear foolish. But such was the way of the world.

"I believe the Bible is true," he eventually said. "I believe that God created the world, but exactly how He created it I cannot be certain. But I do not believe, like some do," he said, thinking about certain professors, "that all of this amazing life came into being by chance. If you study natural history, or indeed any type of science, you cannot help but observe the patterns involved, patterns and an order that suggest a Master Designer at work, rather than the chaotic mess of happenchance. So yes, I believe the Bible can be considered authentic."

Her brow furrowed. "Then you believe that Jesus Christ was a real person."

"Of course." Wait — did she mean to imply that she did not? "There is much evidence from historians of that time to prove His life and death real."

"Such as?"

He paused. *Lord, what were those names*

again? His reading of Hugo Grotius's *The Truth of the Christian Religion* leapt to mind. "Such as the writings of Josephus, Pliny, Thallos, and Africanus."

"Christians, no doubt."

"Not all. Some were Jewish historians, some were Greek, some — such as Celsus and Julian — wrote against Christians. Regardless, they all believed Jesus Christ to be a real person. I am convinced that He certainly lived, and died, and I believe the Bible is true when it states He rose to life again."

She eyed him but said nothing, her closed features giving nothing away. He was tempted to ask what her beliefs were regarding the Bible when Aidan interrupted.

"So, where precisely is this famous fossil? I don't mind standing here while you two discuss theological matters, but I suspect your sister would prefer to be somewhere a little more sheltered."

Remorse panged. He should be more aware of Emma's poor condition, rather than only thinking about her lovely companion. Emma had been a trifle nauseous this morning, and the fact that she had decided to come at all was testament to her good nature rather than her good health.

"Of course. Please, let us go this way."

He led the way past a substantial solitary rock, standing up pillar-like from the sand, glad for the low tide that made entry accessible. He glanced out to the sea, which seemed to recede even more. As laden with nooks as this stretch of coastline was, he did not see this particular section as being of prime interest to smugglers. The stretch of sand was too broad at low tide, and the location, while seeming remote, would be inaccessible during high tide.

They rounded a corner, and he gestured to a narrow stretch of banded rock. "This here is the thing I wanted to show you." He pointed to a series of tiny arched lines.

"What is it?" Miss Hatherleigh said, inching closer.

"Mind your step. It is likely to be a little slippery." He held his hand to Miss Hatherleigh and she grasped it, her gloved fingers warm to his touch.

Exhilaration filled his chest, a joy that made him wonder at the pride he'd feel if — no, faith said it would be *when* — he could one day show his loved ones his most longed-for discovery.

"I believe this to be a very large example of a *cornu ammonis.*"

"Really?" Aidan said, peering closer. "You are certain?"

"Quite certain," Gideon said. "My visits to Lyme to see similar samples confirm it holds all the shape and markings."

"It certainly looks similar to the specimen housed at the British Museum," Aidan said. "Do you intend to extract it?"

Gideon smiled. "That is why you are here, my friend. We could hope that the ammonite might dislodge naturally —"

Miss Hatherleigh gave a sound of disbelief.

"No, really, the soil here is easily erodible and the winter storms have long been helpful in releasing new specimens to the eye. See? It is already somewhat loose on this side. I believe if we are careful, we can extract it today."

"Well, that is remarkable." She gently brushed the specimen, then glanced at her dirt-smudged gloves before tugging them off with a rueful smile and stuffing them in a pocket.

"Gideon, I . . . I do not feel so very well." Emma's voice held the edge of breathlessness.

"Emma? Do you wish to return? I can accompany you," Miss Hatherleigh offered.

"Then I best attend you both," said Gideon.

"No, no," Emma protested. "I am slightly

dizzy, that is all. I'm sure it will soon pass."

"We shall manage well enough," Miss Hatherleigh said, as Aidan murmured to Emma. "It would appear you and Mr. Kenmore have some work to do while we enjoy the fresh air."

Was this her way of saying she had not enjoyed his find? He swallowed disappointment and murmured, "Very well."

"Please do not think I have not enjoyed it," she said quietly, laying a hand on his arm. "But I do not want your sister to feel obliged to stay for my sake when she is not feeling well. And from Mr. Kenmore's questions, he certainly seems keen and able to help."

Heart lighter, he acquiesced, promising they would be done shortly.

CHAPTER ELEVEN

Caroline exhaled. "Well, that was certainly an experience."

"Forgive me," said Emma, still looking a little pale. "I don't know what came over me."

"It is no great matter. I must confess that standing at the base of such a great cliff face is a little overwhelming. But this" — she turned to look at the sea — "this is quite refreshing, is it not?"

She drew in a deep draft of fresh air, which restored balance within. Had she really just touched a young man, clasping his arm as she might her sister? Was she so lost to propriety that such things now seemed normal? For it had seemed normal, and something done more from a heart soft towards him, than from any conscious thought.

A heart soft towards him.

Caroline placed cool hands on hot cheeks.

What on earth was happening to her?

She peeked at her companion. Poor Emma still looked a little pale so she drew her forward to a smooth rock. "Here, come sit down. I'm sure you will feel better soon."

Emma gave a twisted smile but obeyed, looking quietly out to the sea. Behind them came the sound of implements striking stones, a steady patter that contrasted with the screech of gulls and slower surge and wane of sea. They sat quietly for some time until the gentle chipping sound ceased.

Caroline glanced over her shoulder to where she could hear the men talking. "They are like little children over there, excited about pretty baubles."

"Gideon has always had a strong interest in natural history," said Emma.

"It is something I have never really thought about," Caroline admitted. "But I can certainly see its fascination."

"My brother would be pleased to hear you say so," said Emma, a smile glinting in her eyes.

Caroline blushed and looked away. She really shouldn't give rise to speculation, but such experiences had never crossed her path before, and she hadn't lied: she did find these matters interesting. But whether that was enough upon which to base closer acquaintanceship was quite another thing.

The scent of fish wrinkled Caroline's nose. She was about to make a comment about the unpleasant aroma when Emma made a stifled sound. Caroline turned to see her hold a hand to her mouth. "Oh! You poor thing." She wrapped an arm around her shoulders. "Mr. Kirby!"

"Please, it is nothing," Emma said, but she did not shrug off Caroline's supporting arm.

"Emma? What is it?" Mr. Kirby gave Mr. Kenmore the large stone he held then hurried to her side. He glanced at Caroline but she shook her head.

"It is nothing," repeated Emma. "I merely feel a trifle ill."

"Then we best return you to the gig. Are you well enough to walk?"

She rose. Caroline dropped her arm but offered her hand as Emma moved unsteadily from the rock where she had perched.

"Excuse me." Mr. Kirby swept Emma up and carried her along the path, leaving Mr. Kenmore to bear the large stone while Caroline collected the scattered belongings and followed in their wake.

The quiet procession was punctuated by Mr. Kenmore's occasional grunts of exertion.

"That certainly looks heavy," Caroline offered, motioning to the stone.

"To be sure," Mr. Kenmore said, staggering slightly. "We can more carefully extract the ammonite once at the cottage, but I think it will be nearly as large as I've ever seen."

"That is good, is it not?"

"Aye, it is."

She heard a mumbled curse and looked at him.

He flushed. "Forgive me, but I cannot stand to see Emma unwell."

Concern for her friend edged her heart. "I do hope she will feel better soon."

There came a murmur of agreement, then, "How that —" another profanity "— came to hurt her so."

"Surely you don't mean Mr. Kirby?"

He chuckled, albeit a little grimly. "Course not. Gideon's as upright a fellow as ever you'd meet. No, that cur who tricked her into marrying him."

She felt her eyes widen, but she wouldn't ask. She *wouldn't* —

"Who is he?"

He glanced at her, but his lowered brows and flashing eyes held an expression so forbidding that she hastily begged his forgiveness for such impertinence, and hurried ahead. Clearly there was some mystery here.

By the time she reached the carriage Emma was seated in the back, her eyes closed, her expression paler than the Carrera marble statues gracing Aynsley's Long Gallery. Mr. Kirby shot Caroline an apologetic look from where he was preparing the horses for their departure.

"Forgive me, Miss Hatherleigh, but I think it for the best if Emma is returned home as quickly as possible. She is susceptible to colds and I —"

"Of course she should return home. I can stay with her if you think that would help."

"Thank you, but she will have servants who know her condition and can assist."

"Of course," she said, trying not to take offense at how her offer to help had been so summarily dismissed.

Mr. Kenmore arrived, placed his burden in the rear of the gig, then offered Caroline his hand to ascend. She kept her spine ramrod straight as they returned, but then noted poor Emma's pallor and glistening brow, and reached to gently squeeze her hand.

Soon they had arrived at the small cottage, and Emma was being assisted to exit, Mr. Kirby barking orders at his friend to take Miss Hatherleigh home.

Within seconds the brother and sister had entered the building, leaving Caroline to look at Mr. Kenmore uncertainly.

"Forgive him. He is right to consider Emma's health. She has always been delicate, and today she tried to do more than she should," he said, almost angrily.

"If I had known I would never have insisted on going today."

"No, no, it is not your doing. She is stubborn, like her brother." He snapped the reins. "Forgive me, I'm not making much sense, am I?"

"No."

He chuckled, his expression clearing. "It may come as a surprise to you, Miss Hatherleigh, but I have long considered myself like another brother to her."

"It comes as a surprise you consider yourself as a brother."

Mr. Kenmore looked sharply at her, then gave a bitter-sounding laugh. "I suppose I am fool enough to think my affections unobserved."

"If it's any comfort, I believe she is unaware."

"I don't know if that is comfort or not."

"Forgive my impertinence, but how could it be any comfort for her to know such a thing? Is she not married?"

He jerked a nod.

"Then — again, forgive me — how could you ever hope to find happiness with her?"

A sigh sounded, seemingly wrenched from his innermost being. "It be a long road that has no turning."

"Surely society would take a very dim view on such things."

"I find I do not care. Emma has long enchanted me, ever since I knew her as a little girl. It's like her smile has chained my soul forever."

Caroline's heart throbbed in sympathy. Oh, to have someone wax so poetically over her . . .

"I first met Emma when I returned with Gideon to his home during the Long Vacation. Emma's grand smile, her patient spirit, was like balm, soothing my soul. I felt as though I had met an angel. It was then I determined that I would marry her one day, and after I completed my studies I returned and offered my hand, only to be told by her father that he would never countenance an Irish ingrate."

Her breath caught. She had heard her own father make similar derogatory comments, and had never minded them overly. But to hear such discriminatory words from this perspective . . .

"I am sorry."

"I don't want your pity, lass. I just cannot stand to have you think me dishonorable."

"I never thought that!"

"No?" He glanced at her quickly. "Well, regardless of what others think, I will wait forever for her — for that maggoty scoundrel to die and finally free her from the noose of cursed matrimony."

She stared at him. What must it be like to have a man admit he was enchanted by her? To have someone willing to wait for her? To seem almost willing to commit violence for her? The thought was shocking — and also a little thrilling.

"May . . . may I ask what happened?"

He shook his head, and for a moment she thought him affronted and would not answer. Then he sighed. "It was a bad business. Their father was ill, and I like to think that is why he would not entertain my suit. He said something about not wanting Emma taken off to the wilds of west Ireland." He snorted. "Like we don't have doctors over there."

The bitterness in his voice wrenched her heart. Here was passion, but passion tortured by propriety's strictures.

"Next I knew she had been married off to

the most likely candidate, leaving my poor heart torn in pieces. These past two years have been torture. I tried to forget. I traveled, I represented my father's interests at home and abroad, but I could never forget her. Or that scoundrel who married her." His lips pressed together as if to clamp down further words.

Sympathy wrenched. The poor man. To have loved and lost, and yet never given up. "Do . . . do you think she is safe?"

"I pray so," he said. "If ever I see that monster — Forgive me, Miss Hatherleigh. I have a tendency to let my tongue run away with me."

"If it's any comfort, I think you would have made her very happy," she said, thinking of how often he made Emma smile. "I think you still do."

"Well, there is that, I suppose." He released an audible breath. "She does not have an easy road ahead of her, that is for sure and for certain, but I will do what I can to make her smile, and bring some gladness to her heart, for as long as I breathe."

Her eyes pricked, and she swallowed several times to clear her throat. How wonderful, how inspiring, to see such affection in action. Surely this behavior displayed love more than fancy verses or flowers. She sighed. Would she ever be so fortunate as to be loved like that?

Three days later Caroline was disappointed yet unsurprised to see neither the Kirbys nor their friend at services. The minister's prayer for the sick was one echoed sincerely in her heart for Miss Kirby, prayers not being something she was overly familiar with. Still the confusion raged. Mr. Kirby seemed so certain that Jesus Christ was real, that the things in the Bible occurred, but her legacy of unbelief made such simple trust so hard. How was talking to an invisible someone any good, save as a kind of panacea to the soul? Surely it was the hope that someone might be listening that was of greater good, not so much the thought that an invisible someone was actually answering prayer?

Her thoughts tracked back to that unsettling discussion about the Bible, and Mr. Kirby's firm belief in a Creator. She had never really given it much thought. It did seem foolish to believe the world had just magically formed into such order without someone or something being responsible, without a guiding hand, but she never thought that someone might be actively interested in their lives today. She had rather supposed He must have made the world then left them to it. Her brow furrowed. But surely that presupposed belief in a God after all?

"Caroline, people are waiting for you to leave," her grandmother hissed, forcing Caroline to her feet, and her expression to adopt something more appropriate for church. She swallowed a smile. Heaven forbid anyone think she was actually thinking about whether the God they worshipped in such a place actually existed or not.

"Ah, Miss Hatherleigh," the minister intoned, taking her hand. "It was good to see you engrossed in the sermon today."

Heat swept her cheeks. It hadn't been his message that engrossed her. "I wonder, Reverend Holmes, what evidence you can give for the validity of the Bible."

"Caroline!" her grandmother exclaimed.

Reverend Holmes's look of startlement gave way to one of condescension. "I am sure those subjects are not what a young lady should be thinking on."

"Indeed they are not," snapped Grandmama before dragging her away. "What do you mean by asking such questions? And to a minister no less?"

"Who better to ask that question of? Surely he should have a ready answer."

"Well, yes, but to ask such a thing in a public place, where anyone might hear you. Why, one would think you might be one of these bluestockings one reads about, and I cannot think your mother would countenance that."

No. Mama certainly would not wish for her eldest daughter to be spending more time wondering about books and religion than about finding a husband.

"I am sorry if I have embarrassed you, but I have found myself thinking about things I have never considered before."

"Well, it is not seemly and must stop."

She bit back her reply. Perhaps she would not ask, but would do further investigation on her own. It was just a shame the people she thought might best be able to answer her question had not been in church today.

God, where are You?

Gideon gazed out across the garden to where the sea gleamed beyond. But today the vista held no comfort, held no assurance. Yesterday's visit from the doctor had put paid to that.

Emma was pregnant.

The doctor's prognosis was that she might likely die.

The word was a monstrous spider, whose

web was fast spinning across the truths he'd always known. How could a good God allow such things? Emma was innocent, had never harmed a fly much less a person. How would she cope?

He glanced up at the bedroom window beyond which his sister slept, the drugs having dragged her to unconsciousness. He was glad for the precious moments to think, to try to regain order in his brain which had felt in disarray since that dreadful day's visit to the cliff cave.

It seemed ice had overtaken his senses. How could they have not known? Yet the doctor had been clear: the nature of her long-standing illness meant that she had not presented with the usual symptoms. He had been sure about other things also. She was not likely to survive to see her child live. The pregnancy that fiend had forced upon her would sap her strength and steal what meager reserves of energy she had to fight this horrendous disease.

If only things could be as simple as they'd tried to pretend. If only dropping Pratt's name had been all Emma needed to do. If only she could drop that villain's spawn —

He swallowed bile. Muttered a prayer for forgiveness for such thoughts about an innocent child. But how could he prefer that man's child live at the expense of his sister?

The doctor had been so certain. "I am sorry, but in my experience, these conditions are only exacerbated by the extra stresses pregnancy entails, and it is highly likely you will find yourself feeling extremely fatigued and unwell."

When Gideon finally had him alone and had explained an edited version of their circumstances, the doctor had been more forthright. "I think you should prepare for the worst. The father — ?"

"Dead," he lied, ignoring the twinge of conscience.

"Then it is good she has you to provide strength at this time. She will need it."

Somehow, he'd managed to hold it together, had managed to maintain a stoic countenance in front of Tom Ballard and his wife, even Aidan, whose whitened face at the news preceded a hasty escape to the shore. But now . . .

He wiped his eyes, the emotion burning in his chest begging release. How would he ever cope without his sweet sister, without her sunny nature and smile?

Oh, where was God in the midst of this?

He looked up to the heavens, streaked with murky clouds that mirrored his inner despair. Where was hope? Where were those promises?

"God, where are You?"

As if triggered into action, a tiny glimmer of memory stole across his soul. What had been Father's oft-quoted verse? Something from Psalms, about God being his rock and salvation; "my defense, I shall not be moved," he muttered, the words snatched away on the dying wind. He'd always thought he would stand, that his faith would never falter, but right now he felt as though he might be blown far away.

"God, help her."

And God help him. He had so little left to give.

The next day Emma felt a little better, but he was reluctant to leave her alone — or alone with her thoughts. He knew she'd always had a strong conviction of God's love, love that transcended circumstances, but with this latest news he wondered whether her thoughts would press in on her as his had on him. He could only pray her faith remained strong.

He tapped on the bedroom door. "Emma? May I come in?"

At her affirmation he opened the door, relief seeping through his chest at the sight of her sitting up in bed, a Bible opened and to one side. "You look better."

"I feel better. I am sorry for yesterday's tears; I do not know what came over me."

"You never have need to apologize."

She smiled, and patted the side of the bed. He gingerly sat down. "I am not made of glass," she said.

"I know. I just have no wish to cause you pain."

"*You* will never cause me pain."

Her reassurance warmed him, gave tiny wings to hope that dare not speak its name. "Have you thought anymore on what the doctor said?"

She nodded. "I confess I was up half the night thinking through his words. And I cannot help but think it would be best —"

"— to seek a second opinion," he guessed. At her nod, he continued, "Yes, I thought the same."

"Do you, do you think it might be possible?"

"Of course. Aidan has the right idea in thinking a London doctor might know more than a rural man."

"But I hate to think your investigation would be interrupted again by my health."

"You are of far greater importance to me than any long dead creatures," he assured her, clasping her hand and giving it a gentle squeeze. "I shall make preparations for us to leave tomorrow."

CHAPTER TWELVE

They had left.

Caroline tried to not take it personally, conscious of her new resolve to live at peace with others. But, oh, how encompassing such a resolution was: to not be so quick to judge, to try to see things from an alternate perspective, to fight feelings of offense, to realize that other people's actions did not have to impinge on her own state of mind.

For everything about the Kirbys had proved kind, and she knew their reason for departure was perfectly reasonable. Their absence was simply necessary due to Emma's continued poor health, their removal to London because of her need to see specialists, or so Emma's letter had said, hand-delivered by a somber Mr. Kenmore that morning. He had made his own apologies for leaving also, saying he had business to attend to on his father's behalf.

Yes, she knew she shouldn't take these

matters personally, but the challenge from Romans still caused her struggle. She didn't like how their absence compounded her loneliness, making her aware of how few friends she truly possessed. She didn't like this continued rankle in her soul, the awareness that she was less than she'd always believed, that she was, in fact, more absorbed with herself and her own comfort than what she'd previously assumed. And she did not like the sense of helplessness she felt, unable to do anything more for Emma than to wish her well, for she rather doubted God — if He truly existed — would listen to the prayers of one who questioned His existence, or would want to help someone who mistrusted His power to do so. But maybe He'd be willing to overlook Caroline's inadequacies in the face of Emma's superior qualities —

"Excuse me, Miss Hatherleigh. Your grandmother wishes to speak with you in the library."

"Thank you, Dawkins," Caroline said, getting up from her chair and setting Mittens aside before following the butler to the library.

Oh dear. Such a summons never seemed to lead to anything encouraging. In recent days they had barely talked. Perhaps Grandmama was about to take her to task for preferring to spend time in her room.

Her grandmother looked up from where she was being read to by Miss McNell. The frown lines creasing her forehead plunged deeper. "There you are at last."

"Forgive me, Grandmama. I was not aware until now that you were looking for me."

Jezebel hissed at Caroline, causing her to jump, and wonder if that verse about living at peace with others was supposed to extend to felines as well.

"Thank you, Miss McNell. I wish to speak with Caroline alone."

"Of course," murmured Miss McNell, darting a blue-eyed look of curiosity at Caroline as she collected her knitting and book and left.

When the door had shut behind her — and the evil cat — her grandmother turned to her with a look that made Caroline's heart sink. Was she also going to be sent away?

"You puzzle me, my dear."

Caroline pressed her lips together. Likely it was best to stay silent.

"I find I do not know quite what to make of you. When you first arrived, you were quite a missish thing, and did not seem particularly interested in anything beyond your nose."

She winced. There might be *some* truth to that.

"I cannot help but attribute a recent lift in your spirits to your associations with that man and his sister."

"The Kirbys have been very kind and friendly. I enjoyed my time with them very much."

"Hmm. I do hope you are not developing a *tendre* for him?"

"Grandmama!"

"Don't look at me like that, child. It would not be the first time a man of more charm and personality than funds had caused a naïve girl to fall in love with him."

Caroline bit back words of affront, settling for a milder, "I am not in love with anyone."

"Really?" Her grandmother sniffed. "It also would not be the first time someone denied such a thing."

Heat filled her chest. Really, how much longer need she listen to these things? How was she to live at peace with Grandmama hurling hurtful accusations?

"I know your mother wished you to get away from association with the Amherst man, and I don't mind telling you I am not at all unhappy a connection with the Kirby fellow has now been severed as well. He is not the man for you, understand?"

She inclined her head. She understood her grandmother might think so . . .

"I find I cannot abide seeing you mope about the house as if the sun has gone away."

"I am not moping, Grandmama."

"No? Well, if that indeed be the case, I want you to get yourself dressed and ready. We are going out tonight."

Heart sinking, Caroline obeyed.

Still, she thought later when she was being helped into her satin gown — a gown more appropriate for a London soiree than the common Assembly Rooms this town boasted — at least tonight might offer something of a distraction.

Sidmouth's Assembly Rooms were connected to the London Hotel, which, with its position as the town's coaching stop, considered itself quite the premier establishment of the village. Caroline said all that was polite to the hotel proprietor, who was acting tonight in the role of master of ceremonies, and was clearly proud of his venue. But to compare such small rooms to the ones she had visited in Bath or London would be like comparing a mackerel to a whale. Even with its chandelier, there was scarcely anything of significance.

The people consisted of those to whom she'd already been introduced: Lady Dalrymple, the local squire, the owner of the manor. There was the captain of the militia, looking smart in his red coat and side whiskers. A couple from London, here for the sea air. The conversation was — as expected — dreary and insipid, consisting mainly of the dreadful weather, and the dreadful smugglers' latest exploits, and the dreadful shame it was that etcetera, etcetera, etcetera.

As Caroline turned from pretending interest in Miss McNell's story about Jezebel, her gaze was captured by a new arrival. The tall, fair gentleman — for gentleman he must surely be in that well-cut coat and satin knee breeches — glanced around, his gaze alighting on her for a moment before he bowed to her flustered curtsy.

Caroline looked away, embarrassed to be caught staring, yet unsurprised when, moments later, the master of ceremonies was at her side, begging for the opportunity to present his lordship to her.

Grandmama had wandered to the card room, which meant Caroline need decide for herself. She nodded, and seconds later, they were being introduced and the tall man was bowing once again.

"Good evening, Miss Hatherleigh."

"Good evening."

"I was pleased to see someone attending tonight who appears much younger and prettier than I was led to believe is usual."

Heat crept across her cheeks, but his words of flattery seemed empty. Or perhaps that was because his eyes were pale and held no warmth.

"I am sure Sidmouth proves more popular in the summer," she offered.

"Perhaps," he said, glancing sharply around the room. "I am told that this village is quite popular with certain celebrities, that even our King has enjoyed a stay here."

"On several occasions, I believe," she said.

"Hmm. It holds a certain charm I suppose." He put up his eyeglass to examine one particularly colorfully dressed lady, who appeared to have dressed for the Queen's Drawing Rooms, with a number of ostrich feathers jauntily placed in her hair. "How peculiar."

"You have just arrived?" she asked, not liking the way he sneered at the locals, yet uncomfortably aware how much his manner echoed hers from just weeks ago.

"Yes. From farther north."

She nodded. "Then you would be appreciative of the milder clime."

"Why? Are you from the north, too?"

"Well, yes." Aynsley was situated directly north, though she suspected it was not quite what he meant. She had no wish to lie, but neither did she feel like she wanted to give this unknown man too much information.

"Hmm. I wonder if you have ever had the chance to meet some acquaintances of mine. A man whose name is Carstairs, Erasmus Carstairs."

"Why no, I have not," she said, relief filling her at the truth. She glanced around for an escape. Really, this man was most presumptuous, speaking to her as if they were closer than the merest of mere acquaintances. "If you'll excuse me . . ."

"Or perhaps you've seen a lady, auburn-haired, pretty."

He could be describing any number of her acquaintances. "I'm afraid not. Good day, sir," she said, eyeing him in a way she had seen Mama do, before using his moment of bowing as her chance to walk quickly away.

"Who was that?" Miss McNell said, peering at him with not a little curiosity.

"A man who asks a great too many questions."

"Hmm. Where is he from?"

"Somewhere north, so he said."

"Does he have a name?"

Caroline thought back to their introduction. "He is a Lord Pratt, I believe."

Londonberry House
Mayfair, London

"James."

"Gideon." His brother clasped his hand firmly, before turning to their sister. "And Emma. My dear, how are you?"

"I have been better," she murmured.

"Forgive me, but you do not seem at all well. As much as I long to speak with you, perhaps it would be better on the morrow when you are feeling more the thing."

She demurred at first, but soon was persuaded to be taken by the housekeeper to a bedchamber upstairs, leaving the two brothers to face each other in James's study.

"How is your sweet wife?"

"Elizabeth is well, but had no inclination for London, not at this delicate time."

His sister-in-law was increasing, and after two miscarriages, much was hoped for this child to finally give James the heir he needed.

"She is in our prayers."

"And you and Emma have been in ours. Tell me, how is she?"

Gideon told of their late afternoon visit to Dr. Blakeney and his advice for this latest stage of Emma's chronic illness, advice which only concurred with that of Sidmouth's Dr. Fellowes.

His brother paled, the fire crackling in the fireplace the only sound for a long moment. "There is no hope?"

"We need a miracle." *God, grant Emma a miracle,* Gideon begged, before explaining more fully just what the doctor had said.

"If only I had known."

"We have only just learned this ourselves," Gideon said, nettled by the note of self-defense in his tone. "We sought a second opinion, which is why we came here."

James waved an impatient hand. "Never mind that. What are we to do? Emma must be shielded from Pratt at all costs. You obviously have not yet been found, although I cannot like your being in town. He has been sighted."

"What? He's not actually going to show up for Parliament, is he?"

"Perhaps. Who knows? Mayhap he holds some thought that doing his duty in this way will render him to appear responsible."

Gideon snorted. "It would take a lot more than just showing up for anyone to believe that true."

"But what if he does find you? What will you do? You could stay here, or visit the country house, but we both know they are the first places Pratt will try, and I strongly suspect he possesses enough audacity to show up and try to snake his way in."

"Elizabeth?"

"Is with her parents in Oxford while I attend Parliament, and I would not wish to trouble her, not when she's in a delicate condition."

"Kenmore has offered for us to travel to Kilgarvan and stay with his family."

"He still holds a candle for her?" James said, before muttering something under his breath. "He will not thank me, I know, but while he might treat poor Emma kindly, we both know that would only cause more harm if — when — the truth came out. It would be a scandal neither of our houses would easily live down. So I'm afraid I cannot support his offer, generous though it be."

Gideon plunged his head into his hands. "Then I do not know. I simply do not know."

Silence filled the room. Gideon's mind

whirled with unleashed emotion, with frustration, with the doctor's diagnosis.

"I wonder," James eventually said, "do you think it likely that you can remain unknown in Sidmouth?"

"I do not know. I will admit to surprise that Pratt has not found us yet."

"It would seem he did believe you had traveled overseas."

"Perhaps." Gideon shrugged. "But he is wily. I can only hope we are able to remain incognito."

He looked at Gideon curiously. "How much longer do you think you shall continue your search?"

"A week or so? Perhaps more? The winter season is when most cliff movement happens, and that is almost at an end."

"Then after Emma has rested, and if she is in agreement, perhaps it would be wise to return there, at least until arrangements can be made for an alternative location. Although I do not know if I like the fact that we are withholding news about a man's potential heir from him."

"A potential heir that will likely not be born because it will kill his wife first," Gideon snapped.

"We do not know that," James said. "Where is your faith?"

"Where it's always been," Gideon muttered. But barely.

The conversation moved on, but still the feeling of distress remained. Where was his faith? It felt like his faith was at the very bottom of the sea.

CHAPTER THIRTEEN

The reading room at Wallis's Marine Library possessed, in addition to the daily newspapers from London and the most popular periodicals, a most spectacular view across the bay — certainly something far lovelier than anything Bath or London might offer. Caroline looked up from the dissected map she had been assembling to glance once more at the view. Truly, when the sun was shining and with such a vista to behold, it was no wonder that Grandmama enjoyed living here. Why, she could almost believe this little village to be the most charming in all of England.

The sound of a low voice interrupted her musings. She paused, listening, recognition filling her. Her nose wrinkled. *That* man again.

Grandmama had not been pleased upon learning he had so abruptly forced his acquaintanceship upon Caroline. "Pratt? I know of no one by that name, and if that display of manners be his means of recommending himself to others, then I can assure you I have no desire to. It makes me think there is something distinctly untoward about that man."

That man was speaking to someone behind the glass cabinet displaying some of the curious toys and trinkets that made the Marine Library superior to the other circulating library in town kept by a Miss Giles.

". . . a Mr. Carstairs . . . someone who may purport to be his wife . . . red hair . . ."

"Oh, no," came Miss McNell's voice. "I'm afraid we know of no one new to town with that name. The only couple matching that description would be Mr. and Mrs. Kirby."

"*Mrs.* Kirby, did you say?"

"Yes. Or is it miss? I'm afraid I don't remem—"

"Would you be so good as to tell me where I might find them?"

"I'm afraid it would be no good looking for them now. Mrs. Kirby has been quite ill and they have but recently returned to London."

A sound, not unlike a growl, came from him. "And would you happen to have a forwarding direction?"

Caroline listened in growing trepidation.

Oh, let her not mention . . .

"Me?" Miss McNell tinkled with laughter. "Why would I have such a thing? No, they kept to themselves a great deal. Although Mrs. Kirby did seem to become quite good friends with dear Lady Aynsley's grand-daughter."

"Did she indeed?"

"Yes, so she might know something more."

"And where might she be found?"

"I do believe you met her yesterday. Miss Hatherleigh. She is somewhere here around."

Another growl-like sound. "Thank you, madam. You have proved most illuminat-ing."

Caroline shrank down into her seat. What would she do if he should speak to her? Now she knew there was something most definitely peculiar about the man, for why should he be searching for a Mr. Carstairs yesterday then be seeking Mr. Kirby today? Was this the man Emma was hiding from? A shiver of fear goose-fleshed her skin. She had no wish to speak with him further.

She glanced about. If he came to look for her, she had few hiding spots, the room consisting of a large table with chairs and a couple of sofas positioned in front of the book-lined walls. Heart thumping, she rose and hurried to the corner. Fortunately, a large, rather rotund gentleman had taken up residence in the sofa closest to the books, and she might just be able to squeeze between . . .

The sound of approaching footsteps quickened her movements as she maneuvered — most unladylike! — into the tiny space between sofa and wall. She burrowed into the wall, hiding behind the man's bulk, yet positioned so that if she were discovered she could say she was searching for a book.

"Excuse me," she whispered to the now-frowning man providing her screen. "That man is a loathsome creature, and I require your help to shield me."

She did not think her words did Lord Pratt any great disservice; she only hoped she'd done enough to appeal to the stranger's sense of chivalry.

A creak at the threshold suggested Lord Pratt had arrived, which was quickly confirmed by his voice. "Excuse me, I was wondering if you had seen a young lady, a Miss Hatherleigh, I believe?"

Caroline's breath held as the pause stretched unnaturally long.

Then, "I beg your pardon?"

"I am searching for a Miss Hatherleigh. Have you seen her by any chance?"

There came a harrumphing sound, then the plump man said, "I know of no such person, and I take leave to tell you I have no great liking for being interrupted in my reading. If you persist in looking for young ladies to make your sport then may I suggest you visit Lyme or some other place. We certainly don't hold with such carryings on here. Now, be off with you and let this reading room be returned to its original purpose, if you please!"

There came a sound of disapprobation before various creaks suggested the man had moved away. Seconds later came the plump man's whisper, "It is safe now, my dear. Your nasty-looking pursuer has gone."

She exhaled, but didn't stir. "Has he truly left?"

"I can see him passing by the windows as we speak. Perhaps he is going to Lyme to find himself a fancy bird after all." He chuckled at his wit.

She slowly rose, brushing down her clothing to release the worst of the wrinkles. "Oh, thank you so much, sir! Truly, he is not a nice man, and I have no wish to speak with him."

"Then I hope you have no need. And next time, my dear, if I might offer you a piece of fatherly advice, do not be so unwise as to take up with that sort of fellow."

She bit her tongue and offered a nod she hoped looked suitably penitent, and then slowly made her way out to the main room. Here Miss McNell drew forward, hands outstretched. "My dear, we have just been searching for you! I thought you had left."

"No, but I wish to leave now, if you please." Steering her grandmother's companion firmly to the door she murmured, "That man you spoke to earlier is the one Grandmama was complaining about last night."

"Oh, my! Goodness me! Oh, I did not know."

"No," Caroline said, hurrying towards the carriage. "And because you did not know him, it was not at all the thing for you to mention my name to him. What if he should seek to speak with me now you oh-so-obligingly told him I know the Kirbys? There is something most peculiar about him, Miss McNell, and I would not choose to speak with him again if my life depended upon it."

"My dear Miss Hatherleigh!" Miss McNell was almost in tears. "I do not know what to say."

That would be a first. "Then perhaps you should refrain from speaking until you know how matters truly stand."

They attained the carriage and were soon passing along the Esplanade, where a tall fair figure made her shrink in her seat. He turned, and in the moment of passing, stared into the coach, encountering her gaze before she quickly ducked her head.

But not before she'd seen his features harden as his lips twisted in an eerie smile.

The next two days she stayed in her room, not even venturing out of doors as was her wont, instead spending her time with Mittens as she worked on her correspondence. Really, she thought wryly, she seemed to have written more letters this past fortnight than she had the past year. But she could not let the Kirbys remain uninformed about the man who sought their whereabouts. When the bulk of the third day had passed, Grandmama sent for her, and Caroline knew she could keep quiet no longer.

"What is the matter now, child? I declare, you are the most paradoxical of creatures. Wanting to be out, now wanting to be in. What on earth is the matter with you?"

So Caroline told her about the encounter, and something of her suspicions concerning why he would wish to speak with her.

"Well! That is a predicament. What on

earth would he want to have to do with the Kirbys? I know they are not quite of our class, but certainly neither of them seem the sort to get involved in anything untoward."

"I do not trust him," Caroline said. "Why would he enquire so closely about a Mr. Carstairs only to change the next day and enquire about the Kirbys? Something is very odd."

"Carstairs? Now where have I heard . . . ?" Grandmama's wrinkled brow cleared. "No matter. Well, if it be any comfort, I will ensure he is not granted admittance to the estate. Such a description as you have given me should make him quite easy to notice."

"Thank you," Caroline said with a sigh. "It is why I do not wish to go outside, and have no wish to visit the village, for if I was to encounter him then I do not know what I would say."

"I believe you may rest easy and leave that to me, my dear." She nodded decidedly, adding, with a smile for Caroline that for once showed a degree of warmth, "I certainly have no intention of allowing such a vulgar person to cut up all our peace."

The following day at services Caroline was almost inclined to believe Grandmama's words. She saw no sign of Lord Pratt, and no sign of any other strangers. The relief this produced was matched by a new appreciation for the liturgy. It seemed to make sense. She even found the reading of a section of Psalms and some verses from Romans somewhat interesting, having read them only recently herself.

After the service she reached the churchyard, where she followed her grandmother's lead in speaking only with the minister before moving to their waiting carriage. But Grandmama was delayed a moment by Lady Dalrymple, forcing Caroline and Miss McNell to enter alone. Caroline had just settled back against the squabs when a man's voice came through the open door.

"And here she is at last. Miss Hatherleigh, you have proved quite a determined little quarry, have you not?"

What should she do? Ignore him or dismiss him? Miss McNell's worried face gave no clue. She subtly shook her head at her, desperately hoping the woman would not feel it necessary to fill the silence with unnecessary talk, and kept her gaze averted.

"Still avoiding me, I see. One can only wonder why. Indeed, it rather makes a man think you have something to hide. Something about the Kirbys, I believe?"

Caroline bit her tongue until she tasted blood. She would not answer the man. She would not!

"You there!" Grandmama's voice. "What is the meaning of such behavior?"

Caroline peeked across to see Lord Pratt offer a small bow. "I beg your pardon. My name is Pratt —"

"You!"

"Lady Aynsley —"

"Do not address me, sirrah!"

He flinched, the supercilious expression slipping into something more severe. "Forgive me." His voice was hard and cold, matching the expression in his eyes. "I simply wished to speak with Miss Hatherleigh —"

"Who has no desire to speak to you."

"It concerns your friends, the Kirbys —"

"They are not my friends, and neither are they here. Really, such flagrant interest as you have shown rather lends itself to speculation as to its cause."

"I simply wish to speak with them."

"But if they have no wish to communicate with you, then I can say from this encounter that they have my full sympathy." She paused, looking at the sea of interested faces beyond his lordship's cold self, before saying in a carrying voice, "And if I can encourage the good people of this town to have nothing further to do with this man, the better it will be for all of us. Now be off with you," she spoke to Pratt again, resuming her seat within the carriage. "My granddaughter has nothing more to say to the matter. Drive on!"

The carriage started with a jerk, leaving a flinty-eyed Pratt staring at them as they passed, soon followed by the open-mouthed faces of Mrs. Baker and another lady, surrounded by a gaggle of runny-nosed children.

Grandmama huffed out a breath. "Well, I never! The nerve of some people. I do not mind telling you, Caroline, that I am in full sympathy with you — and the Kirbys — in understanding why none of you should wish communication with such a man. There is something quite unholy about that man."

"Indeed."

"I . . . I did not notice it the first time we spoke," Miss McNell quavered, "but now you mention it I see you are quite right. The man is *very* peculiar. Such an unnatural look about him."

"Hmm. Well, I think we should do our best to ensure he leaves without further ado."

"But how?" Caroline wondered.

"There is more than one tradesperson whose livelihood depends on my goodwill. I don't mind telling you I have no scruples in letting people know I have no wish for them to assist a man who seems desirous of bringing fear amongst our neighbors."

"But surely we cannot be truly certain that is his intention," Miss McNell ventured. "It would appear he simply desires to know the Kirbys' whereabouts."

"Which doubtless they would tell him if they had wanted him to know, which leads me to suspect that they did not. No." Grandmama shook her gray head. "I might not have always approved of them as your friends, Caroline, but I certainly have never seen any harm in either of them. So I have no desire to see them brought to harm by one whose very person seems to exude it."

Caroline smiled, her grandmother's support filling her heart with ease for the first time in days. Somehow she knew her grandmother would prove true to her word, and the specter of the Kirbys' past in the form of Lord Pratt would soon be chased away.

London

Gideon glanced across his brother's drawing room to where his sister sat, listlessly staring into the hearth's flickering flames.

He exchanged a speaking glance with James before saying softly, "Emma? What do you think of those options?"

She shrugged in a manner he had not seen since she had been virtually held captive at Pratt's house. He had visited then, only to be fobbed off with thinly smiled excuses and her diffidence, like she had given up, and knew there was nothing to be done.

"Emma," — he seated himself next to her and clasped her cold hand — "what is it you would like to do?"

She shook her head, the bewilderment in her eyes since the doctor's diagnosis seeming to have taken possession of her very soul. "I do not know what to say. I'm so very tired, and it is all so overwhelming."

Gideon suppressed a sigh, then repeated the choices he had mentioned but a minute earlier. "We can stay here in London," cloistered within the walls of James's town house, "or you can go to James's country-seat —"

"We would be pleased to have you," interpolated James.

"— or he could find you another property where you will be safe."

A strand of hair fell across her cheek, gleaming dully in the firelight. "Would you come?"

"Of course."

Her gaze slid up and met his squarely, as if trying to discern his thoughts, before shaking her head. "No, I could not ask you to do that. You have done so much already."

"Emma —"

"Gideon, no. I do not want to interrupt your work any longer. You should return to Devon and continue your search. I . . ." Her voice faded, her shoulders slumped.

His heart twisted. "Would you truly have me be so selfish as to focus on myself when you are in need? How can you say such a thing?"

"But you would have me be so selfish as to insist you stop?"

"You are not insisting; I am, that is different."

"Perhaps it would be best if you were to return," she said. "I . . . perhaps I could return with you."

"But —"

"Truly, I have enjoyed our time there more than anyplace I can remember. And if Dr. Blakeney is happy for me to return, then I do not see why I cannot."

"But wouldn't you rather be in London?"

"Never going out? Never daring to be seen? No, I think not." Her voice held a measure of resolution. She shot a look at their brother. "I am sorry, James."

He inclined his head. "It is understandable."

"Emma," Gideon felt it necessary to say, "please understand that I do not *not* want you with me. I am simply concerned —"

"I know you are," she said, patting his hand. "And I appreciate you more than you could know."

"I just want what is best for you."

"Then it is settled." She pushed upright, her previous lethargy gone, decision now marking her features. "We shall return to Sidmouth."

Further protestation died when a tap on the door was swiftly followed by a footman, bearing a salver holding mail.

"Forgive me, m'lord, but I thought you may want to know this immediately." He glanced apologetically at Gideon. "It appears some correspondence for you was misdirected, sir, and as it came from Devon, I wondered if you might wish to have it at once."

"Thank you," Gideon said, stretching out his hand.

He perused the direction wryly. "No wonder," he said, after the footman had departed. "It was addressed to E. Kirby, so it is a wonder it made it here at all." He glanced at Emma, trepidation rising once again. "Did you tell anyone of our location?"

"Only Caroline."

His heart caught.

"Caroline?" James said with upraised brows.

"Caroline Hatherleigh," Emma supplied. "She is the daughter of Lord Aynsley, and has been such a good friend to me. And to Gideon," she added, her expression holding a new glimmer of cheer.

"Has she indeed?" James said, frowning. "Well, I am glad you have friends, but I cannot be sure that I like others knowing such things. What if Pratt should discover your whereabouts?"

Gideon slit open the seal, scanned the contents, and stifled his groan with an effort, before glancing at his sister. "Forgive me. I should have known it was meant for you." He turned to James. "Miss Hatherleigh is a very proper young lady, and would never do something so scandalous as to write to an unmarried man."

But he could not hand the letter to Emma. Such news might prove too distressing.

"Well? What is it?" James asked.

Gideon cast Emma a look of apology, having no wish to add to his sister's dismay. "It seems Pratt has recently arrived in Sidmouth and has been making enquiries."

Emma gasped. James stretched out a hand, gesturing for the letter with impatient fingers. He read it, his brow furrowing to a greater degree. "Oh dear."

"Caroline is so good to have told us." Emma's breath hitched, her eyes searching him anxiously. "Oh, Gideon, whatever will we do now?"

"But he has been told you are in London." James tapped the letter. "When was this posted?"

"On Thursday."

"And it takes two days for the mail to arrive . . ."

"And this was delayed due to the direction," Gideon said.

James shook his head. "Then unless he is a fool, he will already be on his way here."

Emma blanched. "Oh no."

"Which really means there is only one thing to do," James said, staring hard at Gideon.

He gave a small nod of comprehension — mixed with not a little resignation.

"Emma," Gideon said, taking his sister's hand. "It seems your wish shall be fulfilled; we'd best return to Sidmouth as soon as possible."

"Truly?" Her eyes lit.

"Truly." And he exchanged glances with his brother as Emma wrapped him in a fragile hug.

CHAPTER FOURTEEN

Lord Pratt, so the village whispers suggested, had left for London on Sunday afternoon — displaying no reluctance to travel on the Lord's day. It seemed his high-handedness — or Grandmama's request — had swayed the villagers to closed mouths. The Pratt, as he was now known, had been none too subtle in questioning the villagers, and they took exception to his arrogance as much as to his prying into the lives of people they now regarded as their own.

"Mr. and Mrs. Kirby," asserted Mrs. Goodacre, "have been nothing but friendly, and I don't take to no stranger asking strange questions about people I like. Then the Pratt asked about a Mr. Carstairs. 'Mr. Carstairs,' I said to him, 'has never lived here, and if you can't make up your mind as to know who it is you be asking about, then I have no good mind to tell you!' "

This was related to Caroline with such an

air of triumph that she could only congratulate the apothecary's wife for her quick thinking.

The experience of Mrs. Goodacre seemed a common one, with various other townsfolk relaying their own encounters with the man they now held in disdain. Even her plump savior from the library offered his misgivings, saying to her on the Tuesday, when they happened to again meet at that establishment, how glad he was to hear that his lordship had left town.

"For we certainly don't want the likes of him here. Imagine having the audacity to interrupt a man who is simply trying to read! I don't care what he calls himself; that is *not* my idea of gentlemanly behavior."

Knowing this led Caroline to feel a certain degree of ease, enough that she could venture to attempt some sketching in the garden, doing her best to approximate the likeness of the plants and water features. But though she had visited the village, she had yet to return to the Assembly Rooms. Pratt might have left the village, but the place still held the fingerprints of fear.

She peered closer at the pretty pink shell she had discovered on that excursion with the Kirbys. How were they getting on? She hoped Emma was feeling better, and Mr.

Kirby —

No. She would not think on him. She'd best steer her thoughts away. Best focus on her sketching, on the shell that demanded closer perusal. How would Serena depict such a —

"Miss Hatherleigh."

Breath hitched, then released, as the footman apologized for startling her.

"Lady Aynsley requests your attendance in the drawing room."

Minutes later, her sketchbook fell to the floor as she rushed to clasp Emma in a hug. "You are back!"

"We could not stay away," Emma said, her face pale, but her smile filled with warmth. "London is not a particularly healthful place at the best of times."

And this was certainly not the best of times, Caroline thought, looking at her shadowed features carefully.

"Besides, my brother was keen to resume his searching."

Caroline turned to Mr. Kirby. "I hope you may find what you are looking for, and quickly," she added, thinking on the letter she had written. Had they not received it? Why were they here? What should happen if Pratt returned?

Grandmama sent for tea, a surprising

request, seeing as she normally could neither abide unexpected visitors nor wish them to prolong their stay, and had made no secret of her disapproval of the Kirbys as suitable friends. But judging from her conversation, all centered on the mystery of Lord Pratt and his questions to the villagers and how she — single-handedly! — had persuaded him to leave, it became apparent just what she was doing. To their credit — and her grandmother's obvious disappointment — the Kirbys said little, offering noncommittal answers as to why this man was so insistently curious about them.

It was not long before Grandmama's expression grew bored, and Caroline's impatience mounted. She could only hope Grandmama would feel it necessary to leave soon. For how could she ask the questions she longed to have answered whilst Grandmama and Miss McNell remained?

Salvation came in the unlikely form of Jezebel, whose hacking cough drew all eyes and a cessation of conversation. Within the minute, a most disgusting retching sound was followed by the loathsome sight of a brown, damp mass of . . . something. A something that landed on the hem of Grandmama's gown.

"Good heavens!"

"Oh, dear Lady Aynsley! Oh, poor Jezebel!"

"Poor Jezebel, indeed," Grandmama snapped, casting Miss McNell a look that would have cast lesser mortals to stone. "Get this cleaned up now."

Miss McNell fluttered off to find a servant amid a waft of apologies, clutching Jezebel to her chest as if fearing her pet might be thrown into the sea.

Grandmother rose stiffly. "Please excuse me."

Mr. Kirby stood and offered a bow, and his belief they should leave.

Caroline's chest tightened. But if they did, how would she ever know — ?

"I hope a tiresome cat will not chase you away," Grandmama said, as a servant scuttled in to clean and remove the offending item from view. "I'm sure Caroline can entertain you sufficiently."

"Grandmama, do you want assistance?" she felt obliged to say.

"Beatrice shall attend me. Good day." And with a regal nod to the Kirbys she departed.

Caroline exhaled, turning to meet her guests. "Well, I certainly didn't envisage such drama this afternoon."

"Poor Jezebel," Emma murmured.

A spurt of laughter pushed up. "Poor

Jezebel, indeed."

Amusement tweaked Mr. Kirby's features as Emma released a soft giggle. Already she was looking better, her pale cheeks holding a tinge of rose.

Caroline exhaled, curbing her humor. "Forgive me. I should not laugh, but that wretched cat . . ." She shook her head, forced herself to focus on her guests and ask the question before any further interruption could be made. "I must confess that I am surprised to see you. I trust you received my letter?"

"Thank you, yes. It was what convinced us to return," Emma said.

Mr. Kirby gave a ghost of a smile. "If I were a gambling man, I would stake Pratt has already called upon our brother and demanded to see us."

"And your brother?"

He paused a moment, then said, "He is not easily intimidated, and his servants know to be vigilant. Besides, we have an alternative scheme in mind."

"Which is?"

"My brother found reason to send two servants in a carriage to a house far away in the north near Durham. The servants, strangely enough, hold something of a resemblance to Emma and yours truly, and are making various stops using the name Kirby."

Caroline clapped her hands. "With the intention that he will follow their trail! How very clever."

"It was my idea," he said with a half smile.

"Clever, and so modest, too," she said.

Emma laughed, a sound that seemed to surprise Mr. Kirby as he glanced at her quickly. "You know my brother well, Miss Hatherleigh."

Telltale heat swept through her cheeks. It was so silly to want Emma's words to mean more. To turn the conversation from her embarrassment, she said, "Well, I hope his servants can hold their own. Lord Pratt did not seem the type to let such things escape him, and I cannot imagine he will be best pleased to discover he has been fooled."

"You are correct," Mr. Kirby answered. "Which is why James and I decided the most capable servants would be ones employed from a certain locale not far from Gentleman Jackson's." He smiled with grim self-satisfaction. "I think even that scoundrel will think twice before meddling with an ex-prizefighter and his wife."

Caroline blinked. "You are not serious."

Emma gave another gurgle of amusement, which again drew a keen look from her brother. "I like how dear Gideon thinks someone will mistake a prizefighter's physique for his! Tell me, Miss Hatherleigh, would you mistake my brother's build for that of a prizefighter?"

"Emma!" Mr. Kirby said in a scandalized tone. "Please do not answer that, Miss Hatherleigh."

"Why should she not?" Emma countered. "Miss Hatherleigh might wish to."

"I —" What could she say that would not get her into trouble? Oh, how the lessons of decorum should be used right now! Only . . . she couldn't quite remember them. "I — I have never had opportunity to notice a prizefighter's physique."

"But you have had opportunity to notice my —"

"Emma, that is enough!"

"I think," Caroline said, sure her cheeks must be as red as Mr. Kirby's, "that I would like to know why Lord Pratt was asking about a Mr. Carstairs."

Emma's look of amusement faded, leaving Caroline to regret having asked. She peeked at Mr. Kirby who seemed similarly afflicted.

"That is a good question," he eventually said. "I —"

But his words died as Miss McNell moved

back into the room. "You are still here. Oh, I do hope poor Jezebel didn't cause you to feel any sort of *repulsion* for her, poor thing. I'm afraid she is a little out of sorts, and can only hope, dear Miss Hatherleigh, that your grandmother understands that such a thing is only natural for felines, and . . ."

Caroline shot her guests a look of apology as Grandmama's companion carried on quivering excuses, a look that was met with wry smiles and — when Miss McNell finally paused for breath — Mr. Kirby's apology that he and his sister must away.

He gave his sister a look that pushed Emma to her feet. She offered Caroline a small curtsy and expressed the hope they might meet again soon.

As Miss McNell continued to espouse the wonders of Jezebel to poor Emma, Mr. Kirby took Caroline's proffered hand in both of his and said in a low voice, "Miss Hatherleigh, I am indebted to you. Thank you for sending Emma that information, and for being a good friend to her. Many a time I have heard her thank God that she has found such a friend here in Sidmouth."

Her heart glowed with childlike pleasure. "She said that about me?"

He assented with a smile. "I have not heard her laugh these past days, so your enabling of that has done both her heart and mine a world of good."

Gladness radiated through her chest. "I . . . I am pleased to offer what I can."

"Thank you." He glanced at her hand quite intently — her foolish heart thought it seemed as if he would like to kiss it! — then he let go. "Goodbye."

"Goodbye," she echoed.

And she watched them exit, feeling suddenly forlorn.

The next few days Gideon spent seeing to Emma's comfort. He was glad the return to the little village had met with approval, glad that the salubrious southerly winds this coast was famed for were giving color to her cheeks and vitality to her bones.

He spent time carefully extracting from the stone the large ammonite found on that last ill-fated expedition, polishing it with cloth and water until it held the appearance of embellished metal. The lethargy induced by Emma's illness, her condition that so often flared then waned, was put aside in her enthusiasm, and he felt a sense of pride at recognizing, then retrieving, one of the largest specimens of ammonite ever found.

"It is so large," Emma said, tracing the ridged surface.

"Over twenty inches in diameter."

"It almost seems to hold something of an ancient shield like King Neptune might have used."

But though he smiled, he could not help but want more: the skeleton of the *ichthyosaurus,* the ancient sea dragon of lore.

"Gideon? What is it?"

"Nothing."

"You do not appear as pleased as I imagined. Are you not thankful that you have found such a beautiful specimen?"

"I am, indeed, extremely thankful to God for this. I know I could not have done so without His help."

"Then what is it?" Her brow furrowed. "Are you still worried about Pratt?"

"No, and neither should you be." Well, that wasn't entirely true. But he and James had employed measures other than the ones leading Pratt — hopefully — on a wild goose chase north.

"Then what is it?" Her expression grew mischievous. "Are you concerned about Miss Hatherleigh?"

"I am concerned about her," he admitted, glad to see his words widened her eyes. "I am concerned with how much thought and energy you seem to be putting into something that can clearly never be."

"Not *never* be."

"Not be any time soon," he amended.

"But something you would like to be?"

He fought the inclination to roll his eyes. Perhaps this tease of hers was necessary for her to maintain a happier frame of mind. It gave her some focus, something that took attention from what her future very likely would be. Or wouldn't be.

Swallowing the lump in his throat, he said, "Do you remember why I wanted to discover the secrets of the earth?"

"You said you wanted to reveal God's interior ornaments of the earth."

"Do you think it selfish of me to still wish to discover more?"

"Not at all. If I were you, I would want to pursue all such dreams and even more. I would seek adventure and travel to exotic lands to see as much as I could. But as I cannot, and will not" — her face shadowed — "I need to know that someone is pursuing their passions and living. *Really* living," she added, her eyes shimmering.

He grasped her hands and squeezed gently. The London doctors had said the pregnancy would continue to sap her strength, but despite his pleadings they were reluctant to do anything to save her life. Their reasoning? That an operation to remove the child was highly dangerous, and would likely further weaken her, if not kill her outright. So, she was left carrying the unwanted child which would soon extinguish the life of the sister he desperately wanted alive. Oh, what a tangled coil in which they existed.

"Heavenly Father, help us."

"Amen."

They shared slightly twisted smiles, she blinking rapidly, he willing away the moisture burning at the back of his eyes.

She exhaled, shoulders slumping ever so slightly.

"What can I do for you to make this day easier?"

"Besides stopping this nausea?"

"I wish I could."

"I wish —" A tear trickled down her cheek, and he drew her close to his chest. "I hate that I don't want it," she whispered. "Does that make me evil? A mother who does not want her child?"

What could he say? What would provide comfort, not more guilt or shame? "It makes you honest." He stroked her head. "God sees. He knows. He understands."

"I know, but . . ." She drew in an unsteady breath, and shifted upright. "Listen to me, feeling sorry for myself." She wiped her eyes. "How pitiful I am."

"Not pitiful. Loved."

Her lips tweaked into a semblance of a smile. "You are sweet."

"Now, what can I do to make your day more pleasant?"

"I don't know. I wouldn't mind seeing Caroline, but I suspect her grandmother might not be so keen." She gave another twist of her lips that suggested wryness. "I still think she believes us beneath her, which is ironic, considering . . ."

He shook his head. "It does not matter what she thinks. But if you like, I could ask Miss Hatherleigh to visit?"

"No. I don't think she needs to be disturbed. Mrs. Ballard said she'd take me to the warm sea-bath now that they are in operation once again. Perhaps that might wash off some of this misery."

He offered a smile he hoped encouraged, but his concern remained unabated. Emma's fragile state of mind, her fragile state of health, could not last like this for much longer, that much was patently obvious, and so heartrendingly true.

CHAPTER FIFTEEN

Caroline hoped today's visit to the village would put her in a better frame of mind. News contained in the latest epistle from her mother definitely had not helped. She was expected to return to Aynsley to begin readying for the London season within the fortnight. Within two weeks! How could she leave this place and all she had grown to love within such a short space of time? How could she leave her new friends and return to her former life where she had none? Granted, she would like to see her family members again — to see if the conciliation offered in her letters would have any effect in their day-to-day relationships — but oh, how she would miss the closeness she had started to experience with Grandmama.

And the Kirbys.

She chewed the inside of her bottom lip as the carriage continued its progression to the village. She could not think anymore that Mr. Kirby and his sister were social rungs beneath her. On the contrary, from the London address Emma had given her, it seemed that they had quite noble connections. For who else could afford to live in Grosvenor Square? And who else could afford to employ servants simply to hoax the Pratt into pursuit?

Puzzling over this, she lighted from the carriage at the post office. "I shan't be too long," she told the driver. She hoped to find here souvenirs of her time and suitable gifts for her family. She had previously bought a copy of *Devonshire: The Beauties of Sidmouth Displayed,* a wonderful guide to the town and surrounds. Cecy might enjoy that, being the reader that she was, although she suspected Verity might enjoy something a little more unusual. Perhaps she would ask Mr. Kirby if he could recommend a place where she might purchase an ammonite or two. Such a gift would certainly not be in the usual way.

She was about to enter when a large dark-haired fellow of hulking proportions opened the door, shooting her a quick look from small brown eyes. A sensation of prickles raced up her spine.

Inside, she met Mrs. Baker, whose chatter with a woman of brown hair and sickly children ceased, and then resumed in hushed tones. Caroline searched the shelves, aware with skin-tingling certainty that her name was being talked about. Only why would these two be bandying about her name? She moved to the counter, and paid for her items.

"Miss Hatherleigh," Mrs. Baker said, leaving her companion to draw closer. "It is good to see you getting out and about now."

"Thank you. I find the milder weather is more conducive for such things."

"We were just saying, weren't we, Mrs. Belcher, 'ow we don't take with strangers in our village."

"Which might prove a shame seeing as Sidmouth is considered a fine watering hole for tourists, is it not?"

"Oh, you know what I mean. There be some who don't quite fit in these parts, whereas others seem to know how things ought to be done. Like the Kirbys, for example. They might be a bit peculiar, and keep themselves to themselves, but we don't mind that, do we, Mrs. Belcher?" said Mrs. Baker, throwing a look over her shoulder.

"No, indeed."

"Have to say it was good to see your grandmother giving that Pratt man something to think about." She sniffed. "Poking 'is nose into affairs that don't concern 'im none. We certainly don't want the likes of 'im back 'ere again."

"No. And you have seen no further strangers in town?"

"Apart from the usual tourists? Not that there be many of them, not at this time of year. In fact, I can't think of any, save that man who arrived on the coach when the Kirbys returned. A big man, said his name was Browne or something. I think he's lodging with the widow on Broad Street."

"Was he the man who was just in here?" Caroline asked.

"Aye."

"Who is he?"

"Nobody knows, miss. Although we have our suspicions." Again, another look of significance passed between the two.

Caroline shivered. "You do not think he is likely to hurt anyone, do you?"

"Now what would put such an idea in your 'ead?" Mrs. Baker said. "Like I said, we don't know the man, so for all we know 'e might be as sweet as Don Belcher." This was said with a cackle of laughter and another of those queer sidelong looks. "But it always pays to be vigilant, and let others know if there be something you see out of the ordinary way."

"I will keep that in mind," Caroline said, making hasty excuses and taking her packages to the waiting carriage outside.

Just when she thought visiting the village would be safe again, a new stranger should happen along. What if he was a spy for Lord Pratt? What should she do? Should she warn the Kirbys? Or would Mr. Kirby think her a little goose for getting carried away?

She was just about to ascend the carriage when, as if summoned by her thoughts, she spied the figure of Mr. Kirby coming towards her. She placed her packages inside then called for the driver to wait a few minutes more.

"Good morning, Mr. Kirby."

"Miss Hatherleigh, hello." He glanced at the carriage then back at her, a questioning lift to one brow. "I trust I am not delaying you?"

"Oh no. Not at all. I . . . I had hoped to talk with you." Oh dear. That made her sound desperately bold and improper!

His brows rose, and he assumed a look of polite interest.

She bit her lip. How could she ask about the mysterious man? Was this urge to speak with him borne from concern or was she simply being too forward in wanting his attention? Was she too quick to assume he wished to speak with her? Still, she could make enquiry about his sister. "How is Emma today?"

His face suddenly closed in something akin to pain.

"Mr. Kirby?" Her heart hammered in fear. "Whatever is the matter?"

He shook his head. "Forgive me, I cannot talk about it. It is too —" His words broke away as he cast her a look of such desperation she was obliged by all that was kind and good to step closer and lay a hand on his arm.

"Please, sir. Is there anything I can do?"

His gaze returned to her, and for a moment she could feel the nervous tension riding through his body, the pain communicated with his eyes. "We cannot talk about it here."

Conscious of the villagers observing them most strangely — after all, wasn't Mr. Kirby still supposed by some to be a married man? — she stepped away, dropped her hand, dropped her gaze, breaking the connection. "Forgive me."

"I'm sorry, Miss Hatherleigh. I should not put you in such an awkward position."

Her lips pushed to one side. "Rather, it is I who have made things appear awkward for you." She looked up, studied him closely, saw the strain of care around his eyes. "But you do need to talk with someone, do you not?"

"I . . . perhaps."

"Would it help to speak with Reverend Holmes?"

His lips twisted. "No."

"Is there someone else to whom you could speak?"

Again, she felt that mute appeal like a tangible thing. *You,* his eyes seemed to say. Her pulse increased.

"Would . . . would it help if we spoke?" she finally dared. "You must know I care about Emma," and you, she added silently, "and if I can offer nothing but a sympathetic ear then I would be pleased to do so. We could meet somewhere if you wish."

She cringed as her words hung in the air. How unseemly was such an offer! He would think her completely lost to propriety. She ducked her head. "I am sorry. Please forgive my presumption. I have no desire to intrude in private matters." She half turned to leave.

"Miss Hatherleigh." His raspy voice drew her attention back to his face, to the misery there.

"*Would* it help to talk?"

"Yes. Perhaps. I do not know."

"I do," she said, feeling a strange and

urgent sense of decisiveness. "You should come to the beach where we first met. I will tell Grandmama I am going to sketch. Then we can talk and not be observed."

"Oh, but —"

"I know such things are not very proper, but some things are more important than propriety, would you not agree? And if there is something I can do to help you and your sister, I would be honored. Now, I shall return to Saltings, and expect to see you in an hour."

His lips tweaked into a rueful smile as he bowed. "Your most obedient."

A chuckle escaped. "I do sound a little bit too much like my grandmother, don't I? You will have to forgive me; I'm afraid such presumption comes with being an oldest child. I shall expect to see you there soon."

He inclined his head, she made a short curtsy, and instructed the driver to return to Saltings without delay. As the carriage swept around the bend, she saw the large man she now knew as Browne, standing at the corner of the London Hotel. But he did not seem to be doing anything, save looking at her, and observing Mr. Kirby, leaving her to wonder and shudder again.

Within the hour, she was in the garden at Saltings, in the section overlooking the beach. From this vantage point she could see the various approaches as people moved along the shore. Fortunately, she had seen nobody in the past minutes. Would Mr. Kirby come? Had her instructions been too high-handed? Or had she, once again, misinterpreted things, and did he not wish to come in order to save her from further improper behavior?

"Excuse me, miss? Would you like me to fetch you a shawl? It is growing quite cool and the breeze here holds a nasty bite."

"Yes, please, Mary."

As soon as Mary disappeared from view, Caroline hurried across the back lawn to the gate, walking fast, in an almost half crouch when the bushes were low, until she finally made it to the path that led down to the beach. She stifled a giggle. Oh, how lost to propriety was she, escaping like this, going to meet a man? What ever would Mama say if she knew her proper daughter was acting in this way? A smile twitched; she suspected Verity would approve.

A few steps, a few more, and she was on the beach.

And Mr. Kirby was drawing near, wearing that same rueful expression as before.

"Hello."

"Hello, Miss Hatherleigh."

"I am glad you came."

"I scarcely know why I am here. I really don't know what to say."

She waited, working to ignore the niggle of disappointment at his obvious noninterest. She was here for Emma's sake, she reminded herself.

"Does your grandmother know you are here?"

"Well, no, because she wouldn't have let me come."

"Then I should go. I cannot like meeting in a way that feels clandestine."

She stilled, heart cramping with hurt, her good intentions fading away. "Then I do not know why you have come."

He lifted his hands. Dropped them.

"And I truly did not think you could ever be more missish than I."

His anxious features smoothed into a smile, then he chuckled. "You, Miss Hatherleigh, say the most surprising things sometimes. Just when I think I know who you are . . ." The amusement faded as his gaze grew intent, dropping to her lips.

Her heart fluttered. Well, perhaps he wasn't so unhappy to meet her here, after all.

"Mr. Kirby, I fear that if you do not tell me what is the matter with Emma then our meeting will be construed as something more clandestine than it is."

He blinked, and collected himself. "Forgive me. I . . . I just don't know where to begin."

Perhaps she should help him out. "Emma is not well, is she?"

"No," he said, and then with the air of relief at finally being able to unburden himself, he began to share. "She is a private person, but I do not think she will mind you knowing."

"You do not know what is wrong with her?"

"She has seen doctor after doctor, specialist upon specialist, and none of them quite know." He sighed. "For the past five years she has been prone to episodes of weakness and tremors. Not every day, but enough to give rise to concern, and when they occur she feels a debilitating kind of weakness so that all she can do is rest. Some doctors have mentioned the palsy, but her symptoms are not consistent enough for all specialists to concur."

"Has she been to any of the spa towns? My grandmother vows that Bath's waters have done her a world of good."

He offered a small smile. "We have taken her to every spa town of note in the land,

and she has drunk more waters than might be found in the North Sea. No, I'm afraid her infirmity is of a more enduring nature."

And he told her how Emma's mysterious condition had worsened in past weeks with the recent news that she was expecting.

"Oh my!"

"And now it seems the worst will happen all the sooner, due to this child she has no wish for, all because of the actions of that evil man."

Her eyes blurred, her throat grew tight. "I'm so terribly sorry."

"I have no wish to upset you, but I could not have you in ignorance, not when she considers you her friend."

Her lip was trembling; she bit it.

"Dear Miss Hatherleigh. I feel like I'm a scoundrel, upsetting you like this. Please, forgive me."

"Forgive you?" she said, dashing at her eyes. "There is nothing to forgive you for. You have done everything that is noble and good, sacrificing yourself for dear Emma's sake. I . . . oh, I wish there were something I could do to help."

"Thank you, but there is nothing, save, if you would pray for her, and if you could pay her the occasional visit to lift her spirits. I'm afraid she seems to struggle with maintaining a positive frame of mind these days."

"Something that is completely under-standable. It must be so very hard for you both."

He cleared his throat, then gruffly thanked her and looked away.

Sensing his withdrawal, she quickly said, "I will endeavor to visit her each day, if Grandmama permits. Oh, and may I bring my little pug with me?"

"You have a dog?"

"Mittens is the sweetest thing. She was my only friend here for quite some time, before I met Emma."

"I'm sure Emma will be very pleased to have a visit from you and . . . Mittens, did you say?"

She nodded. "Excellent. I shall call later this afternoon." She turned to go, then swiv-eled to face him again. "Before I go, may I ask if you have heard anything more about Lord Pratt?"

"I received a letter from my brother just this morning. It seems our ruse has worked and our decoys have been followed on their journey to the far north of England."

"Oh, that is good. I just wondered you see."

His brow knit in a way that suggested he did *not* see.

"I wondered about the new visitor in town, a rather large man who looks and walks a bit like a bear. I believe he is called Mr. Browne, or so Mrs. Baker said today."

A smile flitted across his features. "What about him?"

"Well, I thought I saw him following you, or at least," for that wasn't *quite* accurate, "or at least watching you. This morning he was, anyway."

Had her lessons in elocution and deportment at Haverstock's been for naught? Why could she not speak and make sense? Perhaps it had something to do with the way Mr. Kirby was looking at her kindly, albeit — she frowned — in a way an uncle might regard a foolish child?

"I should not worry about any bear-type men if I were you."

"But Mrs. Baker and Mrs. Belcher seemed to think there was something suspicious about him."

"And I certainly would not concern myself with what Mrs. Baker and Mrs. Belcher think. I have a handy notion they would find anyone they did not know suspicious."

"Why do you say that?"

He smiled. "Because I happen to know that both their husbands are deeply involved in the local free-traders movement."

■ ■ ■ ■

The wind nipped at his face as the view of
Lyme's harbor opened up before him. Gideon thought back to yesterday, his lips lifting in a smile, at the moment on the shore
when Miss Hatherleigh's face had dropped
in surprise. He supposed a well-brought-up
young lady would not have even thought
smugglers could be encountered in the village shops or in the churchyard after services. She was truly a sweet innocent. So
her shock, and compassionate concern, had
brought much-needed respite from the
general feeling of hopelessness that so often
swamped his days.

The cart clattered down the steep hill into
Lyme Regis. True to her word, Miss Hatherleigh had visited Emma yesterday, and once
again he was plunged further into indebtedness. For she seemed to know exactly what
to say to lift Emma's spirits, and thus his
own. Her kindly interest never veered too
close to personal matters that might embarrass, and her amusing stories of self-
deprecation far from the proper young lady
she had first appeared, engendered even
warmer feelings towards her.

Today Miss Hatherleigh had provided

another period of respite, with her offer for Emma to spend the day at Saltings, thus releasing him to continue his explorations. He had protested, but Emma eagerly accepted. From the way he had left them, he gathered the day would be spent drawing, in the gardens, with the pug — quite simply the ugliest, laziest dog he had ever seen — and engaging in all manner of frivolities, activities he believed Miss Hatherleigh had specifically designed to provide distraction and amusement.

His heart glowed at her thoughtfulness. She truly was a blessing in their lives, her kindness soothing the tension forever lining his heart. "God, bless her."

The cart driver turned around with an enquiring eye, to which Gideon was forced to shake his head.

He had today at least. They would have to leave soon. Even with Mr. Browne standing guard, he knew it would only be a matter of time before Pratt learned the truth and returned again. He would make the most of each opportunity to scavenge the beach, for such opportunities would likely not exist in his future, when they were forced to go into hiding again somewhere.

"God, help me," he prayed aloud again.

This time the cart driver did not turn

around. Perhaps he was used to the strange ways of some of the visitors in town.

Within a few minutes, he had paid the man and was making his way to the beach, his hunger for discovery rising as he inhaled the tang of brine and as seawater droplets stung his cheeks. He hitched his satchel over his shoulder, gripping the spade and sack more firmly as his feet slithered over the cool wet of mossy rocks.

Ahead on the sand, he saw a group clustered at the base of the ominous dark cliff known as the Black Fen. His pulse increased. Someone had found something?

A man, younger than he by at least half a decade, sprinted past. Gideon hailed him to stop.

"What is that ahead?"

"Did ye not hear? Young Wilmont found hisself a fossil . . ."

Gideon's heart sank, even as he contrived to look enthused. "Really?"

"Aye, they think it be like the crocodile that young Anning found years back."

Gideon refrained from correcting the man's assumption about the Annings' discovery. If people chose to believe it a crocodile, he could not stop them. And initially that appeared to be what the find had suggested, for who had ever thought a world existed, far removed from what was known?

He listened as the man continued, conscious of a great weight dogging his footsteps. He knew he should not be jealous, but Wilmont already had financial backing, and could well afford to spend his days searching without finding. Was it so very wrong to feel such envy?

Ahead, he could see a cluster of men and some ladies gathered around a rock that seemed to have been split in two. His lip curled in disgust. What — people were now resorting to carving up all the rocks in the hopes of discovering fossils? What would be next — employing a small army with pick-axes to slice up the cliffs? Could they not rely on God's good timing and nature's forces to do so?

He nodded to Wilmont, even now gesticulating wildly as he talked about his find.

". . . it was lying like this when I arrived this morning, as if cut from the cliff by God Himself."

Gideon felt a moment's shame. It appeared he had misjudged the man and his willingness to enact extreme measures of excavation and extraction.

"Ah, Mr. Kirby! Tell me, what do you

think of my find?" he asked, almost glee-fully.

He looked at the large vertebrae, about an inch thick, and again felt that twist of envy. "It appears most intriguing. Do you have thoughts on what it might be?"

"One can only hope for an *ichthyosaur,* like Miss Anning discovered."

"And the rest of the skeleton?"

"Will be hard to find," he said, with an air of regret. "Seeing as it broke away from the cliffs, I cannot be sure precisely where it came from."

Gideon managed a tight smile, the rush of gladness at hearing such a thing chased by a qualm of conscience. "Does Miss Anning know yet?"

"No, though I'm sure she soon will."

This last was said with no small measure of pride, but Gideon could not fault him. How hard would it be in this moment of triumph to not appear like one was gloating over one's good fortune? Even if it seemed the good fortune had almost literally fallen into one's lap. Was it truly a victory if one stumbled over such a discovery, rather than achieving it as a reward for one's labor? He quashed his inner acerbity, offered his congratulations, and turned away.

How long would it be until he, too, could

claim a find? He trudged the sandy path along the rock-strewn beach. Perhaps this was a fool's game. Perhaps he had been misled. Perhaps he should have joined all those others in searching these more popular cliffs, and not have pinned all his hopes on Sidmouth holding similar treasure. The sharp stabs of envy rose again. He was running out of time. When would be his turn?

CHAPTER SIXTEEN

The fresh breeze tugged at her curls as Caroline eyed the sketchbook with disfavor. Why was it that no matter how much she tried, her sketches never seemed to be quite right? Perhaps she should have paid more attention in art class to the instructions given by the art master, rather than concentrating quite so much on his handsome features.

Tossing her book aside, she slouched — most unladylike — in the stone seat, watching the sea vista before her. For some reason, today it reminded her of Emma, with its green-gray glints and unruffled surface. Beneath its surface lay depths she had not yet encountered, such depths she wondered if they might forever remain a mystery.

Her brow furrowed. Was it more prudent to hold thoughts and feelings close to your chest, or was it better to let others know of one's concerns? Verity had little guard on her mouth, while Cecy at times seemed to have too much, so that one could never be quite sure what she was thinking. Perhaps it was more judicious to be somewhere in the middle.

A cleared throat made her start.

"Excuse me, miss."

"Yes?" She glanced at the footman.

"You have visitors. Your friends, the Kirbys."

Her heart scampered with anticipation. She pushed the tendrils of hair from her eyes and rose, enquiring of the footman where she might find them, then, after scooping up Mittens, set off in the direction of the south terrace.

As she hastened through the rose garden, up one set of shallow steps and along the flagstone path to the next rise, she wondered what she would say. How could she ask without revealing interest far deeper than she had any right to display? Oh, what did it matter! Friends asked questions about the other's well-being; such actions proved they cared.

Pinning a smile to her face she reached the steps of the terrace and lifted a hand in greeting. "Good afternoon, Mr. Kirby, Emma."

This last she offered a kiss on her cheek. Her heart fluttered. What would it be like to be so free and easy that she could offer Mr. Kirby a similar token of affection?

Suppressing that *most* irrational thought, she continued. "How glad I am to see you! Thank you for coming to rescue me from an afternoon of boredom." She waved her fingers. "You can see I have needed to resort to charcoals in order to entertain myself."

"You poor thing," said Emma, light filling her eyes, in stark contrast to the shadows underneath. "Your life seems almost unbearable."

Caroline chuckled, turning to Mr. Kirby. "Your sister is most unsympathetic today."

He smiled, a smile that trickled gladness through her heart. "She can be most insupportable."

Caroline gestured to the curved stone benches, positioned to best capture the view, then invited them to sit. Emma obeyed, and begged to hold Mittens, a request Caroline gladly fulfilled. Mr. Kirby remained standing, his hands behind his back.

"May I offer you some refreshments?" Caroline asked.

"Thank you, no. We cannot stay too long," Emma said, before bending her head to murmur to the pug.

Caroline eyed her. Today must be one of Emma's good days, for her color was better than her last visit, though her energy seemed to be dissipating fast. How hard her life had been. Perhaps Emma might find some comfort from a pet of her own. One like Mittens, who was happy to be cossetted, only wanting to lie and be stroked, who never raised her bark loudly. She blinked. Perhaps Emma might like to borrow Mittens for a time.

"My sister just wanted to see you," said Mr. Kirby, his deep voice stealing her attention. "She would not let me have a moment's peace until I agreed to escort her here. Apparently Emma's brother simply cannot compete with your conversation."

Caroline's smile at his self-deprecation grew taut as she wondered at his words. Did he mean he had no interest in seeing her himself? She stifled the thought. When would she stop thinking so selfishly?

"Oh, listen to him, as if denying his interest in you himself. Really, Miss Hatherleigh, it cannot be denied that my brother had just as much inclination to visit as I did."

Gladness bloomed across her chest, her cheeks filling with a heat sure to approximate the color filling Mr. Kirby's countenance.

To avoid further embarrassment, she resolved to put into practice her earlier contemplations and ask about her guests. "And how have you both spent your day?"

"I have done nothing much of interest," Emma admitted, before motioning to her brother. "But Gideon on the other hand . . ."

Caroline looked at him expectantly.

He shrugged, and Caroline thought his eyes held a sense of strain. "Really, I have nothing of great import to share."

"How goes your fossil hunting?" she asked.

His lips tightened as he lifted one shoulder in a shrug. "If I am honest, I would say I am more frustrated than anything. The ammonite is all well and good I suppose —"

"Oh, Caroline, you should come and see it," Emma interrupted. "It looks marvelous all polished up."

Strange hurt twinged within when Mr. Kirby made no further invitation, but only shook his head. "I thought by now that I would have found something to make my visit worthwhile."

"I see." She was a fool to wish his words did not strike so closely to her heart.

Conscious she was being watched closely by Emma, she sought to cover her conflicting emotions with an unwavering smile. "What is your next step, do you think?"

"I hope to visit the cliffs nearer Ladram Bay tomorrow."

She nodded. "I hope you find what you are looking for."

He lifted his gaze to hers, and for a long delicious moment, she was trapped in his dark gray gaze. Breath constricted, her midsection all aflutter. She wrenched her gaze away, back to Emma, who was smiling at her in a manner most curious.

A slight sense of panic forced Caroline to say quickly, "I received a letter from home today. It was from my mother, and concerns a Mr. Amherst. Have you heard of him? He is the son of the Earl of Rovingham."

The siblings looked to each other as if uncertain. It would seem they did not recognize the name. Caroline hurried on. "Yes, well, he is a young gentleman I have the misfortune to know." She laughed, uneasily aware that she maligned her former friend. "He has some money, to be sure, but his scandalous behavior in London was such that I can have nothing more to do with him."

She was conscious of the note of pride

that had sounded in her voice, and strove to diminish it with a smile. "You understand what I mean, do you not, Miss Kirby? Some gentlemen are not at all what they seem, and I could never have anything to do with someone who purported to be one thing but then proved to be exactly the opposite."

Emma's face grew pale, and Caroline grew uncomfortably certain that she had again said something that caused distress. But precisely what she had inadvertently said she did not know. A glance at Mr. Kirby revealed that he did not appear much better. Truth be told, he looked a little startled, and — now she thought about it — seemed to be avoiding her eyes. She felt a frown form, and smoothed her brow. What had she said that had caused such angst? Was it something to do with Emma's husband?

"Please excuse us," said Emma, rising to her feet. "I fear I must return home."

"Oh, but . . ." Caroline began, her words failing at the resolute tilt to Emma's chin, the way she glanced at Mr. Kirby and he offered a small nod. Oh, why did he refuse to look at her?

"I'm sorry if I have said something upsetting," she continued. "I did not mean to speak out of turn."

They demurred, but she could tell by the

way brother and sister made their goodbyes and left, still refusing to look her in the eye, that whatever she had unwittingly said had hurt them deeply. Leaving her with trouble clouding her heart, the sure and sorry knowledge she had once again failed her friends, and the accursed heat of tears in her eyes.

Gideon trudged up the beach, his feet sinking in the sand, along with his hopes. Few rocks called for attention. Nothing seemed different today. How much longer would it take? He should give up, on fossil hunting, on other things . . .

His heart clenched again at the memory of yesterday's encounter. He was a fool to think on her; he should have known she would have interest from men who could afford to keep her in the style to which she was obviously very well accustomed. This Amherst man . . . why did he not remember him? It was not as if Gideon had never danced at a London ball. Perhaps such doings had occurred when he was away exploring, or last year, when he'd been too distracted by his sister's worsening situation to notice or care much for anything else.

Yesterday had proved challenging in other ways as well. He'd spent the morning searching the beaches and cliffs near the Beer headland when he'd been accosted by a group of men, Baker and Belcher among them.

"You be looking for anything particular-like?" Belcher had asked in his strong Devonian accent.

Gideon had forced a smile past his uneasiness. "I think you gentlemen are aware that all I search for are the petrifications this area is known for."

"Well, there be none round 'ere," Belcher said, arms crossed.

Should he make a push to stay, or would resistance result in a broken head? He did not like the thought that he was being warned away, but neither could Emma afford for him to be hurt. So, feeling like a whipped schoolboy, he had bowed to their united front and turned away.

He did not wonder at their hostility. Last night had seen a full moon, and with the sea not quite so turbulent, would have proved an excellent night for removing cargo from a ship anchored offshore. He had no wish for any part in their doings; it was the excisemen whose job it was to find such men and deal with their activities.

No, he had enough on his mind without worrying about smugglers and the like.

His chest grew tight. He would give himself one more day. Emma's condition varied daily and so he could not spare much more time. She had been so patient with his quest. His stupid, foolish quest. He glanced at the cliff face. Nothing called for attention, so he trudged farther, farther than he had gone before. Sighed. He had given this quest his best shot. He had searched, he had persisted — nobody could fault his determination. But still the find he sought eluded him. He should give up. Emma needed him to focus attention on her, on her future. And the longer he stayed, the more chance there was that Pratt might discover his whereabouts, and then who knew what may result?

Gideon kicked a stone. Nearly swore as heat traveled from his toes through his booted foot. Fool. He was such a fool. Thinking he knew best. "Should I give up?"

His words were ripped away by the wind, and he glanced over his shoulder to ascertain that nobody had heard his cry to God.

He stumbled over a slippery stone, down to one knee. Pain jarred through his body. What, was God punishing him now? Was it pride that had taken him so far, pride that had stolen so much time? Fool. He was such a fool. How much longer? He should give up.

Besides, what would he even do if he did find a fossil? Even without a perfect specimen, Wilmont's find had already seen his name grace the London papers. He snorted. The man would likely even be invited to speak at the Geological Society. It seemed most unfair that some young, heavily financed whippersnapper could receive such opportunities when Gideon's own efforts had failed. Not that it was likely he would find anything, not with his luck. But even if he did find something, could he afford to let the truth of his name be made public?

Fool. He was such a fool. How much longer? He should just give up.

The refrain sounded in his ears as if spoken aloud. He squinted up at the heavens. The sun was beginning its slow descent. Sweat prickled on his neck. His arms ached with weariness. How much longer? He had no great confidence anymore that anything of significance lurked within these shale and limestone walls. He peered at the rock face, discouragement beating at his heart. Would these rocks yield anything greater than an ammonite? Perhaps James was right, and he should just give up and turn his hand to something that might yield more security.

As if God knew his faithless heart and despised him for it, a gray cloud drew overhead. The warmth from before dissipated, sending a chill shivering down his spine. A drop of water hit his cheek. Another. Then another. Wonderful. He would need to seek shelter. He glanced at the narrow slit in the cliff that denoted a cave entrance. He could only hope it did not prove to be a smuggler's lair, though he rather doubted such a place would be in use today.

He drew within. Inside, the dim space opened out to a cavern the breadth of four men. It held an appearance not unlike that of the cave near Beer he had visited several weeks ago. Save this space seemed naturally weathered, not a place quarried to rough smoothness. An eerie kind of prickling traversed his neck. Surely the free traders would not use this space?

"Hello!" he called out. His voice echoed through the chamber.

There came a scuffling noise behind him — rats? bats? — then, just as he was turning, a glint caught his eye, something hard struck his head, and he collapsed onto the rocky sand-strewn floor.

CHAPTER SEVENTEEN

Caroline looked up from where she sat curled up with her book as the door knocker sounded again. Whoever it was seemed somewhat desperate for admittance. She heard a murmur of voices, then the sound of footsteps before the library door was tapped.

"Come in," she called.

The door opened, admitting Dawkins. "Excuse me, miss, but there is a, *ahem,* person to see you."

A person? That could only mean —

"A Mr. Ballard," he continued.

"Who?"

He cleared his throat. "I believe he said that he works for the Kirbys."

"Oh! In that case, please send him in."

She swung her legs to the floor and stood, brushing out the worst of the wrinkles in her skirt. Good thing it was not Mama to see how much of a degenerate her daughter had become in her overly casual state of repose. While such a pose might hold a great degree of comfort, such was not the posture of a daughter of Aynsley!

Mr. Ballard came in, his face holding an expression that coiled a cold kind of tightness within Caroline's chest. "Yes? What is it?"

He coughed. "Begging your pardon for the interruption, miss, but Miss Emma be wondering if you have seen her brother."

"Why no, I have not."

"Oh." He nodded, then shuffled awkwardly. "Then I best return. Thank ye."

Putting aside both the fascinating speculation as to why Emma had thought he might deign to visit Caroline, and the outrageous urge to ask such a thing, she forced her thoughts to focus on the task at hand.

"He is missing?" she prompted gently.

"Miss Emma be right worried about him, which is most unlike her." He sighed. "Poor thing don't need to be fretting at this time."

"How is Emma today?"

"Not so well, I'm afraid. But I best let her know and resume searching."

She chewed her lip. Would Emma welcome Caroline's support as a friend? Would Grandmama understand Caroline's desire to visit? She would have to; this strange urgency compelled her to go. "Wait. I will come with you."

He looked nonplussed, but agreed nonetheless.

When she summoned Dawkins to request her grandmother's location, he informed her that Grandmama had accompanied Miss McNell on a trip to Lady Dalrymple's house. This news caused a strange twinge of hurt that her grandmother had not bothered to invite Caroline along for the excursion, despite knowing full well that Caroline had nothing to do today. However, as this news did obviate the need to request permission for Caroline's absence, she was not too sorry — for she suspected that Grandmama's permission for Caroline to participate in a hunt for Mr. Kirby might not be forthcoming.

After assuring Dawkins she would return soon, and that no, she didn't need Mary to act as chaperone, she was helped into the gig with Mr. Ballard.

Worries nibbled during the silent journey to the small cottage near the cliff path. Where was Mr. Kirby? How she hoped Emma's illness wouldn't worsen. If only she could search, too.

Soon she was helped down, was escorted inside, was greeting a surprised — and very pale — Emma with a hug, was listening to her friend talk of her concern.

"I have the strangest feeling that all is not well with him, and I could not bear to think . . ."

"Come now," Caroline said, clasping her hand. "Surely he is well. He shall likely return soon. He has probably merely journeyed a fraction farther than on previous occasions."

"Perhaps," Emma said uncertainly. "It is just he did not return for luncheon, and he is usually so good with keeping to the time he says, and I cannot dismiss this horrible feeling that something is wrong."

"I'm sure it is nothing," she said, willing her features not to give rise to the alarm she felt within. For truly, Emma did seem most uneasy. Caroline had certainly never seen her friend look so distressed.

"Forgive me. You must think me most foolish. I should never have bothered you."

"No, no. Not at all. That is, of course," she continued, as a trace of uncertainty stole across her heart, "unless you would prefer me to leave."

"Of course not! I'm so glad you are here. But I did not want to disturb your afternoon."

"Time spent with you is far more important than reading frivolous novels," she said.

"Oh, Caroline, you are so kind."

Her eyes blurred. Had anyone ever said such things to her?

Emma's forehead glistened, her pallor such that Caroline was tempted to call for Mrs. Ballard, then Emma squeezed her hand. "I wish Aidan was here."

"But he is not, and we are, and we shall do all we can."

Emma dragged in an audible breath, as if securing some comfort from the words.

A noise came from the entry. Emma shifted forward. "Mrs. Ballard? Has he returned?"

"Not as yet, I'm afraid, dearie."

"Oh." Emma's face seemed to pale with new horror as she gasped. "Oh no! You don't think *he* would have found Gideon, do you?"

Who would have got Mr. Kirby? Lord Pratt? Or Lord Pratt's henchman, Mr. Browne? But further conjecture had to be put to one side as Emma crumpled. Caroline called to Mrs. Ballard, who rushed to retrieve the medicine, all the while wondering about this extraordinary bond between the siblings. She had certainly never experienced such a close bond with her sisters. A twinge pulled within. Little wonder, as she had been so self-centered, but she was trying to change.

"Please, Emma, do not worry," she murmured.

Emma whispered, "Please stay a moment and let me pray for his safe return."

Caroline nodded, even as impatience stole across her chest, which was quickly followed by shame. If prayer gave Emma some sense of security, who was she to argue?

"Dear heavenly Father, thank You for being with Gideon. Please keep him safe, and return him to us soon. Amen."

"Amen," Caroline echoed, feeling like a fraud.

Mrs. Ballard reentered the room, medicine in hand, shooing Caroline away.

Had this been a mistake to come? Would it be better if she returned home? Oh, where was Mr. Kirby?

Outside, she found Mr. Ballard, whose huffing breaths suggested he'd just returned from the shore. "Do you have any idea where Mr. Kirby may have gone today?"

" 'Fraid not, miss. I just know he was not his usual cheery self this mornin', seemed quite a bit down in the mouth, if you know what I mean."

Guilt writhed within. Had her words yesterday been part of why he was not cheerful? Or was such thinking more evidence of her overweening sense of misplaced pride?

She forced her thoughts to the matter at hand. "And you believe he is out scouring the beaches for fossils?" At his nod, she continued. "East? West? Which way did he indicate he might go?"

"I can't rightly be certain, miss. I couldn't see him just now."

She bit back a word of annoyance and forced herself to think. Where had he said yesterday he would go? What was it . . .

That's right. He'd spoken of "Ladram Bay."

"I beg your pardon, miss?"

"Ladram Bay," she said in a louder voice. "Mr. Kirby intended to go near there, or so he told me yesterday."

She ignored the curious look he gave her and asked, "Where is Ladram Bay?"

He grunted something she did not catch, then moved to the coastal path, so she followed, her pulse accelerating, her feet hurrying along the grassy verge. If Mr. Kirby was in danger . . .

Mr. Ballard glanced over his shoulder, but she waved him on. "Please do not concern yourself with me."

He nodded, touching his forehead, quickly

striding away out of view, leaving her to follow foolishly in his wake, wishing she could have confidence to pray as Emma had earlier.

Was it improper to pray for a young man? Not that she was sure that God would even listen to her, but such a thing felt almost too personal, as if the act might bond them in some strange way. She felt sure Mama would not approve . . .

"Miss! Miss, I see 'im."

Caroline heaved out a breath of relief. There. That was nothing to be worried about. Nothing worth carrying on in this hoydenish fashion. Emma must have mistaken the matter. Mr. Kirby certainly had no need for Caroline's assistance. In fact, her appearance here would be considered far too forward. Perhaps she should turn back —

Her steps stumbled to a halt as she finally saw him. Mr. Kirby appeared to be stumbling himself, and she watched as Mr. Ballard raced to his side, supporting him with an arm, into which Mr. Kirby seemed to half collapse.

"Oh my goodness!" Her fingers flew to her mouth as she pressed another cry of horror back inside. Blood trickled from his head, staining his shirt. Poor man! Had he been attacked? Or had the legacy of crumbling cliffsides done their best?

"Mr. Kirby!" she called, hurrying forward. "Oh, dear Mr. Kirby."

He peered up at her from under the rough bandage Mr. Ballard was fashioning from his cravat. "Miss Hatherleigh. What on earth . . . ?"

"What on earth has happened to you?"

He winced and slumped a little more, as if her words held further weight.

"There be time enough to talk about that, miss," said Mr. Ballard. "Best be getting the lad home and being seen to by a doctor."

"Of course." She bit her lip. Thank goodness Emma was not here to see her brother's injured condition. Speaking of . . .

She glanced behind her. If Emma should see her brother in this state, she would no doubt be filled with the very type of anxiety she had been warned about. It was best she be protected from such a sight. "Would it be helpful if I hurried back and sent Mrs. Ballard for a doctor?"

"Aye, miss, it would."

"Then that is what I shall do." She reached out a hand to touch Mr. Kirby on the shoulder, then dropped it, suddenly conscious of the impropriety. "I shall see you soon."

Without further ado, she turned and, picking up her skirts — how like Verity was she becoming? — ran back along the coastal path, her thoughts, her feet flying, heedless of her reputation. Mr. Kirby had been injured! How could she best disclose the news to Emma without startling her too much? It was obvious she could not sustain too great a shock. Oh, how had he been injured?

Eventually, lungs heaving, mouth tasting of blood, she regained the gate that opened onto the cottage's back garden. She flung it open, slowing her pace and her frantic breathing, to not give Emma reason for fright.

A knock on the door and she entered without waiting for called admittance. "Emma?" she called. "Mrs. Ballard?"

The second of these two appeared, putting a finger to her lips as she closed the door to the bedchamber behind her. "Miss Emma is resting. What have you learned?"

"Mr. Kirby is returning home now, even as we speak. But . . ."

"But what, my dear?"

"It appears he has been injured, so perhaps it might be best to keep Emma from seeing him, at least until he has had a chance to be cleaned up."

"What has happened?"

"I do not know," she admitted. But something about the way the men had spoken urgently before she arrived, made her think it not a mere accident. "Mr. Ballard asked that the doctor be sent for."

"Of course. I will go now. You will remain with Miss Emma? I doubt she is yet asleep, and would be most relieved to know he is safe."

"Yes."

Within the minute, Mrs. Ballard left, leaving Caroline to walk cautiously into Emma's bedchamber. She had not been inside before, and was taken aback at the tables covered in the potions and powders and paraphernalia associated with sickness. Emma was resting on the bed, her eyes closed, but at the creak on the floorboard she opened her eyes. "Gideon?"

"He is safe, he is coming now."

"Thank God," Emma breathed, her voice a mere whisper.

"Yes," Caroline murmured. "Thank God." She forced a smile to her lips. "Please do not be alarmed, but it appears he will need a doctor. Mrs. Ballard has just gone to fetch one."

The worry in her friend's eyes prompted her to add, "But he is strong, and no doubt will be soon on the mend, so please do not worry."

"Yes, miss," Emma said meekly.

A rueful smile escaped. "I suppose I did sound a trifle officious then."

"I do not mind."

"Good. I'm afraid my bossiness must be hereditary."

Emma's soft chuckle almost drowned out the sounds of arrival.

"Excuse me while I go see if that is them now. I shall return in a moment."

"Of course."

Caroline hurried from the room to be greeted by the sight of Mr. Ballard propping up Mr. Kirby's head as he slowly sank onto the bench seat in the hall. Around his head was the bloodied makeshift bandage. Breath constricted in her lungs.

"Quickly, miss," Mr. Ballard urged. "Come hold his head up so I can tie another bandage around him. I'm afraid he's lost a bit of blood, and it wouldn't be good if Miss Emma was to see him like this."

"No, indeed," she said, hurrying forward to stand beside Mr. Kirby and, following Mr. Ballard's instructions, gently holding Mr. Kirby's head, swiping his hair free from the gash she could see.

And she had thought touching Mr. Kirby's

shoulder a breach of etiquette! What would Mama say if she could see her now? What would anyone say if they knew how much this touch elicited heat within; heat, and a strange tenderness that made her want to protect him all her days. She gulped.

"Steady, miss."

"I beg your pardon."

At her words, Mr. Kirby's head tilted up, his gaze capturing hers. "It is I who should be begging yours, Miss Hatherleigh," he said thickly. "Never did I imagine —" He broke off, wincing as Mr. Ballard tightened the bandage.

"There. That should do until the doc gets here, and not a moment too soon if I don't miss my guess," he said, with a jerk of his head to the door.

Caroline turned, straightening at the sight of Emma paused on the threshold.

"Oh, Gideon!" She hurried forward, falling on her knees beside him. "What has happened to you?"

"Just a slight scratch," he said, in a much clearer voice than what he'd used only seconds earlier. "Sorry to alarm you, my dear."

"We did not know where you were."

"I know. I am sorry." He shifted slightly and captured Caroline's attention once more. "I trust you were not unduly alarmed, Miss Hatherleigh."

"I do not think it was undue alarm," she said carefully.

He stilled for a moment before shaking his head slightly at her, as if he did not want her to say anything that might upset his sister. She dipped her head in a slight nod of understanding, turning to Emma with a bright smile.

"Well! We have certainly had an adventure today. Perhaps you might direct me to your kitchen so we can ensure your poor brother has a nice cup of tea."

"That's the thing," Mr. Ballard approved. "You take your good friend here to do so, Miss Emma. I'll warrant a good cup of tea would be just the thing for all concerned."

"If you say so," Emma said uncertainly.

"I do," Caroline said, guiding her from the room, glancing over her shoulder to see Mr. Kirby smile at her wanly before he mouthed, "Thank you."

She was a wonder. A whole sky of wonders. Miss Hatherleigh, she of the noble connections and high sense of propriety, had proved herself to be quite the heroine this afternoon, first agreeing to help search, then sacrificing her reputation in an effort to assist him and keep poor Emma from more worry.

Gideon closed his eyes, the dimness of the room permeating his eyelids. He smiled in the darkness. Miss Hatherleigh, she of the chestnut curls and quick wits. Who would have thought to see her act in such a way, running in a fashion sure to give her grandmother palpitations?

His smile faded. If only he could be sure what had happened. The doctor had visited and said the gash resembled the blow of a cudgel and then asked who would want to see him harmed.

Who, indeed. "Nobody," murmured Gideon. The only man he knew who might wish him injury could not possibly realize he'd returned here. And even if he had, he'd be far more likely to attack in some place far more accessible than a remote beachside cave. Pratt had never been one to do what might inconvenience him in any way.

No, his attacker had not been Pratt. Which left . . . who?

The only other thought left his skin pebbling with trepidation. Had the cave proved to be another site for free traders? If so, had he stumbled onto something he was not supposed to? And if so, what should he do? Inform the authorities? Captain Nicholls of the Customs Land Guard would certainly welcome the news. But if he did so, Gideon would surely be targeted, and he would not wish for his sister to suffer anymore than his foolish actions today had already caused. "Dear God, what do I do?"

He thought back to his earlier ruminations. There had been a moment in the cave before the pain smashed through his skull. What was it he had seen?

Memories whirled, blurred, firmed into recognition.

His eyes snapped open. That's right. He had seen a bone.

CHAPTER EIGHTEEN

Caroline called around the next day with flowers cut from her grandmother's garden, for Miss Kirby, so she had asserted to Grandmama, who, thankfully, remained blissfully unaware of yesterday's adventure. But she could not deny the desire she felt to see how Mr. Kirby fared, and she hoped perhaps that he might enjoy the flowers, too.

"Ah, Miss Hatherleigh," Mr. Ballard said, opening the door. "It is good to see you, miss."

"How is Mr. Kirby?" she said, stepping through to the hall.

"Much better, though he be a trifle anxious to leave."

"What?" she said, stilling. "Surely the doctor has forbidden such a thing."

"That he has, but the young master is insistent. He gets a wee bit bullheaded 'bout some things, you see."

"Does Emma know?"

"Not yet, and it only be because he does not wish to worrit her that he has not yet gone. It be all I can do to keep him here."

"Where — ?"

"In there." He gestured to the drawing room. "Please don't be saying nowt to the mistress. She has enough on her plate without more things to concern her."

"Of course not." She moved to enter the room, but he stayed her with a meaty hand.

"Beggin' your pardon, miss, but I wanted to thank ye for helping yesterday. You've got quite a head on your shoulders."

She nodded. That sounded like a compliment. She glanced at his nodding head and pleased expression; yes, it certainly seemed to be one. Gladness warmed within. "I was only pleased to be able to help."

"That you did, miss. Now, here be the mistress." He walked through and announced, "Here is Miss Hatherleigh come to see you, Miss Emma."

"Caroline!" Emma said, extending welcoming hands from her position on the sofa. "Oh, it is good to see you. I cannot thank you enough for all you did yesterday."

Caroline proffered the flowers to Emma's murmured delight. "It was nothing."

"It was everything," Emma corrected. "I would have been so frightened being here on my own, but your prayers and sense of calm helped me not to panic, and I found myself remembering I need only trust God in the midst of things."

Guilt twisted that her non-faith-laden prayer was being praised, leading her to quickly change the subject. "I am so pleased your health appears improved."

"Good news is a tonic. Oh, the relief to know Gideon is safe."

"How is your brother today?"

"Oh, he seems much better. The doctor warned that he might feel a little strange at times, and that he would almost certainly end up with a few headaches, but when I spoke to him earlier he was quite bright and, indeed, almost perky."

"Really?" Well, he would, Caroline thought, if he wanted to convince everyone of his good health. "And has he said anything about what happened?"

"I'll put these in water, miss," Mrs. Ballard said as she collected the flowers, and gave Caroline a stern look fraught with warning.

Emma replied blithely enough, "He said it must have been a silly rock falling from above."

"I'm sure it was," Caroline agreed. Yet if it was, why had the men appeared so secretive before she had reached them? Surely a rockfall wouldn't result in their wishing to hide such a thing.

"It really is a dangerous pursuit," Emma continued, her forehead pleating. "But Gideon is determined not to forsake his hunt for his precious specimens."

"Well, let us be thankful that he is well," Caroline said, sitting beside her. A slim volume lay facedown on the table. "Tell me, what have you been reading today?"

Emma pulled the book onto her lap. "I have found much comfort in the past hours from these words. This is a collection of psalms."

"Indeed," Caroline said, working to look interested as Emma spoke further on trusting God in challenging times. While she was prepared to concede that God may exist, and that some of the Bible did hold truth, it still seemed a step too far to actually trust someone she could not see, and she was not at all sorry when the door soon opened and Mr. Kirby walked in.

Breath suspended. His head remained bandaged, and his pallor was such as she had never before seen him wear, yet he smiled at her and greeted her warmly enough. In fact, he seemed to hold an even kindlier aspect than she'd come to expect, if the smile reflected in his eyes was to be believed.

"I wanted to add my thanks to that which I'm sure my sister has already expressed. She could not cease praising Miss Hatherleigh's good nature and determination and compassion earlier today."

His smile elicited a curl of pleasure within. "Truly, it was nothing."

"Ah, but that is where you are wrong. Clearly such heroics were something."

"Hardly heroics," she murmured.

"You were heroine enough for our purposes, and for that we thank you."

Heat rushed to her cheeks, leading her to wish to turn the conversation to something else. "May I enquire about your recovery, sir?"

"The doctor says I should take things slowly for the next little while."

"I am glad. So, no permanent injury?"

"The only permanent injury might be to my pride," he said, eyes twinkling in a way reminiscent of his sister's. "I am sure that it is not at all the thing for a gentleman to be seen by a genteel young lady in such a state of disrepair."

"Well, I am glad to see you seem to have recovered something of your health and your wits." She pushed to her feet. "If you'll excuse me, I am sure that I must go."

"Thank you, Miss Hatherleigh, for calling on us," Emma said, moving as if to get up.

"Please, do not trouble yourself. I can see myself out."

"I shall see her out," said Mr. Kirby.

A smirk flitted across his sister's face before she resumed her usual composure, simply thanking Caroline once again for the flowers and the visit.

Mrs. Ballard offered a curtsy, opening the door as Mr. Kirby drew Caroline to the entrance hall.

"Miss Hatherleigh," he said slowly, before looking up with those intense gray eyes. "Thank you for not speculating aloud back there on what the cause for my injury might be."

"Emma believes it to be rockfall, but it is not, is it?"

"I do not like conjecture, but I believe it might be something more to do with the local free-trading community."

She gasped. "Really?"

He smiled, before his features stiffened in a wince. "I am devastated to know that elicits your concern more than does the state of my injuries."

Little did he know how his injuries had kept her awake half the night. But she could not let him know of her worry for him, and strove to cover her concern with a careless smile. "Am I to imply by your comment that you are seeking my sympathy?"

"Not imply, my dear Miss Hatherleigh. I wish it to be plainly known."

"Why you should wish such a thing I do not know."

"I hope one day a reason might be revealed to you."

She bit her lip, wondering at the look in his eyes. Surely he did not mean to suggest he held some interest in her? Was that prideful to assume? But if he did, what would her parents say if Mr. Kirby, a mere commoner, declared his interest in someone whose connections to nobility were so well known?

Gideon watched her as the color rose on her cheeks. That she did not know what to reply was obvious. That he was the cause for her confusion made his heart sing. For if she entertained no thought of him, then surely her answer would have been most plainly said by now.

"Forgive me, Miss Hatherleigh. I should not tease."

She looked startled for a moment, and then her features closed. "No, you should not. That is ungentlemanly."

"Again, I beg your forgiveness."

She nodded stiffly, her eyes not quite meeting his, then murmured a farewell and turned as if to go.

"Miss Hatherleigh?"

She paused.

"I offer my deepest gratitude for all your assistance yesterday. And I would beg your indulgence in not speaking of it to anyone."

Her eyes swiftly rose to his. "You have not spoken to the authorities?"

"I do not know quite what I would say if I did, so I think it best to say nothing at this stage."

"Oh. I just thought . . ."

He drew closer. "You just thought?"

"I just thought that if it were" — she hesitated — "if it were members of a certain section of local society, the authorities might want to be made aware."

"I believe they would."

She stared at him, eyebrows raised, as if waiting for him to say more.

"But I fear that sharing such suspicions might prove detrimental to those I love."

Love.

This last word seemed to fill the space between them. He swallowed. Even in his ill-fated serenade to the dean's daughter he had never breathed such a word. But this young lady, so poised and genteel, made him wish for things that could never be. Caution whispered that he wait until he knew where she stood in matters of faith, but something else beckoned him to think on her, think of what could be if she believed like he did. It was almost as if in her presence he became a different man, one who did not need the plaudits of the scientific community but one who could be content to bask in the sunshine of her friendship; of her warm, compassionate spirits; and, if he were so honored, of her love.

Her cheeks filled with a crimson glow, as if she were as startled by the word as he was, before she dropped her gaze and murmured her farewell and good wishes for his recovery. But he could not regret speaking such a thing aloud. He might have come to the southeast of Devon searching for ancient treasure, but he suspected he had found treasure of a very different kind.

A few days later, Gideon was returning from mailing letters to his brother and Kenmore when a voice called for his attention.

"Kirby."

Gideon turned at the raspy voice. "Good day, Belcher."

The thickset man jerked a nod. "Doc tells

me you got injured." He glanced at Gideon's bandaged head. "What happened?"

Ah, so this was the envoy sent to learn how much he suspected. He would have to play his cards very carefully to ensure Emma's safety. "I believe you are aware that I have something of an interest in fossils and the like."

The broad-faced man stared impassively.

"For months now I have been searching for something to further demonstrate God's remarkable design whilst caring for my family." Gideon offered a small smile. "I certainly have no desire to impede anyone's attempts to provide for their loved ones."

Again, the other man said nothing, but this time Gideon refused to say more until the man at least acknowledged that they were not so very different after all. After all, surely the reasons for smuggling had to be more about desiring money for one's family rather than making some political statement, at least in this poor part of the world.

After staring at him very hard for a few moments more, Belcher finally gave a grunt.

Well, Gideon thought, suppressing a wry smile, he supposed that would have to do. "I may have stumbled across such a specimen in a cave not so very far from here, but you know what these cliffs are like." Beyond

Belcher, he saw Captain Nicholls, the exciseman responsible for the local area. "These cliffs are often prone to mudslides and the like."

Belcher jerked another nod. "You be sayin' the rocks did it."

"I will be saying exactly that," Gideon affirmed, casting the approaching exciseman a look of significance.

"Then I be suggestin' you be stayin' away from such places," Belcher said softly, as Captain Nicholls drew near.

"Thank you for your advice," Gideon said, turning to the exciseman. "Good day to you, sir."

The older man nodded, frowning as he looked between Gideon and Belcher. "Is there a problem here?"

"No problem," Gideon said, as Belcher sidled away.

"That is a nasty looking cut you've sustained," Nicholls said, his gaze dragging back from following Belcher to fix on Gideon.

"It is, isn't it?"

The small eyes narrowed. "Dr. Fellowes tells me it happened several days ago. Do you recall what happened?"

"I couldn't rightly say," Gideon said honestly.

"Would you care to speculate on what might have happened, then?" Nicholls said, staring at him very hard.

"I do not know if that is wise," Gideon admitted.

Nicholls pushed closer and lowered his voice. "If it be fear of the likes of Jem Baker and Don Belcher and company, then let me tell you I have them under surveillance. If there is something you think I should know, then I want you to tell me, understand?"

"I understand perfectly, sir, and I promise that if there is something I think you should know, I shall tell you. Until then . . ."

The captain gave a noise of disgust, shook his head, and strode away.

Gideon exhaled, turning to see Belcher watching him still, so he offered a small smile, which was met with a nod. Such matters as had developed today had made one thing very clear.

Gideon needed to return to that cave as soon as possible.

"Tom, I would like you to do something for me."

"Yessir?"

"I find I have need to return to Ladram Bay area, but I do not know if my headaches would make such a journey wise."

"If you don't mind me saying so, sir, I don't be thinking it wise at all."

"Perhaps not," Gideon agreed. "But I find that I am quite unable to refrain from doing so, which makes the telling of my sister of my whereabouts ill-advised, wouldn't you agree?"

"Just what is it you be askin' of me, sir?"

"I be asking for your assistance, Tom." Gideon smiled. "For I do believe I have finally found it."

"Finally found it?" The older man's eyes bulged. "Is this a jest, sir?"

"I am not sure, of course, which is why I wish to return to make quite certain."

Tom nodded slowly. "Would this have anything to do with that evil-looking character I saw you with earlier?" He made a sound of disgust. "Smugglers are no good, the lot of them; should all be hanged."

"Perhaps," Gideon conceded. "Or perhaps if I show I have no interest in their trade, they might be prepared to overlook my desire to return to their cave."

Tom's eyes bulged. "You think it was them that hurt you?"

"I am nearly certain of it."

"Then why — ?"

"Because you may not know that Mr. Belcher there has a young and growing family who seem quite as sickly as poor Emma. I would not be party to seeing the only means of income denied them."

Tom snorted. "They could get relief from the parish."

"You really think a couple of extra shillings enough to provide for a family?"

"I certainly don't hold with stealing!"

"And I certainly don't begrudge a man desperate to provide for his family," Gideon said softly. "In fact, I find myself in sympathy with such a predicament."

Tom muttered something under his breath before eventually sighing. "When would you be wanting to go?"

"As soon as I can ensure Emma is safe. And for that, I'm afraid I may need to rely on Miss Hatherleigh's good graces once again."

"I don't think you got any trouble with that," Tom said drily.

"No?"

"No." Tom rubbed the sides of his nose. "I think it safe to say that young lady will prove most obliging wherever you are concerned, if you don't mind my saying so."

Gideon grinned, heart leaping at this unexpected confirmation of his innermost hope. "Dear Tom, I don't mind you saying so at all."

■ ■ ■ ■

It was another day before his headaches cleared and the expedition to the cave could be finally arranged. In deference to the free traders, Gideon had thought it prudent to make his intentions known in a more public setting, thus giving the smugglers time to remove their goods if necessary, whilst also providing a degree of security by way of Nicholls knowing his whereabouts, should anything untoward occur. This was done in a loud voice guaranteed to secure the attention of both Belcher and Nicholls after services on Sunday, a time which permitted Emma to arrange a visit with Miss Hatherleigh, which he gathered from their discussion would involve a morning expedition to Sidford, about two miles inland, should Emma's health permit. His sister had seemed well this morning, and he trusted the expedition might also allow for further connection between them, as he couldn't help but persist in this hope that Tom surprisingly had given rise to. She admired him? How he longed for the day when he might finally be able to show himself worthy of such esteem.

He trudged along the damp sand, but this

time, instead of his steps dogged by failure, he felt a sense of anticipation, hope lighting his heart — hope for today's outcome and hope for his future. That is, if his memory had not proved faulty.

And when he attained just beyond the mouth of the cave — further secrets the cave held he had no wish to know — he knew his memory had not led him astray.

"Look," he said to Tom, lifting up the lantern and pointing to a curved section jutting from the rock, the surface worn to a shine. "I thought as much."

"Is that a bone?"

"I believe so. Here, hold the lantern while I see if anything more can be unearthed."

The next hour was spent in painful expectancy as he used the hammer and pick to carefully chip away at the stubborn earth encasing the fragment. Gradually its true shape became evident. His heart leapt. Could it really be . . . ?

"Tom. Tom!"

"Yes, sir?"

"I think this might be — no, I scarce dare hope for such a thing."

"You think it might be another of those backbones like Wilmont found?"

"No. I think this might be something even more wonderful!"

If only he could have Kenmore cast his eye over it. Surely his letter must have now arrived? Further efforts soon released more proof amid a cloud of dust. He dragged in a deep breath. By all that was wonderful —

Gideon started to cough and splutter.

"There, there, master," said Tom, patting him on the back. "P'raps you should go outside and get yourself a nice bit of air."

Gideon nodded, choking on the dust, and stumbled to the entrance. Outside the gleaming sea seemed to dance with the same sense of anticipation he could feel rippling through his soul. Oh, he had to tell somebody! He had to tell Emma, Aidan, James — and Miss Hatherleigh.

CHAPTER NINETEEN

"You have a visitor, miss. Mr. Kirby."

At this time of morning? She placed the book down. "Thank you, Dawkins. I shall be ready directly."

The initial thrill of his visit diminished as misgiving crossed her chest. Was Emma unwell? Had yesterday's visit proved too strenuous? Was something wrong?

Further speculation ceased as the door opened and they exchanged bow and curtsy.

"Mr. Kirby. I trust all is well with Emma."

"Emma? Thank you for your solicitude, she is well. No, this is something else. Miss Hatherleigh, I was hoping you might condescend to accompany us on a short journey to visit the new specimen I found yesterday."

"Oh!" She could see from the way Mr. Kirby's eyes shone and the way he leaned forward, pushing up on his toes, that he barely suppressed excitement. "Whatever it is seems most wonderful."

"It is!" he assured her, before going on to describe — in scientific and very detailed terms — the precise skeleton of a sea dragon–type creature known as an *ichthyosaurus.*

She watched him, eyes bright, hands gesticulating as he explained. He was so far removed from the very proper — and quite frankly, dull — gentlemen of her acquaintance. So interesting and considerate a man . . . It was pointless to deny her attraction any longer. In him she recognized the qualities she had long admired but could never admit to, qualities more to do with compassion for others than correct lineage, qualities that concerned social good rather than personal wealth. Did such things stem from his faith? She shook away the disquieting thought, focusing on the one thing she now knew: her growing esteem was such she feared she might be falling in love with him. And what would her parents say to that?

"Forgive me," he said with a disarming grin. "I can be inclined to prattle away, which becomes apparent when my poor listener's eyes are starting to glaze over."

She lifted a hand to her face, then lowered it, blushing as his grin broadened. "Oh! I do not want you to think I was bored. I enjoy listening to you speak."

"You are too kind."

"My sisters would probably tell you I'm not nearly kind enough," she said wryly, "but ever since meeting you, and Emma, of course, I have been challenged to consider my interactions with others, and I have come to the conclusion they have not always been as they ought."

His expression sobered. "I would not wish you to be disconcerted by what I say."

"But it has been only good! The challenge to be kinder in how I speak and think has to be good, do you not agree?"

"I would hope so." He smiled deep into her eyes.

Her heart quivered. She swallowed, willing away the confusion. But no words would form to save her from embarrassment. She was only conscious of the special warmth lighting his gaze, the small lines feathering out at the corners of his eyes that spoke of tenderness and joy. And his smile, so warm and genuine, one that chased away the shadowed recesses of her heart, one that made his face look lit from within, a smile formed by lips so pliable — even now they were twisted to one side — that she wondered how soft —

"Oh!" She jerked her attention away, feeling her face grow hot.

"Miss Hatherleigh? Have I said something to upset you?"

"No, not at all. Forgive me."

"So, would you be willing to accompany me on a journey to the cave?"

Conscious of the heat still flooding her cheeks and the way her thoughts had revealed just how improper she could be, she drew herself up, arming herself with politeness, and said in a cool tone, "I am not sure it would be considered appropriate."

"I see." His look, his voice, conveyed disappointment. "We would not be alone, of course. Emma is feeling a little stronger today, and has said she will accompany us to the cave mouth. You could bring your maid, and your sketching materials."

Heart torn, she eyed him. Yes, she wanted to go. Yes, she felt an almost desperate desire to spend more time with him. But surely such desires were not ladylike, were not proper. No, best to deny these desires rather than accede to them. But his face now looked sad, as if he'd been hoping for her company, and the lack of it would be like the sun shut out from his day . . .

"It is not that I do not want to go." She grabbed at the nearest excuse. "It is my grandmother. I do not think she would be amenable to such a plan."

"I see. Of course, I should have thought —"

"I will ask her," she rushed on, hating to see the embarrassment in his cheeks, knowing she was the cause of it. "She can be very surprising at times, and when she knows it is of educational value . . ."

His lips drew upward and he nodded solemnly. "I should think such an excursion would prove to be immensely educational in understanding what an undergroundologist does."

"Well, I shall ask her. After all, one cannot remain in ignorance for too long?"

"Indeed not."

"Excuse me." She offered a small curtsy and hurried from the room to find her grandmother in the small chamber she used for writing correspondence, a room that overlooked the sea.

After she apologized for her interruption and made her request, Grandmama looked at her with piercing intent. "Do you think his intentions honorable?"

"Grandmama!"

"Well, what do you expect me to think? A young man asking to escort my granddaughter. What else can it look like?"

"He says it would be educational."

She sniffed. "I'm sure. But exactly what

he would be educating you in I do not care to think on."

Caroline eyed her uncertainly. She did not like feeling ignorant, but her grandmother's words were something of a mystery.

"And I cannot think your spending so much time in this young man's company would meet with your parents' approval. After all, what are his connections? Who are his people?"

"He hasn't asked me to marry him, Grandmama, only to accompany him on a short journey to the cave. You did not mind before."

"Yes, but that was with that Kenmore fellow and Miss Kirby in attendance also."

"Miss Kirby will accompany us again."

"Regardless, those excursions did not involve caves. There is something rather unwholesome about a cave, I think. Dark and dingy places."

"Oh, but —"

"Pray, do not interrupt me. Come on, *think* dear girl. What sort of young man woos in a cave? Certainly, none that possesses any honorable intent."

"I believe Mr. Kirby is honorable," Caroline said stiffly. "He is simply interested in scientific matters, nothing else."

"*Is* he?" Grandmama asked, with another

piercing look.

Caroline's cheeks heated. How she longed to know if he truly did hold her in more regard than simply showing off his find. She could not deny such a thought made her heart gambol like one of Aynsley's spring-time lambs. She met her gaze squarely. "Truly, Grandmama, you should hear him talk about this discovery. He believes it might be the find of the century."

Perhaps that was overstating things a tad, but her grandmother had to hear his passion, and perhaps she could recognize him in his own right, and not existing as a mere satellite around Caroline. Her breath caught. Perhaps Grandmama might even be willing to consider becoming his sponsor!

"Yes, I think perhaps it is best I do hear him speak. Is he here still?"

"I believe so."

"Then I shall speak to him. I want to know more about this young scientific friend of yours."

Gideon waited in the drawing room, not daring to sit down, not daring to pace as he'd like to, in case the stoic footman at the door see him and make a fuss. What was taking her so long? It had to be good, did it not? If it had been a denial, then she would have been back immediately — unless Caroline was even now trying to convince her to change her mind.

He felt his cheeks heat. Somehow it seemed a desecration to think of Miss Hatherleigh by her Christian name in such a setting, as if the cherubs gracing the ceiling could penetrate his thoughts and know him to be unworthy.

But he was unworthy. He knew that only too well. He would never have the title or the wealth this place demanded, although he hoped with his discovery that he might one day have a degree of status.

A noise came from without and he straightened, forcing his lips up in a smile as the door opened, only for his expression to slacken as the dowager sailed in.

"Lady Aynsley." He offered a bow.

"Mr. Kirby." She surveyed him, her critical gaze taking in his several years out-of-date coat and his scuffed boots. "I understand you wish to escort my granddaughter on a certain expedition."

"Yes, your ladyship. It is to a nearby cave —"

"Pray do not interrupt me. I am not in the habit of being interrupted."

"Forgive me," he offered humbly, as the tips of his ears heated.

"I do not understand why you felt it imperative to speak with Caroline before speaking with me." She eyed him in a way that made him feel akin to a loathsome spider.

Was he supposed to answer now? "Forgive me. I did not want your ladyship to be disturbed unless Miss Hatherleigh agreed."

"Hmm." Again, that piercing scrutiny. "Who are your family? What are your connections?"

What? Were such questions indicative that she suspected his interest to be deeper than mere educational purposes? Any answer he might offer seemed to take on a more serious weight. He swallowed, then answered succinctly about his family and education and prospects.

"Londonberry, eh? Well, that certainly throws a different light on matters. Does my granddaughter know?"

"No."

"Is there any reason why such connections should not be made more widely known?"

He studied her. Should he trust her? *Lord?* He sensed affirmation, so began to share about his sister and Lord Pratt, a little surprised by her lack of shock at his revelation.

"I see. Well, I do not know that I would

go about things quite as you have, but I can understand your reasons for doing so. Now there is no need to look at me like that. I will tell nobody, I assure you."

"Thank you, my lady."

She nodded, eyes still fixed on him. "So, your intentions towards my granddaughter are entirely honorable?"

"Of course they are, my lady. I would never give rise to anything that might bring Miss Hatherleigh a moment's shame."

"I should think not."

"All I wish is to escort her and my sister to a recent discovery I have made. There would be no impropriety, I assure you."

"Hmph." Again, that disconcerting stare. "And she would be quite safe?"

"Yes, my lady." He would die rather than let harm come to Miss Hatherleigh, but he sensed such a pronouncement might give rise to speculation which he could not yet afford, so he waited, the line of questions giving rise to hope.

"And she would not be brought into scandal? She is an Aynsley after all."

"I assure you that nobody apart from you and my sister are aware of our excursion." He smiled. "Truly, ma'am, I was simply excited to show off my find to people I thought might be excited with me."

"And what is it you think to have found?"

He explained briefly, and marveled that her eyes did not glaze over.

"Hmm. I admit that does hold a degree of interest."

It did? "You would be very welcome to come also, my lady," he offered.

"Somehow I do not think my accompanying you would be what you were hoping for."

Heat crept up his neck. But perhaps her attendance would be beneficial. If she held some interest in his work, then perhaps she might agree to stand as sponsor — he shook his head.

"I thought not."

"Forgive me, my lady, I did not mean to suggest that. I would appreciate your company, more than you realize, but I would not wish to have you do something you might not wish to."

She chuckled. "My boy, I am always being asked to do things I have no wish for. Your invitation, such as it was, at least holds a mite of interest as a novelty."

"It would be an honor, madam, to have your company —" he began eagerly.

"An honor you will have to forgo, I'm afraid, as it looks rather chilly out. I will permit my granddaughter to attend today, on the proviso that she is attended by my maid, and that I accompany her next time."

Heart soaring, he grinned. "Thank you, my lady. Indeed, it would be a great honor to show you the work. Perhaps on our return today we can show you a specimen, and it will give you a greater understanding as to what it is like."

"Perhaps," she said, giving a regal nod. "Now I best summon my granddaughter and give her my blessing. My blessing for today's venture, nothing more," she added sternly.

But he sensed in her small smile an unspoken "as yet," which warmed his own smile and softened his heart towards her.

A footman was summoned and dispatched, and a few minutes later Miss Hatherleigh entered the room, eyes wide as if she couldn't believe what had transpired.

He turned to her. "You are sure you wish to come?"

"Yes," she murmured. "I will need to change."

"Then hurry up, child. You cannot keep the young gentleman waiting. You've kept him waiting long enough as it is."

With a swift smile for him and a curtsy for her grandmother, Miss Hatherleigh escaped, leaving him with the formidable grandmother once again. "You *will* take care of her?"

"Of course."

She gave a sharp nod, eyeing him in a way that made him think she wasn't entirely convinced.

He lifted his chin, and offered a look he hoped conveyed assurance. "You have my word. Today will be a day she will never forget."

CHAPTER TWENTY

Today had proved a day of wonders, enough to make Caroline almost believe there might be other miracles to be seen from this God the Kirbys trusted. She clutched the bag containing her sketchbook and pencils. From the look Grandmama had given Caroline as they departed, she wondered if perhaps her grandmother was not so hardened to romance after all. Especially not when it was dressed as scientific education. A gurgle of amusement escaped.

Mr. Kirby glanced at her, eyebrows aloft as if enquiring as to the source of her joy.

She shook her head, but offered a smile. Beatrice, Grandmama's maid, was sure to report on all that was said and done, Mary's chaperonage having apparently been deemed unnecessary — or unsatisfactory.

"I am so pleased you were able to come," he said in an undervoice.

"I am also," she whispered in return.

As they pulled up, Caroline spied Emma with the Ballards, apparently awaiting Mr. Kirby's arrival. Emma must have anticipated his success in securing Caroline's consent to come. Her pale cheeks belied the determined set of her chin as she drew close to meet them.

As Mr. Kirby helped Caroline from the carriage, anticipation bubbled within. With Mr. Ballard, he led the way along the path to the beach, Emma and Caroline in tow, Mrs. Ballard staying with the gig. Mr. Kirby looked to be walking on air, his excitement palpable. Surely today would be a day of great discovery.

Eventually they arrived at the cave entrance, which seemed but a gash in the cliff, a narrow opening with a sandy floor and red sandstone boulders guarding the entry. Caroline glanced at Emma who appeared reluctant to enter. "You do not wish to come in?"

She glanced at her brother, then acquiesced. "For a moment. I do not like contained spaces, but I could not miss this wondrous event."

"Of course not," Caroline said, looping her arm through Emma's as they moved to where Mr. Kirby stood holding out his hand at the cave entrance.

"Mind the stones underfoot. It is a little slippery."

"Does the water enter here?" Caroline asked.

"I believe so. It seems the tides have carved out this section of cliff over many years."

"Will the tide enter now?"

"The tides are going out. We shall be safe."

He led the way, one lantern held high, the other hand holding Emma's as they passed over rocks and mossy stones. Caroline followed with Beatrice, and Mr. Ballard behind, holding another lamp, whose light cast eerie shadows.

Caroline shivered and pulled her wrap closer.

"You are not cold?"

"No," she lied.

"It can get a little cool, but we shan't be in here overly long. Ah, look, here we are now." He lifted the lantern whose light fell on a section of rock face that glowed gray. Splicing the stone was an odd linear discoloration, which closer examination revealed to be a series of bones, like that of a skeleton. It was perhaps two to three yards long, with a curved smaller progression of bones that suggested some sort of tail.

"Here it is," Mr. Kirby said, pride evident

in his voice. "I believe it to be an *ichthyosaurus.*"

"Oh, Gideon, how wonderful!" Emma exclaimed.

"Truly remarkable," Caroline agreed. "What sort of creature is it?"

"A sort of sea dragon."

"Sea dragon?" A memory sparked. "Like the creature Miss Anning found?"

"Yes, the very same. Of course it was not a dragon *per se,* but a lizard creature that dwelt in marine environments, and looked something like a dolphin."

"That seems the stuff of fairy tales."

"Yet here it is."

"Here it is," Caroline echoed.

Emma coughed, then looked at them apologetically. "Forgive me, but I wish to return outside."

"Beatrice could go with you."

Emma smiled. "Somehow I do not believe your grandmother would think Mr. Ballard's chaperonage quite enough."

"Indeed she would not, miss," interjected Beatrice, with a heavy frown.

"Mrs. Ballard is nearby. The day has cleared considerably, and the breeze feels warmer than earlier." Emma held up a slim tome. "I shall be quite happy out there with my book."

"I'll take you, miss," Mr. Ballard said. "Come now, watch your step."

As they departed, Caroline turned back to Mr. Kirby. "She will be safe?"

He nodded. "Mrs. Ballard knows what to do."

Her attention returned to the rock face. She reached up, then paused, glancing across. "May I touch it?"

"Of course."

She gingerly touched the ridged remnants of spine, marveling at the texture. "It feels so smooth."

"It has doubtless been weathered by many a wave."

Caroline glanced over her shoulder at the maid, standing several feet away, whose expression revealed profound disapproval. "Does this not accord to your taste, Beatrice?"

"I cannot say that it does, miss." She sniffed, muttering something about dirt and vice and wickedness.

"Would you perhaps feel more comfortable waiting outside with Miss Kirby and Mrs. Ballard?"

"I am here to attend you, miss, at her ladyship's orders." She sniffed again, then shivered.

"Truly, Beatrice, we shall return outside

in a moment. You can be sure Mr. Kirby will behave with all propriety."

"I have my orders, miss."

Caroline glanced at Mr. Kirby and shrugged, which he acknowledged with a half smile.

As Mr. Ballard reentered the chamber, Mr. Kirby dispatched him once more, this time to bring in the larger box of equipment he'd left outside. Caroline couldn't be sure, but with her perpetual sniffing, it sounded as if Beatrice must be falling ill.

Mr. Kirby encouraged her to make a sketch, so she drew out her materials, and, using the light cast by the lantern, began to translate the image of the skeleton to her paper. A sense of wonder balled within. Truly, this was a spectacular sight. How long had this creature been trapped within its rocky tomb? And to think she was one of a handful of others graced to see it. What an honor that Mr. Kirby wished her to see such a thing!

"Have you enough light?"

"Yes, thank you, Mr. Kirby." She quickly sketched in some rocks to give a greater sense of proportion. "I do believe my youngest sister would think this most surprising of me. She is the one with the taste for adventure in our fam—"

Her words broke off as a rumbling sound suddenly shook the small space, followed by shouts and screams, including Caroline's own.

Mr. Kirby jerked her away, holding her hard against his chest as a spectacular crash of rocks tumbled from the cavern ceiling to the floor.

"What's happened?" Caroline cried, heart thumping hard. She blinked, trying to peer through the earthen powder. She started to cough instead, choking against the dirt and grit.

"It appears to have been a rockfall. Here, use your shawl to protect yourself from the dust."

She obeyed, wrapping it around her nose and mouth. "Where is Beatrice?"

A feeble moan soon gave notice of where the maid was.

"Beatrice? Beatrice?"

Another muffled sound came from the other side of the fallen rocks.

"Is she hurt?"

Caroline realized the stupidity of that question almost at once, but Mr. Kirby gave no notice he thought the question a foolish one, simply saying, "I cannot know."

"What will we do?"

She could feel him stiffen before his arm

slowly dropped from around her. "I will need to ascertain whether we can squeeze through, or whether we shall have to do something else."

Something else? "What does that mean?"

By the faint light glowing from the lantern, she could see him as he stripped off his coat. "It may become necessary to dig our way out."

"How on earth can we do that?"

"We, or rather I, will need to remove the rocks one by one. But" — he grunted, picking up a stone from the pile — "I won't know, until I can check, so please be patient." He tossed the stone to the side. "You may want to pray for your grandmother's maid."

"Of course." She bit her lip. "Do you think Emma is safe?"

"I trust so. The Ballards are with her, and Tom will get help," he said. But the note of worry in his voice gave wings to her concern.

Oh, dear God! What would happen if poor Emma had been struck? What if she was hurt? What if she was dead? Panic swelled within, making her breathing labored, forcing her to ever more shallow breaths.

"Caroline, we should pray."

But how? She didn't know any of the customary prayers, like those used by the minister in services. Would God even deign to listen to someone who scarcely believed in Him? What was she supposed to say?

"Heavenly Father," he began, "thank You for Your protection, and for keeping us safe thus far. We ask You to release us from this coil and bring us to safety. In the name of Your Son, Jesus. Amen."

Somehow his soothing tones brought a measure of peace, and she echoed his "Amen" weakly.

But what did these words even mean? If God was in heaven, how could He help on earth? But wouldn't He want to help someone like Emma? After all, she was so good. Beatrice, well, God may want to help her, too, but she didn't seem *quite* so worthy of heavenly assistance.

Mr. Kirby moved to another large rock and started to push. It refused to move. It was wedged tight. He groaned, muttered something under his breath.

"What is it?"

"The rock is too heavy. I cannot move it."

"What? You mean we are stuck here?"

"Not yet. I'll try another."

The lamplight showed that the dust was settling, so she pulled her wrap away from her mouth. The air smelled damp and musty. Still, she dragged in long drafts.

Caroline watched as Mr. Kirby tried valiantly to shift another large stone, his back curving with the effort. He was talking to himself, muttering things that sounded like ". . . all things . . . strengtheneth me!" Yet despite his strenuous efforts, nothing budged.

She moved beside him. "Perhaps I can help."

His look of surprise was chased by one of appreciation. But despite her best efforts, the rock refused to shift.

Mr. Kirby slumped back with a gasp. "It won't move."

Hope sagged. "We are trapped."

"For the moment."

Trapped. They were trapped! She tasted fear, swallowed panic. Felt her chest tighten as the terror soared again. "Beatrice! Mr. Ballard! Help us!"

The scream echoed through the small chamber, ringing through her ears, resounding in her heart. A violent trembling shook her body, dread making her next shriek louder, higher. "Help! Help!"

Mr. Kirby drew near, holding her upper arms, gently stroking them as she might soothe Mittens in a thunderstorm. "Miss Hatherleigh, please, I need you to be brave."

"I *am* being brave," she gasped.

337

"Of course, but I mean really brave. We may well be here for a while before we are rescued, and it won't do us any good if you start panicking. You will exhaust yourself."

"But it might happen again! What if the ceiling collapses? What if you are struck on the head? What if you collapse and die and I am stuck here all alone?"

"Then one day you might find your bones picked over by a mad scientist who will visit this site with a young lady who will exclaim over the smoothness of the bones."

She stared at him, jaw sagging. "You are making light of this?"

"I suppose I am."

"I . . . I cannot believe you!"

"What is the alternative? We spend the next few hours crying and panicking? How will that help anything?"

Gradually his response — or lack of one — stole into her senses. Perhaps he was right. After all, panicking wasn't going to help anyone. "You . . . you are not very sympathetic," she finally managed.

"I tend to be more pragmatic, it's true," he said. "But surely you would prefer that to someone who is panicking worse than you?"

He demonstrated, giving a series of short gasps, fanning his face as if he were an overheated young lady at a ballroom.

Her gaze narrowed. "Now you are making sport of me."

"Not at all," he averred. "I am merely enjoying you."

His words, uttered as they were in that surprisingly serious tone, made her forget their predicament for a few moments, touching her deep within. Did he truly enjoy her company? Even when she was startled into panic? The thought made her pull her spine in, and determine to be braver than she felt. "I am not used to cave-ins."

"And here I was thinking you experienced them on a weekly basis."

A chuckle broke past her indignation. "You are quite abominable."

"I know," he said humbly. "It would seem that I am past hope, though perhaps not past praying for." He returned to the rocks, lifting and shifting the smaller ones aside. "Tell me, my dear Miss Hatherleigh, would you do me the honor of praying for me?"

"I . . ." What was she supposed to say? Why did his words leave her feeling off-kilter? "Oh, very well."

"Thank you." He glanced over his shoulder, smile glinting. "I believe there are some who might think me so reprehensible that I would require very regular prayers. At least on a daily basis."

"A daily basis?"

"Perhaps even an hourly basis. I am sure your grandmother would be one of those thinking I might require precisely that."

His words were enough to make her wonder again about what exactly had transpired between him and Grandmama earlier. Whatever it was had been enough to win her approval, although she imagined Grandmama would never have envisaged something of this nature to occur.

Swallowing a sigh, she moved alongside him once more, determined to show him she was braver than he supposed, and tugged at the rocks to release a smaller one. Wryness twisted her lips. These gloves would be fit for nothing save the bin once this ordeal was over.

Now that her initial panic had abated, the cavern's dimness, lit only by the lamp, held a companionable feel, his grunts of exertion and her stifled sighs breaking down any remaining barriers between them, leading her to ask the questions she had wondered over for several hours now. "You must have had quite the conversation with my grandmother."

"She was not nearly as formidable as I had supposed. Whether that remains the case after this misadventure, however . . ."

"You cannot be blamed. You did not know that this would happen."

"Ah, but I promised her you would be safe."

"And so I am," she insisted. "And with you here, I cannot be lonely."

"No, indeed," he said thoughtfully. "Neither one of us will be quite alone."

The intent look in his eyes only intensified, leaving her further disconcerted. Did he mean to suggest that being alone together like this might lead to far-reaching permanent consequences? She knew what society would say must happen when a young lady was found to have been alone with a young man.

She swallowed, and glanced away. "Should we try to cry for help again?"

"If it makes you feel better. I'm sure Tom has sought help by now."

"Then why can't I hear anyone?"

They stood, listening carefully to the entry chamber. Nothing, not even the sound of breathing. Oh, dear God — was Beatrice dead? She gasped.

"What is it, Miss Hatherleigh?"

"Do — do you think Beatrice is alive?"

His gaze softened, and he reached out a hand to clasp her elbow. "We heard her groans before, so we trust God she still is."

The element of doubt in his voice pricked tears. She tried to sniff them away. "But if she *is* dead, then it is my fault and Grandmama will never forgive me."

"I rather think she will never forgive *me*," he said, with no small degree of dryness. "Miss Hatherleigh, do not worry about this. Worry certainly won't change anything. And please know I will do all I can to protect you."

She dragged in a deep breath, working to keep the fear at bay. Mr. Kirby might not precisely accord with her mother's idea of a gentleman, but he certainly possessed something of the gallant about him. "You are right, of course. Forgive me."

"There is nothing to forgive." He added in an undertone, "On my side at least."

He blamed himself for this? "But you could not have known."

"I confess that I was excited about the find, but I should have more thoroughly ascertained the safety before allowing you to come with me."

"Do not blame yourself. I do not."

"Well, that is something at least. I appreciate your graciousness, Miss Hatherleigh."

Graciousness certainly wasn't a word she had heard applied to her character before, but she found she quite liked it. It was a quality to aspire to. Very well. In the spirit of her newly adopted quality of character she said as graciously as she knew, "Do not trouble yourself, sir."

His lips curved, as if amused. "Ah, but I'm afraid that in order to gain our escape I cannot afford to be untroubled." He gestured to the rocks. "I'm afraid these will not shift by themselves."

"I can help you —"

"Thank you, but I would feel more comfortable if you did not strain yourself anymore."

"Why? Do you think there will be another rockfall?"

"I hope not." He grasped the lantern and swung it in a wide arc, peering most intently at the rockfall, where some rocks remained precariously poised. "I trust you will be safe over here," he said, gesturing to a small ledge. "It would appear to be safeguarded against further falls, at least from overhead."

She shivered.

He drew close again. "Are you cold?"

Caroline denied it, but soon her chattering teeth gave evidence to the contrary.

"Come." He drew her into the broad expanse of his chest, and rubbed her back in gentle soothing circles.

Her breath suspended, then slowly released in a long silent sigh as her shoulders relaxed. Though it was hard to truly relax in his embrace, conscious as she was of the intimacy, at the closeness she had never before experienced with any man — even her own father was not given to embraces! She knew such things would be considered most improper, that if it were made known the scandal would ensure her reputation irretrievably lost, but somehow her body refused to move, her bones feeling like liquid, her limbs betraying her sensibilities by puddling into mush. She *should* move, but the strength evident in his arms gave rise to such feelings of safety and protection, and foolish notions that he would cherish her all his days. She slowly inhaled, drawing in his scent of moss and leather, a scent that stirred awareness deep within, feelings coursing through her she had never known before. Oh, she never wanted to leave . . .

"I hope you don't think my actions too familiar," he murmured against her hair, "but I know sometimes Emma appreciates such things when she is chilled."

Chagrin filled her. He only comforted her because he thought her cold? Oh, how she had misread things!

But then, as she noticed the thump of his heart in her ear increase, and his scent start to tantalize her senses, and the way his hand's gentle pat slowed to something more . . . something more caressing, she thought perhaps she had not misread things after all.

His hold tightened, then he pulled away suddenly, leaving her with a strange mix of feeling bereft, feeling shameless, and yet further guilt at feeling unsatisfied. What kind of wanton young woman was she? This was certainly not how a daughter of Aynsley behaved — Mama would have a fit!

After a moment waiting for the embarrassment to subside from her cheeks, she peeked at him. Despite the dim light she could see his look of discomfiture, which renewed her mortification. Was his offering comfort and warmth so terrible? Or was she terrible for enjoying it so much?

Heart still aflutter, she stripped off the remnants of her gloves, working to clear the tremble from her voice. "So, what do we do now?"

"I . . . I don't know. I will continue shifting rocks, but I fear it will take quite some time."

"Is there an alternative route?" She gestured to the back of the cavern. "Have you ever explored beyond this main room?"

"Well, no. Once I saw the bones in this section I had no wish but to see what else this room contained. When I saw that this was the only deposit here I had no interest in seeing if the cave held anything more." He lifted the lamp, his face illuminated. "Looks like now might be the time to do so."

"Indeed," she said drily, then, conscious just how much she sounded like Mama, chased it with a small smile.

His features eased a mite. "I am so dreadfully sorry for causing this trouble."

"I came of my own free will."

"I just hope —" He stopped, swallowed. "I will see if I can find another way. I confess I do not much like my chances."

"You wish me to stay here? Alone? What if there is another rockfall?"

His worried face smoothed. "If you stay near this ledge then you should be safe." He moved as if to go.

"But what about the lantern — oh, I see."

He gave a somewhat rueful looking smile. "I'm afraid it will be much faster to ascertain if there is an alternative exit with the use of a lantern than without. But please, do not fear, I expect I shan't be long." His lips pushed up. "If it is any comfort, I will

346

sing so you know exactly where I am."

He sang as well? What could this man not do? "Very well."

Seconds later, a baritone voice filled the space, the words of the hymn sung on Sunday providing a modicum of reassurance as the speck of light moved away.

She stifled the fears, working to let the words comfort.

"Give to our God immortal praise, Mercy and truth are all His ways, Wonders of grace to God belong, Repeat His mercies in your song."

Was it sacrilegious to think such circumstances not exactly proof of God's mercy? But perhaps it *was* God's mercy that they had not died. And that Emma was — hopefully — safe outside. And that if Caroline had to be trapped with anyone in a cave, it might as well be with a scientist of undergroundology. Especially this particular intriguing undergroundologist . . .

Caroline peered through the darkness at the speck of light as the singing ceased. "Mr. Kirby?"

No response.

"Mr. Kirby?" she called again, louder this time.

There came the distant sound of rocks being moved, of pebbles scattering. Then the light disappeared to her straining eyes. He had gone? He had gone!

She was alone.

Darkness pressed in, the comfort of the earlier song dissipating like morning mist. Her chest grew tight, her skin grew clammy. He had abandoned her!

Suddenly the singing resumed, a sound that jolted her heart.

"He sent His Son with power to save, From guilt and darkness and the grave, Wonders of grace to God belong, Repeat His mercies in your song."

Her heart clutched at the words. How she wanted to believe that God would save them from this darkness, from this grave! Mr. Kirby seemed to believe it. When he sang, his words held nothing of the polite warble that she was used to hearing from the congregants on Sundays. Instead, his singing conveyed heartfelt, passionate conviction.

Moments later the light reappeared, then grew larger, as the form of Mr. Kirby drew near in the darkness.

"Miss Hatherleigh," he called. "I apologize for alarming you."

"You . . . you have returned," she finally managed, hand on her pounding heart. "That is enough."

He drew nearer. "I *am* sorry for causing

you concern."

At the sight of his softened expression her chest tightened then released. Really, she was being most nonsensical to imagine he thought of her in any way. And she was being even more nonsensical to want him to! She pressed down the foolish inner protests at such a denial and said, in a voice she hoped was not too unsteady, "Did you find anything?"

He grimaced, then said, "I have not found an alternative exit, I'm afraid."

"But you found something," she pressed. "The light disappeared, and you stopped singing."

"Did I? How foolish of me."

"What did you discover?"

He paused for a long moment, long enough for her to grow uneasy. "I'm afraid I discovered something that I do not think you will be best pleased to hear."

"What is it?"

"It appears this cave is not just something that holds clues to an ancient past, but . . ."

"But what? What is it you have found?"

He swallowed, then looked gravely into her eyes. "It appears it is also used by some of the local free traders."

CHAPTER TWENTY-ONE

He watched the moment that sank in, that she realized he talked about —

"Smugglers?" Her hand crept to her mouth. "Do you mean to say smugglers are here? No! Oh *no.*"

As she started to tremble violently he grasped her upper shoulders. "No, no. Miss Hatherleigh, we are the only ones here now, I assure you. But there appears to be evidence that certain others have felt this to be an effective hiding spot, and they have left certain evidence behind."

"What sort of evidence?" she asked, eyes wide.

He could not permit her to see the barrels and crates bound with ropes. It was enough she now knew. If — no, when — the smugglers learned of his and Miss Hatherleigh's sojourn in the cave, they would naturally suspect them to have discovered the free traders' secrets. Gideon's only hope of securing her safety was to ensure she did not see the evidence, so she could truthfully deny all knowledge of such things.

"*What* sort of evidence?" she reiterated, a panicked note in her voice.

What could he say that would dissuade her from insisting on seeing? Somehow he did not think her to be so pliable as his sister. "You mean apart from the skeletons?"

"Skeletons?" she whispered, eyes wider than he thought humanly possible.

He chuckled, the sound bouncing around the cavern. "Not quite." Not at all, truth be told. But he needed to say something, and fast, if he was to convince her to stay where she was and not insist on looking for herself. "Truly, there is nothing but a few bits and pieces that suggest the cave has been used in the past." The very recent past, but she need not know that.

He hurried on. "Nothing to worry about, I assure you. Just as we cannot get out, neither can they get in."

Until rescue time. But he would think about that later.

His words seemed to have turned her thoughts back to their more pressing predicament as her brow furrowed, and she said, "So if there is no other passage, how are we to get out? Will we starve? Will we die in here?"

He picked up her hand and gave it a gentle squeeze. "We shall not die," he promised. *God help us, please don't let us die in here.* "By now I would expect Tom would have summoned help and even now be returning."

"Should we call out again?"

"It cannot hurt."

She began calling out, and he was pleased to hear no note of panic. After a minute, he encouraged her to save her energies, drawing her attention to something he hoped might provide sufficient distraction.

"Miss Hatherleigh, may I enquire as to whether you have ever had geological tendencies?"

"Why, Mr. Kirby," she said, her voice steadying to adopt his playful tone, "I cannot say that I have."

"Then may I encourage you to assist me in such a venture? I understand it may not be the usual thing for a lady of aristocratic birth to engage in, but I believe it could render our time more profitable than calling out and wearying your voice."

He showed her his tools, encouraging her to hold them as he demonstrated in the flickering lamplight how best to use them.

This task grew more challenging, as it necessitated holding her hands. His words faltered, then failed, distracted as he was by the sweet fire stealing through his veins that her nearness induced.

"Am I holding the brush correctly?" she said, turning so her breath wisped along his face.

"Y-yes."

Did she feel the same sweet sensations he did? She was so proper, he did not wish to embarrass her, but surely she must.

He withdrew his hands, turning her attention to something far less potent, encouraging her to use the horsehair brush around the tiny remnants of shells near the floor, while he used the small pick to chip at the rocks blocking the entrance. His mind whirled. He could not admit to her that such actions were mere distraction; he did not like to think how long their rescue might truly take. What if the tide turned? Would it seep inside? Would they drown?

Gideon glanced at the cavern's ceiling. It appeared dry, so perhaps they would not drown — unless tonight was one for a king tide. Regardless, he'd give his last breath to ensure Caroline stayed alive. Then there was the problem of the smugglers. If he could perhaps secure their release that would be best all round, especially if it avoided notice of their entrapment to the local community. "God save us."

"Did you say something?"

"Only a prayer," he said, realizing the longer they worked in silence the longer worry would prey upon her mind. He would need to fill the quiet with chatter to drown her fears.

As he worked, the dim light making it very hard to see, he asked her questions, learning more about her life and family, so very different yet somehow similar to his. He heard about her two younger sisters, Cecilia and Verity, one so shy and sweet, the other hoydenish and headstrong. He learned about their family estate, Aynsley, and knew regret that the cave-in now ensured that he would be thought heedless of their daughter's safety, and unlikely to ever receive an invitation there.

He learned more about Mr. Amherst, and felt a moment's jealousy, before she plainly said such a man was anathema to her, although his bullet wound for escorting a married woman about town was a *trifle* harsh, then concluding that he seemed to hold little purpose for anything save the pursuit of his personal pleasure. Such words buoyed uncertain hopes: did she see in him a greater sense of purpose? Or would she — and her family — deem his hunting for relics of the past as a mere waste of time?

She sighed, then scrambled off the floor. "I do appreciate your thoughtfulness, but I really think my time would be better spent helping you remove the rocks."

He appreciated her kindness, but had no wish to see her injured. Yet admitting to the very real possibility of another rockfall could not aid her peace of mind.

"Thank you, Miss Hatherleigh, but your hands —"

"Are already dirty. And I'd feel so much better knowing my efforts are useful. And surely we could accomplish things faster working together rather than you doing this alone?"

Alone.

Or together.

He swallowed, then muttered a prayer under his breath. She was right. He would have to trust God for her protection.

"Very well." He demonstrated how to use the small pick, then retrieved the larger one.

Hours passed as they chipped away at the rocks and talked, the darkness leading to a sense of openness he'd never before experienced with a young lady. But — he cautioned himself — such mutual vulnerability was not license to indulge in warmer feelings, despite what their earlier embrace had ignited within. Until he knew exactly where she stood on matters of faith, he could not permit himself to think on matters that would only stir frustration.

"I . . . I have been so concerned about Emma."

He glanced at her; her face held tender interest, not the avarice of the crow-like gossips of home, who always enquired so sweetly that he was hard-pressed to know how to counter them. But just as he sensed their desire to know was about personal pride to be first with the news, he also sensed Miss Hatherleigh's interest was far more genuine, and it was this that made him finally say, "My sister has not had an easy time these past years. She . . . is reluctant to have things talked about."

"Well, in that case please do not betray her trust," she said so promptly that he was encouraged to share even more, offering brief snippets of younger days when Emma's health had not been so precarious.

"I'm so sorry," she murmured. "She is such a kind and sweet soul. It is sad she is not well."

His heart glowed at her compassion. "I think it is that sweetness that first attracted the attention of that scoundrel." Memories of his brother-in-law pricked. His movements grew more tense, more frantic as he scraped the dirt with the pick, working to loosen the earth. "Since meeting that fiend while taking the waters near Buxton, she has been pursued relentlessly by him. He must have been attracted to —" our family name and fortune, he almost said, "her sweet nature and looks, but he later proved to be a loathsome sycophant. He charmed her and wooed her and promised her the world until she scarcely knew which way was up or down. We could only grow more uneasy watching her succumb to his manner."

"We?"

"My elder brother and I." James had been suspicious from the start, mistrusting the easy charm that lived in Pratt's words but not in his eyes. But when their father had approved the match — or had been finally worn down by the young man's pleadings — what more could they say? Gideon had ventured so far as to say if the match was not to Emma's liking he would happily take her far away where Pratt would never find her, that she did not need to marry if she held any doubts at all. He'd even wondered about going against his father's wishes and contacting Kenmore to intervene. Would to God he had; Aidan would have proved the much surer man.

But Emma, whether from a desire to not cause a fuss, or to be labeled a jilt, or whether she really had thought Pratt loved her at the time, had not cried off, saying instead that he was simply misunderstood, that he possessed a softer side, a gentleness that did not appear to advantage when in the company of Emma's own far more forthright brothers.

No, Gideon thought, eyes narrowing, his softness instead extended to manipulations and emotional torture, and smothering Emma with his constant need for her that saw him isolate her from her family and friends, to the point that she never met them without his prior approval, approval which resulted in his constant attendance. Any attempt to meet otherwise was thwarted by his servants, who acted like spies upon their mistress.

Once Emma's portion of the Carstairs inheritance had fallen into Pratt's hands, Gideon and James had grown increasingly worried, fearing for the life of their sister as she faded into someone unrecognizable, jumping at every shadow, talking in a hushed voice, her laughter as far from her as fears had used to be.

And he knew Pratt did not take care of her. He knew that man did not insist she see doctors, let alone London specialists. He was controlling, self-centered, and a hypocrite of the highest order, deceiving Emma with his pretense of faith. Gideon's fingers clenched, his chest heated. Such depths of rage the man provoked within him. He was as scum, a swine, a villain, a cur —

"Mr. Kirby? Are you quite all right?"

He exhaled. "Forgive me, Miss Hatherleigh. Thinking about the scoundrel does not bring out my best self, I'm afraid." Rather it evoked him to such feelings of wrath he sometimes dared pray that God would strike Pratt from the earth!

"I believe I would share in your outrage at a man who had hurt my sister in any way."

"So perhaps you can see why it became necessary for me to steal her away."

"What happened?"

Gideon swallowed, remembering. He had certainly not proved his best self on that particular day. "It was eight months after my parents' deaths. They died from cholera, so I suppose it was a blessing Emma was away from home, otherwise she would have certainly succumbed, too." He blinked away the burn. "My brother and I had resorted to unannounced visits, just to check on her. She was always so relieved to see us, and Pratt taken so much by surprise he was sometimes shocked into revealing his true colors. Last November, I turned up one day uninvited and unannounced, gaining entrance via a side door to avoid the servants who often seemed sentry-like in their duties. I could hear raised voices — well, one raised voice, and my sister's tears."

He paused. The cur's accusations that she wasn't really ill, that she liked to pretend she was to gain attention, for the neighbors to feel sorry for her. Emma's sobbed protests that she *was* ill, and right now felt faint, and that she wanted to retire to her room, and his yelled response that forced Gideon's feet to move faster than they had since school days and fling himself past the gaping footmen just as Pratt lifted up a Sevres vase to hurl at Emma.

Gideon stroked the scar on his cheek, evidence of the priceless china striking his face, the blood of which had caused his sister to scream and Gideon to throw himself at Pratt before his stunned servants could respond. Pratt had crashed to the floor, striking his head on an iron fender, knocking him senseless. "I . . . I had to get her away before he hurt her again."

"Is that how you got your scar? By protecting Emma?"

He nodded.

"Then you are a hero!"

His heart warmed at her approbation, but . . . "It would have been much more heroic to have prevented her marriage to that scoundrel in the first place." And thus prevent the villain from impregnating her. But such could not be said.

Silence was a ruthless game.

He'd told the servants in no uncertain terms if they so much as breathed about this he would ensure the marquess would see them imprisoned for aiding and abetting a violent fiend. Their swift removal from the scene and the lack of chase suggested his words had done the trick, initially at least. Regardless, it had been enough for him to carry Emma to his curricle and drive her to James's mansion, during which time they decided it would be best for all concerned if Gideon should move with her under an assumed name. His brother would hint that Gideon had gone overseas, and while that wasn't strictly true, Gideon had managed a quick trip across the sea to the Isle of Wight so James had not completely perjured himself. Even so, Gideon had refused to give even his own brother any clue as to their whereabouts.

"So this is why we are here, where she is safe — as long as nobody learns the truth about who she is and that she is my sister and not my wife."

She bit her lip, as if worried, then slowly said, "But surely some people must know the true situation? The doctor, for instance."

"A few people, yes. The doctor is one of them."

"And my grandmother," she admitted in a whisper. Her brows pressed together in consternation. "I'm so sorry, but I told her weeks ago, when Emma told me. Please forgive me."

So that was why Lady Aynsley had appeared unsurprised this morning. Perhaps Miss Hatherleigh's earlier acknowledgment of his true relationship with his sister had even helped his cause, if her grandmother was inclined to think on him as a potential suitor. He hastened to assure her. "Pray don't worry any longer. I spoke of the matter to her today, and she appeared quite understanding."

"She did? I'm so glad." She released a sigh that seemed to draw up from her toes.

The next few minutes passed in silence as he continued to work at removing the rocks, her uncomplaining spirit digging his admiration deeper. How many other young ladies of noble heritage would have helped so? She was kind, she was thoughtful, she was easy to talk to. But did she believe? He opened his mouth to ask this when she said, "I'm still surprised that you have not met anyone who knows who you are."

"No one." He released a small smile, along with a handful of rocks. "I was never high on society's circles, anyway." Unlike his brother, the heir. Not that he cared. The only circles where he had wished to find approbation were scientific ones. Until now . . .

"Did Lord Pratt not know of your endeavors? Surely you must have considered that he would seek you in a place like this."

"With my name being unknown to the larger community, and with reports of my being overseas, I had hoped that Emma and I could remain incognito for some time still."

"But . . . he discovered your whereabouts. Forgive me, but will he not return?"

The worry of fear wriggled in, an incessant worm of doubt that his plans were not as watertight as he hoped. "I trust that he would think such a thing most unlikely. I hope that as soon as we can extract this specimen, we might be able to leave once more."

"Oh."

She said nothing more for some time, and he grew worried she might wish for nothing more to do with them. It was a fantastical story, one whose grimness spoke less of fairy tale than fears. She bit her lip, and another reason for her sadness pushed into awareness. Surely she did not think he wished to leave her? Or was such a thought vanity to entertain?

He opened his mouth, but her sigh cut off any chance of explanation.

"I am so very sorry for her, and for you," she said, a quiver in her voice. "I cannot imagine how difficult things must have been for you all."

"Thank you. Perhaps you can understand why these things are so hard for Emma to speak of."

"Indeed." She drew in an audible breath. "And I can assure you that I will do all I can to protect her as well. Anything she requires, if there is anything within my power, please do not hesitate to ask."

Warmth filled him at her generosity. "Thank you, Miss Hatherleigh. I hope to never have to ask such things of you, but I appreciate the offer."

Silence stretched between them as he continued chipping away at the rocks. He hoped that his news would not give her a disgust of him, that she would keep her promise to support Emma. Unlike a prior young lady, whose embarrassment at Emma's poor health had led her to shun him, and his singing outside the university dean's house.

"Mr. Kirby, I hope you know how much I value your sharing this with me. I am honored by the fact that you trust me, both with Emma's story, and with all of this today." She gestured to the rock. "Truly, you are quite remarkable, quite heroic, indeed."

Her words ignited a warm glow in his chest. She thought that highly of him?

Such buoyancy of spirits grew increasingly necessary as the long grind of his work became harder. Eventually he felt a small chink in the rock ease then give way. A rock tumbled to the earth with a loud clatter.

"Please be careful, Mr. Kirby," Miss Hatherleigh exclaimed.

"Of course," he assured.

But he would endeavor to be a little more careful in future, in case he dislodged something greater. He painstakingly removed the dirt encrusting another large stone before putting his back into hefting it from its spot. Another heave. Another. There! It was done.

"Oh, Mr. Kirby, you must be incredibly strong," Miss Hatherleigh said.

He murmured something suitably modest even as her words, her look of admiration, filled his chest with pride. He turned to the next rock, something rather more boulder-like, above which poised another large stone. If he could just remove this one then he might be able to see his way to breaking through.

Beyond them, he could hear the low hum of what he hoped were the voices of their rescuers — and not the voices of those wishing to protect their assets still hidden in the recesses of the cavern.

He called out, but when no answer was forthcoming, resumed work on the boulder, easing away the dirt with the small pick. A little more. A little —

A mighty creak was followed by her piercing scream as the rocks tumbled atop of him, smashing into his shoulders and plunging his world into darkness.

CHAPTER TWENTY-TWO

"Oh, Mr. Kirby! Mr. Kirby!" Caroline dropped to her knees, frantically tearing at the rocks that had smashed into his body. His bleeding body. His immobile body.

Her eyes filled with tears. "Mr. Kirby? Oh, dear God! Dear God, what do I do?"

She sank to her knees and leaned close over his face, lifting a dirt encrusted finger to trace his cheek. He did not move. His head bore the gaping wound of a rock smashed into his skull, the blood now trickling past his scalp down his forehead. She pulled at the lace fichu covering her neck and padded it to cover his wound. Blood seeped through her fingers.

"Mr. Kirby! Oh, please do not die!"

Breath came in short bursts. Panic clawed through her throat, expanding within her chest. What if he did die? What would people think about her? About them? Her reputation, her future prospects would all be gone! What if she never saw daylight again?

She shook her head, willing her breathing to steady. How could she care for such things? Nothing mattered other than Mr. Kirby's life.

"Please, Mr. Kirby," she begged. "Please live."

Breath caught on a sob. She pressed on the wound with one hand, used the other to swipe away her tears. Knew her face to now be smeared with dirt and blood.

"God, help us, please."

Her words, uttered like a prayer, filled her ears. Suddenly asking someone unseen for help did not appear so very unreasonable, when she could scarcely see herself. Was prayer so very foolish after all? Was belief? Surely if it made people feel better it could not be all bad.

Her thoughts rolled on. Was God actually interested in her, enough to show her His mercy, as Mr. Kirby had sung about earlier? Would He save them from darkness and the grave? Was it foolish to hope He might bestow another miracle, like the one concerning her grandmother's permission that she'd been so flippant about earlier? Did He care? Or did God consider her to be more like a slave, a mere pawn in His game, much like her own parents tended to consider her, a tool for their own purposes?

Beneath her hand came a faint stirring. The faint glow of the lantern sputtered. She could see Mr. Kirby's eyelids flutter, the long dark lashes caressing his cheeks lift, to reveal pain-tinged gray eyes.

The lantern flickered out.

She shrieked. Panic rose again. "Oh, dear God, please save us!"

Her words echoed in the darkness. Then . . .

"M-miss . . . ?"

The raspy voice pulled her thoughts to focus. "Mr. Kirby! You're awake."

Silence, save for some faint sounds beyond the rock.

"Mr. Kirby. Mr. Kirby!"

Nothing.

Then, "Miss Hatherleigh." His voice was thin, weak. "Ah, my head."

He groaned, and there came a sound of shifting pebbles as if he was trying to move. She felt his arm slowly lift. "No, please do not move. You were struck by a rock, and I'm afraid you have bled quite badly."

"You . . . you are uninjured?"

"I am quite well." Apart from the sting of ragged fingernails, and the ache in her arms, and the panic that still swelled within, kept only at bay by her feeble prayers.

"So . . . glad." He sagged once more; she could feel his head loll to one side.

"Mr. Kirby!"

He gave no response, so she shifted her position and gently hoisted his head into her lap. Pressed a finger under his nose and felt the faintest hush of breath. "Dear God, don't let him die. Please, I'll do anything."

The words echoed around the chamber, striking deep within. Would she do *anything*? Truly?

Her words from earlier mocked her. If — God forbid! — something happened to poor Mr. Kirby, would she really do anything to protect Emma, as she'd recklessly promised? Would she stand up to society's scorn, the conjecture of her friends, her family? Would she be prepared to forgo her reputation in the attempt to keep her friend safe?

The thoughts spun within. Would she *truly*? Or were her words mere spoken air, holding nothing of substance, nothing to rely on?

Was her prayer much the same? Would she really do anything God required of her in order for Mr. Kirby to live? Truly?

She glanced down, dared to trace a finger down one rough cheek, to smooth his matted hair. Her heart escalated, her senses growing tight, as if waiting for something most momentous. Would she?

"Dear God," she finally managed, "I promise to do anything You want if You would only keep Mr. Kirby and poor Emma safe."

She exhaled, feeling a weight of pressure within, ears straining, heart waiting for any kind of response. Surely it could not be that much more absurd to believe that someone invisible might wish to speak with her?

Trust Me.

Caroline jumped. Fear prickled her heart. Mr. Kirby had not moved, his breathing steady as if he remained asleep. Nobody else was here. Were they?

Trust Me.

That same neck-tingling sensation washed over her again. Who was speaking? Or had nobody spoken, and this was God's way of letting her know He heard her prayer?

And what did trusting in God really mean? Was it enough to hope that God would somehow magically sort things out, like a benevolent grandfather might fix a child's broken toy? Or did trusting God mean something deeper, something like what Mr. Kirby had sung about earlier, remembering God's mercies even in the face of certain death? Is that what gave

Emma peace? Did such peace originate in those words she'd read weeks ago in Romans, that belief in Jesus Christ's death and resurrection was enough, that even if things did not go as she might wish, she still had a sure and certain hope for eternity?

New sensations stirred within, forcing her thoughts deeper than before. The Kirbys appeared to regard God as not just a judge but as someone who desired relationship with people, someone who treated people more as friends than slaves. Did God really want to be friends with her?

She stilled, her soul reaching out in desperation. "God?"

Trust Me, that small voice whispered once again.

She blinked in the darkness. Was she mad to think the God who created the universe would actually speak to her? "Help me understand."

Breath shakily released as the thoughts, the emotions, of past months drew into new focus.

Suddenly she could see how her adherence to propriety had proved a form of slavery as much as the servants' blind obedience to Emma's husband, something that allowed pride, allowed sin, to perpetuate. She was no better than Lord Pratt, perhaps even worse, for she had been so quick to try to hide her shortcomings with a smile and good deeds.

But she was *not* good. The words from her Bible reading weeks ago sprang to mind again. So often she had not shown love; she had not been kind. She knew her heart had been poisoned by self-interest, by pride. Nausea washed within, followed by cramping shame. Oh, what measure of sinner was she to have so blindly followed her father's decree, denying God's existence? To have carelessly followed social rules and disregarded matters of eternity?

"God, forgive me." Tears leaked, as a kind of hopelessness loomed within. Oh, how she needed Him, needed His help. "God, *forgive me.*"

A wrenching sob drew from her chest, followed by another, then another. She was helpless against it, her heart cramping with the pain of knowing herself to be so full of guilt. How full of pride she had been! How full of lies, saying one thing and doing another, pretending to admire then being as quick to judge as gossipy Lady Heathcote or Lady Dalrymple. She was no better. She liked being the first with gossip, regardless of how it might affect the subject of which she talked. She liked the feeling of power it gave her, to know things others didn't, to share information for no other purpose than to appear more important than those who did not yet know.

"God, forgive me," she cried, tasting the salt of her tears.

Would He forgive her? She had denied His very existence for years. But somehow in this dark and hopeless place, she could no longer believe He did not exist. Like Mr. Kirby said, surely the world had to have been created by someone, the glories and patterns of nature could not be denied. Surely life, even her own life meager as it was, could not exist in a void, and be purposeless. She shook her head. Why had she never thought on this before?

Oh, how wretched was she.

Oh, how she needed hope.

Oh, how she needed forgiveness.

"God, forgive me." A tidal wave of emotion rolled over her, so embarrassing in its magnitude that a tiny part of her was glad Mr. Kirby remained oblivious.

When it finally subsided, and her tears dried to occasional sniffs, she exhaled once more, and sat in the silence, tear-spent and exhausted.

The verses from Romans whispered within. "The wages of sin is death, but the gift of God is eternal life through Jesus Christ our Lord."

A gift, from God, to her. To refuse such a gift would be foolishness, unthinkable.

"Lord God," she finally dared whisper into the darkness, "I admit I do not know very much at all about this, but I am willing — no, wanting — to trust You. I know I am not good enough, but I believe that Jesus Christ's death paid for my sin, and that You will forgive me. Please help me trust You, help me to understand what You want me to do. And please, *please* help us get out of here, and help poor Mr. Kirby . . ."

Her eyes filled once more, but this time, instead of fear, she felt a sense, deep, deep down, that Someone was in control, and an ease within that felt a little like peace. "And, Lord, please help Emma in her awful situation, and Beatrice." She remembered proper prayers from church. "Amen," she said in a voice ending with a squeak.

She exhaled once more, rubbed her aching forehead, closed her eyes, and slept.

The faintest of sounds dragged him from his slumber. Where — ?

He couldn't see. He couldn't see! Had he been blinded?

He shifted. Groaned at the ache pummeling his head. Nausea rose. Slowly subsided. What had happened?

Eventually the swimming in his head receded to something less intense, allowing him to realize his body lay somewhere hard. Realize his head was cradled somewhere soft. That a hand lay on his chest. Whose? He moved to grasp it, felt its smoothness. From somewhere close drifted the slightest scent of lily of the valley.

Where had he smelled that sweet scent? It had been but recently, in a moment filled with both trepidation and fulfillment. A moment of danger, of closeness . . .

Remembrance struck with awful clarity. "Miss Hatherleigh?"

A stirring came above him. He shifted a little more, felt a corresponding movement, the hand on his chest slide away.

The noises from afar grew louder, a kind of tapping, like one imagined mining pixies might make. His lips twisted. Such fanciful notions meant this had to be a bad dream, did it not?

He closed his eyes, only to open them again seconds later when something like a soft shout invaded his ears. So, he hadn't been mistaken. This wasn't a strange dream. He set himself to listen, could almost make out vague words.

"Miss Hatherleigh?" he tried again. Heaven help them, but if that was the sound of rescuers, she would be mortified to know they had been found in such a compromising position. And heaven help him, but Gideon could barely move.

"Careful!" a male voice, an Irish-accented voice, called. Kenmore was here?

There was a sound of crashing stone, a sound that caused him to wince and the softness in which he lay to jerk. "Miss Hatherleigh!" he tried again.

She released a slow sigh, which was immediately followed by far-off muffled curses, then a light pierced the darkness of the chamber through the tiny gap.

"Gideon? Miss Hatherleigh? Are you in there?"

It *was* Aidan's voice. Relief, deep and profound, swept over him. "We're here!" he called feebly.

"Did you hear that?" Aidan said. "It sounded like someone responded."

Gideon cleared his voice. "We're in here!" he cried more loudly. Pain pierced his temple.

There came a corresponding sound of relief, then Aidan's voice assuring them they would soon be released. "Is Miss Hatherleigh there with you?"

Gideon peered up at the face washed with dirt and tears. His heart wrenched. He was a scoundrel to have his misadventure cause her so much grief. But at least they weren't to be entombed forever. "Miss Hatherleigh," he said urgently. She had to wake up, she had to move before it was discovered that he lay with her in such a way. "Caroline!"

She blinked sleepily at him, her brow creasing. "What?" she squinted. "Did you manage to make the lantern work again?"

"No, no." He pointed feebly at the blocked cave entrance. "We are being rescued."

"Really?"

He nodded. Winced at the arrowing pain.

"Oh, thank God," she breathed, her face lighting with a dirt-smudged smile.

She gazed at him, with such a soft look in her eyes that the sounds around him faded. They seemed to share a tender bond, something new, forged through this experience perhaps, unless it was something infinitesimally deeper, more profound.

He neither knew nor cared what the reason might be, only that her words had triggered an assurance that this young lady did not blame him for what had occurred, and that perhaps in her he had finally found the young lady with whom he might be able to share all his adventures. *God?* The check in his spirit had vanished. Did this mean — ?

"Gideon?" There came the sound of more tapping, another rush of falling rock, then Aidan's voice again. "Gideon? Miss Hatherleigh? Are you both well?"

Gideon glanced at his companion. She nodded, her smile as balm to his heart. "She is well," he called again.

"And you?"

There came another sound of muffled oaths as rocks crashed again, allowing for more light to be shone into the cavern.

"I'm a little headsore," Gideon admitted.

There came a scrabbling sound, then a "Be careful, sir!" before the light was obscured for a moment. Gideon peered up.

Aidan's face peered down. "I see them!"

"Thank God!" came the muffled exclamations.

"Hello, Gideon," said Aidan. "Good evening, Miss Hatherleigh," he said with a grin.

"Is it evening?" she said faintly.

"I'm afraid so. You must forgive our tardiness, but it seems Sidmouth rock has no great desire to move."

"We must beg to differ," Gideon said wryly. "Seems it moves quite quickly on occasion."

Aidan chuckled. "Yes, well, be assured we

are doing our best to get you out as fast as we can. I'm hopeful it will be even faster when I remove myself from this position, but I had to see for myself exactly where you were to ensure you are not hurt by our excavations." He frowned. "Miss Hatherleigh, are you able to move at all?"

"Yes," she said in a weak voice.

"Then would it be too much to ask if you could possibly assist my unfortunate friend over to that ledge over there? I believe it would be safer that way."

"I will try."

Gideon's head was gingerly removed from her lap with a whispered, "I'm sorry. I am sure it aches so."

He tried to reassure her, but the truth was his head felt like it had been cracked in two.

She scrambled to her feet, her skirts covered in dirt and mud. "Here, give me your hand."

At her gentle tug, it felt as though his head might explode. He gritted his teeth as she gingerly wrapped an arm around his shoulders and helped him to his feet. "I feel like such a fool."

"Stop it. You are injured. I'm so glad I can at least help you."

He stumbled to the ledge, the movement causing nausea to ripple through him again.

He groaned, the action triggering a paroxysm within, then to his horror, had no recourse but to cast up his accounts.

Mortification rushed through him as he wiped his mouth. Dear God, please let none of that have splashed on Miss Hatherleigh! But when he finally ventured to glance at her she seemed to regard him with something akin to pity, rather than revulsion.

"Kirby? Are you quite all right in there?"

"Never better," he managed to call, before apologizing to his companion. "I am so sorry."

She smiled gently at him. "Please don't even think about it. You've received such a nasty bump on the head I'm surprised you're even conscious." The faint light showed the sheen of her tears, as she added in a wavering voice, "I thank God you were not killed."

His throat constricted. Those were tears for him? He hated — though a tiny part of him that he despised, loved — to know his welfare mattered to her so.

"Kirby? You are not disgracing yourself in there I hope?" Aidan called.

Gideon winced at his friend's unfortunate choice of words. Would that the other men with him did not misconstrue such things to cause Miss Hatherleigh embarrassment.

"Mr. Kirby has received a very nasty knock on the head," she called.

"Not from your hand, I trust?" said the irrepressible Irish viscount.

There came a barrage of guffaws from beyond the stones, drowning out Miss Hatherleigh's gasp and his own low mutterings, which was swiftly followed by another "look out!" and the crash of tumbling stones.

More light now revealed that a space had been created, a tunnel large enough for a slender man to crawl within. The light was briefly obliterated then grew brighter as the viscount's form somehow scrabbled through.

Aidan's muffled oath as he saw the state of them gave notice of the severity of his injury. "Dear God!" He wrapped Miss Hatherleigh in a one-armed hug, before dropping to his knees to grip Gideon's hands. "I'm ever so glad to see you again, my friend."

"The feeling is mutual. Although your presence is a surprise."

"I headed here from London as soon as your letter arrived." His grin swiftly faded, replaced by a frown as he peered at Gideon's head. "I don't like the look of that at all, not that Miss Hatherleigh hasn't done a splendid job at keeping your blood in."

"I didn't know what else to do," she murmured.

"You've done wonderfully well," he assured her, before turning back to Gideon. "I want to help her get out before high tide arrives." He grimaced. "It is past our ankles already."

"Do it now. She must be kept safe," Gideon said, intent in his gaze and tone.

Aidan nodded. "I'll be back soon."

Gideon offered his own nod, then winced. Miss Hatherleigh was peering at him anxiously, so he hastened to assure her. "I'll see you on the outside soon."

"But perhaps you should go first. I would hate to think —" She bit her lip.

Her solicitude warmed him. "You are very kind, but I could never consider myself a gentleman if I considered my own safety above yours. Go with Kenmore; he will keep you safe."

She still seemed reluctant, but nodded. After taking a moment to collect her sketchbook and reticule, she moved to the hole in the rocks, casting him a final glance to which he responded with a smile he hoped reassured. Aidan grasped her hands and helped her up, then offered gentle encouragement for her to slide through the gap in the rocks. Within minutes he heard the sounds of cheering and her being assisted to the ground on the other side.

"Thank God," he breathed, closing his eyes.

Aidan's voice again. "And now for our hero."

Gideon opened his eyes, saw his friend had slithered through once more. He moved to get up, but a wave of dizziness had him near collapsing into his friend's arms.

"Steady, Gideon. I cannot afford to have you faint. Neither can Emma, remember? She needs you, as will, I fear, that lovely young lady with whom you have spent so much time."

His eyes snapped open. "What do you mean?"

Aidan drew him closer to the hole in the rock. "Merely that your absence has not resulted in prayers being the only thing whispered these past hours."

"Dear God," he managed, barely restraining another release of his stomach contents as the dizziness swarmed again. "Her reputation . . ."

"Will depend upon what you do when you appear on the other side, so it's best to be aware of what will be said, and what may need to be done."

To be done? This time he could not keep back the nausea, noting with a tiny despicable degree of satisfaction that some of it had splashed onto his tormentor's boots.

"Now, now," Aidan said. "Such a course of action need not be so repellant. She is not unlovely to gaze upon."

"Shut up," he managed to groan, as Aidan helped him find handholds.

The rocks felt cool and slippery beneath his grasp. Head swimming with pain, wretchedness cramping his body, he managed to follow the called instructions as his friend boosted him into the narrow space. Blearily, he could see hands reaching towards him, and he stretched to grasp them. Then he was being tugged through, his head screaming, breath heaving, until his shirt caught on a sharp rock. He shifted; pain jerked his skull. Tried again. To no avail.

"Can't move!" he finally gasped.

"Try wriggling a little."

He tried. Wanted to swoon again at the pain. Forced his thoughts to narrow down, to focus on Emma, on Miss Hatherleigh. They both needed the protection of his name. His real name. *Dear God, release me from this coil.* They needed him. He needed them.

Eventually he jerked his garment free from

the offending rock, and he was released to recommence his torturous slide to freedom.

"Here 'e comes!" shouted Mr. Belcher.

The light grew brighter, brighter still. He caught a glimpse of burly men, of ropes, of picks, of lanterns. Of Miss Hatherleigh's worried face, her shivering form wrapped in a blanket. He saw Beatrice, similarly attired, with her bandaged arm and her disapproving mien even now adopting something akin to a sneer.

He slid forward, into waiting arms, caring not that he looked the fool he was, as he splashed down into the encroaching seawater, and tumbled once more into unconsciousness.

CHAPTER TWENTY-THREE

After several days in bed recovering from weariness induced by the shock and a slight chill, Caroline finally emerged from her bedchamber and descended the stairs to the drawing room. Here she found Grandmama playing cards with Miss McNell, a game that stopped abruptly when her presence was announced.

"Caroline," Grandmama said, in a tone Caroline could not decipher. Was she upset, annoyed, displeased? "It is good to see you among the living once again."

"Oh, my dear Miss Hatherleigh," cried Miss McNell. "What a traumatic experience you went through! I'm sure if anything like that had happened to me I would be bed-ridden for the rest of my days."

Judging from the expression Grandmama cast to the ceiling, Caroline wondered if she might wish such an experience upon her companion. "I am feeling a little better now."

"That is good, for I fear we have some news to share that you may not fully appreciate."

"Is it Miss Kirby? She hasn't worsened, has she?"

"Worsened? No. Although there appears to be quite the scandal about her." Grandmama's eyes narrowed. "Did you know she was expecting?"

Caroline swallowed, but she could not lie. "Yes."

"And you did not think it pertinent that I should know this information?"

"I did not want to be accused of passing on gossip, ma'am."

Her grandmother blinked. "Well, that is commendable of you, I suppose."

"Her husband is that Lord Pratt who was here making enquiries about them before, but his cruelty led her brother to enable her escape, which is why they have been living here quietly."

"But he came here for them, so he knew they had once lived here. What on earth made them return?"

"Mr. Kirby believes Lord Pratt would not consider it likely for them to return."

"Well, perhaps. But he certainly went

about things in a most underhanded way!" She shook her head. "I suppose such things could not be helped. But it's too late now."

"What do you mean?"

"What do you think I mean? Your escapade has been in all the papers, my dear."

Oh no.

"That's right," Miss McNell said, head bobbing. "You and Mr. Kirby have become quite celebrated indeed. Such an adventure!"

Such a scandal. If the newspapers had somehow picked up on their story then Caroline's fate was sealed, her marriage prospects dwindling down to one. She gulped, turning her attention to her grandmother, who picked up and waved a cream sheet of paper.

"I'm afraid all of London is talking about you, which must be why I received this letter today. Apparently, we are to expect the joy of your mother's company in the next few days."

"Mother is coming for me?"

"Yes." Her grandmother's smile grew brittle. "It seems that she is shocked at my lack of guardianship over you, or so she's had the audacity to write, and cannot believe that matters have reached a point where her eldest daughter is now obliged to marry a mere second son."

"I beg your pardon?"

"Surely you must have realized what being alone with a young man in the dark for so many hours would entail. As I stand in lieu of your father, Mr. Kirby has come to see me, and I have been forced to grant him my blessing."

"What?"

"Caroline, do not gape so. Try to remember you are a daughter of Aynsley, if you please."

She shut her mouth.

"Mr. Kirby knows his duty, and is prepared to make you an offer."

Caroline's stomach turned. Put like that, it sounded so very clinical, so very proper. Where was the love she thought had dwelled in his eyes, the affection she had supposed in his manner? Had she been mistaken, and he was marrying her from mere duty after all?

"I . . . I don't know what to say."

"I know it must not be what you were hoping for . . ." Grandmama began.

But Caroline barely heard the rest of her words. No, Grandmama was wrong. She had hoped to marry Mr. Kirby — she loved him after all — but not like this. Not because society said he must.

"He is a very well-built young man, with those strong shoulders and arms," twittered Miss McNell. "I have always thought him quite handsome, too, especially if you ignore his scar. One can only wonder how he received such a thing. Do you think it was another accident with rocks? Or perhaps a lovers' tiff?" She giggled. "I think it gives him a dashing look, like that of a swashbuckling pirate. Indeed . . ."

She kept on talking. Caroline said nothing.

"I don't think Caroline cares about his scar," said Grandmama, talking over the top of her companion as was her way. "We are not all supposed to be ornaments of the field."

"I . . . I should speak to him."

"I think you would be better off waiting until your mother arrives, then we can determine what is best to be done. I have my ideas, of course, but your mother has never taken kindly to my influence."

"Of course." Well, naturally Grandmama might think waiting the best option — though such a thought seemed surprisingly humble — but it didn't mean she would submit to it.

No, Caroline had to somehow speak with Mr. Kirby to determine his true feelings before her mother appeared, to discover whether she was being forced into a marriage of obligation where the lack of love — on his side at least — would forever underwhelm and disappoint.

She sought escape as soon as possible. Under the pretext of taking Mittens for a walk in the garden, she — and Mittens — fled the assiduous attentions of Mary and visited the stables. The stables *were* in the gardens, and had required a walk to attain, so technically it wasn't a falsehood. Hurried instructions to the groom soon saw her make her getaway through the servants' drive, a path that took the gig on a route much closer to the sea. She hugged the pug close to her chest. Along this route she could see where the storms of years past had washed away the cliffs, gouging the landscape like a monster had clawed at the red earth.

"That happened a score of years ago, miss," said the groom, apparently noticing her fixed gaze. "There be a place not far from here that lost near sixty acres when the earth slid into the sea."

"Sixty acres?"

"Aye, that be a terrible time," he said.

"Was anyone killed?"

"No, though a few sheep were heard bleating as they tumbled down the hill. It happened at night, so the worst of it weren't seen 'til the morning. A terrible big storm it was."

Mittens whimpered, protesting the close clasp; Caroline loosened her hold a mite. "Is Grandmama's house safe?"

"I surely hope so. But I would not worry if I were you. The worst of storm season is done for another year now, so it likely won't affect you."

"Oh, but . . ." She wasn't concerned for herself. It was Grandmama who had nestled into her affections. Perhaps that was what happened when one started to pray for those in one's life, instead of mentally berating them. One could live more at peace with others, and wish for their best, and not their harm.

These past days in her convalescence she had spent much time in prayer, the absence of all notice save from Mary and the occasional visit from Grandmama allowing much time for thought. She had persuaded Mary to smuggle up the Bible she had read earlier, and found comfort once again from its words. Even if things did not work out as she hoped, she had a new confidence that God would be with her regardless. She would pray and trust He would work this situation out, both for her good and for Mr. Kirby's.

Her thoughts shifted to the arrival of her mother. Mama would not be pleased to know Caroline was forced into this alliance, but she might grow resigned to such a thing if she knew that Caroline was happy. Her chest tightened. But she could only be happy if she knew Mr. Kirby's wishes. Oh, what would Mr. Kirby say? Would he look at her with affection or long-suffering? Had she been misled by what had happened during the cave-in? Playing the memories over and over these past days had made her question everything.

The gig drew into the village and stopped at the end cottage. Caroline stepped down, telling the groom she would be driven home, and instructing him to absent himself to prevent any questioning where he might not want to lie.

Really, she thought, knocking at the door, she was growing quite as much of a wily-pie as her youngest sister. But seeing as she had no reputation left to lose . . .

The door opened, and Mrs. Ballard looked out. "Miss Hatherleigh!" she exclaimed. "We certainly did not expect the pleasure of your company today." She peered at the animal in her arms. "Nor that of your little dog."

"I am sorry for interrupting, but it is imperative that I speak with Mr. Kirby as soon as possible."

"I'm afraid that isn't possible right now."

Her heart caught. "He has left?"

"No, he's simply down at that blessed cave, he and half the village, it appears, judging from all the folk that have headed down that way."

"He is quite recovered, then?"

"Well, I wouldn't say completely recovered, but there was no stopping him."

That was something at least. "And Emma?"

"Ah, poor lass. She's here."

"May I speak with her?"

"Of course. Please, come in." She gestured to the small sitting room Caroline had seen before. "I'll just make sure she's ready."

Caroline walked into the room, whose every surface was now covered with samples of fossils and rocks. Specimens of ammonites and belemnites competed for attention, varying in their color and design, each holding a unique beauty. In one corner gleamed the large ammonite they had found before, polished to a sheen so it resembled a great and curious jewel, like a silver snake-like pendant a giant might have worn. But she knew such things faded in comparison to that which Mr. Kirby was excavating even now.

She placed Mittens on the floor, where she immediately began sniffing around at all the lovely new smells.

"Oh, Caroline!"

At Emma's voice, more breath than sound, Caroline turned, rushing forward to grasp her hands. "Emma, how good to see you." Though Emma did not look at all well. Her eyes appeared sunken and were heavily shadowed, her skin tinged gray. Everywhere she seemed too thin, save for the slight paunch around her middle. Caroline settled her into the sofa and sat beside her, clasping her hand, Caroline's eyes filling with the heat of tears. "My dear friend!"

Emma shook her head, her lips twisting into a plaintive smile. "Please, do not let us talk about me; I cannot bear it. Instead, let me offer my heartfelt thanks at your care for my brother, and to say how *very* glad I am that you are safe."

"And I am glad you were not injured. I was worried about you."

"So my brother told me. It is he you wished to see?" Emma said with a glimmer of the old mischief. "Or so Mrs. Ballard said."

"I . . . I suppose I should see him."

"Especially if one is to be married to him." Caroline bit her lip.

"Caroline? Does this not please you? Forgive me, but I did not think you were completely indifferent to my brother's charm."

Heat suffused her cheeks and she glanced away. "I am not indifferent, it is true."

"I am truly pleased to hear it! I have longed for a sister I can live with."

"Is not your other brother married?"

"Elizabeth is good-hearted, to be sure, but rather taken up in her own interests and affairs, so that I cannot help but feel I'm in her way."

Guilt clamored within. How often would Caroline's actions have made others feel like that? But God was helping Caroline live a different way now. "I don't think you could ever be in someone's way."

"You are always so very kind. It is no wonder Gideon — but enough. You wish to speak with him?"

"Mrs. Ballard said Mr. Kirby is at the cave."

"Mr. Kirby," Emma said with a tiny gurgle of amusement. "I believe you can call him

Gideon now."

"Oh, but . . ." No, she couldn't. Not until things were sorted properly.

"*Gideon* has returned to the cave, both he and Aidan, along with what Mrs. Ballard believes to be most of the town."

"You are not going?"

"I think everyone would prefer I stay here," Emma said, with a return to that ghastly smile.

"I see." But would Emma be safe? What if Lord Pratt had heard Mr. Kirby was back in town? In fact — her heartbeat escalated — how could he have *not* heard, if such matters had been reported in the London newspapers? "Oh dear."

"It is not that bad, I assure you," Emma said, stretching out a hand for Mittens to sniff. "If you want to go, I am quite content to stay here with Mrs. Ballard and your delightful doggie for company."

"But will you be safe? I have no wish to alarm you, but what if your husband appears, or he sends someone to find you?"

"Gideon has promised I'll be safe. Tom is somewhere about, and Aidan has promised to return as soon as possible."

But what about that strange Mr. Browne man? Mr. Kirby might be very clever, but even clever men could be wrong about others sometimes. She swallowed her fears; she did not wish to alarm Emma anymore, especially now she seemed happy to play with Mittens. She would simply pray for God's protection. What could happen in just a few minutes, after all?

Caroline made her excuses and left, following the path down to the beach where she could see a large crowd had gathered outside the mouth of the cave. It seemed as though half of the village's inhabitants were here, as were two donkeys patiently waiting alongside a wooden cart. Excitement buzzed through the murmured conversations, the feeling of anticipation growing as she wove her way to the entrance. She could hear men talking inside, the plink of hammers, the thud of dropped earth, and the chipping of picks on stone.

Mrs. Baker moved alongside her, Mrs. Belcher a step behind. "The donkeys be 'ere for when they get out them bones."

"I see." Caroline cast them a sidelong look. Were they truly the wives of smugglers? Such a thing seemed impossible.

"Glad you be looking well," Mrs. Baker continued. "That must've been quite the adventure."

"One I have no wish to repeat," said Caroline.

"Probably wise," Mrs. Baker said, with a small nod. "Dangerous things lurk in these caves."

"Especially at full moon," Caroline murmured.

Mrs. Baker's eyes widened. "You know?"

"When we were trapped Mr. Kirby mentioned the cave might have been used for certain things."

"He never said anything to my Jem."

"No." Caroline added, "I'm sure he has no wish to cause distress."

Mrs. Baker studied her for a long moment, then nodded, as if satisfied.

"Where is your husband?"

She jerked a thumb at the mouth of the cave. "In there, 'elping your Mr. Kirby."

Her Mr. Kirby? Heat swept her cheeks. So, the gossip had spread through the village also. Oh, how she needed to speak to him, to get matters sorted, to just know his feelings! A pricking sensation made her turn. The bearlike Mr. Browne stared at her. Why would he do so? Who *was* he?

Heartened by Mrs. Baker's affability, she motioned to the man and asked, "Has anyone yet learned about that man?"

Mrs. Baker made a face. "He was seen talking to that exciseman Nicholls. Likely 'e be an exciseman."

Or a spy for Lord Pratt. Caroline saw how Mr. Browne was inching back, away from the crowd of spectators. Was he going to go to the beach cottage? What if he hurt Emma? Her pulse began to hammer.

"You know," she said slowly, "I rather believe he is."

Her words might malign the man, but he was clearly up to no good, and if Mrs. Baker felt it necessary to ensure her husband's activities were kept safe from the man, then Caroline was not responsible for what actions might prevail.

Mrs. Baker looked at Mr. Browne with a hard gaze, before tapping Mrs. Belcher on the shoulder and murmuring in her ear. Seconds later, the two women threaded through the crowd and went and spoke to Mr. Browne. He frowned. They nodded. Caroline watched them leave, until her attention was stolen by an Irish voice.

"Good afternoon, Miss Hatherleigh," said Mr. Kenmore. "I certainly did not expect to see you here. I'm so pleased you are feeling better. Have you come to revisit the scene of great calamity?"

"Thank you, Mr. Kenmore," she said. "I am better, but will admit I do not consider it a great calamity, not when we are now safe."

"And I am certain that Mr. Kirby does not consider such an event a calamity either. Not when he is so fortunate as to gain two precious treasures."

"Two?" she asked.

He gestured inside. "One being a skeleton of an *ichthyosaurus* —"

"Oh, it really is one, then?"

"It is," he confirmed. "The work be slow — it took a blessed long time to remove the rockfall — but everything points to it being just as fine a specimen as that found by Miss Anning. And," he added with an air of satisfaction, "as it seems to be a complete skeleton, it is definitely finer than the remains recently discovered by young Wilmont."

"That is wonderful news!"

"It is."

He studied her with such an incomprehensible look that she had to ask his meaning.

"I am surprised you did not ask about the second treasure this cave released. But perhaps you already know."

"I'm afraid I don't," she admitted.

"So humble," he said, a gleam in his eye.

There came a shout from within, and he excused himself to hurry back inside. She glanced to her right, pushing to her toes, but the figures of Mr. Browne and the two women had disappeared entirely from view.

"Miss Hatherleigh."

The quiet voice belonged to Mr. Kirby. She turned, saw his bandaged head, and felt herself blush, conscious they were under the scrutiny of scores of eyes. "Hello, sir."

"Kenmore mentioned you were out here. I was surprised, but pleasantly so."

"I'm surprised that you were able to return to work so quickly. I'm so glad you are recovered."

"Thank you."

"I didn't mean to hold you up from your work, but I do wish to speak to you."

"We have much to say to each other, I suspect."

She glanced back at the faces surrounding them. "But not here, not now."

"But soon. I suspect we shall be only another hour or so, then begins the real task of getting this to the top."

"I do not wish to detain you. I will go and keep Emma company."

"Kenmore shall accompany you."

"Oh, but —"

"I would not have you without escort. Not when . . ." His voice faded, his eyes warming into something that breathed hope into her heart. Perhaps he did care after all.

Mr. Kenmore reappeared, Mr. Kirby

excused himself to return to the excavation, and Caroline and her Irish escort soon began the long walk to the village. She chewed her inner lip. So much remained uncertain, unresolved.

"What is it, my dear?" Mr. Kenmore asked. "You seem concerned."

"I hope Mr. Kirby will be safe in that cave. I would hate to think another cave-in might occur."

"It is now well braced and supported inside. I cannot think anything untoward will happen."

She exhaled. "I suppose I should simply pray for his protection."

"You believe?" he asked quickly.

"Yes." Conscious of his curious look, she felt compelled to explain. "When we were trapped, and Mr. Kirby was unconscious, I . . . I found myself calling out to God for help." She remembered the assurance found in that moment of hearing *Trust Me.* "And He answered," she added in a wondering voice. "I do not claim much faith, but enough to know we must trust God."

"Indeed we must," he murmured, before clearing his throat. "It is good to see the solicitude you exhibit towards my friend."

Her cheeks warmed. Perhaps he'd think the color due to the exertions of this walk.

"I would feel the same toward any of my acquaintances."

"Of course you would," he agreed. "I have often noted your interest in *my* welfare."

"I am glad you have, as it obviously did not need to be vocalized."

"Obviously, indeed." He chuckled.

But a frisson of unease made her shake her head. "Enough frivolity. You truly think him safe?"

"Yes."

"And Emma?"

"She has some careful watchguards in the Ballards."

"You think Pratt will come again?"

"It is possible, especially after the newspaper reports."

"And if he does, what will they do?"

"As soon as Kirby retrieves the skeleton, he plans to return to London. There, I imagine, he and Emma will ensconce themselves at Grosvenor Square under the protection of their brother, until other matters are resolved."

"Other matters?"

"Surely you want to know about the future?"

The future? Oh, he meant her future. Queasiness rippled within. How she longed to know whether Mr. Kirby's best friend knew of his feelings; how she feared to know he had none. She said carefully, "I know he was honor bound to offer for me, if that's what you mean."

He looked quickly at her. "It was not just honor."

She shook her head. "I know what the gossips would be saying; he must have felt his hand was being forced."

"You truly think so?"

"He has spoken no words to suggest otherwise."

"And you would want him to?"

"I — I . . ." She stumbled to a pause. How could she talk of warmer feelings to this man she scarcely knew? "I would not wish for him to offer for me if he had no, no . . ."

"No attachment?"

She nodded stiffly.

He smiled. "And you must see that I cannot permit my dearest friend to pursue matrimony with someone who holds him in aversion."

"In aversion? I do not think of Mr. Kirby in that way."

"It is becoming plain to me just how you regard our friend."

Oh, what had he seen? Had she been so unguarded? She tossed her head. "You are quite as abominable as he."

"Which is why I must seek his best interests, seeing as we understand each other so well."

She released his arm, and quickened her footsteps away. "I do not wish to speak with you a moment long —"

"Please." He hurried to match her pace. "Please let me finish."

She sighed, drawing in her spine and bracing for whatever else it was he had to say. "What is it, Mr. Kenmore?"

He appeared to wince. "So many errors remain to be rectified. Forgive me, Miss Hatherleigh. I had thought by now you would be made aware — but no matter. I shall explain; it scarcely matters your knowing now. You see, I am not a mister."

"What?" Her footsteps faltered. "Then what — who are you?"

"I trust you shall not see it as a gross deception. I am a viscount, so I should more properly be addressed as Lord Kenmore."

He was the same rank as her father. They were equals.

"I do not understand," she said. "Why the subterfuge?"

"Sometimes dropping accoutrements like titles makes things easier."

She bit her lip. Like Emma had dropped her proper name. Yes, she could certainly understand that.

He held out his hand, helping her across a slippery section of dim path. "Perhaps, my dear Miss Hatherleigh, you will prove so good as to overlook my little ruse and dance with me the next time we meet in a London ballroom."

"Perhaps," she said, dropping his hand. Then, aware how ungracious that sounded, added, "Of course."

"I shall look forward to it."

"Mr. — I mean, Lord Kenmore, is there anything else I should know?"

"There is, but I regret I cannot fully explain. Not until . . . someone else speaks. It is not my place to tell you."

By now they could see the cottage lights aglow, the sun dipping lower in the horizon.

"I suspect that I have spoken out of turn, and made you wish me at the devil rather than helped you see more plainly. The simple fact of the matter is this: Gideon is a decent-hearted, honorable man, and knowing how important propriety is to your family, he has done the honorable thing and proposed marriage rather than see you left abandoned. He would rather endure a loveless marriage and save your reputation than see the actions of last week cause you embarrassment."

Caroline stumbled. So, it was true. Mr. Kirby did not have warmer feelings for her. Pain wrenched so fiercely that she gasped.

"Miss Hatherleigh?"

She waved off his concern and offered arm, willing herself not to give in to base emotion. "It is nothing, just the steep climb."

"I thought —"

"Look, we're almost there!" she said, determinedly changing the subject. "I'm sure Emma will be glad to see us. I shall be sorry when she returns to London. She has proved to be a very good friend." She chattered on, working to ignore the ache inside that shouted of her disappointment. Could she truly marry someone who had only offered out of obligation? Oh, why had she let the tendrils of affection wrap around her heart? Mama had been right; such things were not the Aynsley way. Her footsteps hastened. Really, the sooner she could get back to Saltings — get back to Aynsley! — the better.

"Miss Hatherleigh, I fear my words have upset you. I'm sorry, I did not mean to suggest —"

"I can assure you, Lord Kenmore, that I have no wish for a loveless marriage with Mr. Kirby or with anyone."

"No? But I thought —"

"I still don't know why I am speaking of this to you and not to him." They had reached the gate of the garden. Lord Kenmore opened the gate for her and she hurried to the front door, knocking, before noticing it was ajar. She pushed and stepped inside. "Hello? Mrs. Ballard? Emma?"

Lord Kenmore joined her in the hall. "Hello? Anyone here?"

Before Caroline's emotion-blurred brain could decipher what was happening, a tall figure struck the Irish peer with a heavy stick, and he slumped to the flagstone floor without a sound.

Her breath hitched. Her legs wobbled. Her chest squeezed.

"Hello, Miss Hatherleigh," said Emma's husband. "We meet again at last."

CHAPTER TWENTY-FOUR

The scream rippling from her throat was cut short by the hand clapped over her mouth.

"Now, now, let's have none of that. I'm afraid my dear wife might grow frightened." Pratt dragged Caroline past the slumped figure on the floor to the sitting room and shoved her heavily toward the sofa, where Emma sat motionless, arms crossed over her belly, her haggard, pallid expression suggesting that she was a long way past frightened.

"Oh, Emma," Caroline said, clasping the cold hands, working to keep alarm from her own face. Mr. and Mrs. Ballard were nowhere to be seen; what had Pratt done to them? "Has he hurt you?" Caroline whispered, reaching up to push aside an auburn lock fallen across her friend's eyes.

"It doesn't matter," Emma said faintly, her eyes reddened from tears. "He can kill me, it doesn't matter. But if he hurts you, I shall never forgive myself."

Caroline studied the pale man who possessed a distinct look of menace. "Did Mr. Browne tell you where they were?"

"Who?" He made an impatient noise. "I know no Mr. Browne."

Caroline sent a questioning look at Emma, who shrugged, murmuring, "Gideon had employed someone to be a bodyguard. I believe that was his name."

Oh no! No wonder Mr. Kirby had not been concerned about Mr. Browne. And she had sent him away with Mrs. Baker and Mrs. Belcher to have goodness knows what happen! Nausea swirled within. Dizziness washed around her.

"Such a fool to think anyone could save you. But Carstairs was always a fool."

Who? Where had she heard that name before?

"A fool to imagine I would not learn the truth about the two decoys up north!"

He was talking about Mr. Kirby? "But not such a fool since you followed them," Caroline managed.

A blur of hand, a strike of pain, and fire stung her cheek as she slumped against the sofa, eyes closed against the sharp throbbing, the ringing in her ear. She ran her tongue around the inside of her teeth; they at least all appeared to be there. Was this real? No one had ever raised a hand against her! "How . . . how dare — ?"

"Do not speak," he said, his voice cold as steel. "You are nothing to me."

"Please, please don't hurt her," Caroline faintly heard Emma beg. Somewhere she could hear the sound of her pug barking. Then a thud. Then a whimper. Then silence.

"How could you kick a helpless animal?"

He'd kicked Mittens? Caroline made a moan of protest which he ignored. She opened her eyes to see his pale eyes and raised fist. The fear she tasted arrowed deeper.

"I don't know why I ever bothered with you," he said to Emma. "I would have been better off with you dead! At least I could have married again and got an heir —"

Her next attempt to speak was hushed by Emma's whisper-light touch on her shoulder. "I am sorry," she murmured, but whom she addressed Caroline did not know.

Caroline struggled into a sitting position. "What are you going to do?"

"I am going to take my wife home —"

Emma gave a moue of protest, her horrified eyes flicking to Caroline.

"— but before I do, I have some unfinished business to take care of. Starting with that brother of yours."

"Mr. Kirby will not —"

"You dare still speak? And speak of what you do not know?" He sent an incredulous look to Emma. "Does the" — he called Caroline a most unflattering name she was not entirely sure she knew the precise meaning of — "not know the truth?"

"I know enough truth to know that Emma married a monster."

Another backhanded whack and she was on the floor. Emma started to cry. "No, Caroline, no. He will kill you!"

"No, he won't," Caroline said, staggering to her feet, her jaw burning, her heart thumping in rage. How dare this bully torment Emma so? "He won't kill me, for everyone would know that he killed a viscount's daughter. And he would be hunted down, and then hanged for all to see. Hanged like a common criminal at the crossroads." She eyed Lord Pratt. "Your pride could never bear that, could it?"

He stepped toward her; she stumbled back. "You —" He spat another word most ungodly. "You know nothing about me!"

"I know all about what pride makes one do, and the honor due a family's name." She turned to Emma and managed to push out a somewhat wobbly smile. "I think you should tell him the truth."

"The truth? About what?" he demanded, advancing on Caroline, fist clenched.

"A-about the baby."

"What baby?" He spun to face his wife. "Emma? Are you pregnant?"

Emma pressed her lips together, her fearful gaze flicking from Caroline to the prone body of Lord Kenmore.

A roar of rage filled the room. "Is this true? Have you and that Irish" — another expletive — "been carrying on?" He yanked Emma to her feet. "How long has this been going on for?"

She shook her head, but he ignored her denials, and slapped her hard in the belly to her loud gasp. "How dare you?"

He began to shake her. Caroline wrenched at his arm but he was too strong. His free palm sent her crashing to the floor.

"Stop it!" Caroline begged. "Leave her! Can't you see that she's in pain?"

"Good! I cannot stand the thought of that Irish spawn within my wife. You are mine, you hear me?" Pratt shook Emma harder. "Mine!"

"Are you truly that stupid?" Caroline cried, stumbling upright once more. It did not matter what he might do to her. All that was important was that Emma be protected. "That is your child!"

His head swiveled to Caroline. "You lie."

"Tell him the truth, Emma! Do you want to die?"

But Emma only shook her head, tears rolling down her face. "I don't care anymore. I don't —" She gasped then moaned and clutched her belly, slumping to the floor.

"Dear God! What have you done?" Caroline fell to her knees beside her friend's body, the fear within massing to a new degree of horror. "Get a doctor!"

Pratt stood still, mouth, arms slack.

"Get a doctor!" she screamed. Oh, dear God. Was that blood seeping through Emma's gown?

"That is my child?"

"It won't be if you don't get a doctor. Hurry!"

Dear God, dear God, dear God! The prayer seemed all that she could utter. Tears were seeping, her nose was leaking, her whole body was shaking. What should she do? "Oh, God, *please* help her!"

She pushed to her feet, stared at her bloodied hands, stared back at Emma's misshapen figure, and emitted an ear-piercing scream.

And kept on screaming.

Gideon heard the sound from afar. A high-pitched keening, as if the earth had been rent in two and the angels were despairing. He glanced at the men pushing the cart from behind. "You hear that?"

"It don't sound too good," Belcher said.

The darkness made it hard to move quickly, the donkeys pulling the cart laboring under the weight of the stone. Beneath their feet a fringe of water lapped at their boots. The tide had turned. It had taken far longer than he'd expected, the sun lowering to the sea by the time they finally were out to the cheers of a few remaining spectators. It was good that the townsfolk were excited; no doubt they hoped such an event would put little Sidmouth on the map the way Miss Anning's find had done for Lyme Regis.

He'd even felt prompted to ask men such as Baker and Belcher to assist. He didn't mind the free traders knowing their indebtedness to him for his silence was being repaid this way, and he figured if any of the unscrupulous collectors of fossils were around, these men had enough beef to put a stop to any pretensions.

The sound began again. Unease prickled his spine.

"You think you can guide this to the cottage?" he asked, gesturing to the cart. "I do not like that cry. Someone is in trouble." His heart lurched. Emma couldn't be in trouble, could she? Not with the Ballards protecting her, and Browne, and Kenmore, too. He frowned. The wail didn't sound like her voice, now he came to think of it . . .

"Caroline!"

With shouted instructions to the men, he left the cart and hurried back to the cottage, his feet slipping and sliding on the loose pebbles as he dashed up the path.

Ahead, he could see the cottage lights, could see a group of people gathered by the door. The sound of the screaming, which was growing louder as he neared the cottage, abruptly stopped. "What is it?"

"The door is locked! We can't get in."

Panic clawed at his chest. Where was Browne? What was happening? "Caroline?"

He shouldered the door. He only hurt his side, the door refusing to budge.

"Sir," came Captain Nicholls's voice. "Allow me."

Seconds later, the door crashed in, and he almost toppled over an unconscious Kenmore. But he barely noticed that, so transfixed was he on the scene of horror before him.

Pratt stood in front of Emma's body, one arm wrapped around Miss Hatherleigh's throat.

CHAPTER TWENTY-FIVE

"Emma!" Gideon rushed towards her, but was stopped by Caroline's gasp as Pratt tightened his grip.

"Don't move."

"But Emma —"

"Needs a doctor," Caroline whispered, her eyes locked on his. "Get a doctor!"

He shook his head. "You —"

"Get a doctor, Gideon! She hasn't much time."

He'd wondered what his name would sound like on her tongue; he hadn't imagined hearing it in circumstances like this.

"Go!" she pleaded.

He started to back away, one step behind the next.

"I ought to kill you for what you've done," Pratt snarled.

Gideon ignored him, eyes fixed on the woman he loved, who even now was begging him to leave her to find help for his sister.

"Sir?" A voice behind him. "What has happened — Oh!"

"Captain Nicholls, I would be much obliged to you if you could go and retrieve a doctor right now."

"Sir, I —"

"Now, captain! My sister is —" Horror clogged his throat. She couldn't be dying. Could she?

The sound of steps speeding away fueled hope that the man would do as requested and bring the doctor quickly.

"Pratt, please let Miss Hatherleigh go. She has nothing to do with this."

"I know that you care for her, and if that is so, then it will give me immense pleasure to hurt something you love."

Caroline's wide eyes were fixed on him. Gideon swallowed. There was only one way to protect her. He did not want to have to say this; he hoped she'd understand . . .

"I do not love her."

She gasped.

"What? Are you not betrothed to her?"

"I am," Gideon said, "but only because such a thing became necessary when we were alone together after the cave-in."

Hurt cramped her eyes, pinched her face.

"You do not care for her?"

"You know me," Gideon continued, hating how his every word seemed to flash pain across her face, "I care only for my rocks and fossils."

Pratt's jaw, his grip, slackened. "I . . . I don't understand."

"It's true," Caroline whispered, her eyes burning into Gideon's own. "He only felt a sense of obligation. He's never once told me that he cares. He never even spoke to me about betrothal, he only spoke to my grandmother out of a sense of duty."

Gideon's heart wrenched. She didn't think that, surely? Yet her words carried a ring of truth, a note of pain.

Enough for Pratt to stare at him. "Is that true?"

"I'm afraid so." He swallowed, praying his next words would not be believed by the wrong person. "I've never cared for her save as one might care for an acquaintance."

Her eyes were shiny now, the candlelight picking up one tear, then another as they slid down her cheeks. Dear God, she did not truly believe him, did she? Or was she an actress worthy of Mrs. Siddons, putting on the greatest performance of her life?

"And the poor girl obviously thought you did. How sad to know such disappointment."

A sound came, the scuffle of boots running on cobblestones, the murmur of men's voices. Then Captain Nicholls's voice. "The doctor is here."

"Do not come in —"

"I'm sorry," came Dr. Fellowes's gruff voice, "but I have a duty of care to my patient. Now, what has happened here? Oh, Miss Hatherleigh! Miss Kirby!"

"That's Lady Pratt to you," snapped Gideon's brother-in-law.

The doctor knelt beside Emma, listening closely to her chest.

"Is she alive?" Gideon asked, hating how his voice trembled.

"Yes, but only just." He glanced up. "She needs immediate attention, and I shall need help."

"Captain!" Gideon called.

"Yes, sir?"

"Doctor, tell him what you require."

The doctor gave a list of instructions, starting with the aid of another medical practitioner, ending with the call for soap and hot water.

"Pratt, please, release Miss Hatherleigh and let us focus our attention on Emma," Gideon continued. "You cannot want to see your heir die?"

His arm dropped, then he twisted Caroline roughly to face him. "You spoke the truth?"

Caroline jerked away, escaping to the other side of the room next to the doctor. "Of course I did, you stupid man!" Her voice broke on a sob, the sound heartrending, even as she dropped to her knees beside the too-pale, too-still figure of Emma. "How can you think otherwise of your wife?"

"You cannot have seriously thought Emma was pregnant with another's man's child?" Gideon exclaimed. "How could she have done so?"

Behind him, he heard faint sounds, then a soft curse in an Irish accent. "God bless me, I . . ." A gasp. "What the deuce — ?"

Gideon glanced at him, motioned him to be quiet. "We are having a disagreement, Kenmore, and you would be wise to refrain from making any comment."

"Emma!" he gasped.

"*Wise* to refrain!" Gideon snapped.

"You fiend! May the devil cut off your head and make a year's work of your neck . . ." Aidan cursed, before a "Beg your pardon, Miss Hatherleigh."

She gave a hysteria-tinged laugh. "It scarcely matters. I think you only said what I have been thinking this past hour!" She shot Gideon a look of undiluted scorn.

Aidan raised his brows at Gideon and stumbled to his feet. "How very improper of you, Miss Hatherleigh."

"Oh, there's nothing very proper about me, anymore." She gave another half sob that wrenched Gideon's heart. "It seems I'm so scandal-plagued that my only remedy might be to board a vessel to the colonies."

"But Kirby here would not like —"

Gideon gripped his arm, but Pratt had noticed, his eyes narrowing as he looked between Kenmore, Caroline, and Gideon. "So, you *do* care for her."

"Of course he does," Aidan said.

In a snarl half animal and half human, Pratt lunged to grab Miss Hatherleigh, as her face melded into terror.

Bang!

Caroline's body was the first to move, falling toward Emma. *No* —

Then Pratt's knees began to buckle, his mouth drooping in slackened surprise, as red bloomed across his chest.

"Sorry 'bout that" — this from Belcher, pistol smoking as he entered the hall from the back passage — "but it seems the rogue wanted to hurt your young lady."

Caroline — from where she hovered protectively over Emma — glanced up at Gideon with a fleeting look of raw pain before she turned her face away.

Gideon slumped against the bookcase, willing it to hold him up.

Aidan's voice begged Emma to live.

Hurried footsteps signaled the other doctor's entry, upon which he uttered an oath most un-Hippocratic and joined Dr. Fellowes in attending Emma on the floor.

Captain Nicholls arrived, puffing. "I heard a shot."

Gideon instinctively looked over. Belcher had melted away. He glanced at the others.

"Good God!" Nicholls exclaimed, bending over Pratt's prone body. "Who did this?"

"I've been attending my patient and saw nothing," Dr. Fellowes muttered. "Quick, lift her up. We need to get her into a bed now."

"This way," Caroline said to Aidan, as he lifted his precious burden. She seemed determined not to look at Gideon.

"Well?" Nicholls said, red-faced and angry. "What the blazes happened here? Doctor?"

The doctor muttered, "I arrived here after the shot was fired."

"Kirby?"

Gideon could say. Wouldn't.

"Do you want to let a villain get away with it?"

Gideon looked him steadily in the eye then said, pointing to the figure on the floor, "He won't get away with it anymore."

CHAPTER TWENTY-SIX

London

Six weeks later

And she had thought the exhaustion induced from the cave-in was bad.

Caroline walked to the top of the set, summoned a smile for her partner, and then glanced around the ballroom glittering with the proud and the titled. If only the social challenges of the past few weeks were not to be met in such a headlong way. But Mama had been insistent. Caroline would not be forced to hide away as if she had done something wrong. For she had not. Her only error had been in following poor Mr. Kirby into a cavern — and in believing *dear* Miss McNell would be able to hold her tongue.

She curtsied, then followed the movements of the dance, her feet and actions automatic, her mind free to wander. Around her, the room buzzed with the news of the day. Mrs. Hale, Serena's friend whom Caro-

428

line had met months ago, and her scandal-plagued husband seemed to have risen above the gossip of the past years for him to have received a commendation from Lord Liverpool, and an invitation from the Prince Regent to Carlton House. Mama had been shocked, but agreeably so, as if she anticipated a similar generosity of spirit might be shown toward her own scandal-plagued daughter.

Indeed, Mama must think so, as she had given permission for Ned Amherst to engage Caroline in a dance. Caroline had noticed Ned speak with Major — no, Lieutenant Colonel — Hale, in such a subdued manner it made her wonder what had transpired between them. She had also seen Cecilia notice, and her downcast mien when Ned had moved towards Caroline, and begged for her hand in this dance.

Why Cecy still wished for his attention she knew not, she thought, whirling around the room. Yes, he might be the younger son of an earl, but he treated her in such a shabby fashion, ignoring her, or if he noticed her at all, treating her like the younger sister he never had. Really, Caroline thought crossly, why couldn't young men behave more circumspectly towards young ladies, and not give rise to hopes that only led to disappointment?

Her chest grew tight. The back of her eyes burned. Why hadn't Mr. Kirby so much as spoken to her since that dreadful day? She had thought, she had believed — or was it hoped? — that they had shared a connection, but his words that day had raised only doubts, doubts confirmed when she'd left Sidmouth with no renewed request from him to pay his addresses. It didn't matter what Lord Kenmore said; surely if Mr. Kirby cared he would have said something. The fact that he *had* not said he *did* not. She drew in a savage breath. Oh, what a fool she had been.

"Caro?" Ned said, his green-gold eyes fixed upon her.

"I beg your pardon, I was not attending."

"I know."

He gave a half smile curled into one corner that suggested he was not offended, the sight of which eased a mite of her impatience. He did seem a little different these days, as if the injury he had sustained late last year had worn away some of the reckless confidence she knew in him before. She glanced over his shoulder to where Cecy sat, downcast. Perhaps there might be hope after all.

". . . some good deeds."

Her head snapped up. "I beg your pardon?"

"You need not. I should perhaps instead beg for yours, seeing as my conversation is so dull that it cannot hold your interest."

She felt a moment's shame, before eyeing him narrowly. "What is it you wish to say?"

He smiled, but such a pale imitation of what she remembered she couldn't help but feel a moment's sorrow for him. Had his experience changed him so much? "I was hoping you might advise me on how I might go about performing good deeds."

"Good deeds? I'm afraid I don't quite understand."

"Surely you know what good deeds are, Caro. Why, you're performing one right now, deigning to dance with a man you despise."

"I don't despise you."

"You don't respect me, that is certain. Not that I blame you," he said heavily.

"All this self-deprecation does not become you at all. Please, Ned, if you wish to ask my advice, then do not carry on in such a gloomy manner."

He chuckled, not without mirth. "That's more the Caroline I know."

"What do you mean?"

"You. You accuse me of being morose

when you barely smile yourself."

"You are being ridiculous."

"Am I? I've known you for years, and I know when something is troubling you."

"Whatever troubles I may or may not have are nothing to do with you."

"Really? Because I cannot help but feel that they have a great deal to do with me."

"You are extremely presumptuous!"

"Am I?" His eyes glinted. "Or am I simply wallowing in more guilt, that you would not have fallen into such a predicament if you had not been sent off to South Devon because of my association with you last year?" His smile grew wry. "You cannot deny it. I have heard as much from your rather more forthright little sister."

"Verity told you this?"

He inclined his head.

"She would be better off minding her tongue than sharing all the family secrets."

"She didn't quite share all," he murmured.

Caroline felt herself flush. "I have nothing further to say to you."

"Come now. I certainly did not believe dear Lady Heathcote when she came calling to tell of your adventures by the sea."

"That woman," Caroline muttered.

"Perhaps that might count as one of my good deeds." The music spun to a stop and he bowed over her hand before releasing it.

She caught a glimpse of the misery writ large on Cecy's face. Heart softening, she said, "If you're so desperate for good deeds, then perhaps you should ask Cecy to dance."

He glanced over her shoulder while offering his arm to escort her back to her mother. "That would be like asking my sister to dance."

"Am I not like your sister?"

"You, dear Caro, have always been the most obliging of my obligations."

Heat raced across her chest, and she released his arm. But conscious she could not afford to make another scene, she plastered a smile on her face and moved in a stately manner to the ladies' retiring room, holding her gown as if she had sustained a small tear which required repair. She attained the withdrawing room and sat down in a padded chair, waving away the maid who came forward to offer assistance. "Thank you, no."

She did not need her hem mended; she needed to have space to think, to consider.

Why had Mr. Kirby not spoken to her?

Her bottom lip trembled. How she hated to think herself as wearing her heart on her sleeve as Cecilia did, but she could not release these feelings. How could she share such a bond with someone, only to have him spurn her? How could he be that careless with her reputation?

She released a silent sigh, thinking back on her time in Sidmouth before she was whisked away by her scandalized Mama. Grandmama's proclamation of relief at Caroline's rescue had been swiftly followed by her renewed assertion of Caroline's doomed prospects. "For what gentleman would want a wife known to have been tainted by such an experience?"

No gentleman, it seemed. Not even the one with whom she had shared such a tainting experience. Chagrin cinched her throat. How could she have ever thought him a gentleman?

In a strange and twisted way, she was almost glad he had not spoken to her, glad she did not have to hear whatever excuses he had offered. Mama's arrival, like that of an avenging Fury, had seen Caroline's swift removal, precipitated by her horror at Caroline's blackened eye. Within the space of two days they had left Saltings, Mama's disgust at the scandal she blamed Grandmama for leading to a bitter exchange of words.

Mr. Kirby had apparently called to see

her, but had been barred, his interview with Mama all too brief. Mama had scarcely spoken of the matter on the journey home, her outraged sensibilities such that Caroline had little desire to ask and invite further censure on her head. And she was strangely relieved that Mama had scarcely spoken of the matter; it was good to pretend she could put these matters behind her, to pretend she did not care. For though her heart was bleeding, she could not align herself with someone who had admitted he did not love her.

He did not love her. Her eyes blurred. He did not love her!

She shook her head at her wretchedness, her shoulders slumping. How could she have let herself succumb to such a pitiful state? She was almost as bad as Cecy! Was she destined to live like poor Emma had been, bound in matrimony to one man while secretly caring for another? Oh, that she could stuff these foolish emotions away, and revert to her former thinking, that marriage was simply an alliance, and that she would be happy with a sense of mutual esteem and a degree of affection. How much easier that would be than this wretched half living she now endured, made worse by society's demands that she smile as if she had no cares.

Her heart panged, rebuking her once more for her self-centered thinking. Of course, in comparison to some, she had no real concerns, other than wounded pride and a splintered heart. Such things might recover, much like the angry purple bruising she and poor Mittens had sustained that night, bruising that took weeks to heal. Even now poor Mittens walked with a limp, something the veterinarian had said would likely heal in time. Some things held hope of healing, whereas others . . .

"Dear Lord, please heal dear Emma."

The prayer fluttered to the ceiling. Of poor Emma Caroline knew only that she still clung to life, though the babe had miscarried. She had heard no further talk, not even in tonight's ballroom. And she would not be so foolish as to ask questions that would only provoke the curious to gossip about what they did not, could not, know. No. She might not be able to do much for her friend save pray, but Caroline could give Emma the dignity of not speaking of her pain.

Another, silent prayer for her friend's well-being rose, followed by renewed resolution to remember her example. Emma's quiet grace and dignity sustained a greater quality of ladylikeness than one encountered in most ballrooms.

The sound of the door opening hastened her to brush wet eyes and affix a smile to her lips.

"Here you are!" Mama's voice, accompanied by her now familiar troubled look. "Did somebody have the effrontery to say something to you, my dear?"

"No," Caroline said. "I just needed a moment to gather my thoughts," and gather her courage, "which I now have."

"I see. Let us return then, shall we?"

Caroline acquiesced, and together they reentered the ballroom, her mother scanning the vicinity as if searching for any potential suitors.

"Oh dear," Mama murmured behind her waving fan. "Here comes that dreadful Lord Snowstrem. Really, he is the most tiresome bore. You would do well to avoid dancing with him if you can escape gracefully. One can be sure that whatever is said to him today will be tittered over in all the clubs tomorrow."

"Ah, Miss Hatherleigh." The fat man bowed, his corsets creaking. "Such a lovely addition to the circle here tonight."

"Lord Snowstrem." She curtsied, forcing her lips to curve. *Please God, let him not ask about the past weeks.*

"It must be nice to have opportunity to enjoy oneself with a dance."

"I beg your pardon?"

"After the incident in Devon, wasn't it? Rather a terrible time, I gather."

She said nothing, her artificial smile growing brittle.

"Of course, it must have been helpful to have had the assistance of someone like young Carstairs there."

Who?

"I gather he was quite helpful, eh?"

Again, she had no words. Oh, for her youngest sister's rapier wit right now!

"I perceive you are without a partner. May I be so bold as to solicit you for the next dance?"

Caroline cast a desperate glance at her mother, who seemed similarly struck dumb by the man's impudence, before another voice lilted, "I'm rather afraid you cannot, dear Buffy, as the young lady is promised to me."

Caroline turned gratefully to the newcomer, her mouth falling open foolishly.

Her savior was none other than Lord Kenmore.

"Lord Kenmore," she said, holding out her gloved fingers. "How do you do?"

He bowed, pressing his lips to the back of her hand. "Please forgive my tardiness," he said, eyes watchful under smooth brows.

"Yes, of course," she managed, glancing at Lord Snowstrem. "Excuse me, but I promised Lord Kenmore this dance long ago."

His expression fell, like that of a greedy child whose sweet had been snatched away.

"That's correct, my dear. Shall we dance?" Lord Kenmore held out his hand, then drew her firmly into the set just forming.

"I am surprised to see you in London," she said, when they finally had a moment to speak.

"Forgive me, Miss Hatherleigh. My time has not been my own."

She would not ask him about Mr. Kirby; she would not! Instead she offered a cool smile. "Thank you for coming to my rescue just now. I could not bear to dance with Lord Snowstrem."

"And I could not bear to watch you do so. You must allow me to thank you for agreeing to avert such a spectacle."

Her gaze faltered, her step slowed. "You think me a spectacle?"

"I think" — he murmured in such a low voice she had to peer up at him — "we need to make it look like we are dancing, so we are free to talk about what really is of import."

"You mean Emma?" *His* name she would not speak. "Have you seen her? How is she?"

He smiled, but drew her into the movements of the dance. "We shall talk as soon as we are not being observed. Be patient."

But patience seemed so far away, the dance progression taking an infinitely long time. Yet she knew Lord Kenmore's words to be prudent; Buffy Snowstrem was not the only person watching them with keen curiosity.

Eventually they were released to stand at the head of a set, allowing some small time for them to converse. "You have seen her? Where is she?"

"I have just come from there, and yes, I am happy to report that she is improving slowly," he said.

"And she is safe?"

"She is very safe. She has no one who wants to harm her."

"Thank God," she said.

"I do." His expression sobered. "I am so pleased you are here, and I have opportunity to tell you personally. I know you have been a very good friend to them both."

Both? Was this a test to ascertain her feelings about Mr. Kirby? If so, she would not give him the satisfaction. She smoothed her expression to one of polite interest.

"I see you do not ask about our other friend. I presume Gideon still counts as your friend?" he asked, eyebrows aloft.

She bit a suddenly wobbling bottom lip as tears rushed to escape. She blinked rapidly.

"You may be glad to know that he is well."

"I'm so glad," she managed, her gaze dropping to his starched neckcloth. "Truly."

But if he was well, why had he not contacted her? Her chest grew tight once more.

"If you are so insistent on being glad, may I enquire why your countenance appears to state otherwise? Or am I allowed to guess?"

Her cheeks grew hot. "Please do not tease me, my lord."

"I beg your pardon." And the movement of the dance drew them apart once more.

When next they were together he gazed at her soberly. "It is, however, on his behalf that I attended tonight. I had been all set to refuse the invitation when your estimable family's name was mentioned among the guests, and I found I did not have it in me to decline such an opportune moment."

"What do you mean?"

"I mean, my dear Miss Hatherleigh, that matters were left in some disarray after Sidmouth, and I have come as an emissary of peace."

"My lord, I am tired of hearing nonsense. Won't you say plainly what you mean?"

"Very well."

But at that moment, the music drew to a close, and they were forced to exchange bow and curtsy, then he was obliged to escort her to her parents where she made the introductions. "Father, Mama, this is Lord Kenmore, an acquaintance —"

"A friend," he interjected.

"— I made whilst staying at Saltings. Lord Kenmore, these are my parents, Lord and Lady Aynsley."

She ignored her mother's narrowed eyes whilst she listened to the men exchange views on various matters of Parliament, before the seemingly more important matter of horseflesh was mentioned, forcing her to bite down her impatience.

"Miss Hatherleigh, I wonder if you might honor me with a stroll along the terrace. It is a trifle cooler out, and I fear you must be tired from our earlier exertions."

She made a suitable reply, and having received Mama's permission, soon attained the terrace, sipping from a glass of punch that had been liberated from a footman's tray.

"Now we can speak more freely," Lord Kenmore said. "I know it is most unorthodox to speak of such matters, but I have felt for some time that Kirby's actions after Sidmouth were not as they should have been."

She stared at him. "I beg your pardon?"

"He is too punctilious in his reckonings, and did not want you to feel forced into something for which you had no wish."

"I don't understand."

"Then understand this: after being alone with you for that amount of time in the cave, your reputation was compromised and he should have made you an offer."

"Which he did, at least through Grandmama."

"But he never spoke to you personally, did he?"

"No."

He made an impatient noise, muttered something under his breath. "Such a fool."

"Thank you, Lord Kenmore. That is a fact I am made aware of on an hourly basis."

"My dear, I don't mean you. Gideon is the fool." He shook his head, his lips wry. "You poor thing."

His sympathy stung, unleashing frustration to steam through her chest. Yes, she did feel helpless. Once she'd thought she could hunt down Mr. Kirby and ask him his intentions. But now, after his denial of affection . . . She rather thought even Verity would balk at that!

He remained silent for a long moment. "Would you care to accept his suit if he spoke to you personally?"

"I don't know why this concerns you, sir."

"I mean no disrespect. I only speak to you about this as I'm aware of my friend's despair."

Her heart quickened. "He despairs?"

"Despairs." He nodded solemnly. "One would think that having discovered such a magnificent specimen of an *ichthyosaurus* and having helped save his sister's life, he would not be so utterly wretched, but it appears that is not the case. Apparently he misses his young lady."

"His young lady?"

"Did you not hear Belcher refer to you so? Kirby certainly esteems you in that way."

"But he . . . he denied it to Lord Pratt. He said . . ." The dreaded tears returned, her voice wobbled. "He said he did not care for me."

"And you believed him? Oh, my dear, I assure you such things were said to ensure your safety. If Kirby told me once he told me a hundred times how much he regretted speaking in that way."

He had? Tremulous hope lit within.

"Truly, you have touched him in a way no

one else has."

"But if that is so, why has he not ever said anything to me?" She strove to lower her voice, conscious it had reached a pitch too high. "If he loved me —"

"Loves you," he corrected gently.

"Then why has he still not said anything?"

"Because, I fear, he might have thought his chance with you was gone after that awful night with Pratt."

"I don't understand. Why would he think that?"

He coughed. "I believe he was given to understand not to hope."

"Are you suggesting it is my fault he has said nothing?"

"I'm suggesting he could perhaps do with some encouragement."

She placed a hand to her head, her thoughts, emotions, awhirl. What to do? What to *do*? "I . . . I do not know what to say."

"Shall I perhaps convey your regret at how things ended? Perhaps I could say you still feel a great sense of hurt that he said nothing."

"That is all true, I suppose."

"Then I have your permission?"

What would it matter if he knew she was upset? She nodded.

"You may trust me to deliver the missive in an appropriate manner and style."

"I hope so." She eyed him doubtfully.

He laughed. "Your misgivings are without basis, I assure you." He clasped her hand. "Thank you. You have no idea what a relief it is to know my wife has such a good friend."

"Your what?"

"Oh, did I forget to mention it? Emma and I were married by special license two weeks ago."

Her jaw sagged. "Truly?"

"Truly." His expression grew gleeful.

"How abominable you were not to tell me earlier!"

"It is something of a surprise, I know, and remains something of a secret still — heaven forbid propriety be offended! But we had no desire to put our plans on hold simply because certain societal ladies might believe something had occurred with undue haste."

"Propriety can be overrated," she admitted.

"Exactly so. No, I saw no sense in waiting, and when Emma was well enough to know her mind, I knew I could not delay asking that question I have longed to these many years."

Her eyes blurred, and she managed to say,

"I wish you both every happiness."

"Thank you." He grinned, and then his face grew thoughtful. "It seems sometimes God blesses the undeserving with the greatest gifts."

"Yes."

"Sometimes those gifts might require much patience."

She nodded.

"I trust Emma and I may soon be able to wish you joy also, my dear. Now, let me escort you back to your mother. I fear I have overstayed my time with you, and she will be displeased." He carried on in this jovial manner for a few minutes more, while her head and her heart spun with the ramifications of what he'd said. "Ah, Lady Aynsley, thank you for allowing me the pleasure of your daughter's company. I trust I may be able to call upon you in the not-too-distant future?"

And with a smile to Caroline, and a bow to her mother, he was gone.

CHAPTER TWENTY-SEVEN

Royal Geological Society
London

"And this is why I believe . . ."

A sense of awe filled him as he gazed out at the sea of faces listening expectantly as he continued the evening's dissertation about his recent find. The interest had been immense, both in his find and in the story of his entrapment which could have ended tragically.

He continued speaking, taking questions at the end of the lecture.

"Mr. Kirby, you talk about how you believe these finds speak to an ancient past. Could you tell us, how do you reconcile this with the creation of the world as recorded in the Bible?"

Gideon grasped the lectern a little more firmly, and uttered a silent prayer that his words would make sense and honor God. "I believe man can never hope to fathom all the ways and means of our awesome Creator. We may regard the creation of the world as occurring in seven days in a literal sense or something more metaphorical. Regardless of how God created the world, I do believe it was created by Him, and not just an accident or a collection of random events that somehow formed such intricate unity."

More nodding of heads. He felt a moment's ease within his soul. Encouraged, he continued. "Just think of a babe, and how its very being develops and grows, nearly always into perfection. Science shows us that a child develops from a tiny life within its mother's womb into something that can one day have rational thought, can feed itself. Can we believe such a process to occur by chance? How can we not consider this a miracle?"

Amid more head nodding, he felt his spirit clench. How could he have not considered poor Emma's child a miracle? How could he only see it as being a product of that monster, when in fact it had been his sister's child also? Had been, in fact, a child created by God? Conviction clanged within for his too condemning words, and too faithless prayers.

"A child's growth and birth is, to my

mind, evidence of a Master Designer at work, so if the question concerns whether I believe in God, then I do. Do I believe He has created the world? Yes, I do. Do I believe that the world holds evidence that suggests it has changed over time? Again, I do. Do I believe there are mysteries we are still to search out? Yes, indeed." He eyed the questioner. "And do I believe God created this creature? Yes, I do."

A few more questions and then he was released to hand clasps and patted backs. Gideon exhaled, glad to have reached the conclusion of tonight's proceedings. He met the evening's organizers, was thanked profusely, and then escorted to the front doors. Minutes later he was in a hackney cab, being driven to Portman Square, as his thoughts wandered freely.

The opportunity to speak at tonight's prestigious gathering had been a long-held dream. But he realized now how hollow such a thing was in comparison to other matters.

The past few weeks had been ones of torture interspersed with moments of joy. Feeling sure he would lose Emma, only to have her miraculously restored. He had not let the doctors leech her after the first days, but he was sure the bloodletting had removed some of the toxins the poison of her child had caused. No, the fact that she had returned to health — well, a version of it at least — was truly one of God's miracles. Even the doctors agreed.

His thoughts shifted to another of God's miracles: Aidan's assertion that Miss Hatherleigh owned faith. His heart had eased at that news, as if the acknowledgment that she shared his faith had finally loosed the constraint he'd sensed between them. He was desperate to know more, but such questions had been buried amid later rejection.

Shaking off his moroseness, he focused on another positive — the fact that Aidan had convinced James he should marry Emma. Emma's joy at finally being reunited with the man she had long loved was enough to melt any of James's misgivings, and the fact that it could be done so quietly was another benefit, he knew.

But the benefits of past weeks, though glorious, seemed unsatisfyingly few. The joy of discovering the *ichthyosaurus* had been transitory, Gideon's pride at being visited by members of various natural history societies proving a mere illusion compared to his heartache at losing the chance to court the woman he had hoped to marry.

He still could not fathom how Caroline had misunderstood. Had he been too opaque in his words? Aidan said he had; even Emma had decried Gideon's lack of affection in his manner. Gideon had tried to offer excuse by way of saying that Miss Hatherleigh would not wish to be improper. But he'd been laughed to scorn, and memories would arise of her desperation that last night, when she'd flung those words at him, her blue eyes ice cold as she declared herself scandal-plagued enough to flee to the colonies.

The day after the Pratt encounter, his efforts to present himself to her mother as a suitor had been met with flat refusal. He had barely opened his mouth to speak when she had cut him off, launching into a litany of his faults. Lady Aynsley held a strong resemblance to her daughter, but where Caroline's features grew soft with understanding he feared her mother's never had. The viscountess had instead been bitter and thorough in denouncing his antics, his antecedents, and his manner of dealing with her daughter. Such harsh words spoken had raised his mettle to a point where he had been perhaps too plain in his speech also. But it had been her last words — that Caroline's mother could not wish her daughter beholden to a man Caroline could not love — that had cut the deepest.

And Caroline's refusal to answer his letters had only confirmed his worst suspicions: that Gideon had hurt her, hurt her so deeply she could never forgive him.

The cab rounded a corner and drew to a standstill in front of the tall town house belonging to Kenmore's father. Gideon would usually stay at his brother's London home, but Emma had insisted on Gideon staying with them.

He paid the driver and exited, walking quickly up the steps and entering the front doors. A quick enquiry revealed his sister had retired hours ago — she was feeling tired — and that Kenmore had not returned yet from his visit to a ball tonight.

Feeling too agitated to retire, he strode to the drawing room and settled into a comfortable sofa with today's news sheet to await his new brother-in-law.

He was about halfway through when Aidan entered the room, looking especially dapper in evening dress.

"And here he be, tonight's guest lecturer. How was your evening?"

"Tonight went well, I think. People were responsive. I was a little concerned some might oppose me for offering an alternative to more traditional views, but one cannot deny what has been seen with one's eyes, can one?"

"No," Aidan said, his own eyes gleaming, a strange smile lurking around his mouth. "One most definitely should not dismiss what one sees with one's eyes."

He sat opposite, stretching his legs in front of him, studying Gideon with that curious expression.

"What is it? You keep looking at me like a cat that's got the cream."

"I don't mind admitting that I feel like a cat that has got the cream."

"And what cream is that?"

"Tonight's ball saw one Lieutenant Colonel Hale being courted by those who, until recently, I believe, thought him to be something of a loose fish. One of these runaway marriages that appears to have worked out, and now all is forgiven."

Gideon eyed him, a faint frown pushing between his brows.

"Now, now. There is no need to look at me like that, dear fellow. It's not as if I needed to resort to such an ignominious start to wedded bliss."

"I'm glad."

"Yes, you should be. Not that I didn't think about it."

"What?"

"Oh, yes, I thought about it. Wished I could have contrived some way of undoing time so Emma could have been whisked to safety before another stole her away. But what's done is done and cannot be undone."

"True," Gideon said, his spirits sinking as he studied the news sheet blankly. If only he had not made such a mess of things . . . Tightness filled his chest again.

"Saving, of course, when it can."

He peered up. "I beg your pardon?"

Aidan grinned. "Really, my friend, have you been drinking? You really should not if it affects your ability to reason."

"I rather think it is your cryptic comments that are leading to my state of confusion, because, as you well know, I have certainly not imbibed."

"Then perhaps it is the aftereffects of your knocks on the head."

"Or perhaps it is simply the enigmatic nature of your remarks. I wish you would tell me plainly what it is you wish to say."

Aidan laughed. "You rather put me in mind of someone else I had the pleasure of speaking with tonight."

"Clearly someone of good sense, if they, too, struggled to understand your meaning. Who?"

"Miss Caroline Hatherleigh."

His chest tightened, his pulse increased. "Well, how is she? Does she look well? Does she —" He swallowed. How could he ask the questions whose answers he really wanted to know?

"She seems well, yes, and quite recovered from the ordeal."

"Thank God." The cords binding his heart loosened a notch. "Did she, by chance, mention Emma at all?"

"Yes, she did, and then congratulated me on my good fortune." Aidan chuckled, green eyes mocking. "If that is your none-too-subtle way of asking if she mentioned you at all, then no, she did not."

His spirits plummeted. He knew it was too much to ask, but a tiny part of him still wanted to believe he'd held a tiny corner of her heart.

"You'll be pleased to know that I, on the other hand, did."

"You spoke about me?"

"Of course I did! Who else do you think we would talk about? Poor Prince Leopold? As I'm not personally acquainted with the man I find it hard to exchange much conversation concerning him. You, on the other hand, I will always have much to say about. And share." He grinned mischievously.

Gideon groaned. There was much Aidan could say; much he probably shouldn't say. "Such comments make me tremble with trepidation."

"Truly, that is most unfair. I cannot be held responsible for your unfortunate feelings."

"What did you say?"

"I simply expressed something of what you said to me after learning of her removal."

Oh no. "I hope you didn't say everything of what I said to you — in confidence."

Aidan waved a dismissive hand. "The merest trifle, I assure you."

"You *know* I wish I could have spoken to her, that I knew I should have, despite her mother's objections. But I could not very well force my way inside. And then before I knew it she was gone. I couldn't leave Emma's side, and then, when she began to improve and my letters to Miss Hatherleigh were returned to me, I began to question what I thought I knew, that I could never presume . . ."

"I know your scruples do you credit, but you should not always adhere to them."

His fingers clenched. "*What* did you say?"

"I merely ascertained how such matters were perceived by her. It would appear she was misled by certain things said on the night of Pratt's visit. Not that I was privy to all that was said, being unconscious, you understand."

Hope flickered in his heart. But still, his indignation needed venting. "I cannot believe you discussed such things with her!"

"Well, you certainly would not have."

"No, and for two very good reasons. Her mother refused to entertain my suit, and I would not have Miss Hatherleigh feel compelled to marry me simply because she felt society had forced her to. I —" He stopped himself from saying *love.* "I care for her far too much to have an alliance made in such a way."

Aidan shrugged. "Then perhaps you won't mind knowing what she had to say."

He swallowed. "What did she say?"

"You'll be pleased to know" — he waited, a catlike grin tilting his lips — "that she said much the same."

"What? That she did not want to marry me simply because society thought she should? Well, that makes me very glad indeed," he said sarcastically.

"Erasmus Gideon Kirby Carstairs! Really, this temper of yours needs to be better controlled. How on earth has your dear sister coped?"

"My dear sister did not go out of her way to be provoking, that's how she coped."

"Are you by any chance suggesting that I do? I am mortified."

"Do you have anything else to add, or am I supposed to thank you for burying my hopes?"

"Hopes, is it?" His eyes glinted. "Really, Gideon, you should be more careful about what you say."

"I am not the only one," Gideon muttered. He said in a louder voice, "So there is nothing further. Well, thank you, but I must retire —"

"Not so fast," Aidan said, leaning forward to clasp his wrist in a surprisingly strong grip. "I thought you might want to hear the rest of this."

"I thought perhaps I would also, only you never got around to saying it."

"Forgive me. It is simply this: Miss Hatherleigh assured me she would not be opposed to your suit if she knew it was not made from societal obligation but rather engendered from . . . warmer feelings, shall we say."

His pulse spiked. "She told you this?"

"Yes." Aidan smiled complacently, flicking at a speck of dust on his coat of superfine.

"Or did you have the effrontery to ask her this?"

Aidan opened his eyes in a look that somehow mingled mischief with hurt surprise. "Do you truly think me capable of such solecism?"

"Yes."

He sighed. "I am forever misunderstood."

"You are forever meddling."

"But are you not pleased by my efforts? Now at least you know you can pursue your young lady and you shall not be rebuffed. At least, not by her," he added thoughtfully.

"But rebuffed by her parents."

"Perhaps," he shrugged. "Perhaps not. I still cannot understand why you did not present Lady Aynsley with all the facts when given the chance."

"But I did."

"To Miss Hatherleigh's mother?"

"Well, no. I never got the chance. I did admit all to her grandmother. I assumed she would mention my connections."

"It would appear she did not. Perhaps, dear friend, if you were to avail Miss Hatherleigh's parents of such information, you might find a different response. It's not as if you come completely titleless or unendowed. I imagine it cannot hurt your cause to have a marquess for a brother."

"You think these things are important to her parents?"

"Indubitably."

"But I do not have the estates, or any fortune."

"But you do have a house, and a tidy competence, as I recall."

He sighed, memories of his last encounter with Caroline's mother rushing through his mind. He would have explained, had she given him opportunity to speak. "How did her parents seem?"

Another shrug. "Like most parents of unmarried girls. Eager to encourage a young man's attention, yet aiming for the top of the trees."

Exactly. Somewhere he would never be.

"You know, now I recall a certain Mr. Amherst dancing with your pretty Miss Hatherleigh."

His fingers clenched.

Aidan laughed. "Ah, but if you be too shy to chase her, then it would be a grand shame to let her sit on the shelf all alone. Not when someone could offer her his name, and he be a family friend and neighbor."

"She doesn't love him," he gritted out.

"Perhaps not, but give them time. Somehow I do not think he possesses the necessary scruples to be concerned about the niceties of cutting my dear friend out."

"I know you are funning, but I do not find this amusing."

"And neither do I like the thought of my friend sitting on his hands when he has a young lady practically begging him to find courage to pay his addresses."

Gideon swallowed. "You think I lack courage, do you?"

"I think you possess too many nice notions, and if you only ever play by the rules then you will be hurt as surely as if you play with none. Wouldn't you like to know what possibilities may be, rather than wish you had tried but never attempted the thing? If you could just speak with her, find out from her own lips and give yourself a chance rather than taking yourself out of the game before it even begins, then you can worry about the parents and what they may say. You may find that they don't mind her being married to a marquess's brother after all."

Gideon sighed. "You are quite the Machiavellian, aren't you?"

"I've already been told I'm abominable tonight, so I suppose that is something of an improvement."

A chuckle escaped despite himself. "Miss

Hatherleigh?"

"The very same."

"She knows you well."

"Don't sound too cocky my friend. She has said the same about you."

"Has she?"

"Oh, yes. But that was before she admitted that she found such a person rather appealing, so I gather from that remark that there is hope for me yet."

Gideon threw a cushion at him. "You truly are abominable."

"I know."

And they shared grins, and started to plan Gideon's attack.

CHAPTER TWENTY-EIGHT

Caroline had just concluded her shopping in the bazaar when she was hailed by a voice from a passing carriage. "Miss Hatherleigh!"

Caroline turned and saw Lady Heathcote. Her heart sank, she made her curtsy. "How are you?"

"Very well, thank you, my dear. Tell me, is your dear mother with you?"

"She is just inside with Cecilia, finishing up their shopping."

"Ah, good. I wanted just a quick word with you while she is busy. I hope you don't mind?"

Caroline gritted her teeth in a polite smile and acquiesced, obeying the gestured summons to climb up into the landau.

The older lady said in a hushed voice, "It is about your time in Devon."

What a surprise.

"I simply could not believe it when I read

it in the papers! To think, a dear neighbor of mine embroiled in such an adventure! Now, tell me all, how is the young man? Did he recover, or was he left with irreversible injuries?"

Caroline stared at her. Had she not heard about the more recent mishap in Sidmouth? Not that she would tell her. Disgust churned within at the ghoulish gleam she could see. "I believe he is quite recovered," she said carefully.

"Oh." Disappointment filled her faded eyes. "Well, I suppose that is for the best. Has he come to pay his addresses to you? I imagine it is not *quite* the way one would wish to receive a marriage proposal, but when such a misfortune occurs, one must be prepared to do what is right."

Caroline swallowed. How could she answer this, when she had no answers, and even less desire to give further fuel to this wicked speculation? She knew Verity would offer a blunt assessment of Lady Heathcote's nosiness; that Cecilia would shrivel into a pink ball of fluster and confusion. But what could she say that would be true and yet still allow her to behave in a manner befitting a daughter of Aynsley? *Lord, give me wisdom.*

"Lady Heathcote," she said slowly, "I

must beg for your forbearance in this matter. You see, I have no desire to be the scuttlebutt of society, and I am sure you, as such a good friend of our family, would have no wish to see my affairs talked over as if I meant nothing more than a person unknown to you. You would not wish that, would you?"

She gazed into the faded eyes, gladdened to see the surprised chagrin in the dilated pupils, before Lady Heathcote nodded vigorously. "Well, of *course* I would not wish you to be subject to such things. How dreadful some people are, gossiping about people they do not know."

"When it is far preferable to gossip about people we do know, is it not?" Caroline said sweetly.

"Exactly," Lady Heathcote said. "Which is why I simply must ask —"

"Please, do not let me keep you," Caroline said, opening the door and stepping down. "I'm sure you have many important and productive things with which to fill your day. Goodbye."

Lady Heathcote blushed and stuttered her excuses, releasing Caroline to catch her breath and school her countenance as she moved to wait within the Aynsley carriage. Her mother and Cecy soon arrived, shoving various bags and hatboxes at the footman before accepting help to ascend the carriage steps.

"Caroline? You seem a little flustered," Mama said, peering at her.

"Lady Heathcote wanted a word."

"With you?" At Caroline's nod, Mama sighed. "One can only guess why."

"She wanted to know all about my adventures in Devon," Caroline confirmed.

Mama eyed Caroline in her disconcerting way. "And did you share *all* about your adventures?"

"Not quite all."

She nodded, as if satisfied, then gave the command to move.

As the carriage jerked into motion, Mama studied Caroline again. "I suppose she wanted to know whether your reputation has been salvaged or not by a proposal from that ridiculous man."

She swallowed. "Mr. Kirby is not ridiculous."

"How that man could even hope to aspire to my daughter I do not know."

Caroline said nothing. The reassurance she had felt from Lord Kenmore's words concerning Mr. Kirby's affection had faded during the night, and she was left in the quagmire of uncertainty between hope and despair. For it was all well and good for him to say such things, but until Mr. Kirby spoke of his heart, she could not be truly assured.

Mother eyed her for a long moment more, to which Caroline returned a bland look, before her attention turned to Cecilia and discussion over whether she wear her new pink sarcenet tonight at the Sefton's ball. "I do think that color becomes you very well," Caroline offered.

Cecy looked surprised, as if she had not expected Caroline's compliment, which determined her to do more to show Cecy and Verity her true affections. God might not permit her to marry the man she loved, but she knew He wanted her to love the family she had.

The carriage pulled up in front of the town house, and a footman toddled down the steps to assist them — and their pack-ages — inside.

The silver salver bore witness to visits paid while they were out. Mama rifled through the cards on the tray. "The Marquess of Londonberry! Well, I wonder what your father has done to earn his notice. And the Viscount Kenmore. I don't know who that is, do you?"

Caroline's pulse accelerated. She knew

exactly who the latter was, and suspected why he had come to call, and possibly even with whom. "Mother, Lord Kenmore is the man we met last night."

The butler cleared his throat. "If you please, m'lady, Lord Kenmore said he would return in an hour or so."

"Well! He must be very keen to see us. I wonder what he wants." She looked hard at Caroline, causing an internal squirm. "Do you have any notion of what he wants?"

"It is customary, is it not, for a gentleman to call on his dancing partners from the previous evening?"

"It is customary to acknowledge such things with a note or a posy, not necessarily a social call. Well, I suppose you had best go change and we'll wait to see what he has to say for himself."

A short time later, while Mary was arranging Caroline's hair in the bedchamber, she heard a carriage arrive, and hurried to the window and glanced down. Lord Kenmore descended from the carriage steps, holding out his hand to —

Emma! And there was Mr. Kirby! Her fingers flew to her mouth. Her pulse heightened. What would be said? What did he want?

"Miss? If you don't let me finish fixing

your hair you'll resemble a scarecrow, make no doubt about that. Now, come sit down and let's get you looking as a daughter of a viscount ought."

She meekly acquiesced, and sat just long enough for Mary to finish braiding her hair into something appropriate. "There you are now, miss. Very pretty. Especially with the young gentlemen downstairs."

Caroline shot her a darkling look, then shot up and out the door. Surely their guests would have been plagued by her mother's questions long enough.

But to her surprise, it was her father, not her mother, who greeted her as she entered the morning room. "Ah, here she is. Caroline, I believe you know Lord Kenmore, oh, and Mr. and Miss Kirby, too."

Caroline ignored the heart pang, and offered a greeting and curtsy. She stole a peek at Mr. Kirby. He seemed much healthier looking than the last time she had seen him, his countenance more open, his scar gleaming palely on his tanned cheek, his gray eyes intent on her. Emma, too, seemed far happier, though still very frail, her movements stiff, her color wan, with shadows under her eyes.

She extended her hands to Emma. "How wonderful to see you again! You have been in my prayers." She gave Emma a light hug and whispered, "Congratulations."

"Thank you," Emma murmured, eyes shining with a soft peace Caroline had not seen before, and envied.

She turned to her father. Perhaps if she maintained the conversational ball she might be able to avoid speaking directly with Mr. Kirby. And prevent her father from noticing Emma's sudden radiance. "Father, I am truly thankful to have spent time in Sidmouth. I can only imagine how very lovely it is in spring. Grandmama talked about the daffodils that bloom atop Peak Hill."

"I recall Mrs. Baker saying something of the sort," Emma agreed.

"There is so much natural beauty in Sidmouth and its surrounds. I only wish I had my sketches here to show you what I mean."

"Oh, but I have brought one, Miss Hatherleigh," Emma said, withdrawing a piece of paper from her reticule. "I wanted to return this to you. It is the sketch you drew in the cave." She turned to Caroline's father. "I wish I had something of your daughter's talent with drawing . . ."

They exchanged quiet conversation, freeing Caroline to examine the piece of paper, as memories surged of the cave-in. "It seems a lifetime ago," she murmured.

"I have thought the same," Mr. Kirby's baritone voice said from beside her.

She stilled. How had he got there? Were Lord Kenmore and Emma maintaining Father's attention sufficiently to allow them a few moments of private conversation? Did she even want to speak with Mr. Kirby? She turned, and placed the paper on a nearby walnut bureau. Was he here only from obligation?

"I am pleased to see you looking well, Miss Hatherleigh," he continued. "Looking very well," he added in a voice just for her.

Her insides curled with pleasure. She would have to give Mary an extra coin for her good work today. But . . . but she would never let him know how much her heart still hurt, that his words from weeks ago still caused her pain.

"I am very glad you are safe. I find it hard to forget that dreadful day," he said.

"As do I," she admitted, with a shiver.

"Please, do not dwell on the less pleasant aspects. For myself, I count it as one of the most fortunate days of my life."

She glanced swiftly at him. "How can you say that when Emma was injured so terribly?"

"That, of course, was not something any

of us wanted. But this dreadful situation has finally led to good, would you not agree?" he said, motioning to the happy couple.

Well, yes. She glanced down, confusion muddling her brain. How could he look at her as if he cared, then not say anything to the matter? Was she such a fool as to believe he cared when he did not? What was it he had said to Pratt? That he cared only for his sister and his fossils? Is that why he had not spoken to her?

"I suppose you are glad you finally found your fossil," she said in a flat voice.

His brow puckered. "Well, yes."

There. Confirmation. She bit her lip, felt the burn in the back of her eyes. She drew back, half turned to join the conversation Lord Kenmore still valiantly sustained.

"Finding such a thing was indeed quite marvelous," Mr. Kirby continued, his words halting her movement. "But not as marvelous as another discovery I made."

He paused, as if waiting for her to ask him what discovery it was. But she could not ask to be rejected once again.

"You do not ask me," he continued in a low voice of disappointment.

Her heart prodded. Was she not supposed to live at peace with others? Was she letting pride sway her actions yet again? She swallowed, and finally said, "What discovery is that, sir?"

"My treasure."

She looked up. "Did you find smugglers' gold?"

"No, something far more valuable." He smiled. "I realized my treasure did not consist of gold, and was not to be found in the past, but was standing before me all the time."

His touch on her arm sent heat soaring through her skin, escalating her pulse and her breathing. No, he didn't mean her. Did he?

"Miss Hatherleigh, dearest Caroline . . ."

Her pulse scampered.

"I learned more of your character through that experience, and prior, when we were trapped in the cave, than I would have in a month of snatched conversations in ballrooms. I thank God for that, I assure you. I thank God for *you.*"

"You . . . you exaggerate."

"I simply tell the truth," he said, honesty writ in his eyes. "And then, later, when Kenmore told me of your faith, well, you cannot know how glad I was to learn this, to feel that we both could share in what I consider the most important part of life."

She glanced down once again. But if this was so, why had he not spoken to her until now? Why had he not sought an interview with her father?

Further questions were cut short by the entrance of Mama, whose apologies at her delayed arrival and murmurs about a useless maid soon faded as she glanced at the guest seated close to Caroline. "The nerve!" she hissed, before casting him a narrow look then turning her back on him, making her disapprobation very plain.

"Mr. Kirby," Father said, the warning in his voice and eyes enough to shift him away from her. "My mother wrote to explain a little about matters in Sidmouth —"

Caroline's breath hitched. Oh, what had Grandmama said?

"— and the accident you underwent. I am pleased to see you have made a recovery. May I ask when you propose to return to your scientific work?"

"I have already returned, sir," he said. "My work does not require me to stay only along the shore. While in London I have made use of my time in visiting various scientific societies and sharing about my discoveries."

"I see. And may I ask how long you have been in London?"

"For the past fortnight."

Two weeks and she had not known? Caroline turned to him, brows raised. He offered a small smile that looked tinged with apology.

"You must forgive us for not calling upon you sooner," Mr. Kirby said. "Had I but known of your stay in town I would have ensured we were here the first available hour."

"It matters not," Father said, to which Mama agreed most vehemently.

"I am so glad you think so," Lord Kenmore said, eyes dancing. "I do feel myself to be something in error, especially as Emma here has been desiring to renew her acquaintance with Miss Hatherleigh."

Father cleared his throat. "I fail to see why such a thing should be of your doing, sir. Surely such a thing should be the responsibility of a father, or at the very least, a brother."

"I know," he said humbly. "It is simply that one always tries to do one's best when one is accounted a host," he added, neatly avoiding any mention of his secret marriage.

"Our father died a year ago, Lord Aynsley," Mr. Kirby said, eyes watchful.

"Oh? And who might your father be? I'm afraid I do not recall any Kirbys of our acquaintance."

"Of course," he said, bowing his head. "Kirby was my mother's maiden name." He glanced at Caroline, eyes filled with apology. "Please forgive my slight bending of the truth. You must know that I could not afford to be known by my family name, not with Pratt certain to search for us."

"And what exactly is your family name, sir?" Mama asked, her expression of disdain for Mr. Kirby thawing to curiosity. "Surely the deception is no longer necessary."

"Again, I must beg pardon."

"Your name, sir?"

"Of course, madam," he said, bowing slightly. "My family name is Carstairs. My father was the Marquess of Londonberry."

Gideon glanced at Caroline as he said that, saw her widening eyes, her whitened cheeks, the way her gasp echoed her mother's.

"I beg your pardon. Did you say your father *was* the Marquess of Londonberry?"

"Yes, my lady."

"Then, then" — Lady Aynsley's eyes were almost popping from their sockets — "then are *you* the Marquess of Londonberry?"

He smiled at her obvious shock and delayed approval, and the disappointment he knew was sure to be hers. "I'm afraid that title has gone to my brother. I am known as Carstairs."

"Carstairs, not Kirby?"

"Carstairs," he affirmed.

"Oh. But I suppose you cannot be merely a mister, not if you're a marquess's son. Well! This is quite the turn up!"

Gideon glanced at Caroline who still seemed shocked. "I am sorry I did not tell you before. For one reason or another, it was never the correct time."

She blinked. "You did not think being trapped together for nearly five hours constituted enough time?"

Now it was his turn to blink. He hadn't expected her response to be quite so . . . blunt. "Please forgive me," he said, as humbly as he could.

"Well, my *lord,*" her mother said again, glancing between them both. "Did you not think such information might have proved helpful when you approached me to offer for my daughter's hand?"

"You did?" Caroline said, her eyes filled with confusion. "I thought —" She pressed her lips together.

"You did not know?" he asked her, before questioning Lady Aynsley with upraised brows. "I sent letters which were returned to me."

"It is most improper for a single gentleman to write to a young lady. And Caroline certainly needed no such distractions," she said with a shrug. "And it would seem I was right in withholding such information, as you have obviously withheld rather crucial aspects of your own life, sir."

He bit his tongue, aiming for a conciliatory tone. Nothing would be gained from speaking what he really felt. "Lady Aynsley," Gideon finally said, "I must beg your forgiveness in not being completely open concerning my family's name and connections. Such an omission was in no way an attempt to deceive, but simply to protect. I will say, however, that I did impart this information to Miss Hatherleigh's grandmother, which may be why she was initially supportive of my suit."

"But she is not responsible for Caroline."

He inclined his head. "I believed it to be otherwise, at least while Miss Hatherleigh was in Sidmouth. I will also own to being vain enough that I wished to win Miss Hatherleigh's heart and not just her sense of obligation."

He glanced at Caroline; her mouth had sagged once more. He smiled, and returned his attention to her mother. "I know my being a mere second son does not, perhaps, endear my suit as much as a grander title may, but I love her, so again, I ask for your permission to pay my addresses to her." He turned to Caroline again. "That is, if you would be so good as to receive them."

Her eyes filled with tears, and she dipped her head.

Gladness filled his heart.

"Oh! Well. Well, you should rather speak with Lord Aynsley."

"Of course," he said, turning to Caroline's father, who nodded, with something like approval in his eyes, before murmuring about meeting tonight at Brook's.

Hope kindling, he smiled at Caroline again. "I hope you do not find my suit too distasteful."

"I do not find it distasteful at all," she whispered.

"Then perhaps you might agree to accompany me to the Park tomorrow. I believe I saw some roses there that are almost the same color as your cheeks, and I would like to compare the two shades."

She blushed to that satisfying color he'd remembered, before giving a shy nod.

"Lord Aynsley? I trust I might have permission to escort your daughter?"

"Yes, yes, of course. If Caroline should wish it, of course."

"Does she wish it?" he asked her, again in a low voice.

"Yes," she whispered.

"Then I look forward to seeing you on the morrow."

And, heart singing, he joined the others in making his adieus, and planning how he could best present his case to Lord Aynsley tonight.

CHAPTER TWENTY-NINE

The next day Mr. Gideon Kirby — no, Lord Carstairs! — called in at four in the afternoon, the earliest time considered appropriate for a drive. Caroline was waiting, her hair tucked up under a hat of pale pink, her pelisse a richer shade that did wonders for her complexion, or so Mama and Mary assured her. After chatting briefly with Mama — her father absent, having matters to attend in town — he escorted Caroline to the carriage, where they were greeted by Emma and Lord Kenmore. She knew their attendance was for propriety's sake, but never did she wish more for propriety to be abandoned.

Gideon tucked the robe around her, his very nearness intoxicating. He glanced up. "I hope today will not prove too cool for you."

She smiled, assuring him it would not. From the warm look in his eyes, she rather suspected she would not notice the temperature at all.

Her heart thrilled, and she barely noticed the brisk spring breeze or the others' small talk as the carriage drove to Hyde Park, passing along the path where the plane trees arched overhead. Emma and Lord Kenmore chatted about inconsequential things, but Caroline could barely summon polite responses. A night of sleepless dreaming had left her too nervous to speak. She suspected she knew what Gideon wished to say to her, had spent half the night envisaging how he would say it, the other half practicing her reply. She had found some comfort in reading her Bible and praying. She only wished she might not disgrace herself by appearing too eager.

The carriage pulled alongside the lake, slowing to a halt.

Gideon glanced at her. "Would you care to join me for a stroll?"

Caroline glanced at the others, but Emma shook her head. "Please, go and enjoy a walk. It is such a lovely day, and the flowers are so pretty. But if you don't mind I think I'd prefer to stay here."

"I shall stay here with you," Lord Kenmore said. "Go, don't worry about us."

Caroline bit her lip, but she supposed if

they cared not for the proprieties then she would not either. Besides, there were so few people about, one need scarcely be concerned.

Gideon was waiting for her, holding out his hand. She took it, feeling the strength in his fingers as he helped her down. "I promise we shan't be too long."

"Take your time," Lord Kenmore called.

Heat filled her cheeks.

For a few minutes, she could think of nothing to say, conscious of the fact that Gideon's friend and sister no doubt watched them still. Such knowledge made her spine stiff, the old lessons in decorum still holding sway. Then, gradually, she grew aware of the heat of his nearness, of his delectable scent, of all sorts of feelings she suspected her mother would think *most* improper.

"Emma seems to be feeling better," she murmured once they were out of earshot, glad to find something normal to speak on.

"She is tired, but very happy." He smiled. "She would not listen to reason, and insisted on coming today."

"I have missed her," she said.

"You have been missed."

Did his words hold additional significance? His look certainly seemed to suggest so.

"I trust all has been resolved since . . .

since . . ."

"Since that awful day? Yes. I'm glad to say it appears to be the case."

"What will happen since Pratt's . . ." She swallowed.

"Since Pratt's death? I imagine the estate will go to his cousin who is next in line. Pratt always thought him a poor choice because his cousin is a clergyman and has been known to squander — Pratt's words — his income on establishing orphanages and the like."

"He sounds a very good man."

"He is, which is why Pratt despised him. But as far as Emma is concerned, she is entitled to what remains of the monies settled upon her at her marriage, which won't be insubstantial. Of course, if she had birthed a child, things would be far more complicated . . ." His voice trailed away.

She nodded, as memories rose again of that fatal day. "Such a terrible time it was."

"And yet you were so brave. How did you do it?"

"Do what, sir?"

"Risk your life for Emma's. I will never forget you flinging yourself to protect her."

"I . . . I had no thought for myself. All I could think was that I could not let her be hurt anymore."

"And this, while you were hurt yourself?" He stopped, turned to face her, and clasped her hands. "I know my words on that night hurt you deeply. I can never forgive myself for upsetting you so. I only wanted to protect you, for I feared that if Pratt knew the extent of my regard, he would only try to injure you further. Please, say you will forgive me."

"Of course I do," she said softly.

"You are so good."

Her conscience smote her. "But I fear you will have to forgive me. I did not know Mr. Browne was in your employ, and I . . . I might have suggested to Mrs. Baker that he was linked to the excisemen. That was why he wasn't there to protect Emma. I'm so utterly sorry."

"So that was why he was found locked in a hotel cellar," he said softly, his face taking on a rueful expression. "I should have trusted you with the truth. Again, I am sorry."

"It is no matter. Unless he was hurt?"

"Rather, he was ashamed at allowing his curiosity to overcome his orders, and embarrassed to have been taken in by two women like Mrs. Baker and Mrs. Belcher, and then allowing himself to be bound. He is unlikely to live down that shame or find similar employment anytime soon."

Caroline bit her lip. Poor man. "But at least Emma is safe now, and seems so much happier and healthier."

"And yet not everything is as it ought to be."

Her brows rose, and he guided her underneath a graceful willow, where they were half obscured by dangling leaves.

"Yes." He gently squeezed her hands. "There is one very important thing left to rectify. I do not know how I could have ever not known you in my life. You are wise, and witty, and courageous, and clever, and so very much more lovely than anyone I have ever beheld."

Caroline's chest throbbed with a hundred emotions. She tamped down the elation with a self-deprecating, "You are somewhat blinded, sir."

He chuckled, shaking his head. "No, not at all. Instead, since I have met you, I feel as though the scales have fallen from my eyes." He lifted her hand to his lips. "I love you. You are the woman I have been praying for these many years. Please, dearest Caroline, won't you make me the happiest man in the world and consent to be my wife?"

Her heart fluttered. This clever, intriguing man wanted to marry her? "Sir —"

"Gideon," he pressed.

"Gideon." She felt a blush. How bold it was to speak his Christian name aloud!

"I love to hear my name upon your lips. But, my dearest, I have one further confession."

"What is that?"

"My name. It is not truly Gideon, although it was one I was christened with. My first name is Erasmus."

"Erasmus?"

"Unfortunate, is it not? Perhaps you can understand why I prefer Gideon."

"Gideon, the brave soldier, who slew the enemies of the Lord."

"You think of him like that? I always think of him as the man who put God to the test."

"We all test God at times, do we not?"

"Yes." He paused, licked his bottom lip. "I feel like I am being tested now. You cannot know how much it has hurt me, knowing you doubted my regard."

She lowered her gaze. How could she have doubted him?

"Let me assure you, my dearest Caroline, that I love you, and that no one else has ever truly lived within my heart." His voice dropped to a half whisper. "Please, stop this Gideon from feeling tested and let me know if you can find it in your heart to believe that I love you."

She swallowed, and nodded.

"And will you consent to marry me?"

"I am conscious of the tremendous honor you do me —"

"But?" His face drooped with disappointment.

"And I would be honored to marry you," she finished in a whisper.

His smile illuminated his face, and before she could take another breath, he had moved swiftly to capture her lips with his.

A dizzying array of sensations swirled within. The joy of knowing she was sought! The scandal should they be seen. The ardor stirring deep within as his fingers reached to her cheek, then moved to cradle her head as he deepened the kiss.

Oh . . .

Was this what passion felt like? Her insides stirred with strange heat, her chest seemed like it might burst. She felt herself grow breathless. Who knew a man of science would know how to thoroughly kiss a woman like this?

The sound of a snapped twig drew their lips apart and their attention to where Lord Kenmore stood, arms crossed, amusement creasing his lips upwards.

"From the looks of that it would appear

matters have been resolved satisfactorily."

"They have," Gideon said, grinning at her, before picking up her hand and pressing it with his warm lips. "Caroline has consented to marry me."

Lord Kenmore bowed. "Then I felicitate you, Miss Hatherleigh. You could not have chosen a better man." He turned to his friend. "And I felicitate you, for you could not have chosen better either."

"Thank you," Caroline said, shyness stealing over her.

"And may I encourage you both to swift nuptials, as judging from the intensity I saw displayed here a moment ago, it would appear that such haste might be necessary."

"Kenmore!"

Caroline ducked her head, the heat of mortification streaming through her.

"Ah, Miss Hatherleigh, please forgive me. I am rather pleased to know you bring my friend such happiness."

"Then please refrain from making my betrothed feel otherwise," Gideon said, wrapping an arm around her protectively. "I would not have her embarrassed by you."

"Again, I offer my apologies, Miss Hatherleigh. But you must be aware that in marrying my friend you will inevitably be placed in situations where encounters with me may well bring a certain degree of embarrassment at times."

"I understand," she said. "Just as long as you understand that most of those times the embarrassment will not be of my doing, and thus, not mine to share."

This sally elicited a chuckle from both men, and for Gideon to hold her hand a little tighter. "See? I knew I had chosen well."

"You need someone with quick wits for when your own are so sadly lacking."

By now they were returning to where Emma awaited them, a smile on her face. "I can tell from the delight on your faces that the answer must have been positive."

They had all known?

"Congratulations, dearest Caroline! I'm so very glad to welcome you to the family."

Caroline was engulfed in a close hug, most unlike the polite pats and stiff embraces her family tended to use.

"He really is the best of brothers, you know."

"Even better than the marquess?"

"Oh, James is good, too, but he's ever so busy. I do hope you can meet him soon."

"I hope so, too."

"I know he called upon you recently and, as he attends Parliament, I expect he will call again soon."

"I'm sure my father would be very pleased to further their acquaintance."

"Your father said as much when I spoke with him at his club last night. Come," said Gideon, smiling at them both. "Let us return so we can deliver the glad tidings."

"I hope Mama will be pleased."

And, to Caroline's great delight — and not a small amount of relief — she finally was.

CHAPTER THIRTY

Aynsley, Somerset
June

The day that would make her a wife held every promise of good in the blue and cloudless skies. Various household members woke early, with so many tasks to accomplish before the service at ten, or in Caroline's case, unable to sleep due to the excitement thrumming through her veins. How she hoped all would go well. How she hoped she'd look her best. Her gown was a beautiful concoction of ivory silk overlaid with Brussels lace, which also trimmed the ruffled décolletage and the hem and veil. Never had she felt more beautiful than when she had tried on her gown; how she hoped Gideon thought so, too.

One member of the family seemed to hold little regard for the day's events, though, a fact evidenced when Mama steamed into Caroline's bedchamber as she was dressing to inform her that Verity was missing.

"Missing?"

"She cannot be found anywhere," Mama said with a groan. "Really, she is simply the most abominable child."

"Scarcely a child," Caroline said, adjusting her veil. "She is just turned seventeen."

"Exactly! You would think she would know better, but she's not nearly ready to be presented, let alone think about being married."

Caroline couldn't really see her headstrong, flighty sister as marriage material. It would take a very strong man to deal with her.

"Cecilia thinks she has gone off for an early morning ride. Can you imagine? On such an auspicious day!"

"I'm sure she will return in time," Caroline murmured, wincing as Mary dug a pin in to hold the veil more securely.

"Sorry, miss," Mary murmured, to Caroline's waving off of her concern.

"Well, I wish she would hurry up and return," Mama complained. "I know she was not in favor of the dress, but truly, this running off and hiding is immature in the extreme."

"Perhaps she has not run off, Mama. It could be that she is simply unaware of the time."

"Since when did you start making excuses for your sister? No. It is simply unacceptable that she should wish to spoil your day with her silly antics."

"I am sure she has no wish to spoil today," Caroline said firmly. "She is not selfish."

"Perhaps not. But she is heedless, and headstrong. Heaven help any man who might wish to marry her. I think Verity would as soon eat such a foolish man for breakfast."

A smile crept past Caroline's trepidation. She truly could not see any man ever gaining the upper hand with her hellfire little sister.

The Aynsley chapel having been deemed too small for the guests traveling from afar, the church of St. Michael and Mary had been appropriated in the village that bore their family name. As they passed in the carriage along the way, villagers waved and occasionally tossed flowers, their bright smiles smoothing away the tension from before.

Caroline relaxed. Verity had been found — so Cecy said — but further details she did not disclose, save to say she had been slightly injured. While this caused Caroline's prayers to rise, she worked to tamp down her worries. Cecy had said Verity's injury was no cause for alarm; she did not need to worry anymore.

The rich scent of her bouquet of creamy roses filled the carriage with sweetness. She drew in the heady aroma, then exhaled. Today she was going to marry a truly remarkable man whom she loved very much. She glanced at her father; a rare pleased expression filled his face as he acknowledged the tributes from the estate's people.

"It is good to see you receiving proper respect," he said, nodding to the genial grocer. "I am glad that people know what is due."

"I am glad you are glad," she said, squeezing his arm with affection.

They pulled up to the stone church, the Norman stone and square tower giving a kind of solid reassurance about the vows she was about to make. Her father stepped from the carriage and handed her down, where she was met by her mother and Cecilia.

"Verity's inside," Mama hissed. "She's limping, but I told her nothing she did was to spoil her sister's big day."

"But if she is in pain, Mama —" Caroline began.

"Then she will perhaps learn to consider what she is about. Though that might be a trifle too much to ask."

The bells began ringing. Cecy said fretfully, "The service needs to start, Mama."

"The service can only start when we are there. Now, Caroline, I have to say you look very lovely." She minutely adjusted Caroline's veil, smoothed down her gown. "The Marquess and his family are here, and Lord and Lady Bevington have arrived."

"I'm so glad Serena could make it." Caroline smiled. "And Gideon?"

"His lordship is awaiting your arrival, so I suppose we best go in."

Mother and Cecilia offered her kisses on the cheek, then hurried through the doors inside the church to take their seats. Caroline turned to her father who gave her a warm smile. "You look lovely, my dear."

"Thank you, Father." Was it vainglorious to admit that she felt lovely? But she did, the joyous glow filling her heart deeper than appreciation for a compliment; today felt ordained by God.

The doors were opened once more and, clutching her father's arm, she walked slowly down the aisle, following Mama's advice to neither hurry like an underbred young miss nor adopt a step that suggested she was older than Methuselah.

She glanced up, saw Gideon standing straight and tall in front of the altar. Her heart swelled. He was here — and he would be her husband! Suddenly she did not care if her eagerness made her scamper to the front, but her father's hand on hers restrained her to a sensible pace.

"Remember, you are still a daughter of Aynsley," he murmured.

But not for much longer. Soon she would be a bride of Carstairs.

At last she reached her place, and she could finally meet Gideon's gaze.

His smile filled his face, and hers quickly followed. So much for avoiding the appearance of eagerness.

Reverend Poole welcomed them and began the marriage ceremony. "Dearly beloved, we are gathered together here in the sight of God, and in the face of this congregation, to join together this man and this woman in holy matrimony, which is an honorable estate, instituted of God in the time of man's innocency, signifying unto us the mystical union that is betwixt Christ and His church, which holy estate Christ adorned and beautified with His presence, and first miracle that He wrought, in Cana of Galilee, and is commended of Saint Paul to be honorable among all men . . ."

He continued, Caroline listening carefully, as these references to biblical events resonated within. How glad she was to now know Christ, and know, through His help, she would be able to help and comfort her Gideon, in times of both adversity and prosperity.

"If any man can show just cause why they may not be lawfully joined together, let him now speak, or else hereafter forever hold his peace."

No impediments raised — not that there were any, Caroline thought with a smile — the minister addressed Gideon. "Erasmus Gideon Kirby Carstairs, wilt thou have this woman to be thy wedded wife, to live together after God's ordinance in the holy estate of matrimony? Wilt thou love her, comfort her, honor and keep her, in sickness and in health, and, forsaking all others, keep thee only unto her, so long as ye both shall live?"

"I will."

Her heart glowed at his firm voice, giving her an extra measure of confidence when Reverend Poole asked about her intention. "I will."

There was a titter across the room, as if people were amused by her slightly overloud response, but she could not hide her anticipation. Propriety was greatly overrated, after all.

"Who giveth this woman to be married to this man?"

"I do," said Father.

Her right hand was held by Gideon's right hand, as he repeated the vows.

"I, Erasmus Gideon Kirby Carstairs, take thee, Caroline Elizabeth Hatherleigh to be my wedded wife, to have and to hold from this day forward, for better for worse, for richer for poorer, in sickness and in health, to love and to cherish, till death us do part, according to God's holy ordinance, and thereto I plight thee my troth."

When it came time for Caroline to repeat such vows, her words held resolve, conviction swelling within her, as if drawing up from the very soles of her feet.

The ring was blessed and placed on her fourth finger, as Gideon declared, "With this ring I thee wed, with my body I thee worship, and with all my worldly goods I thee endow. In the name of the Father, and of the Son, and of the Holy Ghost. Amen."

She smiled, turning to meet Gideon's grin. He gently squeezed the hand he still held, helping her to kneel.

As the minister prayed over them, Caroline closed her eyes, absorbing the words of blessing as if taking them into her very bones. Yes, she would keep the vow and covenant betwixt them made. Yes, she would do all in her power to love this man, to remain in peace, and do him good, all her days. Yes, she would do so empowered through the grace of God through Jesus Christ our Lord.

"Amen."

Their right hands were joined together. "Those whom God hath joined together let no man put asunder." Reverend Poole turned to the congregation. "Forasmuch as Erasmus Gideon Kirby Carstairs and Caroline Elizabeth Hatherleigh have consented together in holy wedlock, and have witnessed the same before God and this company, and thereto have given and pledged their troth either to the other, and have declared the same by the giving and receiving of a ring, and by the joining of hands, I pronounce that they be man and wife together, in the name of the Father, and of the Son, and of the Holy Ghost. Amen."

They were married! Her heart swelled with happiness until it seemed she might burst.

The minister pronounced a blessing. "God the Father, God the Son, God the

Holy Ghost, preserve and keep you; the Lord mercifully with his favor look upon you, and so fill you with all spiritual benediction and grace, that ye may so live together in this life, that in the world to come ye may have life everlasting. Amen."

Communion followed, and the reading of Psalm 67, and prayers for children, then they signed the register.

They turned to face the congregation as the minister cleared his throat. "I present to you Mr. and Mrs. Erasmus Gideon Kirby Carstairs."

Moisture gathered in her eyes and she held on to Gideon's arm almost blindly as they made slow progress down the aisle, stopped as they were many times by well-wishers. Eventually they gained outside and shook the minister's hand before they were showered with rose petals and herbs to signify new life.

"Congratulations," Cecy said, encasing her in a hug, the first of many such embraces that demonstrated warm affection rather than the cold propriety Caroline had once thought fitting.

Verity drew near, offering her congratulations, her pale, strained features drawing Caroline's enquiry of concern.

" 'Tis nothing but a fall," her sister stated,

though Caroline wondered if that was all. "Look, Caro, your husband is ready to take you away."

Gideon helped her into the flower-bedecked carriage then drew out a bag of coins with which to shower their well-wishers.

As he tossed the coins by the handful, small children scrambled to collect them. "You are so generous," she murmured.

"I feel as rich as Croesus today." The children waved their thanks, and Gideon waved in response. "And no," he continued, turning back to her, "it has nothing to do with marriage settlements."

The warm, intent look in his eyes drew a delighted shiver. She knew he meant her.

"Have I mentioned how beautiful you look today?"

"No."

The carriage jerked into motion, the driver encouraging the horses to Aynsley where the wedding breakfast would be held.

"Then allow me to rectify that immediately. You, my dearest Caroline, are the loveliest creature my eyes have ever had the good fortune to behold."

More of such sentiments punctuated the journey, as did his warm lips against her hand, her wrist, and once — scandalous though it be, in public as they were — on the lips.

The long stretch of Aynsley's façade drew near. Inside Caroline knew the servants had been bustling all morning preparing for the feast, those ranked higher who had attended services would have sped back here in order to ensure everything was ready on time. Aynsley had certainly entertained well over the years, but it wasn't every day so many noble connections would fill its rooms.

The carriage neared and servants scurried out to help them inside.

The wedding breakfast consisted of delicious flavors and champagne, but what Caroline remembered most were the faces. The still slightly stunned expressions of her mother and father, as if they couldn't quite believe they'd agreed for their daughter to marry the mere heir to a marquess.

Her grandmother's pleased countenance, as she nodded during the speeches.

The love suffusing the faces of Emma and Lord Kenmore as they exchanged looks of adoration.

James and Elizabeth, as they smiled at each other, and then at their tiny daughter.

The joy filling Serena's features, their earlier conversation leading to mutual professions of faith and renewed warmth between them.

The pain suffusing Ned Amherst's face.

Cecilia gazing mournfully after Ned.

Verity's look of impatience as she scratched at her dress, her leg bound and propped on a chair.

And her wonderful, wonderful Gideon — it would take more time to grow used to the other name — whose eyes and lips told her again and again that he thought her to be truly the most beautiful young lady in all of the world.

Later, after handing her into the coach that would take them to his estate in Lancashire, he said, "I love you, you know," before pressing his lips once more to hers.

"I know," she said, when she could finally draw breath. "And I love you, Gideon."

She smiled. Her wonderful Gideon. Wonderfully brave, wonderfully clever, wonderfully kind. Her hero.

And she waved farewell to Aynsley, and set her face to her future.

AUTHOR'S NOTE

I've long been fascinated by Mary Anning, the nineteenth-century "miracle child" and finder of some of the most remarkable fossils in England, on whom it is reputed the tongue twister "She sells seashells by the seashore" is based. But I didn't want to write her story; Tracy Chevalier has already done that in the excellent *Remarkable Creatures.* So I wanted to write a story that referenced her and something of the fossil-hunting mania in early 1800s England. With two sons, I suppose it was inevitable that I would eventually succumb to the world of dinosaurs.

For this I used a number of reference books, including *Rocks, Fossils and Dinosaurs* (edited by Busby & Coenraads), *Fossil Revolution* (Douglas Palmer), and *Bones of Contention* (Paul Chambers), and I was extremely blessed to borrow a copy of *The*

Observer's Book of British Geology from my lovely church friend Joan Freere. Together these resources helped shape this story, but as it's fictional, some of the elements were changed to suit my purposes. The ichthyosaurus Gideon discovered is loosely based on discoveries made around that time. While most ichthyosaurii have been discovered in Jurassic-era formations, it is interesting that in 2017 an ichthyosaurus considered to be the largest found in the UK was found directly north of Sidmouth in Triassic-era cliffs — which lends weight to the idea that such things could be found around the Sidmouth area also. (Regardless, I'm not a scientist, and this is fiction!)

The descriptions of Sidmouth were based on the 1810 pictorial guide referenced in *The Beauties of Sidmouth Displayed* by Edmund Butcher, published by J. Wallis — a fabulous account of Sidmouth from two hundred years ago.

Another book referenced in this novel is the 1809 reprint of *The Truth of the Christian Religion* by Hugo Grotius and John Clarke, which listed ancient writers' accounts of biblical and early church history, including the truth of Jesus Christ as a real person, whose life, death, and resurrection were noted by those ancient writers of Greek,

508

Jewish, and other traditions.

It is not my intention to discuss evolution or get into lengthy arguments about the creation story; I do believe God created the world, and I wanted to show how a scientific Christian man might approach such things in Regency times, before the scientific world became heavily skewed to evolutionary theory.

On a different note, Emma's mysterious medical condition I imagine as something not unlike lupus, or an autoimmune disease the likes of which would have been especially hard to diagnose let alone treat with Regency-era medical knowledge. My understanding is that this disease presents with days when it flares, and days when it can be in remission, which can account for the varying levels of energy and wellness Emma portrays, and the great concern physicians held for her life with the complications pregnancy presents.

Domestic violence is an all-too-prevalent issue touched on in this book. Studies have reported that in Australia, one woman a week is murdered by her current or former partner; in the US, reports from the Bureau of Justice indicate two or more women are murdered *every day* by current or former romantic partners. In Regency times, women had little recourse when faced with an abusive husband; as far as the law was concerned, wives were regarded much like their husband's property. In today's world, women are still sometimes blamed for being victims. Monica McLaughlin, deputy director of public policy at the US National Network to End Domestic Violence suggests victim-blaming should be replaced by simply offering to help. So instead of asking, "Why don't you just leave?" ask how you can help. Say: "I feel scared for you and can see these threats are real."

In other words, loving others enough to be honest, and to keep asking until you see those who are bound set free.

On a happier note, I'd like to thank my friend Vicky Smalko, whose suggestion it was to include a Regency wedding in one of my books. The service depicted is from the Anglican Book of Common Prayer, the "Form of Solemnisation of Matrimony." It's fascinating to see the similarities and differences to wedding services today — I hope you enjoy that, too.

For behind-the-book details and a discussion guide, and to sign up for my newsletter, please visit www.carolynmillerauthor.com.

If you have enjoyed reading this or any of

the other books in the Regency Brides series, please consider leaving a review at Goodreads, Amazon, or wherever you purchase.

ACKNOWLEDGMENTS

Thank You, God, for giving this gift of creativity, and the amazing opportunity to express it. Thank You for patiently loving us, and offering us hope through Jesus Christ.

Thank you, Joshua, for your love and encouragement. I appreciate your willingness to read my stories and all the support you give in so many ways. I love you!

Thank you, Caitlin, Jackson, Asher, and Tim — I love you, I'm so proud of you, and I'm so grateful you understand why I spend so much time in imaginary worlds.

To my family, church family, and friends whose support, encouragement, and prayers I value and have needed — thank you. Big thanks to Roslyn, Jacqueline, and Brooke for being patient in reading through so many of my manuscripts, and for offering suggestions to make my stories sing. Big thanks also to Joan Freere and Vicky Smalko for assistance in loaning materials and ideas to help ground this story in greater authenticity.

Thank you, Tamela Hancock Murray, my agent, for helping this little Australian negotiate the big wide American market.

Thank you to the authors and bloggers who have endorsed and encouraged and opened doors along the way: you are a blessing! Thanks to my Aussie writer friends — I appreciate you.

To the Ladies of Influence — your support and encouragement are gold!

To the fabulous team at Kregel: thank you for believing in me, and for making *A Hero for Miss Hatherleigh* shine.

Finally, thank you to my readers. Thank you for buying my books and for spreading the love for these Regency romances. I treasure your kind messages of support and lovely reviews.

I hope you enjoyed Caroline's story.

God bless you.

ABOUT THE AUTHOR

Award-winning author **Carolyn Miller** lives in the beautiful Southern Highlands of New South Wales, Australia. She is married, with four gorgeous children, who all love to read (and write.)

A longtime lover of Regency romance, Carolyn's novels have won a number of Romance Writers of American (RWA) and American Christian Fiction Writers (ACFW) contests as well as the Australian Omega Christian Writers Award. She is a member of American Christian Fiction Writers and Australasian Christian Writers. Her favourite authors are classics like Jane Austen (of course!), Georgette Heyer, and Agatha Christie, but she also enjoys contemporary authors like Susan May Warren and Becky Wade.

Her stories are fun and witty, yet also deal with real issues, such as dealing with forgiveness, the nature of really loving versus 'true love', and other challenges we all face at different times.